Train

Train

Pete Dexter

W F HOWES LTD

This large print edition published in 2004 by
W F Howes Ltd
Units 6/7, Victoria Mills, Fowke Street
Rothley, Leicester LE7 7PJ

1 3 5 7 9 10 8 6 4 2

First published in the United Kingdom in 2004 by
William Heinemann

A CIP catalogue record for this book is available
from the British Library

ISBN 1 84505 672 8

Typeset by Palimpsest Book Production Limited,
Polmont, Stirlingshire
Printed and bound in Great Britain
by Antony Rowe Ltd, Chippenham, Wilts.

For my friend Dr. Ploof

CHAPTER 1

PHILADELPHIA

January 1948

At this point in the story, Packard had never fallen in love, and didn't trust what he'd heard of the lingo (forever, my darling, with all my heart, till the end of time, more than life itself, with every fiber of my being, oh my darling Clementine, etc.). It sounded out of control to him, and messy.

He had spent maybe a thousand Sundays in church, though—make that four hundred—and then two edgy years on a battleship in the Pacific Ocean, and then five very edgy days in the Pacific Ocean without the battleship, and before any of that, he'd deliberately and often put himself in places where he saw awful things happen not only to people who deserved it but also to people who just seemed to stumble in at the wrong time, walking into the picture as the shutter clicked, through no fault of their own.

Which is to say that by now Packard recognized praying when he heard it, and knew the kind of deals people would offer up, the promises they

1

would make, when they were in over their heads. And that, from what he'd heard, was what it— love—was about.

Later on, however, something in the feminine line, in fact, came along, custom-fit, and Packard, to his enormous surprise, found himself apeshit in tow. Although not *every-fiber-of-my-being* apeshit in tow. Of long habit, Packard only gave in quietly, without losing his dignity.

And much later on, when he was tamed and had the advantages of maturity and the long view, he would come to realize that everything that had happened was inevitable, that he was, after all, a human being, and it was therefore not in his nature to keep things simple.

Even the psychologist who did the pre-employment interview had seen something on Packard's horizon.

"Perhaps," he said, "you need someone to share this with."

Packard had just described for the psychologist not his loveless life but his heavy cruiser, the *Indianapolis*, burning to the waterline in the night, and the days and nights of floating around in the Pacific Ocean with the sharks and burned and dying shipmates. The sharks came morning and evening, at mealtime, and stayed about as long as it would take you to eat dinner. Packard to this day did not eat at regular hours, but aside from that, on the occasions when he asked himself how he felt, he felt approximately like the same person.

People he'd known before the war, on the other hand, said he'd changed, but he couldn't see it himself. As his grandmother had pointed out a long time ago, he wasn't a real sweetheart to begin with.

Packard, by the way, had not brought any of this up to the psychologist himself. All he wanted was a job, and all the psychologist wanted was to keep his job, and he was required by the city's insurers to review applicants' military records and inquire specifically in regard to Purple Hearts.

The psychologist assumed a certain casual baritone authority that made Packard want to slap him, and he sat beneath his diplomas in a cheap suit, absently listening to an abbreviated history of Packard's wartime adventures, pinching his chin, making fifteen-dollar-an-hour dimples and grunts. He nodded from time to time, as if he'd heard it all before.

Then, when the half hour was over, he said, "Perhaps you need someone to share this with."

But it was all a dance anyway. War heroes could get work at any fire department they wanted.

Before this, right after the war, Packard had run into a nun in a bar in San Diego. The kind that didn't talk, although she did play the English horn. She'd given that up, though—her vows, not the horn—and was on the way to Philadelphia, trying to make up for lost time. He was given to understand the city had quite a symphony orchestra.

3

Packard was not by nature an optimist, but it was encouraging, coming home to America and being fucked half to death night and day for a month, but even in all the confusion and maneuvering—she seemed to expect him to bend back over himself, the way her horn bent—Packard became gradually aware that he was no closer to the girl than he'd been to all the other bodies, alive and dead, that he'd been around since he left home.

So he got closer for a little while, and then spent twice that long getting farther away. He stayed in Philadelphia, though, and thought he might never leave.

He loved the Italian neighborhoods; the Irish, he could take or leave. He loved the baseball, and the movement of the city—the Mummers and the restaurants and the clubs. He snuck off once in a while to the art museum when he was looking for women. He even went once to the symphony orchestra, thinking she might throw him a bone for old times' sake, but she wasn't there in the horn section, and he guessed she hadn't practiced enough at the convent to make the cut.

The city, though, was crawling with life. At least it had been then. Lately, it was slower.

Lately, he'd lie in bed after a fire, naked, hawking up soot, his eyes stinging, lying in the smell of smoke and sweat and rubber, and see himself being walled in. Something was building around him, always at the same numbing crawl, walling him in. He witnessed this phenomenon from a familiar, removed perspective—from his earliest memory, he'd had a facility to see himself from a distance. Sometimes when he thought about it, it seemed like he'd been someplace else, watching himself, for most of his life.

He'd been in the department two years now, and was already famous for the chances he took. The feeling afterwards wasn't the same as it had been in the beginning, though. By now, in fact, there was no feeling afterwards. He was disconnected.

And so, needing a hobby, Packard became a runner.

Here was Packard's training schedule: Midnight, he would walk into a neighborhood where he did not belong, say Kensington or the Devil's Pocket. He'd sit down in a bar, order a beer, and insult one of the locals. The easiest way to insult one was to use a word he didn't understand. *Avuncular, bulbous, crescendo.* Say the word *avuncular*, the next thing you knew, fifteen of them had bats and were chasing you down the street, screaming "Kill the queer."

And the beauty part, as they said in the Pocket, was that they meant it. If they caught you, you were dead. Packard, however, was in excellent shape and undefeated, and eventually went looking for better competition.

Packard had his hands in his jacket, feeling around for his keys, when he noticed the car. His pockets were full of his regular stuff—change, matches, a couple of wieners for the dog, loose cigarettes, rubbers that had fallen out of a vending machine in a bar down on Race Street in Chinatown when he'd pulled the lever for Alka-Seltzer. The dog was a stray, all mange and scabs, with hideous black tits and a fifty-pound head. She didn't want to be touched, and Packard didn't want to touch her; it was enough for them both just to hand over the wieners—one when he left his place, one when he came back. The dog would bare her teeth before she accepted it—reminding him of the rules—and then swallow it whole. It wasn't much, but the truth was it felt better the next morning than it had with the nun.

The dog wasn't around tonight, and Packard had a sudden, unsettled premonition that something had happened, that she wasn't coming back. He was loyal, even if he hadn't been a real sweetheart to start with.

It was snowing, and the whole city had stopped. The neighborhood streets were narrow and clogged with cars, some of them packed to the windows by the snowplows, some high-centered or simply stuck in ice ruts and left in their own tracks. Earlier in the winter, a fire had burned half a block in Tasker Homes before the trucks could even get to the houses. Four dead, trapped and innocent of everything except not having money to heat the apartment. At least that night, they were.

Packard looked again at the car, knowing who

it was. He stood motionless, the dog still on his mind, trying to focus, trying to get the moment to hold still and feel it. Nothing.

The snow was filthy and wet and black all around him. Traction could be a problem. He'd left his car on South Street tonight and walked back to the apartment from a pool hall. He had tennis shoes on and his feet were freezing. Where would the dog be, a night like this?

He'd gone into the place with a ten-dollar bill, bought a beer and gotten into a fifty-dollar game of nine ball, knowing what could happen, but all night long he couldn't lose on purpose, and ended up six hundred ahead, and then spent a hundred of it buying drinks and tipping. He'd gotten himself a little drunk.

The car windows were fogged—that was the first thing he noticed—then a faint glow inside as one of them lit a cigarette. Then, at two o'clock in the morning in South Philadelphia, standing outside on the coldest night of the year, he suddenly felt alone.

A minute later they were out of the car, one of them with a crowbar, the other with a bat. They wore loafers and leather caps and long camel-hair coats, and slipped on the ice as they separated and then closed in. There was no reason for them to hurry, though. Packard didn't want a head start.

The younger one, who still had the cigarette in his mouth, came in a wide circle around a puddle frozen over with ice and then found himself behind another, smaller puddle. He hesitated a moment and then jumped, skidded when he hit the sidewalk, and went into the air backward, turning as he fell, like a child who decides too late that he doesn't want to go down the slide. Then he hit, and lay still a moment, and the crowbar rang on the cement.

"Albert, for Christ's sake," the older one said, "you'll wake up the whole neighborhood."

He came up off the sidewalk slowly, holding his knee, limping and furious, and wiped at the dirt on his coat. Then he picked up the crowbar and began to beat it against the parking meter, slipping half off his feet again as he swung.

"All right, Albert," the man said, "that's enough."

And the kid stopped.

The man looked at Packard almost apologetically. Packard had seen him a few times before—he was not from this neighborhood, but was from some neighborhood, somebody who'd come up the old way, gotten his nose spread a few times, his ears lopped, and had made something of himself in the business. Packard noticed that he'd spent some money on his shoes—Packard knew clothes and shoes, especially shoes—and nothing on his teeth. The locals had called the man Mr. Bambi when they told Packard that he'd been around looking for him. "You're a nice guy, Packard," they'd said, "pay him his money."

It was eleven hundred dollars, and they'd been

after him for six, seven weeks, and at that moment Packard could have written a good check for eleven hundred dollars five hundred times in a row. One of his great-grandfathers had invented tire tread, and nobody in the family had worked for a living since. Packard had been connected to money all his life.

Mr. Bambi stood beneath the streetlamp, casting a gorilla's shadow across the cement. The shadow looked healthier than Mr. Bambi did—younger, and you couldn't see his teeth.

"You don't mind my asking," he said, "what was the plan?"

That was the question all right. *What was the plan?*

"Fuck, Mr. Bambi," the kid said, "I tink I bwoke my leg."

Packard had seen the kid before, too, hanging around with his friends, always in new clothes, combing his greasy hair over and over, talking to girls who never even looked up. The kid had lost an index finger somewhere in his travels, and sometimes stuck the stub in his nose for the girls as they walked by. And still they didn't pay attention.

Go figure women, right?

"What do you say we go inside where it's warm," Mr. Bambi said, "take care of this like gentlemen." He sounded like a reasonable man.

The kid was still limping around, holding his knee. "He tinks he's got a bwoken leg," Packard said. "Maybe you should take him to the hospital."

Hearing that Packard was laughing at him, the kid ran at him with his eyes closed, swinging the crowbar at his head. Packard took a step backward and fell into Mr. Bambi, who was surprised and stumbled and then pushed him away. It wasn't an angry push, though; in some way, he was still asking if they couldn't all just be reasonable.

Then they closed in, the kid feinting with the crowbar, Mr. Bambi coming straight on, looking resigned, and Packard waited, timing the kid's swing, and then went right past him and up the sidewalk.

He ran flat-footed for traction, and it felt slower this way, but he could hear them behind him and knew where they were, and could tell by the ragged breathing that they were not used to running. He slowed down, not wanting to lose them yet, and led them a block like that, the kid yelling bloody murder, Mr. Bambi not wasting his air, just trying to keep up.

Another block, and Packard heard them slow and stop. He stopped too, grabbed his knee and limped around in a circle, imitating the kid.

They came after him again, balls out, and he ran ahead, running easily, feeling light and happy, crossing the street.

He thought he'd been hit by a car. One second he was there, the next second he wasn't. Then there was a blur of mange and teeth somewhere on the edge of his vision. It brought to mind the night he was lifted out of his bunk in the Pacific. But there were no lights now, no sound except the footsteps behind him, only the animal's terrible breath before she closed down on the junction of his neck and shoulder.

She was still mauling him when they caught up; it seemed like a long time. They stood there awhile with their hands on their knees, catching their breath, watching, and then the kid stepped forward with the crowbar over his head, but Mr. Bambi was looking at the strange turns Packard's leg took as it lay in the snow, and stopped him. He watched a little longer and then kicked her away. He winked at Packard and held off the boy.

"Too many cooks in the kitchen," he said.

Packard was lying across the side of a snowbank, which he estimated was as steep and cold as the row-house roofs above him. He had been hurt before, and knew that afterwards he would not remember the pain. If he were pushed, he could describe it, tell you something about it, but the experience itself, it was gone when it was gone. Like a palm job, he thought, looking at the kid. But if you wanted to talk about pain—which was not the same thing as remembering it—you might as well ask the old women out on their stoops all summer about having babies. They could talk to you about pain.

Packard saw the kid was excited in a damp,

queer-bait way, and hoped, speaking of palm jobs, that he never got even that close to a girl in his life.

He was a hard case, and he had been hurt before, if never in quite this way. His leg, at least, was broken in ways he couldn't figure out. He went in and out of focus. He'd thought before about what it would be like if they caught him, if he'd try to give them the money or just smile and find out where it all led.

It never occurred to him that it could turn out anything like this; that he'd be alone in the street, not knowing whether to laugh or cry, double-crossed and heartbroken over a dog that wasn't even his.

In the end, when the focus began to come back, it was from another place. It was hard to say exactly where, but approximately from one of the row-house roofs. He began to see himself and the street clearly, though, see the whole mess he was in, and then it changed and it was the mess *he*—the other he—was in, and it was all suddenly secondhand.

The ambulance arrived much later, and the medics found him lying half-conscious in the snow and saw the leg—told him he might lose the leg—and gave him a shot of morphine for the pain and wrote in their report later that the victim was delirious, that nothing they said would make him stop laughing.

CHAPTER 2

BROOKLINE

Los Angeles, March 1953

The fat man couldn't turn it loose. Got the sun in the sky, birds in the trees, shine on his shoes—everything a gentleman need but two wives and a death wish, as the old saying went—but he still just stood there froze over the ball, the seconds ticking away, like somebody couldn't pee for the nurse.

And yellow pants, speaking of urination.

The boy was a few steps behind the fat man and to the side, carrying his bag. He'd been standing by watching half the morning, and there was something about the fat man he still couldn't place. Something familiar that reminded him of something else. The boy waited for the connection to come, not trying to hurry it along. Connections came to him all the time—people to things and things to people, things to each other, surprises and amusements out of the thin air—it wasn't anything he did to cause it, and sometimes, like now, he knew one was there before he knew what it was.

And sometimes, of course, it turned out to be a surprise but not no amusement at all.

The boy was almost eighteen years old, but innocent-looking for that age, still hadn't grown into his feet, and when he spoke, it was soft and mumbled, where you could barely tell what he said. He was known around these environs as Train.

The fat man's weight hung over his belt in bags in front and over the sides, and his thighs moved around under those big loose pants—it looked like children hiding in the curtains. He took a long breath and then went still, with eyes like a strangling.

This same thing been going on long enough now that it lost its comical aspect. Then a ripple passed across his face, like a fish swam up to the surface, and they all saw it and knew it was time to shut up and hold still, and for a little while nobody moved, nobody dare to move, because any little perturbation now, any flutterance in the air, and they got to all go back and start over from the beginning. The breeze itself stopped blowing.

The boy held his breath, and held the bag—his hand went over the irons to keep them quiet—and then the fat man sighed, like the news on this shot was already in, feeling that old, familiar misery stalking him again, and picked the club almost straight up off the ground.

Which was a relief to all concerned.

Once the swing was safely begun, Train went squint-eyed, as he sometimes did to diversify himself when things was slow, and watched the whole scene transmogrified around to Little Big-horn, Montana. (The boy picked up that word off a tote, a retired justice of the peace from someplace down south, who found it himself in the *Reader's Digest's* "It Pays to Increase Your Word Power," and ever since, every time he hit it into the water or out into the yards and houses and streets beyond the course, he turned to his playing partners and said, "Gentlemen, you have witnessed an officer of the court transmogrified to human shit," and that was surefire material for the regular associates of his, no matter how many times they heard it before.)

The fat man lifted the club higher, pulling himself up with it, and Train saw Custer, all wore-out, fighting to the end in his yellow pants, standing his ground and swinging at the redskins with an empty rifle as they floated past on their war ponies. The last white man alive.

There was a thought.

And then, just like the movie, here come the tomahawk, cutting down through the sky, death on a stick, and then a wet, heavy noise when it hit home. And then Custer was gone as fast as he come, and the club head had took a divot half a foot deep, and the ball itself squirted almost straight right, off the cart path toward the trees.

Time slowed down and everybody went numb-mouth at once. The ball ran like a jail break, and the boy knew to a certainty that even though it was only a twosome, this round was surely three hours a side, and there wasn't no chance in hell he was finishing in time to carry two bags today. They gone out late in the first place—didn't get on the first tee till 10:22—and as soon as the fat man had hit it once, Train realized that his wet dreams was better organized than his tote's golf swing.

He looked back up the fairway now to keep the fat man from seeing what he was thinking. Not that he would necessarily know exactly what it was, but they were all quick to notice cheek in their caddies.

The fat man, though, was still staring at the spot where the ball gone into the trees, like he was offering it one last chance to give itself up and come out, and then without any warning he wheeled around and sent the club in there too, a sound vomiting up out of him that wasn't in any *Reader's Digest*, or any dictionary, that didn't have letters to spell it, a sound as old as the ancient game of golf itself. He grunted with the effort and the shaft winked in the sun as it crossed the morning sky.

"They must of left the sprinklers on all night," the fat man said after he got back in control of his deportment again. He lifted his shirt to look at the line of mud that had splashed up, and Train saw a patch of wild red hair on the hanging underside of his belly, and the skin beneath it was faintly blue with veins. "It's getting worst than the public courses," he said, "the way History keeps this thing." And then, glancing at his stomach, as if something there reminded him of it, he said, "Maybe he got his pecker stuck in Helen Sears' storm drain last night. . . ."

The man he was playing with started to laugh at that, got about halfway home. He didn't make no laughing sound, just the motion, and it was hard to tell what he was thinking. He was a guest, though, not a member, so he didn't know who Helen Sears was, didn't know nothing about the situation. Just walked around so far looking like something out here might amuse him. What it was, Train couldn't say. The name tag on his golf bag was from Hillcrest, said Mr. Miller Packard, but Train named him "the Mile Away Man" on the first tee, on account it seemed like in all that amusement, the man was someplace else half the time, like not everything was getting through. It was an old habit, naming his totes; there was five or six he called "the Living Dead." Not out loud, of course, only to himself, behind his expressionless face.

Train, whose name was Lionel Walk, Jr., kept to himself and always had. The other caddies laughed at their totes back in the shed, imitated what they said and how they limped, but then they picked up the bag and it was "Yessir" and "No sir" and "Thank you, sir," all the way around. The boy did not have the loose-ness for that, but expected that someday he would. From what he seen, the world conducted

17

its business by who was there when you was talking.

Even the members themself watched what they said, he noticed, at least around each other. Or until they started to playing bad. Around the working people, of course, they didn't care. For instance, they been calling the greens superintendent "History" all year, sometimes right to his face. As in "He's history." Not that it bothered the superintendent any. He started calling himself that lately, in fact, seemed pleased with the idea he had them wanting to fire him.

It was the custom at Brookline when you got mad enough to throw your sticks, the first thing you did when you come back to your senses was to blame it on History, but these days it was more connected to his romance with Helen Sears than his habit of sitting around on his ass all day reading books while the course went to hell. She was even driving him to work now. Bud Sears was dead since Halloween, but that wasn't the point. The point—at least the way History explained it—was that you die and then the *greenskeeper* just walks in the front door and heads to the liquor cabinet, probably wearing your shoes. It was everything wrong with being old and rich, the core of the apple: scavengers was everywhere.

It tickled History to death.

Sometimes in the morning when there was extra work out on the course, History called down to the caddy shed for Train and paid him three dollars for

18

the day to run the mowers or fill divots or punch the greens or whatever it was had to be done. He used Train because he was strong—stronger than the rest of the grounds crew could believe, looking at him—and a fast learner, and never complained that he had too much to do. When Train was finished, History was usually back in the storage barn, sitting around on his ass drinking a martini and reading *The Great Gatsby*. He'd been inside that same book ever since he started up with Helen Sears, seemed like he couldn't get enough of the story. Sometimes he read parts of it out loud. He kept gin, vermouth, and a bottle of olives on the same shelf with the motor oil, and one afternoon he showed Train how to make a dry martini, and told him that anything further he needed to know about the country club set he would find in the pages of F. Scott Fitzgerald.

The fat man was drinking gin since the second hole. Train recognized the aroma from his afternoon in the barn with History and F. Scott. The fat man, of course, didn't appreciate it the way History did. Sniffing and twirling and all that. History become so satisfied with the flossy life at Mrs. Sears' house and how he looked with a martini in his hand, that he enjoyed to play with a drink these days as much as he did drinking it.

The fat man took it straight from the thermos and closed his eyes and shook like a dog that run through the sprinkler and said, "Ah, breakfast." He said that same joke every hole, again and again, the way golfers did. The drinking hadn't untied him yet, though, where he could just step over the ball and hit it without all that quivering around and waiting.

Earlier, he'd offered the thermos once to Mr. Packard, who was lost in his thoughts at the time and jumped back like somebody showed him a snake, and then said no, no thank you, it was still a little early in the day for him.

The fat man had another shooter and returned the thermos to Train, did this in the same fashion he handed back his clubs, or held out his hand for a ball, without admitting the boy was there, but it didn't matter to Train if he looked at him or not, any more than it mattered if he fell in the pond and drown. He knew Sweet wouldn't have give him the tote in the first place if he was a tipper. The kind of totes Train got lately were the kind that won two dollars and handed their caddy a quarter, and went home thinking everybody had a wonderful time. And none of them—not even the old ones who had turned kind and sweet when their balls dried up—nobody ever talked to Train like he could do nothing but carry a golf bag, except to be a fireman or a policeman, the sort of thing they thought of themself back when they were children.

So Train guessed he got on Sweet's bad side; he didn't know how. There was always somebody on it, though, and whoever that was stayed there usually till somebody else took their place. He guessed maybe it was just his turn.

The other caddy—the one carrying Mr. Packard's sticks—was called Florida. From what the old-timers said, Florida come to Los Angeles before there was sunshine, and all the time since he'd been walking this same course in Brentwood, and all that time it was "Lawdy, Lawdy" whenever a ball went into the water or the trees, like it was the first time he'd seen white people treated so cruelly, always laying a "sir" in there somewhere, as if the act of carrying the man's golf clubs wasn't enough to prove he had the right intentions. His favorite word, though, was *eviscerate*. The tote hit a good shot, he said something like, "Well, Florida, I believe I got both cheeks into that one," and Florida would wipe at his eye and shake his head and say, "Indeed, sir. You done *eviscerate* that one." And if they was winning, that would make them smile; some of them even walked around the course saying "You done eviscerate that one" to each other.

Other things made them smile when they lost. Bitter things, and when Florida saw that coming, he knew how to disappear. He still be there holding the bag, but somehow the tote didn't see him anymore. Florida had an eye that leaked, and the tips of his fingers were whiter than any white man's skin, and Sweet always give him good totes, every time out. Sweet took care of him, no one knew why. Train heard that once he'd got a fifty-dollar tip, just

21

put it in his pocket and went back to the wooden, tin-roofed shed where they all waited for their jobs, and never said a word. He had no interest in anybody down there, especially Sweet, and saved his socializing and smiling for the golf course. He was like Mr. Boyd the golf pro—good-natured for professional reasons only.

Train stopped now near the trees where the fat man's ball disappeared after it hit the cart path. Brookline had more trees than any country club in Los Angeles County—somebody actually counted the damn trees—and the members were oddly proud of that, like they grown them themself.

"You see where it went in, Miller?" the fat man said.

Mr. Packard looked back up the tree line. "The ball or the club?" he said.

The fat man crashed off into the trees and a different kind of laugh played at the corners of Mr. Packard's mouth. He was easygoing in some way that was the opposite of what you expected. It caught you by surprise. Still, it was clear to Train there was a bad side there and you didn't want no part of it.

Train adjusted the bag across his shoulder and followed the fat man in, picking up the three wood that he thrown and wiping off the dirt. There was nineteen clubs in the bag and he had to lift them up like you do flowers in a vase, shake them loose at the bottom to get this one in too. He counted them again to make sure: nineteen. The heaviest bag he carried all spring.

The fat man was out of sight about a minute, and by the time Train caught up, he was standing over a perfect, white, unmarked Spalding Dot golf ball, a ball that never hit any cart path. And it was laying there in a perfect opening in the trees, maybe eight feet across and about that high, wide open to the green. Train stopped and took the bag off his shoulder and felt embarrassed in some way, like he caught him picking his nose. The fat man looked at him, letting him know he didn't care what he saw, or what he thought. Train glanced away, keeping himself out of it. Just like Florida.

"Three iron," the fat man said, and held out his hand. It was the wrong iron—he needed to get the ball up in the air—but then, when your game recalled Custer's last stand, most of the time there wasn't no right iron in the bag anyway. Golf was like that, as cruel as a clubfoot.

Mr. Packard's voice came to them from the other side of the foliage. "You find it, Pink?"

"Yeah," the fat man said, "I got it over here."

He looked once again at Train and then stepped back over the ball. He took a practice swing, his stomach rolling beneath his shirt, the head of the club scraping the overhead leaves. He stepped back and took another swing, ripping into the branches this time, and then another. Train thought of a saying he heard recently: Rules are made to be broken. Which was not necessarily a golf saying,

23

he knew, but the golf course is where he heard it. There was always a philosopher in a foursome, and some days Train played their sayings back in his head to pass the time, found the right situation to use one on every hole. Some of the sayings were comical and some of them were resentful, but either way, they all came down to the same thing, which was disappointment. Disappointment was the only thing about the game that lasted. You could try not to get your hopes up, but you might as well tell the cat not to kill the birds. Things work the way they work.

There were other things they said, too. There were jokes; sometimes Train heard the same one three or four times a round. The old golfers forgot which ones they'd already told, and which ones they already heard, and walked around all day laughing, wondering why life never seemed this sweet to them when they were young and could enjoy it. One day when the wind blew in so dry and hot there was nobody to tote, Train spent an afternoon in the shed with a scorecard and a pencil, writing down all the jokes he heard about players that killed their wives accidentally and had to take an unplayable lie to remove the ball. Or the wife got hit by lightning, or bit by a snake, which all came to the same thing. There was twenty-six jokes about dead wives that he could remember. Train had never caddied for women—they didn't let them play at Brookline, except a nine-hole scramble on Halloween night—and wondered if they told jokes about their husbands too. He thought about Bud Sears then, and his wife Helen fucking the ears off old History, and thought they probably did.

The fat man finished with the foliage, and half the limb was in pieces on the ground and the air smelled like cut wood and the leaves did not touch the club head when he swung. Then he skulled it anyway, the shot coming out low and hot, headed into the pond, but it caught the lip of a bunker instead, caromed sideways, and rolled out into the fairway 155 yards from the green.

"You cunt," the fat man said, almost like whispering in her ear, and dropped the club on the ground. Train picked it up and followed him out of the trees. Another saying come to him— The wrong place at the wrong time—and he had the sudden realization that that was the direction things was going ever since he got up.

"You see that, Miller?" the fat man said. "The whore don't hit the trap, it's on the green."

Mr. Packard had that Mile Away Man look on his face, but he turned back to the tee box, saw there was nobody waiting, in spite of how long it took the fat man over the ball, and said, "Hit another one. I don't care."

The fat man seem to considered that, then shook his head like he couldn't bring himself to break the rules. "No, fuck, we got a bet. . . ."

Train seen by now that Mr. Packard had his bait in the water, even if he wasn't paying no attention to the game, but now it occurred to him that the fat

25

man might be doing the same thing. Mr. Packard was the golfer—he was giving the fat man a stroke a hole—but who was in the boat and who was in the water, that was anybody's guess now. It was about money, though; the two of them wasn't friends.

Mr. Packard came to his own ball and turned back to Florida. "What's left?" he said. Florida put the clubs down and squinted at the green.

"Two ten, sir, but most of the gentlemens say it seem to play an extra club."

Mr. Packard thought it over, then took an old, scarred persimmon wood from his bag and hit the ball high over the pond. It landed just on the cut of the green, thirty feet below the hole. Train noticed he quit the swing a little short again, like something was bothering with his knee.

As they were walking up, the fat man moved closer to Mr. Packard, breathing hard from catching up, and said, "Miller, you don't mind, I just as soon trade caddies at the turn. . . ." He looked back quickly at Train and said, "This fucking kid I got is giving me the willies. I don't think he can talk."

Train walked up the fairway behind him, carrying his bag, feeling the blood in his face. They got to the fat man's ball, and this time, to prove his point, he said, "Okay, sport, what do I got left?"

Train didn't answer. Florida scanned the scene in a leisurely way, but when his eyes fell across Train, they was a four-alarm fire. One of the players got upset with a caddy, sometime they

26

all did, cost everybody their gratuity. He looked away and the sweet, ignorant expression returned to his face.

"See what I'm talking about?" the fat man said.

Mr. Packard didn't like to be brought into it. "C'mon, Pink," he said, "it's your own course. You know what you got left."

"That ain't the point," the fat man said. "You missed my point." Then he stepped directly in front of Train and pronounced each word distinctly, so there couldn't be any mistakes over what the point was. "All right," he said, "go slow, Nee-gro. What do I got left?"

Train looked at the green, at the pond. There was a dead carp floating in some brown froth near the bank. They stocked carp to eat the froth, keep the ponds looking nice, but there were more dead fish all the time, and if there was something worse-looking than brown froth on the pond, it was a carp floating in it. It smelled too.

Train wouldn't answer.

"You understand English, correct?"

He nodded, and now he felt Mr. Packard looking at him too, curious if he was afflicted, and Train still didn't say a word. It felt exactly like Miss Binion handed him the chalk and said, "Lionel, perhaps you would like to diagram this sentence for the class." That's how much chance he had.

"Let me ast it a different way," the fat man said. He was beginning to enjoy it now. "If it was you standing here, and I was carrying the bag"—he smiled at Mr. Packard to make sure he was catching this—"if I was toting your bag, and you come up to this shot, what club would you ast me for to hit it?"

Train looked at the green.

"You played this course, ain't you?" the fat man said. "Monday mornings, the caddies all come out here and have a big time. . . ."

Train nodded, and then was sorry he gave him even that.

"And you supposed to be a caddy, ain't you, sport?" When Train didn't answer, the fat man slipped into his Negro dialect and said, "You-all is a caddy, right?"

Train nodded again, wishing he hadn't, wishing that he could take off his shoes and walk away. Just like that, drop the clubs, kiss my ass, and walk up the fairway barefoot, while the grass was still cool. Instead, he stood still, and the fat man reached into the bag and came out with the thermos. Looking at him the whole time. He filled the lid and drank it down, and this time he didn't shiver afterwards.

"So it's Monday morning, Leroy. What is you-all gone hit?"

It was quiet again while they waited. He heard Florida say "Lawdy" under his breath.

"Nine iron," he said.

The fat man screwed the lid on the thermos, looking surprised. "A nine iron?" He put his fingers on Train's arm and squeezed. "You must be stronger than you looks."

Train held still.

"Then what the fuck, Leroy, give us the nine." Train pulled the iron out of the bag and the fat man gave him the thermos to put away.

He swung the club once, a slower, easy practice swing, then looked again at Mr. Packard, and then at Train. "You says the nine, sho enough?"

The fat man stood over the ball only a few seconds, not nearly as long as before, and then his stomach rolled up—Train glimpsing that awful pelt of hair—and then it dropped back over his belt and the ball came off the club straight and high, a bit of the divot still stuck to the face, and the fat man held a finishing pose while it was in the air. Showing Mr. Packard his real game now, let him feel the hook in his mouth.

"Be the stick," the fat man said.

Mr. Packard gave Train a quick look of amusement, and the ball hung there in the sky, perfectly on line, right until it disappeared into the pond. About ten feet short of the far bank. The fat man opened his hands and the club dropped behind his shoulder.

"The nine iron," he said, almost like he was asking a question.

The wrong place at the wrong time, that was the expression.

"Yessir," Train said.

"Yessir? Yessir what? You seen where it went?"

Train looked at the pond and saw a line of bubbles.

29

"I liked him better when he couldn't talk," the fat man said, making a joke of it, but then he took a step closer and Train saw the flat shine in his eyes and knew it was trouble. He'd heard that sometimes a member forgot himself when things went wrong and slapped his caddy. It was against the rules at Brookline, and after it happened, the member had to cool down and give the caddy something to take care of it.

The way the caddies looked at it—most of them—the members was feeble enough, it was like finding a dollar in your shoe. There were some, though, that didn't see it that way. Some of them wouldn't take the money, and sometimes if they stared too long at the man after it happened, made his sand tingle, the member would say something to Mr. Boyd in the pro shop after the round, and the caddy had to go home and think over what else he could do for a living.

The fat man wasn't feeble, though; he looked like he moved furniture.

"Pink . . ."

Mr. Packard said his name, and everything stopped. Didn't say it any particular way that you'd remember—in fact, you could almost hear a chuckle inside the word—but something was rolling down on Train, right on top of him, and just like that it turned around and rolled the other way. A moment passed and then the fat man smiled.

"I was only fucking with him, Miller," he said. "He's fucking with me, I'm fucking with him. He's a smart boy, he knows that." Then he turned and looked at Train again. "That's right, ain't it, Leroy? You're a smart boy. . . ."

Train couldn't answer. Back to that.

"We all seen you got a sense of humor. . . ."

Train picked up the nine iron and waited for the fat man to start down the fairway. Waited the way a Mexican would for the problem to go away. There were days he wished he could be Mexican himself—give up toting the bags and just work on the ground crew for History, come out early and rake the traps or weed the flowers. He could always make things grow. But the Mexicans was all illegal, and the club hired them by the day, first come, first serve, and didn't pay them but a dollar for ten hours, and even then Train sometimes saw them fighting in the morning over a place in line. Train guessed it was better work than picking fruit, and guessed they would caddy if the club would let them.

Carrying the bags, Train got a dollar and a half for eighteen holes, plus whatever the tote gave him at the end. Sometimes in the summer, when the sun set at eight-thirty or nine, he made twelve, fourteen dollars. He liked to lie in bed at home at the end of those days and take an ink pen and color in George Washington's eyes. Color them blue. He gave half the money to his mother, rolled the other half up in a sock and put it in his drawer with the other socks, didn't look any different from them. Then there was two socks, and then there was three. He always knew exactly how much was in the socks, and sometimes at night he pulled one on his foot, just to see how it felt to push his toes in there with all those dollar bills.

This particular morning, though, he wouldn't minded being a dollar-a-day Mexican in a flower bed. The fat man was staring at him again, trying to see if Train was laughing at him. Train could tell sometimes what white people were thinking, and was afraid it went the other direction too. He heard Mr. Packard again, sounded like he was fooling in a way, and in a way it didn't. "So what are we going to do, Pink? We waiting for the kid to apologize for you hitting the ball in the water?"

"Miller, you mind?" There was a bad note in that, stepped over the line between them, and the fat man heard it too, and then tried to change it after it was already out of his mouth. Tried to pull back the reins. Even now, mad as a snake and the best shot he hit all day laying in the pond, he seemed a little afraid. Like he worked for Mr. Packard, only it wasn't that. Train guessed that he'd seen the man's bad side, or maybe just knew it was there, the way Train did.

"Lookit," the fat man said, "I'm the one down five, one and three. This is between me and him."

"If that's what's bothering you, forget the bet," Mr. Packard said. "We're just hacking it around today anyway."

"No," the fat man said. "Fuck no, a bet is a bet." Train heard in his voice how bad he wanted to win, and knew then the way it would turn out. You wanted something too much, it never came.

Florida was sweating. He'd set his bag down and was standing beside it, looking out of focus. The fat man pulled the thermos out again and had another drink. Loose lips sink ships, that was an expression he heard out here too. Fat lips sink ships. Train liked the sound of that. Mr. Packard was watching the fat man too, and then he looked around and seem to chuckle again without making noise and said, "You know, Pink, I been thinking maybe we ought to call it a day."

"I never said I didn't want to play," the fat man said. He was eager to clear up the misunderstanding, couldn't get his feet under him fast enough. "I only said this fucking kid's spooky, is all," he said. "I didn't mean nothing about you. I just want to switch caddies at the turn."

"Fine with me," Mr. Packard said, "unless the boy's gotten too attached to you to change sides." And then he looked over at Train and winked.

So Train and Florida traded bags, and Florida stumbled backward under the new weight, then caught himself, rattling the clubs.

"Now I got a problem with you?" the fat man said, trying to make it all a joke again.

"No sir," Florida said. "I just eventuated to lost my balance."

The fat man bust out laughing at that—*eventuated*—and somehow the word changed everything. One word, and the game was relaxed and easy, and Train's troubles with the fat man seemed like the grudges that people hold without remembering what they were about, the kind they just kept there to occupy the space. Harmless. The sun was warm and the air smelled sweet and the new bag was lighter and comfortable against his shoulder, and five minutes later Florida was on the way to the next world.

He'd set the fat man's bag down beside the green, taken a handkerchief out of his back pocket and wiped at his neck, and then smiled in a peculiar way, a confusion passing over his face, and then pitched onto the ground.

Mr. Packard got down next to him and rolled him over and loosened his shoelaces and his shirt. Florida's eyes looked hungry, and white foam spilled out his mouth and down over his lips and chin and his neck.

"He's taking a fit," the fat man said.

Florida was curling into himself now, his arms tight against his chest, fighting to breathe. And then he seemed to relax. That fast.

"It's a fit," the fat man said again. He hadn't looked at Florida, though. Train noticed that he hadn't looked. "I seen them do this before; sometimes they swallowed their tongue."

Mr. Packard spoke to Train like the fat man wasn't there. "Run back to the clubhouse," he said. "Tell them to call an ambulance." There was nothing hurried in the way he said it, though, and Train knew there was nothing to hurry for.

Train let go of the bag, surprised at the clatter it made when it hit the ground, and noticed something shiny just peeking out one of the pockets; for an instant it caught his reflection.

He sprinted fifty yards along the cart path, thinking of Florida, scared to death, and then kicked off his shoes and moved into the grassy fairway, running directly into the golfers behind him. There were four of them standing together on the tee, leaning against their clubs. Two of them hitched up their pants over their stomach, two underneath it. One or two, it looked like they might be carrying a baby. Scabs on their hands and arms and faces; Train had been noticing for a while now that there was a certain age when old men begun to look like they been dragged home behind the car.

"Hey! Where you think you're going, son?"

And: "This here is a golf course, Leroy, not a racetrack . . . ."

Some of the members called all the caddies Leroy.

And then one of them speaking to another: "Is that one of ours?" The golf course did strange things with sound. Sometimes late in the afternoon you could hear a whisper across the fairway.

One of the golfers hit a ball at him—at least he seemed to hit it at him—but it sailed out over the fence, and Train paid no attention and kept coming, straight into them. They quit shouting and then edged away from the tee, decided that

35

the runaway caddy problem was something they'd take up with the pro back at the clubhouse instead of handling it themself.

Train went straight over the tee box without breaking stride. Once he was past it he heard them yelling again, but now he couldn't make out the words. There was another group ahead of him then, waiting in the rough behind the old foursome, and Train headed off into the trees before any of them could yell at him too.

The air was damp in the shade, and the branches seemed to grab onto his legs. He became conscious of the sounds—his feet slapping against the ground, the brushing of his pants legs as he ran, his own breathing. The cracks of old limbs breaking off trees. He was sweating, and it felt cool and safe in there, being out of sight, and just as that thought arrived, his foot hit a root and he was spinning, deaf with pain, and the next second he broke back into the sunlight, crossing the third fairway just behind another foursome, and noticed his little toe was pointed off to the side, like a thumb, and was bleeding where the nail was torn.

There was a wide creek separating this fairway from the eighth, and he ran through it, too spent to jump, dropping into the stinking muck at the bottom all the way to his knees, stumbling, falling, then pulling out and scrambling up the other side. The fall used him up and stole what was left of his breath, and he thought he heard someone laughing. The sound could have been coming up out of his own chest, though.

He headed up the long slope of the ninth hole, keeping close to the cart path now, his legs beginning to go soft. He closed his eyes and pictured Florida falling face-first onto the green, the look of confusion that come just before. He pictured the foam spilling out his mouth and nose, and knew he was drained inside too, every plug in there pulled at once. He pictured those things, and willed himself up the hill to the clubhouse, as if there was something up there that could change what had happened.

When he opened his eyes again, the building rose up in front of him and the sun was blinding off the windows where the white men sat and drank after they'd played golf. To his certain knowledge, there had never been a bleeding nigger without his shoes on inside the clubhouse at Brookline, but he ran directly over the practice green anyway, disturbing a gentleman in orange pants who was practicing one-foot putts, and through the glass doors that led into the lounge.

It was dark and cool inside, the air as still as a cave, and he stopped in his tracks and waited to see what would happen. Expecting they might shoot him. The bartender was a huge, sweet-smelling Negro called Richard, and he was staring at Train, seemed to have stopped breathing. Four ancient ladies were in a corner playing cards, a halo of cigarette smoke hanging over the table. He noticed their hands. Diamonds and bones. One of them looked up at him and smiled.

The bartender was coming around the bar now, looking left and right to see who else might have been afflicted by what just come in the door. His hair glistened under the overhead lights, and Train could not shake the feeling that he was about to be shot, and then it occurred to him, as the bartender came across the rug, that when he dropped Mr. Miller's golf bag, what was peeking out the pocket was the nose of a pistol.

The bartender was smiling to keep the ladies from panicking. He came very close to Train before he spoke, and then leaned in so no one else could hear.

"Rooster, I ever see you again, it better be through that door, runnin' the other way," he said. Train could smell the pomade he used to conk his hair. He stepped back a little, needing some space to talk. The bartender glanced again at the ladies in the corner. One of them had her cigarette in a long white holder and picked it up now and had a pull. Diamonds and bones.

The bartender took his arm and headed him back toward the door. It crossed Train's mind that he might not be able to explain what happened, but suddenly the words were right there, as easy as they were for Sweet or anybody else. "There's a man died," he said.

He felt the pressure change on his arm. "What man?" the bartender said.

"Florida," Train said. "Pitched onto the green and died."

"A caddy?"

"Florida. You know old Florida . . . ."

"No sir," the bartender said, "I do not." He studied Train a moment longer, then escorted him the rest of the way out of the lounge.

Train waited until he was back outside to tell the bartender that he was supposed to call the ambulance. He could see the ladies had to be protected from the sight of himself.

"This ain't the place to come for no caddy pitched onto the green," the bartender said.

"It's where the man told me to come," Train said.

"What man?"

"The man playing golf, said to tell Richard to call somebody right away." He was surprised at how easily the lie came out of his mouth. His mother was ordinarily pleased to tell anyone who would listen that Lionel was the only child born with the male organ in the Walk family history that wasn't an accomplished liar by the time he was three years old. She said the rest of them, it was the reason they learned to talk. He didn't know if that was true—if there was any Walk family men around, he hadn't met them—but it was correct that he couldn't bring himself to tell stories. He didn't have the looseness about him for that.

"This man say who am I supposed to call?" The bartender noticed Train's toe then, and took a step

39

back. Train looked at it too, and it occurred to him for the first time that he come to the wrong place. That when the man said the clubhouse, he meant the pro shop.

"Just like it was a member," he said, "that's what the man said to do." Half a dozen of them had died out on the course in the two years Train been working here, maybe one or two more. The old-timers would talk about it for a month, until every one of them had said the same thing to each other—"Well, I see old Bud Sears finally shot his age"—proud that another soldier died in his two-color shoes. In some way it wasn't unrelated to having the most trees of any golf course in Los Angeles County.

The bartender used one finger and reached carefully through his hair and scratched a spot on his scalp, trying to figure out if calling an ambulance for a caddy could get him in trouble. Then he took a comb out of his back pocket and went over the spot, still thinking. "You go on back there," he said, "tell them Richard took care of everything." Train nodded, but he didn't move. "I'll take care of it," the bartender said, impatient to get Train away from the clubhouse.

"You don't know where he's at."

"Well then, where is he, nigger?"

"Sixth green." Train pointed, and the bartender looked out in that general direction, then went back into the lounge. He was staring Train in the eye as he locked the door against the chance that

40

there was any more like him out there waiting to come in.

Train walked to the edge of the green, past the man practicing short putts, and sat down and pulled on the toe until he heard it pop. Then he tore off the nail, which only been hanging by a piece of skin anyway. He had calmed down enough to feel these things exactly, and the pain rolled up at him in waves, the way his stomach did when he was scared.

He stood up and walked back down the long slope of the ninth hole and headed for the sixth green, leaving small round spots of blood on the grass. You come along later, you might think it was a dog had hurt his paw.

Florida was the same place he had been before, only he seemed smaller now, like he dried up. Mr. Packard was sitting on the grass next to him, his thoughts in a distant land. The fat man was off the green, sitting on his own bag, holding the thermos between his legs. Train saw all this as he jogged down the fairway—favoring the injured foot, not really hurrying anymore, just jogging for appearance sake—past the same old men who shouted at him before. There was several groups of them now, backed up and mean. The club had its rules about starting times and the speed of play. Train kept his eyes straight ahead and he stopped only once, to pick up his shoes.

Mr. Packard looked up and watched Train come

41

the last thirty yards. He seemed tired. "They call an ambulance?" he said.

"Yessir." Train didn't want to, but he had a quick look at Florida anyway, saw that Mr. Packard had closed the lids over his eyes. Somewhere behind them a golfer yelled "*Four!*" and Mr. Packard looked slowly back in that direction. Chuckled in some way that was not amusement at all.

"You wonder what gets into people," he said, and if whoever was back there could see the way they were being looked at, they wouldn't be shouting anymore. Train realized suddenly that Mr. Packard was talking to him, not to the fat man. That in fact he might be talking about the fat man.

"Yessir," he said.

Mr. Packard set his hand on Florida's chest. "Half of them can barely swing a golf club, like Pink over there, but their half-dollar Nassau, or whatever it is, it's still the reason everybody else was put here on earth," he said. Pink looked up at the insult but didn't say nothing.

Mr. Packard thought about things a minute, then did that chuckle again. "I guess they're old and they feel it slipping away," he said. "Maybe it doesn't seem possible to a kid your age, but it does slip away."

The fat man poured himself another drink.

Train looked at Florida again. It was true that he couldn't see himself laid out across the sixth green dead, still trying to smile, but he already knew he could be laid out somewhere. He'd known that a long time. He sat down to put on his shoes.

"So what are we supposed to do here?" the fat man said.

Mr. Packard said, "I think I'll wait. I think I'll sit here and wait until somebody comes and takes care of this man's body."

The ambulance rolled over the hill with the light flashing but no siren, leaving tire marks in the fairway. The members wouldn't like it when they found out who it was for. Mr. Packard stood close and watched them load Florida into the back, and then closed the back door himself, making sure it was shut tight. Nobody wanted to see Florida slide back out onto the golf course.

The fat man carried his own bag awhile and then quit at the turn, said he'd lost his timing waiting for the ambulance. "Maybe I can get a couple of players, we can come back out Thursday or Friday," he said. *Players* meant gamblers. Brookline itself had the oldest membership of any course in Southern California, average seventy-three years old, and the richest, and probably the cheapest. You didn't commonly see big stakes unless somebody brought in outside money.

Mr. Packard didn't seem to care one way or the other. He just appear tired of the whole situation. "Whatever you want," he said.

The fat man went into his pocket and came

out with a roll of bills. There were rules against gambling at Brookline, but then, there were rules against everything. Probably against carrying guns, if anybody thought of it yet. The only rules that counted, though, were who could play and what they could wear. And time, of course. Time was important. "What do I owe you?" he said.

Mr. Packard looked away like it didn't matter. Like after what happened, he didn't even know.

"I lost the side and four presses, right?" the fat man said, flipping through the bills.

"Five," Mr. Packard said.

The fat man looked at him a moment, then flipped two more bills off the end of the roll and pulled all the bills he had counted away from the rest of the money. It reminded Train of a card trick, the way he handled his money, and he saw that the fat man did a lot of business out of his pocket. He handed the bills to Mr. Packard, who never even looked to make sure it was right.

"Maybe next time we won't be sitting around forty-five minutes while somebody dies," the fat man said.

Mr. Packard said, "He looked like he was dying as fast as he could." The fat man didn't look up at that, couldn't meet his gaze, and Mr. Packard chuckled again and put the money in Train's hand.

"Give this to the old man's wife, would you?" he said, still staring at the fat man.

Train looked at the money, felt it sliding out

44

his hand. Twenty-dollar bills everywhere. The fat man was also looking, trying to sort out the exact nature of this new insult. Mr. Packard waited him out, enjoying it again, in no hurry at all.

The fat man shook his head. "Shit," he said. Like he just saw life's grand design, as often happened in golf. "Good luck on that."

"Keep five for yourself," Mr. Packard said to Train, "and see that she gets the rest."

Train folded the money over on itself so it would fit in his pocket. It felt as thick as a sandwich. The fat man said "shit" again, and then he laughed in that bitter way they sometimes did after they lost money. Mr. Packard said, "What is that, Pink, three hundred?"

"Three fifty," the fat man said, as if that was a much different thing than just losing three. "A hundred for the side, fifty a press . . ."

"All right, fat man, I'll bet you the three fifty back that—" He stopped for a moment and looked at Train. "What was your name?"

"Lionel Walk, Jr.," Train said.

"I'll bet you the three fifty back that Mr. Walk here does the right thing."

The fat man looked at him a minute, trying to figure it out. "Fuck it, Miller," he said finally, "the old man probably didn't even have a wife."

Train cleaned the clubs and set them out on the drop stand near the driveway; then he walked down the path past the machine shed and the storage barn to the tin-roof caddy's shed and bought himself a grape Nehi out of the machine. He sat down in the corner with the nine iron that he'd found in the reeds near the pond a year ago, on the same hole where Florida just died. It was a Tommy Armour autograph, with a thin blade and a smooth, hard grip. The shaft was spotted with rust, so he knew it already been there awhile when he found it. He played with it on Mondays, but took it to work every day, took it home every night, not wanting to get on the bus anymore without something in his hands. There were people living in cardboard boxes—or garages or tents—all over Darktown and Watts who took what they could.

He held the club about halfway up the shaft and absently began to bounce a ball off the blade. Straight up and down, then spinning it one way, then the other. He left the Nehi on the bench between himself and another caddy named Plural Lincoln, who was referred to as No-Tank by the other caddies when he wasn't on the premises. Plural had little broke-looking hands hanging at the end of his huge arms. Little bitty feet too. He minded his own business and smelled like fresh laundry, but nobody took his good nature for granted.

Even in the morning, when the room was crowded before anybody went out yet, he had that bench to himself. The only soul would sit down next to him was Train. Plural looked over now and noticed the Nehi, picked it up and had a swallow.

The ball was out of round, and Train could feel the shape of it right through the shaft of the club, as if he was tossing it up and down in his hand. He sensed from bounce to bounce which side of the ball would land on the face of the club when it came back. He hardly had to look.

He sat in the corner with his Nehi and his golf club, Plural a yard away, and the other caddies played cards or slept. Except for the ball and the nine iron, the caddy room was in slow motion, like it always was until the phone rang, and then Sweet would answer it and look over to see who he had and what shape they were in, and decide who went out to the first tee. For those few seconds it took to make up his mind, everyone sat up like they was posing for a picture.

Sweet had a sign on the wire mesh that said he was superintendent of caddies, and an identical one on his space in the parking lot. He had a hair-trigger temper and fingernails as long as a hairdresser. He knew all the members by name, but not by their faces, and remembered which ones would give a caddy a decent tip and which ones couldn't bring themself to do it. He had a diamond set in one of his front teeth and drove a three-year-old yellow Cadillac that he parked in his reserved spot next to the superintendent of greens. He had once been incarcerated at the state prison at Vacaville, for the criminally insane. He was light-skinned and handsome, and people whispered that he had a thousand women in his book, that he even slipped in and out the sheets with the members' wives.

People said he liked the old ones best.

He kept behind his wire cage all day, and padlocked it at night. The lock wasn't much, but nobody had ever broke in to see what was there. Once you crossed Sweet like that, you might as well look for other work.

Train sat in the corner, thinking. He didn't know how to find Florida's wife, or even if he had one. He didn't know where he lived, and he didn't know his real name, the one that would be in the telephone book. He looked at Sweet, sitting behind his cage smoking a Lucky Strike, his eyes half-closed. A contented man. Train didn't want him paying attention to him now, holding all that cash, but he was the only one who would know Florida's address, or even the family name.

Train put the club down on the bench and walked over to the cage. Sweet raised his eyes, and Train had a distinct, last-minute thought not to let him find out what was in his pocket. That was followed by another thought, just as distinct, that somehow he already knew.

"So, man," he said, "Florida just up and died."

"Yes he did," Train said. "He passed away."

Sweet smiled at that, a secret smile. "Did he said he done *eviscerated* when he went?"

"He didn't say nothing," Train said. He decided not to ask Sweet about Florida's name, and turned to sit back down.

"What is it y'all wanted?" Sweet said behind him.

Train stopped, didn't look back there. "Nothing," he said.

"You just come over here to pass the time."

Train didn't answer. He felt the money in his pocket, and wished he'd put it in his sock, where it wouldn't show.

"Nigger, I ast you what it was."

Train turned back around. "It was did you had his address," he said.

"Who?"

"Florida."

Sweet studied him, putting it together. "What you want that for?"

"I got something for his people," Train said.

"What's that?"

Everything he said made Sweet more curious. "Something from the man he was toting," he said.

Sweet stood up, and that was a sure sign of trouble. He avoided movement, went all day usually without standing up. He wanted something, he sent a caddy for it, usually one named Arthur, a coal black Oklahoma boy about Train's age, and twice as big. Arthur's flesh moved like the tides beneath his T-shirt, and he smelled like baby powder and never spoke to nobody but Sweet. Everybody was afraid of Arthur except Plural and Sweet himself.

"Let me see that," Sweet said.

"It's for Florida's people," he said, "for his wife."

"Let me see," Sweet said again, and stood by the opening in the wire cage, waiting. The other caddies were watching, and Train went into his pocket, felt the crumbs in there from some crackers he'd brought to eat that morning and crushed on the run to the clubhouse, and then the ridge of bills. There was nothing for it now but to take them out, and he did that, and cracker crumbs spilled down over his pants legs and shoes.

Train passed the bills through the opening in the cage. Out on the edge of his vision, Train saw Plural stand halfway up, looking at the money, probably trying to remember if some of it was supposed to be his. A long time ago Plural was a knockout artist, twenty-some fights in a row, and then they moved him up to the Hollywood Legion Stadium and he run into a different class of fighter, one that had good legs and wind and took him past six rounds, and that's how Plural Lincoln found out there wasn't any seventh round in him. No matter what he did, how far he ran, how long he trained, six was as far as he could go. These days he sometimes sat on the floor and argued with people that wasn't there over his share of the purse. You naturally knew not to move suddenly when he was like that. Other times he was like an old man who seen everything twice and decided it was all funny. Sweet always checked to see which Plural he had on his hands before he sent him out. However he was,

50

though, when people had to walk by, they always give it enough room that he couldn't reach out and grab them.

Sweet counted the money with his left hand, moving the bills back one at a time from the roll, keeping track in his head.

"I'll take care of this," he said when he'd finished. Plural sat back against the locker, no longer interested. He picked up the Nehi again and had another drink.

"It's for Florida's people," Train said.

Sweet nodded, but he'd quit listening back when he saw the money. "The man told me I was supposed to take it over," Train said.

Sweet looked up from the money. "Where you gone go?" he said.

"That's what I was asking, where Florida live."

"And how you gone get there if you find out?"

Train had thought about that too, and didn't know the answer. "Take the bus," he said.

"The bus don't go where Florida live. He clear the hell out somewhere in the valley. And the missus is jumpy, ain't let you in the door."

"He must of got home somehow," Train said.

"I tole you I'll take care of it," he said. "I got to go over there anyways tonight and tell them Florida passed on. That's in my description here, what I'm supposed to do."

Train stood still a minute, then turned around and went back to his spot next to Plural. He thought about the Mile Away Man offering to

51

bet three hundred and fifty dollars that he would do the right thing.

Sweet gave him a good tote that afternoon, and it wasn't till sunset, when he was walking the road out to the street and Sweet came past him in his Cadillac, blowing dust and little pieces of rock behind him, that Train remembered that five dollars of the money was supposed to be his.

It made him feel better somehow, that Sweet had stole five dollars from him too.

He went to the movies that night, thinking of Florida. The show was Gene Autry, and Train went in even though he'd sat through it one night the week before. The horse was named Champion, and it had guns for a bridle. Train preferred movies where nobody sang, but sitting in the theater kept him out of the way until his mother's new friend went to sleep. The friend's name was Mayflower. He had some beers last Sunday, dropped his arm across Train's shoulders while they was all talking, his hand at the nape of his neck, and then squeezed Train and tried to pull him closer, tried to controlled his head. Train tightened himself and held away, and they fought secretly in front of his mother over that two or three inches of space, with polite looks on their faces, Mayflower squeezing so hard Train felt the shaking in his arm.

And then the squeezing stopped and the hand slid off, and he and Mayflower looked at each other with a cold understanding of what was possible between them. And his mother was sitting there the whole time, seeing what was happening, hoping that everything she knew about men and their territory didn't apply to her own house. Train could feel the weight of Mayflower's hand a long time after it left, and there was a numbness down the back of his head.

"You two stop that roughhousing," she said, "before you tear up my kitchen." She wished one of them would leave; he saw that, and knew which one it was.

Mayflower was a short, powerful man with a shiny scar that ran the width of his neck, like a collar. It rose up off his skin half an inch, and his mother kissed it sometimes and said it suited him, kept him from being too pretty. And so there was that too. Somewhere along the line Mayflower had found out he could be helpless himself, probably lying on the floor while people watched him bleed.

Train was glad of that, and when he looked back up on the screen, Gene Autry was sitting on the back of that beautiful horse, playing his guitar.

It was midnight when the last show finished. He walked out into the empty lobby and caught the bus home to Darktown. Some Mexican boys got on a few blocks later, loud and full of liquor, and they looked at Train awhile, but he had the nine iron with him, and they decided he wasn't what they was looking for after all.

The lights were out at the house and he let himself in the back door, so the dog would hear him coming. He was half deaf now, and sometimes you came in the front way and surprised him, it scared him so bad, he pissed on the floor. The dog's nerves was already shot from being run over when Train found him, but he got worse with age, and worse again when Mayflower moved in. Sometimes now he flinched at a shadow passing over his head.

Train slipped through the screen door, closing it quietly behind him, and then turned on the kitchen light. The dog was lying in the far corner, squinting. Train leaned his nine iron against the table and opened the refrigerator, got himself some ice tea and a piece of chicken.

The dog stayed where it was. Train pulled the skin off the chicken and held it under the table, but the dog didn't move. "Lucky?" he said, and the animal dragged his tail once or twice across the floor, but he still didn't come. Train stood up and took the chicken skin to him. The dog picked it delicately from his fingers—Train feeling only his breath—chewed once or twice on it, and then dropped it on the floor. Train knelt down next to him and smoothed the animal's head.

"You got to go outside?" he said. It was the dog's habit to eat a little of whatever Train had and then take his whistle in the yard. He didn't eat much these days; he was old and tired. "Come on, then," Train said, and tugged gently at his collar. The animal whined a little, and Train moved behind

54

him, got his hands underneath, and lifted him up. He held him there a moment, feeling the heart pounding against his ribs, until he was sure the dog had his feet under him, and then let him go. He walked to the back door, unlocked it and opened it up, and called him again.

The dog moved a few steps toward the open door and then stopped, seemed like he forgot how to walk. Train went back and picked him up and carried him outside. "What's wrong with you tonight?" he said.

The animal yipped when Train set him down in the yard, and Train checked his hands for blood. It wasn't like him to complain. Train had found the dog in the road, run over and left for dead, and carried him home, squeezing him to keep him from falling out of his arms, and the dog never made any noise at all. That was eleven years ago, and his mother said when she saw him coming up the road that day, the dog looked as big as he did. Strangely, when he remembered it, he saw it through her eyes too.

It was a small yard, enclosed in a wood-plank fence eight feet high, and there was grass back there, a curiosity in Darktown. Train had brought the seed home from the course a little at a time in his pants pocket. The dog stood still a moment, almost like he was lost, and then sniffed the ground, found a spot he liked and squatted to take his whistle. Train had never seen the dog squat before—even after he been run over—and it troubled him, the way small things were changing. The things he was losing a little at a time. He heard his mother behind him then, coming into the kitchen.

She had brushed her hair and was wrapped up in a Japanese robe Mayflower said he got in the war in Korea. Risked his life overseas and then gave her the souvenir. There was a sleep line across her face, but except for that, she was perfect. Her skin was tender, like a girl's, and her features looked good, even when she didn't fix herself up with lipstick and rouge.

"I heard you talking, baby," she said. She spoke softly, not wanting to wake Mayflower up. "Thought maybe you'd brought somebody home." Seemed like one way or another she was always pushing him now to grow up faster, get on with his life.

She came over and kissed his cheek, her slippers sliding against the floor, and Train smelled Ipana toothpaste. If burglars woke her up at four in the morning, she'd go to the bathroom and brush her teeth before she called the police. "There's some chicken in the icebox."

Train looked out at the dog. "Something wrong with his legs," he said.

"Sometimes it happens like that, Lionel," she said. "All at once." She seemed to wanted the dog out of the house too.

He was quiet, staring out the screen door, blinking tears. The dog stood up by himself and began

56

slowly walking back toward the kitchen. "It isn't right to let a creature suffer," she said.

"He was rolling in the grass this morning," he said.

She nodded, weighing that. "Still . . ."

He waited, but she'd finished. He wiped at his eyes with his sleeve.

"Even if he ain't much at night," Train said, "if he's rolling in the grass in the morning, then he's still got his mornings."

"Floyd says he could take care of it for you."

Train was shaking his head. "No." he said.

"Save you that heartache is all."

"No," he said again. Floyd was Mayflower, his given name. Train said "No" one more time, louder than before, and she looked back toward the bedroom and lowered her voice, knowing he would lower his.

"His intentions is good, Lionel," she said quietly. And now they were back in another conversation, one they'd been having off and on ever since Mayflower moved in. The day he brought his things into the house, that was the same day he let Train see who he was. Until then, he was courting them both.

"Tell him not to bother the dog," he said.

"Lord, Floyd ain't gone do nothing to that poor hound. He ain't like that."

Train nodded, and then opened the screen door, and the dog came through slowly and then limped over the linoleum floor to his spot in the corner.

"You see?" she said. "That's how they go, baby. They legs up and quit." There was a noise from the other end of the house, and she kissed him on the cheek again and said she had to get back to bed.

He got up at 4:30, his eyes sleep-crusted in the corners, worried about the dog, and walked out to the kitchen and found him more like his old self. He stood up at least, and walked outside on his own to whistle. Train made himself some bacon and eggs, and dropped a piece of white bread into the pan afterwards, soaking up the fat, and held it in front of the animal's nose until he took it. He didn't swallow it whole like he used to, but he didn't spit it out either.

Train ate his own breakfast, scraped the dishes, then washed his face and hands in the sink—there was almost no water pressure again this morning, not nearly enough to shower—and caught the 5:30 bus to work. He decided in the night to get there early and talk to Sweet about the money before anybody else showed up. Sweet had a hair trigger, but Train noticed that usually his temper had a purpose—it wasn't the kind of temper that made him blind and crazy—and he might not go off at all if there was nobody there to see it.

The bus let off just as the sun came up. The sprinklers was already on in the fairways, the water moving back and forth in perfect high arcs, not a breath of wind. Not even the grass had water pressure troubles in Brentwood. He walked from the street down the service road toward the caddy shed, practicing what he was going to say. Halfway there, though, he noticed Sweet's car wasn't in its usual place in the parking lot. Sweet never parked anywhere but that same spot—he was more jealous of the spot than the Cadillac itself—and he was always at work before they turned on the sprinklers.

Whatever business he had with the club manager or the pro, that was when he did it, before the members showed up and saw 'an unnecessary nigger in the clubhouse. But the Cadillac was gone, and the shed was still locked up, and Train walked out in back, where last Christmas some members had nailed a fruit basket against the side of the building for the caddies to play basketball while they was waiting for totes. He found some golf balls from the practice range and began hitting soft little shots off the dirt, opening the blade of his nine iron and cutting under the balls, almost without touching them, lifting them up against the side of the shack until he found the right spot and began dropping them through the hoop.

Just like Bob Cousy at the foul line.

He did this for half an hour, until after they turned off the sprinklers and he heard the tractors out on the course, cutting the grass; until he'd dropped nine in a row through the fruit hoop. That was his lucky number, nine. Born on the twenty-ninth day of the ninth month in the year 1935.

59

The ninth ball in a row dropped through the hoop, and a few seconds later he heard Sweet's Cadillac coming into the parking lot at fifty miles an hour, throwing up pebbles and dust, and took that for a good sign.

And then he saw there was another Cadillac in the lot too, gleaming in the sun. He couldn't tell what color it was, blue or black, but it was parked close to the driveway, overlooking the caddy shed, somebody in it, relaxing against the seat, maybe watching.

Train felt himself trying to hide the club. He was always thinking that today was the day somebody might come around about his missing nine iron.

Train heard Sweet open the car door and slam it shut; then Sweet come down the slope of the hill toward the shed and went past Train without saying a word, smelling stale—most days he splashed himself with toilet water—and opened the padlock to the shed. He stepped inside, hurrying, and then unlocked the cage. He sat down back there and began drawing plans on a pad of paper. He was in a hurry, like there was something he wanted to get wrote down before he forgot.

Train walked in behind him, then went over and hung his hands in the wire separating the two sides of the room, but didn't try to get any closer. The cage was off-limits.

It looked like Sweet was drawing the rooms of a house. The lines were zigzag and jagged, some places the drawing looked like he'd stabbed it.

He waited for Sweet to look up and see him so they could talk.

A little time passed, and then it was almost seven o'clock, and the other caddies begun coming in. One and two at a time, smoking Luckys and eating a jelly roll or a sausage. Some of them come to work with hangovers or without cleaning up, some of them talking about the cars they want to buy, or the girls they want to fuck. Henry Disharoon wanted everybody to smell his finger.

Sweet looked up at Henry, and the caddies noticed he was drawing pictures, and the room went quiet. Everybody knew not to bother Sweet when he was drawing, even though they never seen him at it before. The next time Sweet looked around, it was to ask if anybody knowed where Arthur was at. He paid no attention to Train, still standing there by the cage.

The phone began to ring, and Sweet handed out the totes. The caddies saw he was still drawing his picture, and nobody complained about who they got. They just put on they hats and went out to the first tee when he told them to go. Train went to a spot on the bench near Plural and took a seat.

Arthur come in finally at eight o'clock, and him and Sweet whispered awhile, and then Sweet showed him the picture he made. They whispered some more about that, and afterwards Sweet leaned back in his chair and relaxed, looked more like his old self.

Train got up and walked to the cage again. Sweet was staring at the tips of his shoes.

"Sweet?"

And now that Sweet looked up, Train was already sorry he bothered him at all. "Wait your turn, man," he said.

"I had to ast you a question," he heard himself say.

Sweet squinted up at him now like he couldn't place the face.

"About Florida."

"I took care of that."

Train could feel the stir go through the room. "You took care of it?"

"What did I just say, cat? I said I took care of it."

Train stood there, not knowing what else to do. If he walked away, it was like he given him permission. So he stayed where he was, and then Sweet looked at him again and Train saw the clouds rolling in. "Man, what do you *want*?" he said.

Train caught the glint off Sweet's diamond tooth. "It was the widow," he said, "I was supposed to get a receipt from the widow."

"Receipt? What re-cept you talkin' about?"

"The man that give me the money, he said he want a receipt from Florida's wife."

Sweet stood up and stepped a little closer to the

62

cage and cocked his head, as if he couldn't decide if it was his eyes seeing this shit or his ears hearing it. "What for?" he said.

"Him and another man had a bet," Train said. "Would I give her the money or not."

"And what kind of receipt this man want?"

"I don't know," Train said. "Something from the widow is all I know."

Sweet studied him, and Train could feel all the eyes in the room on the back of his head; everybody there known he was lying. Sweet said, "What's this cat's name?" And as he said that, he unlocked the cage door.

"Mr. Packard, I think," Train said. "From Hillsdale . . ."

Sweet nodded, like this was all reasonable after all, and come through the door. A little sideways, Train noticed. "An old man with that lizard look?" Sweet said. "Mr. Packard?"

Train looked around at the other caddies, and there was something exciting going on, but he couldn't quite tell what it was. "No," he said, "he wasn't old."

Sweet was moving closer, still trying to place the name.

"He was a guest," Train said, "played with that fat man named Pinky."

"Pinky . . ." Sweet said, and took another step closer, still walking a little sideways, and now Train felt it coming. "Don't believe I am familiar with that name."

63

"That's the only name he called him," Train said.

Sweet nodded, as if that was the point, as if everything was reasonable. As if Train was blind and stupid both.

And for some reason, being treated like he was blind and stupid, Train acted like it. "Whoever that fat man is you sent out with me and Florida," he said. And he was sorry that he brung up Florida's name into it again.

He saw the glint off Sweet's front tooth, and then the glint off the pool cue. He knew it was a pool cue; in the instant before Sweet laid it across his ear Train saw the polished wood and the design markings in perfect detail. And then he heard a clicking noise, about like somebody turn off a light switch, and the lights in fact went out. When he woke up, he was on the cool earth floor; his leg was up under him and felt like it had went to sleep. Someone was yelling.

Train looked up and the sky was full of Sweet. He was standing over him, hollering things Train was just beginning to pick up . . . "Nigger call me a thief better come down here with something on his person" . . . blowing little specks of white foam off his lips, and every now and then he brought the pool cue down across Train's leg or his arm, or slammed it on the floor next to his head.

Train lay as still as he could, waiting for Sweet to let him up. He felt blood running down his neck, but he couldn't tell where it was from. The words come and went, and every now and again he went back to how next time Train better "come down here with something on his person."

And then he heard Plural. "That's it," he said. "The boy has had enough."

And as quick as it started, it stopped. Sweet straightened up, looking at Train from two sides, like a paint job he just finished, then turned around and walked back into the cage and locked the door.

"That's it," Plural said.

Train lay still, getting himself right. He pushed himself up and lost his balance and rolled over on the floor. The other caddies watched him, and watched Sweet, and Plural, and nobody cared to help him up. Henry Disharoon sniffed at his finger and Plural seem to go to sleep.

Train become aware again of the blood on his arm and on his hand. It was pooled near him on the floor, and he saw that he'd slipped in it when he tried to rise off the floor. He sat up, getting his arms around his knees. The room seem to come up with him, like it was stuck to his head. He looked around at the other caddies, couldn't remember nobody's name. He dropped his head onto his arms and waited, and when the room stopped moving on him he pushed himself up on his feet.

Train walked back to his spot in the corner slowly, his hand touching the lockers along the wall for balance, and sat down. His head was suddenly too heavy for his neck to hold it, and he leaned back into the wall. A little later he felt blood dripping onto his shoulder. He thought it was an insect at first.

He was suddenly thirsty. He lifted his head to see if things was cleared enough to walk, and then got up and weaved over to the soda machine. It occurred to him that no one had said a word since Sweet went back into the cage. In all that time—how much time was it?— he hadn't heard nothing but an empty hum, like the background noise when the operator called long-distance.

He put a nickel in the machine and pulled out a grape Nehi. He took a sip, which tasted different than it should, and then held the bottle against his forehead and walked back to the corner. On the way he glanced sideways and caught Sweet staring at him through the cage. Sweet looked away; Train dropped back onto the bench and then lay down.

The Nehi was cold and sweet going down and stung his nose coming back up. When that happened, the other caddies moved further away. Some of them even got closer to Plural. Train got up again and rinsed out his shirt with the hose where they all drank water.

The phone rung and Sweet answered. He listened a moment, then called out two of the caddies and told them to report to the first tee. His voice turned nicely cheerful, like he was trying to line up everybody on his side.

Train glanced at the clock; it was only 8:30.

All morning long, Sweet sent caddies to the first tee. By eleven o'clock, there was nobody left in the shed but Train and Sweet. An hour later, the first caddies out came back in, and some of them waited around to see if they would get another tote. Train stayed where he was. There was a big lump over his ear—felt like he was growing another head—and the skin was ripped open and crusty to the touch.

He waited to see if Sweet would let him work.

He found himself thinking about dogs, how they come back humble after they been beat. The reason didn't matter, if the man was drunk and mean or he just come home in a mood to beat the dog, the dog was still sorry. It never crossed their mind it wasn't their fault. And then suddenly it came to him that Mayflower had beat Lucky so bad he couldn't walk. And that his mother knew what happened too.

Arthur had gone out early, and now he came back in and sat down to eat lunch. He opened his thermos and peeled the wax paper off his sandwich, mayonnaise leaking out the sides and through the bottom, looked like it weighed five pounds. Every fly in Los Angeles County was there in two minutes. Train felt his insides getting ready to heave up again, moving right to the edge.

Sweet had another glance at the picture he made,

67

and then the phone rung again and he picked it up. He listened a minute and then hung up and sent Henry Disharoon and three other caddies back out to the first tee.

A few minutes later Henry Disharoon came back in. Sweet looked up from his desk, staring out through the wire, annoyed to see this nigger back in front of him when he just sent him out. "You sick, man?" he said.

Henry Disharoon shook his head. "Cat says he wants somebody else."

"Who?"

Henry shrugged. Sweet picked up his telephone and dialed a number. He said, "Is they a problem up there, Mr. Dugan?"

He listened a minute and then shook his head. "No sir, he ain't available. No sir . . . All I could do was to sent up somebody else for him in his place." He listened a moment longer, then hung up the phone.

"Arthur," he said, "go on up to the first and see if you can't make these people satisfied."

Arthur paused a minute, then set what was left of his sandwich on the bench and got up, wiped his mouth and hands on his shirt and headed out. About half the flies went with him; the other half stayed with the sandwich. Five minutes later he came back in, never said a word, just went back to the sandwich and resumed where he left off. There was a wet spot on the bench where he'd laid it.

Sweet's phone rung again. "I told you, sir," he

said, "he ain't available today. Yessir, I'm sure. I'm settin' right here. . . ."

Over on the bench, Arthur had finished eating and taken a knife out of his pocket and closed his eyes and was running his finger along the length of the blade. Train thought he heard him humming.

Sweet put the phone back in the cradle and looked over at Plural. He said, "No-Tank, go on up and scare these fucking white people off the tee." But before Plural could get up off the floor, the starter, who was supposed to keep the pace of play going, was standing in the doorway. Another man waited just outside. The starter was from Scotland, a people that was always angry anyway, and he stepped inside and turned to the man behind him and motioned him in. Train saw who it was.

"Is he here, then?" the starter said.

The Mile Away Man nodded at Train. "Over there," he said.

"He's right bloody there," the starter said to Sweet, pointing. "What the devil's got into you, man? He's right there. . . ."

Sweet come out of his chair, as if to check for himself. "Aw, shit, Mr. Dugan," he said. "I forgot his name was Lionel, everybody just call him Train. . . ."

But the starter didn't have no time for that. "Come on, lad, come on," he said, and Train got to his feet. "We've backed up one foursome already, waiting on this business."

Train staggered in the sunlight but then got

69

himself right and walked up the path to the first tee. The Mile Away Man was up ahead with Dugan, the starter, who was saying malfeasance of some sort was all you ever got when you gave the Negro authority, even over other Negroes. You had to expect it, he said.

It was the fat man again, and two players that Train never seen. They'd all hit their shots and were standing around with their caddies when Train finally got to the tee. Nobody looked too happy about waiting all this time while Mr. Packard handpicked his caddy, but it didn't look like none of them were going to say it out loud.

Mr. Packard walked straight to the box, got ready to hit, and then stopped. "Have I introduced you all to Mr. Walk?" he said. Nobody thought it was funny but Mr. Packard himself. He chuckled the way he did and dropped a ball on the ground and then swung without even teeing it up, and was walking after it before it hit the ground. On the way down the fairway, one of the other men came over to make sure of the bets. He had a cigarette in his lips and didn't take it out to talk. He sounded smooth and low, like the radio, like this was old business to him, but Train saw that he was afraid of Mr. Packard too, just like Pink.

"So what's the game?" he said.

"Whatever you want, I guess."

"Pink says it's two hundred a side, a hundred a

press. And it looks like we get two strokes on the front, one on the back."

Mr. Packard nodded and moved away, like he preferred to walk with Train. "I thought it might tickle you to see how this comes out," he said. The other man had gone back to Pink, unsure if Mr. Packard had agreed to anything or not.

The partner they gave Mr. Packard was a wild man, bigger and younger than Pink, called everything he hit *cunt*. The kind of player would hit six balls out of bounds in a row, then hit one good one and think the last shot was how he played golf. And every time Pink or his partner fuck something up, it seemed like Mr. Packard's partner did something twice as bad. Like he did it on purpose.

Mr. Packard never said a word; three holes went by, then four, just kept on enjoying the sunshine and Mother Nature, never complained when Pink went into the trees again and found his ball laying in the open, or when he hit it into the creek and then made his drop fifty yards closer to the green than where he gone in. It seemed like Mr. Packard was out on the course all alone, and if he knew there was anybody there with him, it was only Train.

The fat man pulled out his flask and had a drink. He handed it to his partner and then smiled. "Funny fucking game, Miller," he said to Mr. Packard, "funny fucking game. One day, you can't find your own willie; the next day, the world's a hundred-dollar blow job. Of course, it looks like

71

History turned off the water last night, so at least today you can hit the ball off the fairway."

"Lose some weight, Pink," Mr. Packard said. "You'll be able to find willie easier." Then he turned and watched his partner hit a shot deep into the trees. "You cunt," the man said, and then turned to his caddy for another ball. "This is a provisional," he said, "if I can't find the other one."

Mr. Packard looked off into the trees. "Have the fat man help you," he said. "He's good at finding balls."

Pink was about to have another pull off the flask when Mr. Packard said that, and he stopped and brought his hand down slowly and screwed on the top. He'd been slapped in public, but everybody act like they didn't notice.

They came to the sixth hole, the hole where Florida pitched over on the green, and Mr. Packard moved closer to Train again as they walked down the fairway. Train was afraid he was going to ask about the money for Florida's widow.

Instead, he looked at Train's head and whistled. "That's a pretty nice knot," he said.

Train nodded, caught himself just before he said thank you. Train reached up and felt the spot. It was swollen and ragged. Mr. Packard was walking too close, making him nervous.

They went another fifty yards in silence, and then stopped to wait while Pink hit his ball. It rolled up about the same spot it was the last time they played. Mr. Packard was admiring the lump again, from a different angle. "Looks like something's building a nest," he said.

They came to Mr. Packard's ball next, and he took out his four wood and hit it a little fat, favoring his knee, and dropped it into the pond. It was the first bad shot he hit all morning, and Pink could not keep the smile off his face.

"Shit, I thought that was right there," he said.

"No," Mr. Packard said, "no, it wasn't."

"Yo, Pink," his partner said. "What do you tell a woman with two black eyes?"

Pink smiled at that. "What?"

"Nothing, she's already been told twice."

The other players hit their shots and then it was Pink's turn again. He stood in the middle of the fairway, just behind the 150-yard marker, and took the five iron out of his bag. He took a practice swing—he was swinging better today, and Train guessed that the extra players made him feel safer around Mr. Packard—and then hit the ball to the green, where it bounced once and rolled past the pin twenty feet.

He turned and held the club up close to Train's eyes, where he could see the number on the blade. "Five iron, Leroy," he said. "It's the five."

He dropped the club for his caddy to pick up and took out the flask and had another drink. His eyes watered and he shook and said, "Ah, breakfast." And that was when the connection Train been waiting for finally come around, what he reminded him of. It was one of the young wives around the

73

club, married to a member of the walking dead, and she had a bulldog she took everywhere she went— mostly to the pool, where she could tan herself in the mornings. She was young and pretty, and they always had on a ribbon of the same color, the wife and the dog, and every time Train saw them, the dog was always on the brakes, trying to shit, when she was pulling it to the car. That was what it was, the bulldog and the lady; everything want to go their own way at once. That was the fat man from behind.

The man screwed the top on the flask, carefree and happy, and begun walking down the fairway as light as air.

Train started to walk along too, but Mr. Packard stood where he was, like he still out there in the unknown regions. He looked at the pond and the green a little while, then had a look up, like he was just noticing the day. He said, "Pink?" and the fat man stopped. "You know, I was just thinking, if we're going to do this, let's do it."

Pink squinted at him, suspicious. "What now?"

"Double or nothing, from right here."

"Double or nothing what?" he said.

"For the day. Whatever it is at the end."

"How we going to bet on something now, we don't even know what it is?"

"An aloha press," Mr. Packard said. "You must have heard of that. One nine iron, from right here. Double or nothing for the whole day."

"Fuck, Miller, I seen you play." The fat man

74

was annoyed and relieved at the same time, like Mr. Packard worried him for nothing.

"Not me," Mr. Packard said. "Mr. Walk here."

Pink looked at Train, and suddenly Train couldn't feel his feet. He tried to remember if he could feel them before. His toe—he knew he could feel that. That been hurting all day. Pink smiled, to show Mr. Packard he been around the block before.

"What's the bet, exactly?" he said.

Mr. Packard shrugged. "Just what I said. Double or nothing, whatever it is at the end. Mr. Walk hits a nine iron from right here and it's inside your ball."

Pink looked at Train again, then back at the green and grinned. "How many tries?" he said.

"One swing, just like we were playing golf."

It was quiet a minute while Pink thought it over. The other two men seemed like they would prefer to be somewhere else, and looked off in other directions.

"One try, from right where you're standing, inside my ball," Pink said.

Mr. Packard was starting to looked bored.

"Double or nothing, the whole day."

Train stood still, trying to figure out how he got into this, how he was going to get out. Strangely, though, there was something working the other direction too, that wanted to be part of it. He felt Pink sizing him up.

"What's the catch?" Pink said.

Mr. Packard gave him that soft grin he had, and

when he answered, he sounded surprised the fat man would think something like that. "The *catch*?" he said. "There isn't any catch. Yesterday you asked Lionel Walk, Jr., here what he would hit from this spot, and he said a nine iron. So we'll hand him a nine iron and see if he can do it."

The two other men looked at each other, didn't seem to understand.

"And if he can, he can," Mr. Packard said, "and if he can't, he can't."

"One try, from where you're standing."

"It's your big day, fat man," he said, "the world's a hundred-dollar blow job." There was more of the taste of the bad side in his voice all the time, although you had to be paying attention to hear it. He grinned at the golfers Pink had brought along, the proof of what was going on. "I'm just giving you a chance to make it twice as good."

Pink began to nod. "All right," he said.

Then he turned to his partner and said, "What the fuck, right?"

The man looked around and shrugged.

Train stood where he was, wondering what he was supposed to do now. "This all right with you?" Mr. Packard said. "You don't want to do it, you don't have to."

"Wait a minute, I thought we had a bet."

"We got a bet, Pink," he said, sounded like he was talking to a slow child. "Now I'm finding out if Mr. Walk wants to participate in it." He waited. Train's mouth tasted like he'd been licking stamps.

Mr. Packard took his bag off Train's shoulder and dropped it on the ground. The caddies never dropped clubs like that; the members was always checking them for dings and scratches, but Mr. Packard didn't care how his clubs looked, didn't seem to care about nothing but a good time was had by all. Taking something away from Pink. He bent down, looking through the irons, and pulled one out.

"That's the nine?" Pink said.

"You know," Mr. Packard said, looking at the other two men, "all these questions might make a person wonder if everything here's on the square."

Pink stared at the ground and kept his mouth shut.

Mr. Packard handed Train the nine iron, dropped a ball on the grass, and stepped out of the way. Train moved the club up and down in the air, feeling it. It was heavier at the bottom than his club, less flex in the shaft. The grip was soft and he could hold on to it without squeezing. He felt the men waiting and stepped up to the ball, had a quick look at the green and let it go. Without looking, he knew where it was.

They walked down the fairway, Mr. Packard toting the bag, would not let Train touch it. "No sir," he said, "not on your life. You're the stick, I just carry the bag." Having a big time with Pink now.

Pink was up ahead. He never said a word when

Train hit his shot; he never looked at him again all day, and he tried not to even look at the green, where Train's ball was laying almost in the dent it made when it hit, five feet from the pin.

And then Mr. Packard took a drop at the far edge of the pond and chipped it in for par, and Pink didn't seem to see that neither. He got to the point by now that he didn't care about the niceties of the game or how he looked in front of his friends, which in the game of golf was as bad as you could be beat.

Everything changed.

Pink saw he couldn't get his money back from yesterday, and everything that was easy before, he had to think about it now. And then Mr. Packard stopped his partner before he hit his driver off the tee, and said, "Edgar, your name is Edgar, right? Is there a club in your bag somewhere that you hit better than that?" Might have been the first time he spoke directly to him all day.

The man named Edgar turned around, not happily to be interrupted.

"Something you hit straight?"

"Straight?"

"You know, afterwards you can find the ball?"

Edgar took this expression on his face like somebody just tried to explain algebra, then looked over at Pink, not knowing what to do. Pink turned away. Whatever they worked out before they started, it floated to the top now and wouldn't flush.

"I like my mashie," Edgar said.

"Then why don't you hit your mashie?" Mr. Packard said.

Edgar looked off into the distance. "I can't get there with an iron," he said.

Mr. Packard almost whispered. "Then hit it twice," he said.

Edgar took the mashie instead of the driver and hit it a little ways up the fairway.

"There you go," Mr. Packard said. "You've still got the ball; you just saved yourself fifty cents."

After that, Edgar hit the mashie all the time, sometimes in the direction Mr. Packard pointed him, and pretty soon the match came back to even, and a hole after that, him and Mr. Packard was ahead, and all the presses had moved over to the other side. All of it double or nothing. Pink went to the parking lot between nines and refilled his flask; him and his partner was no longer speaking.

Train watched all this happen, but he still couldn't say afterwards how much of it Mr. Packard did and how much of it Pink did to himself. He knew Pink and the other two had got together before it started, but Mr. Packard was winning all the money again anyway, and seeing it all turning around like that, the fat man lost what little swing he had and was even worst than he was the day before, couldn't pull the trigger on nothing, and it didn't any of it, as far as Train could see, have a thing to do with golf.

They were walking up the fifteenth fairway into a hot breeze that had come up from the east, when

Mr. Packard fell in next to him again, matching him step for step. He lit a cigarette as they walked, cupping his hand to keep the match going, and then glanced again at Train's head.

"So, what are you going to do for that?" he said. Train didn't understand him at first. "Your head . . ."

"Ice," he said. "It won't look so bad when it's iced."

"I mean what are you going to do?"

Train kept walking. He was afraid that the other three caddies might hear it if Mr. Packard said anything else, get him in more trouble with Sweet than he already was. In two years, this was the first time anybody ever come down to the shed to pick out somebody to tote his bag. The first time somebody told Sweet what to do in his own office.

Train shook his head. "He's the boss," he said.

Mr. Packard nodded, almost like he was agreeing with him. "I know what you mean," he said.

It stopped Train in his tracks, to think somebody like that knew what he meant. And then he suddenly remembered how happy it felt, walking up the fairway with Mr. Packard carrying the bag, biting his cheek to keep from smiling. He never had a day before when everything went so wrong and right all at the same time.

When they stopped again, Pink reached into his bag for his liquor, threw his head back to drink, and seemed to stagger under the weight of the flask.

★   ★   ★

80

At the end of the round, Pink went back into his pocket for the roll of bills. Mr. Packard watched him count it out—two thousand at least—seemed to satisfy him more to watch it counted out than the money did itself when he handed it over. The other man, the one who had come over to make sure of the bets as they walked up the first fairway, made a show of paying Edgar his money too, counting out the hundreds slow so Mr. Packard would see.

Right in front of all three of them, Mr. Packard turned to Train and shook his head in that easygoing way he had and said, "As soon as they're in the parking lot, he'll get it back."

"Yessir," Train said quietly.

"You saw that too?"

The other three men were looking, but suddenly Train didn't care. He had a feeling, in fact, that he was under Mr. Packard's protection. Like the man might adopt him. Which, of course, didn't made no more sense than anything else did today.

"Yessir."

The men looked at each other and decided to ignore that, like they suddenly gone deaf. Which half of the members at Brookline was anyway.

"Well, I guess if you're going to do something," Mr. Packard said, "you got to go ahead and do it." And then he gave Train fifty dollars for the tote.

Train took his money and walked out to the dirt road without going back down to the caddy shed. He didn't want to see Sweet again, be reminded of what happened earlier.

81

About a hundred yards from the street, Mr. Packard came by in the dark Caddy. He pulled over and stopped, and Train heard the whine of the window motor and watched his face appear. He still couldn't tell if the car was blue or black.

"Mr. Walk," he said.

Train nodded politely. "Yessir . . ."

"You need a lift?"

He looked back down the road, afraid of the man suddenly, and afraid someone would see them talking. "No sir," he said, "I'll just take the bus."

Mr. Packard nodded and rolled the window up and was on his way.

Train walked up the road into the Cadillac's exhaust. He had a lump behind his ear, fifty-two dollars in his pocket, and a slow headache. His shirt was wrinkled from where he washed out the blood. He was thirsty and tired, and he hadn't eaten since five that morning. Hadn't felt like food once and still didn't.

He let himself think then about how it would be riding home in the Cadillac, getting out in front of the house with fifty dollars in his pocket.

He stumbled then, light-headed and excited. He been hurt, though, and remembered the last time he bled out like this his mother took him to the butcher to drink cow blood to put back what he lost. Thinking of that, he dry-heaved up right there on the side of the road, again and again and again, heaved until his stomach felt like something in there wrung it out.

CHAPTER 3

NORAH

The Georgia Peach, *Newport Beach Marina*

They'd come over the side early in the morning, an hour before sunrise, rowing out in the dark from the marina in a stolen wooden dinghy, neither of them able to swim.

The *Georgia Peach* was moored half a mile offshore, barely inside the protection of the stone inlet. Seventy-two feet, two masts, all teak. It had brass fixtures, new Dacron sails, two lifeboats, the best navigation system money could buy.

There was an ornate Parker double-barreled shotgun in a closet in the main cabin, a wedding gift from one of Alec's attorneys—he'd bought the boat and married her all in the same week—but it had never been fired, or even loaded. He'd admired the weapon, thanked the attorney twice, and later, alone with her, he wondered out loud if he was supposed to buy a pickup truck to hang it in the window. He did not like guns, and would give an intruder whatever he wanted, up to and including the boat itself, before he'd shoot him over it.

He was twenty-nine years older than she was,

and enjoyed watching her with younger men, or perhaps it was that he enjoyed watching the young men with her. For a long time now, it was the only sex they'd had, this watching her with younger men. She was never sure what he was thinking afterwards.

The boat had four cabins and slept eight, although the guests never stayed overnight. The captain was a taut, meticulous Mexican who spoke passable English and lived on board ten months a year, February through November, sleeping in the smallest compartment, which was in the bow. Each December, he returned home to Baja and his wife. They had no children. Once, when they were all drunk together, he'd recited the names: Pedrito, Maria, Gaspar, Hector, Veronica. He had begun crying then, and it took her a moment to understand that they had named them, all the babies his wife could not carry to full term. And she saw the reason for that, instinctively understood his attachment to those tiny things that had been alive once, and she also wept, as much for herself as the Mexican.

Later, they were both ashamed.

The Mexican maintained the boat—he had been working on a compression problem the day before, making a list of the parts he needed to replace a piston—and kept his small cabin spotless. He had an intrinsic understanding of the way mechanical things worked, and sometimes, when Alec was below, she felt him watching her on deck. His name was Pedro Ruiz, and they killed him first, shot him in bed.

The shot was not as loud as she would have imagined; no louder, on reflection, than the boat's own noises at night, creaking and settling under its enormous weight, but it was somehow out of place, and she started awake, then lay still, trying to decide what had caused it. She listened for the Mexican, but there was no movement from the bow. Alec was awake too, propped up against half a dozen pillows—his habitual position in bed, as close to flat as he could get without setting off a certain chest pain that felt like a heart attack, even after all the visits to the doctor. "If you can cause it by lying down," the doctor always said, "it's not your heart."

He had a peculiar, ironic expression on his face now, as if he knew what was coming, as if this was what he'd expected all along.

He was always a restless sleeper on the boat, up a dozen times a night to tinkle a few drops in the forward head—he did not use the one closer to their cabin, for fear of waking her—and then sometimes climbing the stairs to the deck to smoke a cigar and check the sky. Several years earlier, he had been upstairs at home in the bathroom when the plane hit, shaving for a fund-raiser they were holding for eight Negroes who had been sentenced to the electric chair in Waycross, Georgia, and was somehow uninjured, even as the famous Howard Hughes bounced his experimental XF-II off their roof, set a neighbor's yard on fire, and half-killed himself in the process.

That was 1946, and Mr. Hughes, she had heard, was still recovering from his injuries. The Negroes were dead, and the carpenters had been up there on the second story of her house on and off ever since, trying now for the tenth or twentieth time to exactly match the lattice pattern along the roof line with the part that had gone untouched. Alec wouldn't let it go until it was exactly right. He'd considered suing Mr. Hughes and his airplane company, but instead accepted a settlement and took the episode as a reminder that in this world you cannot buy safety—one minute you are studying your chin in the mirror; the next minute you are shaving in the outdoors—and in small ways over the years, he became more reckless in his behavior. He worked less and drank more, and was not as careful as he once had been of whom he invited to the boat. Which is to say he was not as careful of her, and she did not mind that at all. One way or another, men had been trying to protect her or save her all her life. She brought that out in them, even after she had stopped trying.

They lay still, listening. The boat yawned and creaked, and she heard uncertain footsteps, and then an angry whisper. He sighed and reached for the overhead lamp. The sheet fell off his chest and she could see the bones in his arms. Thin arms, for a man of his size. A happy red face beneath hair so white she could spot it across the room in the dark; loose breasts, like a bear.

There was another noise, something breaking in the galley. Alec found the light and stood up. "Stay here," he said, and walked to the door and opened it.

"Pedro?"

There was no answer. He squinted out into the darkened galley and then turned to look back at her, his stomach casting an enormous shadow against the far wall, and then he raised his eyebrows in an operatic gesture, and she saw he was clowning and laughed out loud.

"What was it?" she said.

He stepped up, as if to move through the threshold, and then stopped suddenly, bent at the waist, and shivered. And then she saw something dripping from his nipple, and then from his elbow, and then he sat down carefully on the floor, back inside the main cabin, and then lay down. He tried to speak, but that's where they had cut him.

His legs were thin and hairless, and he kicked at the men as they walked in. He made another noise, trying to say something, to maintain a place for himself in the room, but they stepped over him, paying no attention.

The first one through the threshold was light-skinned, perhaps a mulatto. The second was enormous, as black as the open door. She pulled up the sheet to cover her breasts, and her husband moved on the floor, turning halfway over, knocking the mulatto off balance. The mulatto steadied himself and looked down at him for a moment with the same interest he might have had in a dying fish flopping around on the deck with the lure still in its mouth. She saw it clearly, they'd left the knife in his throat. It seemed to be lodged in his spine. He jerked again, and this time the mulatto moved a step away and waited for him to die.

The bigger one stood just inside the threshold, watching her. In no hurry at all. There was a line of sweat beneath his hair, and he was breathing through his mouth. She caught glimpses of his tongue.

The mulatto looked around the cabin as if he were thinking of buying it. Alec moved again, more up and down than sideways, and a different noise came out of him, this entirely from the opening in his throat. They had been married eleven years. The mulatto smiled. "I thought you be screamin' and all by now," he said. He nodded quickly at the floor, as if to remind her what was there.

Behind him, the big one nodded too, as if he were thinking the same thing.

"Let me ast you something," the mulatto said. "He still get it up or not?"

She wasn't looking directly at the floor now, but she still saw the movements there, which were smaller all the time, and the noises he made as he tried to breathe had turned wet.

She thought of the shotgun in the closet.

The big one picked up her panties off the dressing table. He held them up, as if he were trying to decide which side was the front and which side was the back, and then a moment later he was on top of her, pressing her into the mattress. He was twice as thick as Alec; his fingers stunk and pushed into her mouth, pinching her lip against her teeth, and then cutting it, and she opened a little, trying to reason with him, and he forced the panties in, first into her cheek and then between her teeth until they had filled her mouth and propped it open. Then he rolled her over and tied her hands with one of her husband's belts. She thought the bones in her arms would snap under the weight.

He pushed off her and stood up. She turned herself on the bed and saw that the mulatto had already taken off his pants. Alec was still now, and the wash of blood had stopped and pooled, moving gradually back and forth with the rocking of the boat. She wondered if that is where they would leave her when they had finished, lying on the floor with Alec.

"Man, this ain't the time," the big one said.

The mulatto was older, though, and seemed to be in charge. "I live for the day," he said, and came onto the bed.

Her heels dug into the sheet and she walked herself back to the headboard and then up it a foot or two. He moved suddenly, slapping her face. Her head rolled and she kicked out at him, and he caught her leg and lifted it, and for a brief moment they felt each other's strength, staring into each other's eyes, and then he jerked at the leg, turning her over again. His arms pressed into her neck and she felt the other one take her ankles, pulling one leg away from the other until there was enough space between them for the mulatto to force in a knee. She tried to kick, but the one holding her ankles tightened down until she thought again of snapping bones.

And she stopped fighting then and cried out into the panties, a muffled, dry sound, and felt her legs spread wide apart, so wide that the muscles cramped, and then there was a noise, a soft pop, like a bit of tendon as you cut through a steak.

She couldn't see Alec now, and there was no sound at all from that side of the bed. She was alone; she saw that more clearly than anything in the room. The mulatto reached beneath her and she cried out again.

"Come on, now," he said, as if he were trying to talk her into this. As if he were courting. She rose up, trying to stop the pain, and that seemed to please him. "That's it, sweetheart," he said. "Give it up."

She took the second one in that same position, lying on her face, but with all his weight pressing against the points of her shoulders. He had been reluctant to rape her—the mulatto talked him into it: "Man, you got to ask yourself, you pass on this, when it gone come along again?"—but once inside, he seemed to be trying to kill her.

Afterwards, they went above to start the engines. The engines were diesels, though, nothing like a car's. She heard the starter turning over, again and again. She guessed they had never stolen a boat before. She sat up, remembering an outraged letter she had written to the *Times* regarding the paper's coverage of the eight Negroes from Waycross, saying that even if they were guilty of the specific crime of murder, any act of violence between the Negroes and the white race had to be understood in a political context. She could remember the words, the exact words.

Upstairs, they had begun to argue. "I thought you said you drove one of these motherfuckers, man."

"I told you I seen how they did it; I didn't say I been driving it myself."

They tried the starter again, but she knew they hadn't primed the engine, and knew it wouldn't catch. Especially not with the bad piston. She noticed light in the porthole to her right and then, turning left, saw it was still dark there. So she was facing north. There was a certain comfort in that, in any kind of bearings at all, but then, turning her head, she saw him again on the floor, and felt herself begin to break.

"The lady got to know something about this," the mulatto said.

There was no answer.

"What's wrong with that, man? You depressing me now with your attitude. . . ."

"Bring her up here where people can see her is what's wrong."

She stared at her husband's body, unable, for some reason, to look anywhere else.

"They ain't nobody gone see nothing."

"Man, the sun coming up, and sailing people get up early to catch the breeze."

It was quiet a little while and then the mulatto said, "Well, we either got to sail it or sink it."

It was quiet again, and she imagined them studying the maze of stays and ropes and wenches and pulleys, the size of the hull. It would be dawning on them now that they couldn't sail it or sink it.

They came back downstairs, and without a word the mulatto began slapping her again, back and forth. Her ears rang and blood dropped off the end of her nose onto her breasts. The other one reached down, just out of sight, and pulled once, violently, as if he were starting a lawn mower, and came up with the knife that had been buried in the bone of her husband's neck.

She tried to beg them not to do that to him, not to do anything more.

He gave the knife to the mulatto. The mulatto reached into her mouth and pulled out the panties. Her cheeks and the roof of her mouth were dry and her jaw had cramped. "We all ears, sweetheart," he said.

She couldn't speak. He touched one of her breasts, smoothing blood over the nipple, and then pinched it hard between his thumb and the knuckle of his index finger. He looked up at her, as if asking for permission.

She looked back, not knowing what he wanted. And nodded anyway.

"You sure now," he said.

"What?"

And then his hand moved, so fast she didn't really see it, and then she felt him let go of her nipple, and then she saw the knife, and the blood, and realized he hadn't let go at all.

He put it into his shirt pocket, and then she lost her hold and begged them for things that she couldn't even name. The room was lighter now, the sun peeking through the portholes in the west wall of the cabin. The other man stood huge and black in the background, watching.

They gave her a towel for the bleeding, and a shirt, and then a speedboat came past, engines screaming, its hull slapping the water. They waited until the sound had faded away and then the mulatto spoke again, sounding calm.

"You had time to think this over now?" he said. She didn't answer. "Because now I gone ast you one question: You want to start this boat for me or not?"

She looked back at the floor. From this angle, she could see the wide black yawn in his neck. "You wondering, What good is that? Right?" the mulatto said.

He was afraid of something. Maybe the motor-boat, or maybe someone had seen them up there trying to start the engines. Or maybe that he was this close to something and losing it. "Well," he said, sitting down beside her, "the situation here is different than it look. You know how sometime you don't like somebody, but then you do? Like fighters after the big match."

She heard herself laugh out loud. He smiled again, surprised, and then he laughed with her and nodded toward the huge Negro in the door and pretended to shiver. "You heard him ast me could he have the other titty, didn't you?" he said. And she stopped laughing.

The one at the door moved closer and sat down on the other side of the bed, so that she was between them. She felt the heat off the second one's body, smelled baby powder. And grass. He smelled like grass.

"I believe she beginning to like us," the mulatto said. The big one was not in a joking mood, though. They heard another boat and went quiet until it passed, their eyes moving everywhere, meeting sometimes across the bed, sometimes looking at her. The air was thick with the odor of grass and baby powder and the mulatto's cologne and their sweat and hers.

"Now here's what we gone do," the mulatto said. "We gone all go upstairs and start up the engines." The big one looked at him, surprised, but didn't argue. "And then, once we on the road, we gone put you in one of them little boats up there and take this one for ourself."

He studied her as he said this, to see how he was doing. "Unlest you want to come along." The big one moved then, but she didn't see it clearly. One of her eyes was swollen shut.

"You see the situation here?" the mulatto said.

She waited. He looked quickly at his partner.

"Like *Mutiny on the Bounty*," he said. "You been to that, right? Where they left off the captain and took the boat themself?"

She wondered again where they were going to kill her, if they would carry her back down here to do it.

"C'mon, man," the big one said. He wanted to do what he wanted to do.

The mulatto couldn't make up his mind. "I just gone give her a chance to collaborate to start this motherfucker," he said, "let her think it over." Then he seemed to think it over too. A few seconds passed; the boat rocked up and back, as if it were breathing.

"The doctor they got at Vacaville?" he said. "I had to talk to him every Monday morning, ten-thirty, and then group session at four, every damn week, even after he already diagnoses I was a classic psychopath, without the ability to feel remorse. Said I couldn't put myself in nobody else's place. Thirty months, I had to do every day, on account I couldn't feel remorse."

She sat still; they sat still. It came to her that

95

she was supposed to say something now, but she didn't know what might save her. "Tell me the truth about something," the mulatto said softly.

She nodded again. She looked quickly at the big one, and then away. He wanted to do what he wanted to do.

"You ever knowed anybody like that, that felt remorseful over what they done? I don't mean if they got caught. Just sit around cryin' over something that's already past? What is your opinion on that?"

She felt him watching her, waiting to hear her lie. Whatever she said, he would hear the lie, and that would be it. That was what he was waiting for; then he'd let the other one do what he wanted.

"I don't like doctors," she said.

And that stopped him cold, and then he started to smile. She didn't know what else to say, and so she only nodded, and her skin stuck to itself where the blood was drying on her neck, and then pulled loose.

The mulatto kept smiling, and in some way believed he had won her over. "You see that, Arthur? I told you, man. She gone start the motherfucking ship."

They untied her, and when she stood up the towel fell from beneath the shirt, and as they went up the narrow stairway she felt fresh blood on her stomach. She was behind the big one, and smelled the baby powder on his pants. He stopped, halfway through the threshold, checking for other boats, and a moment later he reached down and picked her up by the arm, lifted her the way you lift a child, and it hurt her breast, but then the air was clean again, and cool, and she felt the sun.

The mulatto appeared a moment later and had a look around. There were other boats, but none of them close by. No one would see what happened; the only record would be what these two remembered themselves. The unfairness of that stirred her, that all that would be left of this was what they remembered.

She pulled herself to her feet, and stumbled over a rope. She would have fallen, but the big one caught her by the hair from behind and pulled her upright. She touched her face—she had been touching her face all her life; even as a child, she'd known she was beautiful—and did not recognize the shape.

He let her go, but stayed so close she could hear noises in his stomach. She walked to the back of the boat to the wheel. They both followed her, but unsure of their footing, afraid of the edges. The wind came up a little and there were whitecaps beyond the wall protecting the inlet.

She sat down at the pilot's deck and saw that they'd left the ignition key on. Red lights all the way across the control panel. She left the key where it was and pushed the button on the other side of the panel, the one that warmed the fuel.

"What you doing there?" the mulatto said. He

97

was standing to the side, watching, throwing a shadow over her arms.

"It's a diesel," she said. "You have to prime it."

The mulatto looked across the water. There was movement on the decks of two of the sailboats. One of them a ninety-footer out of Seattle that had been moored there since before she and Alec came on the boat. "How long this gone take?" he said.

"Not too long."

The big one towered behind her, his head a few inches from the boom. The boom was metal and she had once knocked herself out, bumping into it as she came up from below in the night.

She held the button down until her finger ached, using all the battery she could. "It don't take this long," the mulatto said.

The big one stared at him.

"I watched them before," the mulatto said.

The big one said, "How come you ain't watch *how* they do it when you watching how long it took?"

"How the fuck you gone see what people doing with those little switches, man?"

"All I know," the big one said, "you said you could drive it."

"Shit, nigger, you the one supposed to be mechanically inclined."

Then the big one bent over to see what she was doing. "It don't take this long," he said, repeating what the mulatto had said, and she felt his breath on her scalp.

Then his hand was in her hair again, closing down, pulling out little pieces of her scalp. "You gone do it soon," he said, "or else we going back downstairs."

"I was you, I'd do what I could," the mulatto said. "Arthur got a general resentment of white girls."

He let go of her hair, and she moved her hand to the starter button. The engine turned over slowly, right on the edge, and then caught. The mulatto smiled, relieved. He looked around again, and none of the boats was coming over for a closer look; no one was watching.

She got up and went back to the wheel and pushed the throttle all the way up, moving the tachometer needle up past three thousand, past the red line, until the engine sounded like it was screaming. She saw the look on the mulatto's face. "Charging the batteries," she shouted over the noise; her voice was dry and caught on the words. She turned away, as if to go back down.

There was movement from the other side. The sun came through the swollen tissue of her eye the same way it would come through a shade, and she could just make out the shape of the big one's head.

"Where you going?" he said.

"The toilet," she said. "I have to do my toilet."

"No, ma'am," he said. Something formal in it, like a remembered courtesy from before, when things were different. The engine was still screaming; Alec never ran it over two thousand in his life.

"I have to," she said.

He shrugged.

It was easier than she thought. She felt it on her legs, and then on her feet. She wasn't sure if she'd done it on purpose, or if it had just happened. Some of it splashed, and that was what drew their attention.

The boat moved and she reached up and grabbed the boom to steady herself, the puddle growing at her feet, both of them still watching, the mulatto beginning to smile, and then she pushed against the boom with all her weight.

The boom swung the foot or so that the ties allowed it to move, hitting the bigger one across the eye. He was there next to her, and then he was falling backward, into the stairwell. One of his hands grabbed the railing, and the woodwork pulled out under his weight. His face disappeared and she heard him fall the rest of the way down.

The mulatto reached for her, smiling at what she'd done, and she pushed the boom at him too. He ducked easily, chuckling at this situation, and tried again. She crossed the open stairwell, and the mulatto came around it after her, holding on to the railing because he was afraid of the water, and she turned away from him and jumped.

She heard the engine cough once before she hit the water then regain itself at a slightly different pitch.

★   ★   ★

She swam hard for fifty yards and then turned on her back to take off the shirt, and saw them standing together on the deck, arguing. The exhaust was pouring black smoke. She got out of the shirt, and the going was easier.

When she looked again, five minutes later, they were at the bow, tugging at the anchor line, but the engine had quit. She put her face in the water and did not look back again until she reached the marina.

A fisherman in a small aluminum boat pulled her out. He had two days' worth of whiskers and bloodshot eyes, and smelled of the bait he'd been tossing into the hold. He straightened his T-shirt across his stomach before he introduced himself.

"Harry Marquart," he said, and offered her his hand. The blood from her breast trickled down her stomach and her eyes burned from the salt water. He was staring at her, and she asked for a blanket. He might have been sixty years old, and his head and hands were crusted with sun cancer. He had no blanket, but he found a worn checkered shirt without buttons and gave it to her, apologizing for the smell of gasoline, and then he stepped back and stared past her for a moment, out over the water at the sailboat.

"You're a strong swimmer," he said.

She was still on the fisherman's boat when the police arrived. There were only two of them: one in uniform and a sergeant in a suit. The uniform had a patch that said *Orange County Sheriff's Department*. The sergeant's suit was tailored, and his hair had just been cut and his shoes were expensive and shined. He stepped easily from the pier into the small boat, and said "Excuse me" when he moved the fisherman out of the seat next to her and took it himself. The fisherman had been holding on to her shoulder, sneaking looks beneath the shirt. She could not say if he was drawn to her, or simply to the grotesque, or if those were different things.

"They're still on the boat," the fisherman said. "Drinking beer and laughing, having themselves a big nigger party."

She did not like that word, and particularly did not like being the cause of its use. The fisherman handed the sergeant his binoculars.

The sergeant studied the sailboat, using the same hand to hold the binoculars and focus, then looked back at her.

"That's a long way out," he said. His voice was calm and sensible, in no hurry. She nodded, feeling herself shake. She had been shaking ever since Mr. Marquart pulled her out of the water.

The sergeant moved—he was over on her right side, and she couldn't see him well—and then she felt his coat on her shoulders. The lining was smooth and had a nice weight. "Let's see what we've got," he said, and he gently touched her face and turned it. He leaned closer, looking at one side and then the other. "It's not so bad," he said. He touched her lips, looking at her teeth, and then moved her jaw back and forth. "Does that hurt?"

"My breast," she said.

"I know," he said. "Mr. Marquart mentioned it when he called in his report." He turned and told the uniformed cop to find out what had happened to the ambulance. When he looked back at her, she saw that his eyes were dark brown, almost black. He smiled at her, as if to tell her losing a nipple wasn't so serious. She shook violently, cold and frightened.

"Is it all right if I look?" He had a soft way of speaking that made things seem easier than they were.

And she nodded, wanting him to see what they'd done. He opened the jacket, holding it carefully away from her skin. A moment passed. "The bleeding's almost stopped," he said. And then a moment later: "They've got doctors up in Hollywood, they can fix things so they won't even show."

She shook her head. She didn't want it fixed, not when nothing else could be. She touched herself, pressed her fingers into the spot, and for a moment the pain seemed to block out the sun, and she bent over it, trying to stay inside that one moment, trying to stop shaking, bending into her own lap.

He laid his hand across her spine and waited.

He seemed to know when it had passed, even though she hadn't moved. He took his hand off and said, "So there they are, just sitting out on the boat, waiting." He made things simple. It was reassuring to have them laid out in order. She needed some sort of order.

She looked up, blinking tears. "I don't think they can swim," she said, "and they don't know how to sail."

He nodded and smiled, as if that was what he expected.

"And the engine's thrown a rod."

He looked back out over the water to the boat. "You were out there alone?"

She paused, not knowing where to begin. "They killed the men," she said.

"How many?" Quietly, no sign of alarm.

"Two. The captain and my husband."

He held her hand a moment, just held her hand. The one in uniform was running toward them up the dock now, out of breath.

"I'm sorry," she said, "I thought I already said that." He just held her hand, and for the first time she thought of how she must look.

"The call's in," said the one in uniform. "They're on the way, but they don't know where the ambulance is." He was only a shape, something dark against the sky.

"Are there guns on board?" the sergeant said.

"A shotgun," she said, "and I think they have one of their own." It occurred to her that she hadn't seen their gun, that she hadn't seen the body of Pedro Ruiz. That he might not even be dead.

"I suppose he could still be alive," she said.

"Your husband?"

"No," she said, "not my husband."

"Is there any chance?" he said.

That brought her out of it for a minute. "No," she said, "no chance at all."

He looked back out toward the boat. "We'll take care of it now," he said.

She wept, thinking now it would finally be in someone else's hands. Doctors and nurses and police. They would take care of her; they would take care of Alec, and Pedro, and they would take care of the Negroes too. She thought of them on the boat, and she was suddenly angry.

The uniformed cop moved closer to the sergeant and spoke quietly, as if he didn't want her to hear. "You want me to call us some backup?"

The sergeant thought a minute and said, "There's no hurry on that. They aren't going anywhere."

She could hear the siren then, a long ways off. They sat together for a little while, neither of them speaking; then he said, "I'm Miller Packard."

She was thinking of what they had done, of killing him without ever giving him a chance. Without giving either of them a chance. "They must have come on board on the stern," she said, and then realized how little it mattered.

He patted her hand, telling her in a different

way that he would take care of things now. She felt moisture seeping from her closed eye, and was furious all over again. "Could I go along?" she said. "Is that against the rules?"

He smiled at that, laughing at some bigger picture, not making any sound. "I don't know if that's the best thing right now," he said.

She looked out toward the boat, the *Georgia Peach*. "I don't want to wake up at four o'clock in the morning the rest of my life, thinking they're in the room," she said, and saying it, she realized it was true. It wasn't the reason, but it was true.

"They won't seem like the same people, you know," he said.

"Good," she said, "I want to see how they are now."

She turned to look at him, looked him full in the face, not trying to hide what they had done to her, and knew that he would take care of her, that he would give her whatever she wanted.

"Okay," he said. Just like that.

"I'm sorry," she said, "I've forgotten your name."

Mr. Marquart took them back out to the *Peach*. There was a chop now, even inside the marina, and her head pounded as the little whaler bounced against the water. The old man sat at the outboard, squinting into the breeze, primed for a fight, and she sat in front of him, still wrapped in the sergeant's coat. He and the uniformed cop were in front. The uniformed cop had a shotgun now—he'd come back with it from the car—and held it across his chest. His calf was braced against the railing of Mr. Marquart's boat. He did not like this, two Negroes and only two police; he did not like having her along. He'd asked twice if the sergeant wanted backup or the Coast Guard, and then had quit asking. He was afraid, though; she saw that.

The sergeant was sitting on the bait box, one arm dropped over the side into the rush of water, like a boy taking his first ride in a boat. There was nothing in his aspect that suggested what was waiting ahead. When they were perhaps fifty feet away, the sergeant gave Mr. Marquart a signal and he cut the engine to a crawl.

When she looked up again, the mulatto was standing on deck, holding on to one of the stays supporting the forward mast, looking out at the boat. He was wearing one of Alec's blazers, drinking a beer. She guessed he knew it was over and was trying to make as much of the good life as he could while the boat was still his. The sergeant motioned to Mr. Marquart again, and the little boat crept in closer. The cop in the uniform pointed the shotgun at the mulatto and aimed down the barrel, but there was no need for it. He was like a child now.

The fishing boat came about and the mulatto stared at her a moment, then raised the beer and seemed to wave. The sergeant stood up.

"Where's the other one?" he said.

"Hurt. The missus hit him upside the head with the mast and he gone back downstairs to lay down."

The sergeant looked at her to see if that was true, and she nodded. "Get him up here," he said.

"Cain't," the mulatto said. "He all pukin' and moanin'." He looked at her again and grinned. Like they were together in this.

"John," the sergeant said to the uniformed cop, "give me the shotgun."

The mulatto saw that the sergeant had said all he was going to. "Wait a minute now," he said. "I just thought after what the missus been through and all, she wouldn't like to be seeing any more of that nigger so soon."

The sergeant took the shotgun from the uniformed cop.

"All right, boss," said the mulatto, "all right, whatever you want."

He moved carefully to the stairway, his body correcting for each pitch of the boat, and started down. When he was out of sight, Mr. Marquart eased the fishing boat next to the *Georgia Peach*, and the sergeant reached up, laid the shotgun carefully across one of the seat cushions, and then, as easily as stepping into a bathtub, he took off his shoes and pulled himself up there too. He was strong and moved easily, but then his foot caught as he brought his leg over the railing, and it hurt him.

★　　★　　★

She heard them inside, quarreling again. The sergeant left the shotgun where it was on the cushion even when the mulatto appeared again at the top of the stairway, the other one a step behind. She was still below them in the fishing boat, and at the sight of the second Negro, she thought she could smell baby powder and grass.

The uniformed cop went on board next. The soles of his shoes would leave marks on the deck. She thought of Alec, dead in the cabin downstairs, who could not fathom a human being stepping onto a deck with black shoes. Who could not fathom the messes people left for someone else to clean up.

The huge Negro came out of the stairway, sweating, and stumbled to the side, where he sat down, his head falling back against the gunwale. He closed his eyes. The boats were both rocking, and his head appeared and disappeared from her view. She noticed there was dry blood caked from his ear down his neck—the evidence that she'd hurt him.

The mulatto was having a look around. "Things get out of hand, doesn't they?" he said brightly. "One thing lead to the next."

He looked into the fishing boat, as if she could verify what he said, and she saw the size of what was ahead. Attorneys, the questions, the trials. Photographers, reporters, insurance agents, business partners, funerals.

The sergeant now held the shotgun in one hand, absently rubbing his knee with the other, while the uniformed cop turned the mulatto around and put handcuffs on his wrists. The other Negro sat up suddenly and vomited down the front of his shirt, then closed his eyes and leaned back against the gunwale. She felt sick too, but held on. The sergeant looked up at the masts, at the rolled sails and sheets and the lines. "You don't mind my asking," he said to the mulatto, "what in the world were you two thinking?"

The mulatto began smiling and shaking his head. He was relieved to hear the sergeant talking to him in this way, like another person. He was good at talking with white people; he knew how it was done. "We wasn't, sir," he said. "And that's a fact. We wasn't thinking this out at all."

The uniformed cop went downstairs, and his absence seemed to make the mulatto nervous. "No sir," he said, "truly I don't know how something like this ever come to pass. Truly I don't."

The sergeant didn't reply to that; he'd turned ice-cold the moment the mulatto began sidling up. Even considering where they were, she was surprised at the suddenness of his change in mood. She was good at reading men and hadn't seen anything like that coming.

"Excuse me, sir? These cuffs is pretty tight."

The uniformed cop came back up, gagging, and went right to the huge Negro. Without a word, he took a blackjack out of his pocket and hit him half a dozen times across the side of his head. There was a deep, solid noise each time the jack landed.

The uniformed cop set his feet to swing the jack again, but the sergeant stopped him. "John," he said, "it's a waste of time."

Something in the words scared the mulatto. She thought of the way he was in the cabin earlier, the things he had said, how good he had been at scaring her.

"No, sir," he said. "We got time to work this out, sir. Plenty of time . . ."

The sergeant turned back to the fishing boat and looked again at her. The uniformed cop grabbed one of the huge Negro's hands and tried to put handcuffs on him too, but his wrists were too big. Then the Negro moved his head to the side and fresh blood dripped from his ear.

"I don't see nothing; I don't hear nothing," Mr. Marquart said. "Whatever happens here, I look the other way."

The sergeant nodded, as if Mr. Marquart was important in this, as if he mattered. "It's safe now," he said to her.

He waited; they all waited, and behind him, the huge Negro's face appeared and disappeared with the motion of the boats, and the mulatto stood with his shoulders at a strange angle to accommodate the handcuffs.

"Excuse me, sir," the mulatto said again. "I seemed to lost the feelings in my hands."

The sergeant gave no indication that he'd heard him. She was unsure of herself now, uncertain of what she wanted. "Do you need me to identify them?" she said.

"No," he said, and smiled at that too. "It's them."

She stood up and made her way to the edge of the fishing boat. The sergeant leaned over the railing and helped her up. He was strong and solid. The first thing she saw when she'd gotten her feet on deck was the big Negro, reclined against the gunwale. His shirt was wet in front and it clung to his skin.

She was still holding on to the policeman, and the smell came up to her out of the stairwell. She looked away, quietly panicked, realizing that it wasn't over. Thinking it might be endless.

"They shot the Mexican in the head," said the cop who had been downstairs. "The second one's back here, and it's a mess." He seemed to remember her then, and pulled himself up. "Sorry," he said.

The big one opened his eyes. They were bulbous and wet. He looked directly at her a moment, then up at the masts, and seemed puzzled to find himself out on the water in a seventy-two-foot sailboat on Sunday morning. She realized it was a mistake, asking to come with them back out here. She turned to him, the sergeant. She had her hand on his forearm.

"Some other things happened," she said quietly.

He held her up.

"Sir?" said the mulatto, "could I please have

112

a word with you, sir? They's often situations in life that ain't quite the way they seem." He was begging now, and she noticed again that he was wearing Alec's blazer. "What the missus is trying to tell you is that they is some of this she don't want to come out."

The sergeant turned and spoke in that calm way to the other policeman. "John," he said, "maybe you ought to go back to the marina now and take Mr. Marquart's statement."

The uniformed cop turned and looked at him a moment, making sure he understood, then shrugged and climbed back over the side of the sailboat and sat down with Mr. Marquart, who pull-started the motor. The sergeant thanked Mr. Marquart for his time and co-operation, and told him to send the county a bill for the gas. Then he told the other policeman to call the Coast Guard for a tow.

"You sure you don't need some help with this?" the uniformed cop said. "I don't mind."

"No, it's all right."

"Remember that big one's not cuffed."

"I remember."

The sergeant nodded at Mr. Marquart, and the old man adjusted the throttle and dropped the motor into gear and started back across the water.

"Now we can talk," said the mulatto, as if this were a new start. But he knew better.

The big Negro had been staring at the sergeant

for the last few minutes and now he spoke. "I know you, man," he said.

The sergeant looked up, nothing unpleasant in it, the first time he'd acknowledged he was there.

The big Negro said, "Out at Brookline." He turned to the mulatto and said, "Man, this here's the cat come in wanted to pick his own caddy."

The mulatto nodded at that, but it didn't make him happy.

"You said you want your own caddy," the huge one said, and he chuckled. "You want Train."

"Arthur," said the mulatto, "shut the fuck up. I'm trying to talk to these people about how this all happen."

"Man, talking ain't gone help," Arthur said. "You can't see that? It's beyond the talking stage." Then he leaned back again into the gunwale and closed his eyes.

A moment passed, and then the sergeant sighed and picked up the shotgun. He broke the breach to check the load, then closed it again. Arthur's eyes opened at the sound. He began to sit up, and the shot tore away his shoulder and the side of his neck. He was strangely still for a moment. A pink mist floated out behind him, and then gravity took his head sideways and down, in the direction of the missing part of his neck. There were tiny noises then as the bits and specks fell into the water.

"Wait a minute," the mulatto said. "Wait a minute here. We had a misunderstanding, sir. All this situation need to be sorted out . . . ."

The sergeant nodded again, as if this were, in fact, something they would sort out, as if this were all ordinary Sunday-morning sailboat business, and then he turned himself a little and the shotgun turned with him.

Time was confused. She sat looking at the huge body, still lost in that instant when the noise deafened her and the air turned pink over the water. She thought of her husband struggling on the floor, of the way he had held it off, and how this Negro had gone so easily away.

The mulatto was right. There had been a misunderstanding. She was a member of the National Association for the Advancement of Colored People. She lived in Beverly Hills, California, and made a point of using her NAACP membership card for identification every place she wrote a check. She and Alec had gone ahead, for pity sake, and hosted the fund-raiser for the convicted Negroes in a neighbor's yard two hours after Howard Hughes flew his airplane into her house.

Nothing she'd done for them mattered, though. She saw that. When the wires actually touched, good intentions and bad intentions were all the same.

"Sir, I ain't tried to escape here. I ain't tried nothing. . . ." He looked at her, looking for help.

The sergeant took his finger off the trigger and set the shotgun against the hatch door. She saw the relief in the mulatto's expression, and almost in the same instant the sergeant crossed the deck, picked him up by the waist of his trousers, and threw him over the railing. A foot caught in a stay going over, and one of his loafers fell off his foot and back onto the deck.

His eyes found hers again as he went over, held her there an instant, and then he was gone. There was a small splash when he hit the water, and then there were other noises, and then it was quiet. The sergeant picked up the loafer and tossed it over too, then came back to her and sat down.

He had his thoughts; she had hers.

A little time passed, and she suddenly pictured the mulatto, wild-eyed and stiff, somewhere in the current beneath the boat. She wondered if he might still have some thread of consciousness, if he might still know who he was and what he had done to her. And realize what had been done to him.

She had no idea if that was possible; she'd lost track of time.

"You don't have to say anything," he said softly.

And that was true, and it wasn't. She knew there would be statements to give, that she would have to go over what happened in the cabin again and again, every detail, every word they'd said. And she knew that she would have to say the Negroes were trying to escape. And she would do that— give them all the statements they wanted, testify in court, if it came to that. Truth and lies, whatever they wanted. The wires had touched and intentions didn't matter, and somehow in the confusion, she'd been claimed by the wrong side.

A single part of it, though, was beyond the claim. She looked away, afraid somehow that he already knew, and in that moment the name came to her—she heard the name, as if he'd spoken it himself. *Sweet.*

Friday night, in the same cabin where her husband was now lying on the floor, he'd called himself Sweet.

CHAPTER 4

DARKTOWN

The deputies filled half a row of the parking lot with cruisers at seven o'clock Monday morning, but the caddies were already out on the course—Monday mornings, the club encouraged the employees to play golf themselves, to teach them respect for the game—and because his own parish priest and the head of the Police Benevolent Association were both members at Brookline, the lieutenant in charge would not allow his men to drive their cars down onto the course to round them up.

The lieutenant didn't play the game himself, but he'd dealt with the country club set before and knew how they felt about their fairways.

And so eight officers in heavy black shoes and buttoned collars started down the first hole, walking, and then turned up the second, and followed the golf course that way until they began catching up with the caddies. It was already seventy-five degrees, headed into the nineties.

Three other deputies—including the lieutenant—

went to the clubhouse and served the manager with a search warrant, and then followed him down the gravel path to the caddy shed and began tearing the place apart, beginning with the desk behind the wire screen where Sweet kept his business. It took them less time to pick the lock than it took Sweet to open it with his key, and a few seconds more to find the metal box hanging behind the drawer from a shoelace. There were seventeen twenty-dollar bills inside, and they chased off the manager and split it four ways—five bills for each of them and two for the captain back at the station.

Beneath the money was a small black notebook, filled with names and addresses and phone numbers and dates. The lieutenant opened the book, fanned through the pages, and noticed all the names were women, at least the ones that were written out. Some of it was only initials. He put the book in his coat pocket, thinking it might turn into something for him later. That he might like to visit some of the women personally, see what they looked like, maybe ask one or two how they ended up in a notebook like this anyway. No? Well, maybe their husbands might have some idea. He didn't mind watching women squirm, didn't mind at all.

Next, the policemen went to the lockers where the caddies kept their belongings, and it was slower going. The caddies didn't keep things tidy, the way they were behind the wire cage. Sandwiches, liquor, cigarettes, playing cards, small amounts of marijuana, large amounts of marijuana, bus passes, old calendars with pictures of cars and half-naked girls. A syringe, a catcher's mitt, a starfish. A package of morning glory seeds, cigars. There were also articles of clothing, mostly hats and bright-colored sweaters with figures of golfers knitted into the front and back. Clothes the caddies wouldn't wear themselves, but were not inclined to throw away. They'd heard what sweaters with golfers knitted into the stomach cost up in the pro shop.

Everything the deputies found that they didn't want or couldn't use themselves was tossed into the middle of the floor, to be picked through and swept up later by less senior members of the force. Then the empty lockers were pitched onto the floor too so that the policemen could look behind them. The lockers went over, and then the roaches and silverfish washed out, thousands of them, rolling up over the officers' shoes and the cuffs of their pants, crossing the room like surf. One of the deputies yelled, and the panic spread, and then they were all stomping the floor harder than you had to stomp to kill bugs, trying to make examples of the ones they got, and then one of the deputies injured his heel, aggravating an old baseball injury, and the other two helped him to the doorway, where they waited for the bugs to find their way back into the cracks in the walls and corners, out of the light.

The deputies stood in the doorway, shaking their pants, feeling phantom roaches on their legs. There were two umbrellas behind the lockers—the spokes and handles anyway; the cloth had been eaten away a long time ago—an ancient leather golf bag, some dusty bottles of soda pop and beer, a single snakeskin cowboy boot, and, not far from it, what appeared to be the bones of a human leg. The deputies stopped cold when they found the bones, looked at each other, silently considering the paperwork, and tossed them into the middle of the floor with the rest of it.

Train was headed up the slope of the short rough along the ninth fairway when the deputies and caddies rounded the corner of the dogleg behind him. Looked like bad weather rolling in. The caddies were out in front of the officers, eighteen or twenty of them, and the officers were herding them along with their nightsticks, keeping the slackers going. Some of the officers were smoking cigarettes; some of them were carrying their shoes and limping.

Train hid his golf club and sat down against a tree to wait. He was always expecting for somebody to come along, ask where did he get a Tommy Armour autograph in the first place. He watched them climb the long hill, began to hear their voices. He supposed he was done golfing for the day, but he'd been forcing it anyway; couldn't stop himself trying to make the ball go to the pin instead of letting it go. That was the knack, or his sense of it: The shot was already there somewhere, and he just got out of the way and let it go home. But then, some days you could, and some days you couldn't.

Like some days the radio station came in nice and clear, and some days you had to keep moving the dial because of the static out on the edges.

He put the ball in his pants pocket, remembering where it had been, on the chance that they let everybody loose once they had them all rounded up. There was no sense in that, of course, but the law did things that nobody understood but the law itself.

The deputies were tired and blistered and sweating, in no mood at all for golfing niggers. One of them had took out his pistol and held it in his hand as he walked. They took the caddies back to the shed and set them down against the outside wall, directly in the sun, to wait for the paddy wagons. Some of the caddies were nervous, and one named Roger Ennis tried to confess to a liquor store robbery, but the cops guarding them were out in the sun too, and they told him to sit still and shut the fuck up.

The club manager came partway down the hill and then stalled when he seen what was going on, and then tilted his head back a minute, like he might have a nosebleed, before he come the rest of the way down. He was a thin man in pressed slacks and loafers with tassels.

The manager put one hand on his rump and bent at the waist—an old lady's posture, like she's scolding the children—and counted the caddies sitting against the shed. He used a finger to count, keeping track of where he was at in that long line of black faces. Then he turned to the lieutenant in charge, looking like somebody would rather just went back up the hill.

"You're taking them all?" he said.

Even with the extra hundred dollars in his pocket, the lieutenant did not care for loafers with tassles. "Well, sir, I don't see how we can straighten it out here," he said.

The manager nodded, as if he saw the officer's reasoning. Train guessed he was used to that, to seeing other people's point of view. "I gotcha," he said, looking again at the caddies, "but the situation from this side of the fence is that we have tee times starting at one o'clock, front and back, and now I've got no caddies. The mayor himself is scheduled for two-twelve."

The lieutenant waited a minute before he answered, like he was reminding himself where he was. "Well, sir," he said finally, "I appreciate your situation, the mayor being a member out here and all, but it comes right down to it, it's even more complicated than that." The lieutenant took a breath and closed his eyes to calm down, but the fuse had been lit. "You might say the situation is that somebody's supposed to be in charge out here, and there's a criminal enterprise being run right under your fucking nose, and now good people been killed for no reason, and if that means fucking Eleanor Roosevelt herself has got to fix her own divots today, then that's what's going to happen. That is the fucking situation from this side of the fence." The lieutenant's face had turned red by now, and the club manager was nodding a long time before he finished.

"Of course," he said. "I understand completely. . . ."

"So if I was you, I'd go back inside my fucking office, where the air condition was on, and have a good cry and then call up all the dignitaries and golfers and tell them that until further notice they got to carry their own fucking bags."

The man with the loafers sighed. Being club manager, he was immune to crude language and personal insults. "Easier said than done," he said.

"To tell you the truth, sir," the lieutenant said, "being ass-deep in Democrats at nine-thirty in the morning is not what I was hoping for today either." And then he turned away from the manager to watch the paddy wagons negotiate the gravel path from the parking lot down to the shed.

There was only two wagons, and they put half of the people in one of them, half in the other. They had benches along each wall inside, and tiny windows above them and in the doors. All the windows were locked shut and covered with wire, and the air inside was hot and close, just like it came out of the people's lungs. Nobody spoke except when the wagon hit a bump or they slammed on the brakes or turned a sharp corner, and the caddies fell off their seats and cracked heads, and then they all were blaming each other for where they fell, like

124

there was some established rules for riding around in the back of a paddy wagon.

Train was standing at one of the windows, holding on to the wire for balance, his feet spread a yard apart. He wasn't surprised at what was happening; he heard before that the police liked to throw you around in the back of the wagon.

The siren was going—he noticed, though, that they didn't turned it on until they was clear of Brentwood—and Train watched the street pass by outside, women with shopping bags who stopped what they were doing to stare. He imagined his mother, her expression when she found out they'd taken him to jail. And just at the moment that thought came into his mind, the driver slammed on the brakes and people flew everywhere. A person of some sort rolled into Train's knees and he fell sideways, his feet suddenly where his head was a second before, and then he come down hard and his knee slammed into somebody's face. It was soft and bony at the same time, reminded him of an eggshell. The wagon stopped dead and didn't move.

Train lay on the floor and a man lay across his feet, and then he rolled off and looked for a while at the ceiling. Train saw it was Plural, and hoped he was unconscious, or at least didn't see who he was in the dark. He tried to move farther away, but there were bodies behind him and no place to go. He went to stand up, but there was people leaning on him from above.

Plural reached up and touched his eyebrow. He was cut there, and the blood ran down the side of his nose and dripped off his ear. His mouth was cut too. The wagon started up again and then hit a pothole, and Plural's head bounced against the floor. Presently, he wiped off the blood and sat up. Train could tell he didn't know where he was.

Plural squinted up toward the light from the window and said, "It was a slip. Absolutely wasn't no punch; it was a slip. . . ."

They unloaded the wagons in front of the police station, and the caddies went up the steps single file, most of them handcuffed and shackled. They'd run out of cuffs and shackles both just before they got to Train, and he was grateful for that, and not only because he didn't get throwed around so bad in the back of the wagon. As long as he could remember, he always panicked at being closed in. He didn't even like being hugged.

They squeezed the caddies into a single holding cell and took the cuffs and shackles off the ones who were cuffed and shackled. Plural made himself comfortable in a corner, blotted the blood off the cut on his eye with the sleeve of his shirt, and the rest of the caddies saw he was bleeding and was as scared of him as they were of the police. And stayed as far away as they could. When the deputy with the key got to him, Plural smiled up at him and said, "We ain't gone steal your handcuffs, boss."

A few minutes later, they came in and lifted Plural up by his shirt and took him away.

They kept the caddies in the holding cell most of the day, taking them out one at a time. Train didn't speak to anyone, keeping himself still to fight off the trepidation. Fifteen, twenty minutes would pass and then the deputies would come unlock the big door, the banging noise echoing off the walls and ceiling, and pick out another prisoner and lead him away for questioning. Finally, late in the afternoon, they came and got Train.

Two deputies in uniforms walked him down a long hallway, nobody speaking, just the sounds of those hard shoes on the linoleum floor. They passed a room where a man was saying, "The mentality of the colored suspect is often childlike, which does not make him less dangerous. What has to be done in that case is visual communication. Show-and-tell. The young lady here, on the other hand, she might only need somebody to explain the situation. . . ."

Somebody said "yessir," and Train saw there was a woman in the room with the men—loose-legged, chewing gum, and appeared to be in custody.

They pushed Train through the next door, into a small room with a large mirror set into one of the cement walls. There was a single wooden table against the opposite wall with a paper spike sitting on it, about half-loaded with spiked papers, and a radio, and a pile of folders. All that on one side.

The other side was bare. There was chairs at both ends of the table, but Train didn't try to sit down until the deputy in charge came in and pointed him into the one he wanted him to sit in. Train noticed the place smelled of Chinese food.

Train couldn't say for sure, but the deputy in charge did not appear to be a correct shade of white. He come into the room with his face glazed and wet, resembled a doughnut you don't want to eat, and dropped into his chair like everything weighted too much for him to hold it up anymore. His face was that morbid color, and there was also pink patches here and there, like somebody been swatting flies off his cheeks. He was carrying an open container of noodles of some kind, eating it with chopsticks, and after he sat down, he cleared some of the folders away with his elbow to make room for himself to eat. There were other containers on the cabinets, most of them left wide open, with dried rice and sauce on the sides and chopsticks laying in the corners.

"Name?"

Train recognized the voice, the man from the other room, talking about colored suspects. He could tell from the way the cop talked that there were people behind the mirror, watching. He had that old feeling that somebody was about to make an example of him for others to heed. That was one of the worse things they could do, make you an example for others to heed.

"Lionel Walk."

"Age?"

"Seventeen, sir."

"Address?"

Train gave him his mother's address.

"Social Security number?"

"Excuse me?"

The policeman looked up at Train, and then quickly glanced past him at the mirror in the wall. "You got a Social Security card, Lionel?"

"No sir, I don't believe I'm old enough for that."

The cop posed in a certain way and shook his head, like this was a show for the people behind the mirror. "America's just a free ride for you all, right?"

"No sir, it don't seem like it so far."

The deputy narrowed his eyes and stared at him a long time. Train felt his eyes, and he felt the eyes staring at him from behind. "You see that over there?" the deputy in charge said.

Train turned the direction he pointed. There was something spilled on the floor.

"You know what that is?"

"Look like something spilled. . . ."

"You goddamn right, something spilled. It spilled out of one of you people's heads."

Train sat still, looking at the spot. It was pink, maybe sweet-and-sour sauce.

"Now, I'm only going to tell you this once, my friend. I had it up to here with caddies. I heard more lies this afternoon than I could write down, and on top of that, of course, was one of you come in here, accused me of stealing his purse, his fucking purse. A full-grown man." He waited a minute, glanced again at the mirror. "You can see how a person can run out of patience," he said.

Train turned back to the deputy and waited, never considered explaining the kind of purse Plural meant.

"All right now," he said, "let's go through this slowly. How long you known Clarence Holmes?"

Train sat still, trying to remember where he'd heard the name. The cop stared at him, waiting. Train shook his head.

"You don't know him?"

"No sir."

"You work for him, and you don't know him."

"Who?"

"I told you, Clarence Holmes."

"You mean Sweet?"

"Tell me the truth," the deputy said, "are you-all this stupid around each other, or you just do it to fuck with white people's sensibilities?"

"I never heard him called nothing but Sweet," Train said.

The deputy noticed the difference in Train's voice. "Did that make you angry, Lionel," he said, "when I called you stupid?"

Train kept himself quiet. The deputy in charge held him there, staring, a minute longer, and then sighed and resumed to questioning.

"All right," he said, "how long you been in Mr. Holmes' employment?"

"I ain't been in his employment," Train said, and the deputy shook his head and laughed.

"Employment," he said. "That means work."

"I don't work for Clarence Holmes," Train said, "I work for Brookline Country Club."

"So now all of a sudden you know his name."

Train looked the deputy in the eye for the first time. He knew it was dangerous, like staring down a bad dog, but sometimes that would keep one off. "You just told me his name," he said.

They sat still for a little while, and then the deputy in charge begun to hum, and Train seen he was pleased with the way things was going. Then he seem to forgot about Train a minute or two and fussed with his chopsticks and his noodles. He was a fussy fat man with saggy tits and his own habits. Looked like the kind of man that went into the bathroom for two hours at a time. He wrapped a load of the noodles around the sticks and bent down to meet it. Then he looked up, with noodles hanging down his chin, and spoke as he worked them into his mouth.

"Would you say you and Mr. Holmes was friends?"

"No sir."

"But you associated with him socially. . . ."

"No sir, I ain't associated with this at all."

The deputy sat up suddenly and slammed his hand down on his desk, not far from the paper spike. "That isn't what I'm hearing," he said. "That isn't what I'm hearing at all." The noise startled Train, and he moved back in his chair.

Train stared at the spike, and the deputy noticed it and slammed his hand down in the same spot again, showing him he meant business. The folders jumped and settled, and Train jumped with them. The deputy pressed into him. "All right, then," he said, "what about Arthur Tobin?"

Train tried to remember if Arthur's last name was Tobin. He didn't want to get any more questions wrong.

"You know him or not?"

"I know a boy name Arthur, but I don't know it's the same one."

"Big buck?"

Train nodded.

"Black as a sewer . . ."

Train nodded again. The deputy picked up his chopsticks and moved the little carton of noodles. "You hang out with Arthur after work, do you?"

"No sir."

The deputy nodded, as if he'd caught him in a lie. "You and Arthur and Clarence never drive that big Caddy down to Orange County, do you? Maybe down by the marina or some nice white neighborhood and see what you can find?"

"What caddy?" He thought for a moment that the deputy was asking about one of the Brookline caddies.

"Now you telling me you don't know Clarence's ride?"

"Sweet got a Cadillac, but I never been in it."

The deputy wrote that down. "That's your statement, your official statement, that you never been near that car?"

Nothing was clear now, yes or no. It was you been *in* it one minute and *near* it the next. Train didn't want to make no official statement.

"You know what perjury is, my friend?" Playing again to the mirror.

"I been near Sweet's car," he said. "I just never been in it."

"And so if we found your prints inside that car, that would mean you been lying."

"My prints?"

"Fingerprints. You heard of fingerprints. . . ."

Train tried to imagine how his fingerprints could have got in Sweet's car. And then he remembered the money, the twenty-dollar bills that were supposed to be for Florida's wife, and he knew they had him. "They was some money, had my prints on it," he said.

"How much money?"

"I don't know. They was some twenties. . . ."

"You make so much money out there carrying golf bags, you can't keep track how much it is? Is that what you're telling me?"

"I don't—"

The deputy stood up over the desk, everything trembling under his clothes, and his face went a

133

worst color than it already was. "You goddamn right, you don't," he yelled, and spit flew out of his mouth, and then he slammed down his hand again, but this time his foot seemed to slide underneath the desk, maybe on noodles, and he tried to catch hisself at the same time, and the spike went into the palm of his hand and come out between the knuckles. Train sat still, horrified, and the deputy grabbed himself by the wrist and stared at what had happened. He moved his head to look at it from below and above, like he was puzzled what it was.

For a moment, there wasn't any blood at all, at least on the side Train could see, and then the margin of the wound turned blue, and then a little blood pooled around the spike and then rolled down the back of his hand, and then the deputy's face drained like somebody inside him pulled the cork, and he fainted.

Train stood up for a better look, and then sat back down and waited. Thinking it might be a trick. He looked at the mirror, then at the door. Nothing happened, nobody came. The deputy lay on the floor, the spike still stuck through his hand, his feet jerking little jerks like a baby in his booties.

Train pictured how this would looked from the door when the other deputies finally come in, and soon, without really knowing he was doing it, he got up and walked out.

The hallway was empty. At the far end he

could see sunlight. Glass doors and sunlight. He walked a few steps toward the light, past the room where he'd felt somebody watching behind the mirror. The door was closed, but there was noises inside, things moving against each other, somebody breathing hard and thumping, getting his spurs jingled. He knew that sound all right, heard his mother all the time trying to shush Mayflower in the night.

Mayflower, of course, had his own ways of doing what he did. Always wanted Train to know it when he had it inside her.

Train was through the glass doors and in the street before he saw the car and heard brakes. There was a man behind the windshield, seemed to be yelling at him, and then blowing his horn. Train never broke stride, lit across the street, headed north, and was up in Chinatown before he remembered he'd gave them his name and address.

He let himself in through the back door. There was a light on in front, outside on the porch, but the house itself was dark. There wasn't no sheriff's department cars waiting for him in the street, no neighbors on their steps or at the windows. The dog was lying under the table, and he made that sweet squinting expression and dragged his tail across the floor when Train turned on the light.

He went to the icebox and found a plate of fried potatoes and some sliced ham. He made a sandwich and ate the potatoes cold, barely tasting the food. A piece of meat dropped out from between the bread slices, and he picked it up and took it to Lucky, holding it under his nose until he knew what it was.

He heard a noise, and when he turned around Mayflower was leaning against the doorway. His stomach and chest swelled out over his undershorts and he was absently holding his business; his knuckles were the size of your eyeballs. One side of his face was flat from the pillow. "Well, well," he said. "The convict on the run."

Train tasted cold potatoes and the ham coming back at him. He tried to hold on to everything at once. "They was here about three hours ago," Mayflower said.

"Who?"

Mayflower chuckled to himself over that. "The sheriff, man. Who you think?"

"For what?"

"For what? You stick one, give them your momma's address, they gone come around. That's the way of the world. They tell me I got to call them when you show up or I'm an accessory too."

"I didn't stick him," he said. "The police did it himself."

Mayflower shrugged; didn't matter to him how it happened. "They come in here, tore up your room, upset your mother. . . ."

"Where is she?"

"I took her over to her sister's, she wouldn't be

136

around when they come again. She all convulsed the whole time they was going through the house; she keeps saying, 'Oh, no, he couldn't of did that. . . .'" Then, making his voice high, he said, "'My baby couldn't of did that.'"

He walked past Mayflower, feeling the man's heat, feeling his eyes, and went to his room. His mattress had been tossed off the bed, all his drawers were open, his comic books and clothes thrown over the floor, the closet door partially off its hinges. His socks was unrolled, and he knew even before he looked that the money was gone. Four hundred and sixty-eight dollars.

"They probably a reward out on your ass by now," Mayflower said. "I ought to call, see what it is."

Train began picking his things up off the floor, putting them back in the drawers. Taking his time, just cleaning up the room; he saw that it disappointed Mayflower he wasn't all convulsed himself. He took his time.

"If I was you, man," Mayflower said, "I'd be stuffing chicken legs in my pockets on the way out."

Train didn't turn around. He'd suddenly begun to cry. Almost eighteen years old, and he still cried. There was nothing he could do about it. Not just because he was scared but the sadness too. The sadness of things came up on him at unexpected times, before he was ready for it. He rolled his socks into pairs again and put them and his underwear back where they belonged and closed the drawers. Then, keeping his back to Mayflower, he slid his mattress back in place too. He wiped his cheeks against his shirtsleeves and began to make his bed.

"You hear me, man? They coming back. . . ."

Train took his time, tucking in the corners. His mother had been a nurse's aide once at Wadsworth Hospital, way up on Wilshire, the vets' hospital, showed him how to make a bed. She said the lesson she learned from that job was that the hospital made some people nicer and some of them worse.

When Train had stopped crying and was sure he could talk again, he turned around. Mayflower was standing in the doorway, still holding his business. Reminding him somehow of what everything between them was all about.

"Jail or the road," Mayflower said, "that's how the old song goes."

They looked at each other a little while, the house changing hands right in that room, in that moment, and then Mayflower went into another room and come out with his money clip. His fingers crawled through a dozen bills—ones—and he handed them to Train. "You see your mother again, don't forget to tell her I done this," he said. "She likes me being nice to you."

An hour later, walking the streets of Darktown, smelling the sewage—which was somehow always

138

worst at night—telling stories out loud to see how they would sound to the deputies when they got him, Train stopped at a all-night market run by some kind of slants that seem to smile too much for this neighborhood, and got a grape Nehi. He took the money Mayflower given him out of his pocket and saw the blue circles colored over George Washington's eyes.

Later on, he couldn't remember going back; no idea how he got there or where the chair leg was from. It was oak or maple—something heavy—rounded at the bottom and squared at the top. It was still in his hand when she come back to the house and saw him in the kitchen, and saw what he'd done.

Train spent the night pressed into the cool glass window of a bus, staring out at the city from one end of the line to the other, all the way from downtown to the place it turned around in Venice. All night long, people got on and off, drunk and laughing.

In the morning, he went back to work.

It made his lips tremble, walking up the drive-way, but he had no place else to go, and no thoughts where he could hide after what had happened, and for now he only wanted to be someplace he knew.

He walked along the driveway and heard the familiar sound of the sprinklers. He stopped a moment and watched the sun make a rainbow in the spray, and smelled the fresh-cut grass, and the place seemed strangely unchanged—the square two-story white building, the flowers, the outbuildings, the empty parking lot—everything that happened yesterday was invisible. He didn't know what else he expected, but it felt strange.

He walked along toward the club, and it came to him slowly that it was not impossible he was invisible too. The thought took his breath. That even after what happened, he could just blended back into the scenery, into everything alive and dead that was the same today as it was yesterday. That he could just go back, with everything else, to the way things was.

Down to the caddy shed, though, things wasn't the same. The place was tore up and there was a new man sitting at Sweet's desk, a white man with glasses on going through a pile of papers, and he told Train, without looking up, that anybody wanted to come back to work had to submit an application. Train looked around the room. The lockers were on the floor, everything in them spilt out. Clothes, umbrellas, sandwiches, bones . . . The bones stopped him, but not for long. It was the kind of thing in his life that if nobody else mentioned it, neither did he. The wire cage had been torn down, and he noticed Sweet's pool cue lying in the rubble with everything else.

It seemed like the whole room was turned upside

down and shook, and everything come out of the pockets and then dropped back on the ground.

Train leaned over the desk to look at the man's papers, trying to see what kind of application it was. The man made a face, like he smelled something bad, and Train backed away and began to leave, just wanted to get back outside where things looked familiar. Get back to that thought he had walking up the driveway, that he could go back to who he was. The man pointed off in the general direction of the door. "Service entrance," he said. "That's where they're taking applications."

Train followed the cement path around the back of the clubhouse to the service entrance, where a table had been set up and the club manager was conducting interviews. The line of applicants was twenty yards long. The manager was wearing a light blue sport coat and sunglasses and had a carnation pinned to the collar of his jacket.

Plural was up near the front of the line in a clean white T-shirt, but the sleeves didn't look right because of the muscles in his shoulders. Plural always kept himself clean—a clean shirt and shined shoes—and he always smelled like fresh laundry. The sun shined off his skin, and you could see the color of it beneath the shirt where he'd begun to sweat. Train moved up toward the front without getting closer to the line itself, the other men watching him every step to make sure he didn't try to cut in. He been around people who were hungry before, and seen them do sudden,

141.

violent things without no reason you could call a reason. Been around enough of them to know that the way some of them look at it, a place in line or an old comb that they found that morning, or a baby bottle left on a bench, that was all the excuse they need.

At the front of the line, Plural was standing politely now with his hands behind his back, sweating through his shirt, offering the manager his lumpy, smiling face even while the man told him that due to the present circumstances, none of the former caddies at Brookline was being rehired at this time. "The board of directors has taken the position that there is no way to separate the wheat from the chaff, and decided to make a clean breast of it," he said, like that would be good news for all concerned.

Plural kept his hands politely behind his back and waited until the manager had finished, and then he said, "Yessir, I understand your positions, but that clean titty bi'niss ain't concerned with me. I never had no dog in that fight."

The manager took off his sunglasses and repeated what he'd just said about the board of directors, but went through it slower this time. Under the present circumstances, none of the former caddies was being rehired. Perhaps at a later date, but not at the present. Plural took off his own sunglasses, showing him a home-stitched eyebrow, and leaned in close to the manager and then cocked his head birdlike for a better look. Every inch closer he got, the manager moved that much away.

"Yessir," Plural said, "I see what you trying to say. But what I'm saying, under the present circumstances, I don't need that rehiring business, due to I wasn't never unhired in the first place."

"I'm afraid that's what I'm talking about," the man said. "You no longer have a job." He looked around behind him, about to yell for help.

Plural stood up suddenly, and the manager jumped at the movement.

"The man took it away?" he said.

The manager nodded elaborately, relieved, like they just had a breakthrough. "Yessir," he said, "I'm afraid that's it. Your position has been withdrawn."

Plural stood still a moment, seemed to be collecting that, and then when he had it all, he just turned around and walked away.

The manager closed his eyes for a minute and slumped in his chair. When Train looked back at him again, he was feeling his pulse.

Train caught up to Plural, didn't know particularly why, except he seem to felt safer that way, and they headed in the direction of the street. Train and Plural, walking together. Plural smelling like a clean sheet.

"Well, sometime it happen like that, you know," Plural said. "You come in for your money, and the man took it to cover the expenses. That's how it goes." He looked over at Train. "How you did, Lionel?" he said. "You win or lose, man?"

143

Train stumbled over that. Wasn't nobody had called him Lionel around here in the two years of his employedment, and Plural never talked to anybody but himself anyway. He stole a look, thinking that all the time Plural was sitting alone in the caddy shed, people calling him No-Tank—in front of him, but not exactly to his face—you couldn't tell what the man was thinking. People just assumed it was some craziness about some fight or another that mashed up his brain in the first place.

Plural looked back at the clubhouse as he walked away. "Suppose I got to steal somebody's chickens over this however," he said. "It don't pay the bills, but it's something to eat." Plural laughed at what he just said, picturing it somehow, and Train saw that one of his teeth was broke. Train wondered if he had did that himself with his knee in the back of the paddy wagon when the deputies hit the breaks. Either that or the deputies did it later. Plural nudged him in the ribs with his elbow, playful, hurting him without meaning to.

"Ain't that how it goes?" he said. "You look in the damn mirror all morning, can't remember did you won or lost."

They walked together a little ways, Plural talking about stealing the man's chickens, trying to remember if he won or lost.

Days passed and nothing happened. Nothing in the *Mirror News* on Mayflower, no sheriffs asking around where he was. Train began thinking more and more that the world might of decided to let him alone.

He spent days looking for work and slept at night at Sugars Gym, where Plural stayed. Been there about four years now. Mr. Sugars wore big straw hats and checked Train's arms for needle tracks before he let him in, and then told him he wasn't running no Salvation Army. The reason he let him stay, he said, was that now he had Plural around the premises at night to keep the neighborhood kids from stealing his gloves and cups, and he had Train to keep Plural from setting the place on fire. "You don't smoke yourself, do you?"

"No sir," Train said. "It made me dizzy."

The gym was on the border of north Watts, less than a mile from his mother's house, and Train played with the idea sometimes about going over, dropping in to see her and old Lucky, but he never took even a step that direction. The truth was, he was afraid to go home, afraid that she might look at him now the way she did when she come into the kitchen and saw him holding the table leg in his hand. Thought the dog might be scart of him too. He thought about that and then wandered off to wonder again where he got a table leg from, to keep himself from thinking about what she stopped and stared at when she come in the door. Now he thought about it, she might not of even noticed the table leg if he hadn't dropped it and woke up the dog, who yelped and scrambled his toenails on the floor, tried to get his feet under him. Train thought it must of reminded him of that feeling when he was hit by that car and rolled across the road.

But whatever the dog thought, he seen something jumping in his mother's throat, and he could not stand to see her scared of him like that again.

Wednesday night. He climbed the stairs to the gym in the dark, up into the heat, and found Plural sitting alone in the ring, his back against the turnbuckle, smoking some hemp, reading the *Darktown Standard*. The room's walls was plastered with old fight posters, and it stunk the way gyms stink.

Train had gone out early, got on the buses and went to country clubs. He'd found a *Herald Express* and a *Mirror News* both on the bus floors and looked again for a story about Mayflower, but there still wasn't nothing. Just like it didn't happen. He tried to imagine what his mother told the deputies. She was pretty enough; if it was the right officer, they might take her word that she just come home and found him like that, maybe write down that he was fixing the sink and the light socket at the same time. Then, if it was the right officer, they might of just carted Mayflower out of there, just because she was pretty, and then took his ass out into the desert and left it.

Train imagined those gray eyes staring at the stars night after night.

He had no luck at the country clubs. Nobody

wanted no caddy that never caddied before, and when Train told them he been at Brookline, they suddenly remembered they didn't have no openings at the present time. By now, the scandal out there passed through country clubs all over the city, until some of the members at Brookline had even quit their own club over the rumors. Didn't want nobody thinking some caddy slipped off into the foliage with their wives.

Train lay down on the mat that he hauled up onto a plywood shelf for a bed—just like Plural's—and worried his way around a familiar circle. It begun with the dog, wondering where did he think Train was these days. Then he worried if his mother remembered to feed him. Then he wondered where was his bowl. Train pictured the scene in the kitchen, with Mayflower lying there leaking out his personality through the crack in his head, and it bothered him that he couldn't find the dog bowl in the picture. He could see Mayflower; he could see dirt around the heels of his feet as he lay on the floor, the cigarette in the ashtray. Then he pictured the ashtray in the deputy's office, and how that one looked impaled on his spike. Seemed like all he could think of was the messes in the rooms he left.

That brought him to his own room, all tore up when he got home, and then how the house looked when he came back later, and he knew it wasn't his house anymore, and then he could see his mother again, the exact look on her face when she pushed him out the door. He could hear the bolt go into the lock and knew that was that, and then he imagined her turning back into the house to get herself used to what was lying on her kitchen floor.

He remembered how the dog woke up and tried to scrambled when the chair leg hit the floor. Maybe thought he was dreaming all the rest.

Plural got up slowly, washed his face in the sink, washed out his T-shirt, and then crawled into the shelf above Train. He had thin calves and tiny misshapen feet, and Train watched them hang for a while over the edge while he finished the paper, and then he lay down up there and they disappeared.

Plural never turned off the lights and never slept but an hour or two at a time. He would be quiet at first, and then he start to tossed and turn, and a little later he would make a whinny noise, and then before long he would tossed and turn himself into the wall, push his face into it where he couldn't breathe. That scared him awake, and the next minute he was in the ring naked, shadowboxing and talking about stealing chickens.

Train would lie still and watch him break a sweat—he had to break a sweat to go back to sleep—and without understanding nothing about the sport of boxing, he recognized something about what Plural was doing, saw that the movement made some perfect kind of sense. That's how Plural slept, got up to shadowbox two or three times every night.

"Well," Plural said above him now, "I see they's

two boys finally cut each other up over to Paradise Developments." He sounded disappointed, like he'd been warning this would happen all along. Train sat up and leaned out until he could make out a little of Plural.

"Paradise?"

Plural chuckled. "Oh, yes, they got big ideas over there."

Plural's arm come over the side and gave him up the paper, and Train noticed again how his hands was small and lumpy, but perfectly formed—not like his feet—delicate, like a girl's.

Train had seen the *Standard* before. It was for sale all over Darktown; he supposed in Watts too. There was usually an article on the front page how a professor proved Jesus was a Negro or a little girl was run over by a white man's truck right out in front of her house. And there was always something about the war. An article where somebody fought for his country and came home debilitated and couldn't get work. From the pictures, there was more colored people lying around with one leg than two.

The story about the stabbings was on the front page. The participants, the story said, were both young Negroes, gave their names and ages, said they were members of the maintenance crew. The man that owned Paradise Developments said he went down to the barn and found the one on the tractor first. "It's just some kind of tragic misunderstanding," he said.

The reporter was named Lutheran Hollingsworth. Looking over the rest of the page, Train saw that the same reporter had his name attached to every story.

"They could be something for you there," Plural said.

"Look like they could be something for us both," Train said. He been thinking lately it wouldn't be a bad idea to get Plural out of the gym now and again, get his mind off stealing chickens. Not to get too comfortable not working.

"Not me," he said, "I'm strictly an indoor man now."

A tall link fence ran the perimeter of the golf course, and there was a sign every fifty yards.

PARADISE DEVELOPMENTS, MODERN HOUSING
AND GOLF INQUIRE WITHIN

From outside the gate, Train could see places in the fairways where the sun had baked the grass brown. The parking lot was half-full, and most of the cars was not much better than no car at all. Nothing like Brookline. A delivery truck rolled past him and into the driveway, the tires chewing the gravel and broken glass, and parked outside the double-wide trailer that seem to been the clubhouse.

Train took a few minutes to get calmed down for the interview—waited until the deliveryman returned to his truck with the empties and left—and then tucked in his shirt all the way around and went in.

Coming out of the morning sun, it took him a minute to see the people inside: two men standing at the cash register, and a woman behind it. He heard them before he could make them out. The man said he wanted their money back; the woman was trying to hold them off. Train been hearing one version or another of this same conversation every day of his life. She was a big heavy woman—taller than either of the men—with dirty jeans and a wide cowboy belt and a sunburn.

"Lady, if I wanted to play a cow pasture," the smaller man said, "I'd have gone out to the farm." The one with him nodded along, as if that was what he'd done too. The woman behind the cash register had pale eyes. It looked like she'd been smoking a thin black cigar when this started, the ashes spilled out now on a plate next to the remains of a sandwich. White bread with lipstick prints. A crack ran the length of the window that overlooked the first tee.

"If the course was so bad," the woman said, "how come you played eighteen holes before you decided to ask for your money back?" She sounded like she'd smoked cigars a long time, and that her voice wasn't never in the soprano section to begin with.

"I have played golf all over the state," said the

151

smaller one, "and never saw a course in this kind of shape."

The man with him nodded again, like it went for him too.

The woman at the cash register picked a piece of tabacco off her tongue, sizing them up. Then she noticed Train. A certain disappointment passed over her face, like she was hoping for something better. "Shit," she said, looking the little one up and down, "why don't you go join a nice country club like everybody else? I understand they keep them in wonderful shape."

The customer looked around the double-wide and said, "You got a very nice situation here yourself, dear." The woman saw sarcasm was his strong suit, and without another word, she opened the cash register and took out two five-dollar bills and threw them across the counter.

"Don't come back," she said. "I never forget a face."

"But I bet you'd like to," said the little one.

"I was wondering if they might be some opportunities," Train said. His voice sounded strange to him whenever he asked for anything. Asking went against his nature. "Something outside."

The woman was still watching the door where the customers went. "Myself," she said, scratching her head, "I just as soon be robbed by somebody with a gun." She began writing something down, stopped to bite off a hangnail, then

152

looked at Train. "That isn't what you're doing, is it?"

"No ma'am, I was here about an opening."

She finished what she was writing and stuck it in the open cash register. Her hair was dyed so blond, it was almost white. "You run a tractor?" she said.

"Yes ma'am."

"You know what a Triplex is? You run one of those too?"

"Yes ma'am."

"What height you mow greens?"

"Depend on the rain, the time of year," Train said. "Usually three-eighths."

A moment passed, and then the woman scratched at her hairline again, found something there, and closed her eyes and pulled. Her fingers come out pinching a tick still attached to a little piece of her scalp. She held it up to the light, the legs all walking away; Train thought it must be wondering why it wasn't moving. The woman set the tick carefully on the edge of her lower front teeth and bit down. There was a tiny pop and then she spit on the floor and made a face.

"Where did you say you worked previously?" she said, but she couldn't get the tick taste out of her mouth now and wasn't paying attention.

Train stumbled and froze, not wanting to say Brookline. The woman suddenly looked at him more closely and said, "Is it prison? You're kind of young for that." He realized his face was soured up like he'd put the tick in his mouth too.

"No ma'am," Train said. "I never been in prison."

"No," the woman said, reconsidering him, nodding, "I guess not. Well, if you can run a tractor, I don't care where you been. You're not a socialist, are you? I only ask because we had one of those out here already, and that was enough. The boy would not take a bath."

The woman's name was Whitey Stafford, and she walked down the dirt path to the storage barn sore-legged and stiff, like a truck driver. She seemed old to Train, maybe forty, but it was hard to say when they were heavyset. Halfway to the barn, she stopped and picked a weed.

"Let me give you the lay of the land around here," she said. "The first thing is, I shouldn't ought to tell you this. The second thing is, I been employed by Mr. Cooper clear back to the termite business, and I know how the man thinks."

Train stood still, no idea in the world what this was about. "Cooper's Discount Bug and Rodent Extermination?" she said. "He put up those tents over your house, defumigate the insects and made a million dollars, but that bug dust left him a little skippy, if you know what I mean, and then one day a girl came out from the newspaper, doing a write-up on people who have jobs that nobody else wants to do, and the next thing I know, she's hanging around in his office all the time, and then Mr. Cooper quits getting his regular haircut every week, and the next thing is, he's talking about doing something more important with his life than killing roaches.

"I saw it coming as soon as she walked in the door—she's that bohemian type they all like. I know what the man is thinking before he does. He moved his second wife out of the house—I was surprised that one even noticed, if you know what I mean—and moved this one in and married her. She's a photographer, half his age and probably twice as smart. Which, when you get right down to it, ain't that hard.

"Well, she moved in and been in his new place a week or two when she decided she could smell death on him when he came home from work. She's an artist and can't work with the odor of death in her nostrils. So Mr. Cooper went ahead and built her a studio—by then, she already quit the job at the paper to devote her energies to art and poetry and leading Mr. Cooper around by the pecker—but she could smell death just as bad over there as she could in the house. I was office manager at that place eight years, I never smelled a thing. The money didn't bother her, though. She never said there was anything wrong with the way that smelled.

"So the next thing I know, Mr. Cooper sold the business to some Chinese and gave all his work clothes to the Salvation Army and took up golf. Like I'm going to work for some Chinaman. And before long, of course, he gets tired of telling people he used to be the bug exterminating king of Southern California and starts looking around for something else to do, and the idea hits him, a golf course. And not just a golf course, he's going to build a real estate development around it. He thought she'd like that, golf being on the other end of things socially from the pest business."

They got closer to the barn, and Train began picking up bottles and paper cups off the ground. She walked ahead, didn't seem to notice.

"And she said, 'You mean like a country club? Rich old Republicans?' And he thought about that, as much as he is capable of thinking with his dick in her mouth—excuse my French—and decides his project will be integrated. Integrated housing on a golf course, he calls it the idea of a lifetime."

She stopped, out of breath, and noticed Train had an armload of trash. "I talk too much," she said again.

"All right," she said, "they started out in there, in the barn; she had them posing. Grown men, one of them with a wife and a backwards child. He was the superintendent of greens, Don Lance Peters; the other was Freddy Short. Freddy was the socialist. She had them take off their shirts, asked how they decided who was the boss and who was the assistant. That's as much as the third boy back there heard. That boy's name is Lester, and he's a good boy, but you tell him to dig a hole, you also got to go back out and tell him to stop, if you know what I mean."

The woman had a key ring in her belt and went through it, looking for the one to open the padlock on the barn door. "A few minutes later, they commenced fighting," she said, "and then one of them picked up a screwdriver, the other got a mower blade, and the first one got a sickle, and then the other one got something I don't even know what the hell they call it, and they came all the way up the hill like that, stabbing and hacking away, all the way out to the road." She looked in the direction the fight had gone. "The oldest story in the book," she said.

Train nodded, all of this making exactly as much sense as eating ticks. She tried key after key, seemed to pick them at random, and it looked to him like she kept trying the same two over and over.

"And you know what she did? She took pictures. Followed them right up the hill with that camera. Click, click, click. Did everything but ask them to smile. Afterwards, Freddy Short's lying in the road and Don Lance Peters comes back to the barn, climbs up on the tractor, and bleeds out. You see what I mean? A man learns how to kill bugs and he thinks he knows the ways of the world. That's how they are. Once they get a taste of success, you can't tell them a thing."

She looked at him now, waiting for some kind of answer.

"Well, I just mind my own business," he said.

She stared at him a little longer, trying to see if he'd meant to insult her. He saw how she'd took it that way, but he knew enough not to try to explain it, that he'd only make it worse. She held him there on the edge another minute and then shrugged. "I warned you I was a talker," she said.

And then, still looking for the key, she said, "Right now, the whole place looks like Mexico. Weeds growing in the bunkers; the greens ain't been punched since we got here. Trees down where they're cleaning the homesites. Plus, we got grasshoppers and wasp nests in the ground. The famous bug killer can't even keep the bugs off his own damn golf course. The first four people that asked for refunds were attacked by hornets—did I tell you that? I told Mr. Cooper, and after all these years he just looked at me, like I was this *disappointment* to him, or like it might not even be true. He doesn't trust anybody but his sweet little photographer.

"It's been one thing after another," she said, still trying the same keys, "ever since we bought the place. Police, lawyers, refunds, dissatisfied customers, permit problems, investigators, insurance men, reporters. Anybody you can think of in this world you don't want to talk to has come to the door. And the grass stops growing for no one. I'd put Lester on the mower, but Christ knows he'd end up in Nevada."

She found the key to the padlock then and

they went into the barn. Train walked over to the tractor, an old rusted-out John Deere with huge iron wheels and vertical exhaust and a chair cushion for a seat, and pulled himself up.

She watched him from the ground. Train paused when he got up even with the seat, seeing that this was where the one that had made it back to the barn sat down to die. He stepped over and eased himself into it anyway. He had on tan JCPenney & Co. pants, the best trousers he owned, but he didn't want the woman to think he was afraid to get his pants dirty. Did not think it would do to get on her bad side at all, unless you was married to the boss.

"An honest day's work for an honest day's pay," she said, "that's the man's motto." A piece of a butterfly wing was struck to the tractor wheel, and she picked it off and tasted it, and then spit it out. She looked at him quickly then, in a different way. "That and keep your shirt on around Mrs. Cooper."

And when she spit again, it had something to do with the new wife. Like in spite of what she said about him, Whitey could have an interest in Mr. Cooper too.

Train took a moment, looking over the controls, and then pulled out the choke and started the engine.

It was hot and shadeless on the course and the old tractor shook, even going down the fairways, and

159

the smoke came up out of a hole in the muffler and into his face. It was nothing like the tractors they had at Brookline, and it was nothing like the fairways. There were no big trees here, only one pond on each nine, at the fifth hole and the sixteenth, rocks in the bunkers. The greens were dry and spotted with disease, and the fence that went around the property was pushed down a dozen places. The lots that was cleared for houses looked like scabs. He saw a spot where bums or kids had lit a fire and sat around drinking beer. The blow of dry grass and dust came up into his face when he made his turns, and he smelled grasshopper juice and saw lizards and snakes everywhere he looked.

Once, for no reason, he turned the engine off and let the tractor coast a few yards, listening to the grasshoppers and the dry metallic sound of the mower blades. Then it was quiet, and he sat still, looking half a mile back to the barn, and everything he saw made him happy, right down to the vultures picking over the remains of a jackrabbit beside the fourteenth green.

He didn't know what the job paid, or what there was to it beyond driving the machinery and keeping his shirt on around Mr. Cooper's new wife, but it felt good to have something again, something of his own. He finished in the heat of the late afternoon and drove into the storage barn and parked. He spent an hour cleaning and sharpening the mower blades and added two quarts of oil to the engine. Then he rinsed out the cushion that he'd been setting on and laid it outside to dry. His pants clung to his behind, and when he pulled them away, he saw they were stained with blood. It took him a minute to see what had happened, that he must have sweated on the seat.

By the time he left the barn, the office was closed and the gate was locked to the street. He climbed the fence to get out and caught the bus, conscious of his pants, worried that some pretty girl might see him and think he was the kind of boy that saw a puddle of blood somewhere and sat down in it on purpose.

That whoever she was would look at him and think that this life had left him skippy too.

CHAPTER 5

PARADISE DEVELOPMENTS

Train was in the barn alone when she came in with her cameras hanging from her neck. He was eating lunch.

Her hair was dark and straight, pulled back into pigtails to make her look like a little girl. She was wearing a T-shirt, and the camera straps lay across her chest, and she wasn't any little girl. Beyond that, you couldn't say if she was pretty or not. She stopped when she saw him, like she was surprised, and sat down on the floor, crossing her legs Indian-style, and watched him eat. Curious. Train noticed his sandwich had lost its taste.

After awhile, she looked up at the heavy pine beams that ran the length of the barn. Swallow nests and wasp nests, ropes, tractor tires, a pully—everything looked like it was there a hundred years ago. There was windows in the walls near the ceilings, covered with spiderwebs, that gave the room most of its light. Her eyes came back to Train, caught him looking at her.

"It's all right to look at me if you want to," she said.

"Yes ma'am," he said, "thank you." He began to smile politely, but got caught in the middle of it staring at the camera straps, and for one long moment he couldn't move his face. His cheeks had froze. He got hold of himself and looked away, in the direction of the door.

She laughed a movie star laugh, pulling him back in her direction.

"After all," she said, "I'm looking at you."

Train nodded and then turned away in another direction. He heard her take a picture or two. "I suppose by now Whitey's told you the stories," she said.

"This and that," he said. "None of my business. . . ."

"I mean about what happened." It was quiet again and he nodded, and then, in a lower voice, like she was telling him a secret, she said, "It was extraordinary." And now he did look at her, right into the camera, to see what she meant. "You could taste the hate that had built up between those two men as soon as you walked in. It must have been going on for years, around each other every day, blaming each other for the way white people had been treating them all their lives, looking at each other, smelling each other, and suddenly there it was, all out in the open. . . ."

She seemed excited, like it was about to happen again.

"I don't know the gentlemen myself," he said.

"You know what I'm talking about," she said, but he didn't. She leaned forward and played with the focus, and he noticed the word *Nikon* printed across the top. She looked at him through the camera while she twisted the lens back and forth. It reminded him of the way a child might press his forehead against yours and turn, trying to see what you look like up close.

"An intelligent face," she said, like she was talking to somebody else, "not handsome, exactly, but great intensity. Great intensity in the eyes." And then the shutter clicked a dozen more times and she let the camera down.

"Eyes tell their own story," she said, "I've learned that." And then she leaned forward again and squinted, staring at Train's eyes for a long time, like she was waiting for them to do something unusual.

Train wrapped the rest of his sandwich back in the wax paper and put it away for later. "I'm susan," she said, "no capital *S*. Just susan." Train nodded. He knew from his frequent conversations with Whitey that the girl had gave up on last names when she married Mr. Cooper, but he didn't know that she'd gave up capital letters. A moment passed. "And you would be . . ."

"I would be Lionel Walk," he said.

She lifted the other camera, fooling with the focus. "And what does Lionel Walk do around here?" She talked like anything was possible between them, and he felt her voice wake up the spider; something shaking the web.

"This and that. Just work for Mr. Cooper, like everybody else."

She made a face at the name, and then began taking more pictures, faster pictures, the shutter going off every second or two. "What does Cooper pay you?" she said. Then, before he could answer, she said, "No, wait, let me guess. Three dollars a day."

Train didn't reply to that. Mr. Cooper had a rule about not telling anybody what you made. She spread her legs wider, as if to steady herself, and said, "Tell me a story, about what you're doing here." Train looked at the way she was sitting and put the heel of his hand against his pocket to push down the stiffness, forgetting she could see him through the camera. Then he remembered, and the more embarrassed he turned, the faster she took the pictures.

"Not much of a story," he said.

"It can't just be this," she said, and lowered the camera. She looked around the barn. "This is so boring. . . ."

Train shrugged. "Here we both are," he said, and she smiled at that like it was the brightest thing anybody told her all month.

"Do you have a girlfriend?" she said, and the erection crawled up his pants. Might as well try to push down the rising moon. She began taking her pictures again.

"Excused me, ma'am," Train said, and got up to leave. "Excused me, but I got a piece of equipment broke out on eleven." And she laughed again at that; she could see why he had to leave. "I got to go take care of it," he said, "before somebody drive it back to the barn and spill oil all over the course." Thinking that adding to the story would make it sound true. Then he walked past her a little sideways, hiding himself, and then outside into the heat.

That was how it started with susan, no capital *S*.

Friday was payday. Mr. Cooper come by late in the afternoon every week to study the receipts and personally hand out the money. He wore jeans and a shirt and tie—maybe to keep his wife and the bankers both happy—and smoked all the time, nervous with the cigarette, rolling it around in his fingers like the combination to the safe. He coughed when he went to talk, did that so much he seemed not to notice it himself, just pulled out his handkerchief and waited until it stopped and then spit what come up into the hankie and had a look and then folded it back up and went on with his business.

The crew was up to seven employees, which was one or two less than they needed, and Mr. Cooper always looked them in the eyes when he paid them and made a point to ask after their mother or wife, or how they were doing in school. Must have been one of the principles of pest control, but he never actually listened to the answers, though. Train knew Mr. Cooper liked him to look him in the eye back, but he had trouble making himself do that, with what he was thinking all the time about his wife.

Sometimes on Friday night, susan come along with Mr. Cooper and sat outside in the car, but she had all the pictures of this place she wanted now, and was working in the developing room on her gallery show, and never come in. Train heard her once telling Mr. Cooper how she didn't like the way the trailer smelled with all the people in there sweating. Said she hated the smell of the crew.

By now she also come back down to the barn and taken more pictures of Train, did that a few times, and then one day she perplexed her face into a question and asked would he do her a favor, would he pose for her without his shoes. And he did, and then she asked would he take off his shirt and pose with the tow chain around his neck. And then she asked what she could do for him now he done all this for her, and when he didn't say nothing, she done it anyway. Took him in her hand. It went on like that, three or four times a week, all month long, always in her hand, sometimes with her mouth up close to his ear. Never let him touch her back.

Afterwards once, she run her fingers over his lips, her eyes wide open, watching him, waiting. "Now you know what you taste like," she said.

And then one day, she said, "It's a little boring,

isn't it?" Like there was something else he was supposed to do. He didn't know what it might be, and didn't know if it was polite to ask, and then she was disappointed—he could see that—and then she was angry, and whenever he passed near her after that, she looked through him in a way that reminded him of the membership back at Brookline—that's how interested she was now.

After awhile, he thought she might have even forgot which one of the ground crew he was. Even with his intelligent face, she wasn't the kind of girl who made it a point to remember all the names of all the help.

The money came in yellow envelopes, and Mr. Cooper waited till everybody was there in the trailer and then issued his warning that employees was not to discuss what they made. He did that every Friday. And then he told them again about the idea of a lifetime: racial harmony in the future, and how it would all start with the condition of the golf course when the buyers come out here to look. The grounds crew was all his ambassadors.

The room was full and warm tonight, people sweating and excited to be loose for the weekend. Some of them drinking wine over by the radio, some of them watching a dominoes game in the corner. Mr. Cooper suddenly looked up, and Whitey had to tell Lester to turn off the damn radio, and they all waited, and then Mr. Cooper begun passing out the envelopes, checking each one before he let it out of his hand.

The envelopes was laid out in alphabetical order, and by the time he got to Lionel Walk, Train and him was the only ones left in the room. It made Train nervous to be alone with the man like that, with the wife sitting right outside in the car. Train was always afraid what the man was going to say, that he was going to tell him something he didn't want to hear. That worried him, and then the man was also trying somehow to get closer to Train than he was.

Mr. Cooper opened his envelope—the way he'd done with all the others—and slid the money halfway out, separating the bills with the tip of his pencil to make sure it was right. Then he tucked the money back in and sized Train up. Train could tell from the noise outside that the traffic had picked up out on the street, and he wanted to leave before the buses filled up with drunks. Friday was a hard night to ride the bus; somebody was always falling asleep on your shoulder, and sometimes one of them had a hand in your pocket too. But Mr. Cooper wasn't ready yet to turn him loose. He took off his reading glasses and said, "I've noticed we've been going through a lot of gas."

"I don't know about that," Train said.

Mr. Cooper shrugged. "The last couple of months, we're up fifty gallons."

"I don't know," Train said again.

"You're not running the tractor extra?"

"Run the tractor six days a week, just like always. Unless it rains, but it ain't. Using more oil, is all."

"And you haven't noticed anything untoward," the old man said.

"Untoward what?"

"It's a word that means out of the way, improper." Train began to worry that Mr. Cooper heard something of what been going on in the barn with his new wife. But it wasn't that. "Untoward . . . You haven't noticed anyone driving their car down to the barn at night, or early in the morning?"

Train didn't answer, but he seen Whitey down there at closing in her Chevy pickup.

"No sir," he said. "Nothing like that."

Mr. Cooper took three dollar bills out of his own pocket and laid them next to Train's envelope. Three dollars, a day's work. "I've been watching you," he said. "You're a boy that's going to make something of himself in life."

"Yessir, thank you." He picked up his envelope and put it in his shirt pocket. Mr. Cooper picked up the three bills and stuck them in there too.

"What do they all call you again? Train?"

"Yessir, most do."

Mr. Cooper smiled. "Lionel Train . . . very good." Train smiled along too. That fast, Mr. Cooper turned around, as if Train's smiling was the signal for him to stop. "Well, someday, son," he said, "later on, when you're in business for yourself, you may come to find out that no matter how well you treat them, people steal. If you allow it to happen, they will steal. It's the bane of small business." It seem like he was gone talk that old-timers talk now, something from long ago.

"I expect so," Train said, just wanting to get out the damn room.

"I lost a foreman once," Mr. Cooper said, "a man that I knew for fifteen years. He went into a house at night that we'd sealed up for fumigation— he was going to take some jewelry—and was found still in the lady's boudoir the next day. It turned out he'd been stealing all along, right under my nose, and the poison had weakened his lungs and heart. And that last night, he was too weak to make it out."

Mr. Cooper had a long coughing fit and then lit a cigarette. "And in some way," he said, "I suppose I allowed it to happen." He leaned over and spit between his feet. "If that man were here today," he said, "I'd sit him down and buy him a cold beer and then you'd know what I'd ask him?"

"No sir."

"I'd ask him what was the point? He was well paid, well treated. What made him steal?" Train was not sure now if Mr. Cooper was talking to him or Whitey or the dead foreman. He flashed again on susan. He didn't think you could say he'd took anything there, although, like Mr. Cooper, he had to admit he did allowed it to happen.

171

Mr. Cooper was answering his own question. "He wouldn't know," he said, "except it's human nature. A perfectly good man, dead for no reason. When you keep a man honest, you do everyone a favor." He patted Train's shirt pocket and left his hand there a second, and Train felt its heat.

"There is nothing more valuable in business," he said, "than a man you can trust."

Walking to the street, Train glanced quickly at the car, where the new wife was sitting with the door open, smoking, waiting for Mr. Cooper to finish paying the help. She looked at him a long second, her mouth still open behind a scarf of smoke, as if she just had some thought that surprised her, and then she smiled and crossed her legs, because she was bored, and watched the moon rise in his pants.

The bus came late, packed like a hamper. Train got on and stood in the aisle, holding on to an overhead strap. A block up the street, it stopped again. More people got on; nobody got off. A woman bumped into him from behind, and Train touched his shirt to make sure the envelope was still in his pocket. He felt drops of sweat fall from his armpits down his ribs, and fought off the panic at being closed in.

He closed his eyes, thinking of other things. Food—his mother's food—the smell of chicken cooking, the feel of old Lucky's head under his hand. Mr. Cooper's new wife looking at him through the smoke, looking at him in that way and crossing her legs. Mr. Cooper's hand on his shirt pocket.

The bus stopped and started, started and stopped, and then it stopped again, and then he was suddenly pushing his way off, not caring where he was, what neighborhood he was in, and then he was back outside and he stood still for a moment in the street, breathing the cool air. He heard the air brakes release and the bus began to roll, and he looked up and saw a blind lady framed in the pale light of the window. Her eyes were milk, and she looked just beyond him, like she knew he was there and was trying to find him. Train turned away from the face and ran.

He went a long time—sometime on the sidewalk, sometime out in the street itself, dodging traffic—all the way back to the golf course, but the gates were locked when he got there, and Mr. Cooper's car was gone. And he knew it was too late to give him back his three dollars and tell him he didn't want to watch out for nobody stealing his gasoline. That he didn't want to be the one to watch.

He sat down against the fence, dripping sweat, exhausted, and tried to figure out what he was doing, scared to death and running a mile through traffic on a Friday night over a blind lady in the bus window.

Mr. Cooper's new wife came down to the barn one more time. It was a Tuesday afternoon, and the sun was down below the windows, turning the whole place a strange color in the minutes before it set.

Train was stretched out on the floor, working on the mower blades. Somebody thrown a piece of barbed wire over the fence in the night, maybe eight or ten feet of it, and Lester run over it in the morning with the mower and wrapped it up like Christmas. Train was lying down for leverage with two pairs of pliers, cutting the wire away. Lester was sitting on a gas can in the corner, watching him work. Scared to death. The rest of the crew was long gone.

Lester wasn't allowed to drive the tractor, and he was afraid Mr. Cooper would fire him if he found out what he did. He was crying when he come back looking for Train to tell him what happened, and he was still there crying when Whitey come down later to see why the hell nobody was out mowing.

Train told her the tractor was broke and he had to transmogrify a gasket. By now, they both knew he had took over the golf course, even though she come down time to time and acted like she was still in charge, warning him one way or another to stay away from Mr. Cooper. If there was anybody going to be his right-hand man, it was her. The woman was loud and bossy and tasted everything on the course, but she didn't understand how things ran or what made things grow, and neither did nobody else. Mr. Cooper had hired his ground crew on the basis of various shades of skin color, how they would look when prospective buyers come by to visit, and there wasn't nobody but Train around that knew how to keep a lawn green, much less a golf course.

Lester stood up without a word when the new wife came into the barn, and walked crablike toward the door, never turning his back. You had to tell him everything twice because he always thought you was teasing him the first time you said it, but nobody had to tell him to stay away from her. He had been down here when the fight started, seen the trouble she could get you in.

Train stopped working and looked at her from his back. He had a cramp in his hand, and when he held it up and flexed it, he saw it was cut and bleeding from the wire. "Does it hurt?" she said, but it was only a curiosity, not like it mattered if he answered her yes or no. This girl had took pictures while two men hacked each other to death over her that spring; she didn't have much impression over a few cuts somebody got fixing a mower blade.

He shook his hand and blotted the cuts against his pants. He noticed she didn't have her cameras with her, wondered if she'd took up something new. She lifted up her skirt like a girl wading in a creek and walked over the wire Train had cut out and tossed on the floor, then stopped right over him, looking down. There was no underpants; she didn't wear underpants. Train looked another way, but she stood there holding her skirt, looking at him like a puppy.

"You're a strange one, aren't you?" she said.

175

"I don't know," he said. "What was the other ones like?"

A minute passed and she glanced at the door and said, "It's all right. Cooper's up in the office." Cooper. She always called him Cooper. She moved a little, drawing his eye to the bait. He lay tight and still, losing an argument with his business. He remembered that word for it suddenly—his *business*. It was what his mother called it when he was young.

When Mr. Cooper's new wife spoke to him again, her tone was changed, like he'd hurt her feelings. "I only came down to invite you to an exhibit," she said.

"I got to get this wire untangled from the mower blade," he said. "Thank you all the same." And went back to work. He heard her move then, bending over. She leaned under the tractor and got close to his ear to talk—she always like to talked close to his ear—to watch what it did to him.

"It's my pictures," she said. "You're in some of my pictures. I thought you might like to come to the opening and see them." He lay still as long as he could, and then felt his business pop loose from his underwear, and it stuck straight up in his pants. Lying on his back, the bottom of his T-shirt lay across his stomach, leaving that much of his skin exposed, and he suddenly felt her fingers, very lightly, touching his stomach. "Here's the card," she said, still close to his ear, and slipped it beneath the elastic of his underpants, and in that

176

same moment, the spider began to crawl. "It's got the address and the time, if you feel like it," she said, but he barely heard the words.

It blew through like the Southern Pacific, like to shook him out of his shoes, the milk spilling all over him and into his pants and everywhere else. She left her hand where it was until the last spasms passed, and his lap begun to feel cool and sticky, and then he heard her say, "Oh my," and she was gone.

When he was alone again, he rolled over and got to his feet. He looked at his pants and then at the card. The exhibit was called "Images from the Working Life, by susan," and was sponsored by Southern California Artists for a Better World.

He put the card in his pocket and looked around the barn. He thought of the place as his own, and realized suddenly that all she had to do was go up that hill and tell Mr. Cooper he looked at her sideways, and that was that. It was the other side of disappearing into the scenery. Tomorrow the barn and the tractors and mowers would still be where they was, Whitey would still be stealing gas, Lester would still be running over wires, and you had to known the place firsthand to realize Train was missing.

He knew that what just happened didn't matter enough to her to do that to him, but he thought she might like to do it to Mr. Cooper.

CHAPTER 6

BEVERLY HILLS

D r. Speers came by at noon to change her dressing, four days after she had been raped. He was old and clumsy and smelled of cough syrup, and it hurt when he pulled off the tape. It didn't make sense, but little things hurt more now than before. There were carpenters on the roof, hammering, and the ceiling moaned beneath their shoes. He wore an Omega wristwatch and a class of 1929 ring from Southern Methodist and gave her another shot of penicillin against the chance that one of the Negroes had been carrying a venereal disease. Sometimes in the female, he said, screwing the last half inch of a Camel into the ashtray, the disease could exist without any symptoms at all.

The doorbell rang again five minutes after he left. She had just washed down two of the sedatives the doctor left her, and was on the way up to the guest room on the second floor, as far from the hammering as she could get, to take a nap. She stopped on the stairway and considered the

178

front door, thinking it was probably lawyers. Her husband had left the sort of money behind that lawyers didn't like to lose touch with, even for a few days.

She took a moment, thinking of the cool feel of the sheets, and then went to the door instead, and saw who it was, and tried to remember if she had at least brushed her hair.

They sat together in the kitchen, beneath the hammering. She offered him a beer, and was surprised when he took it—she assumed he was on duty somewhere—and then opened one for herself. It was almost one o'clock, and she was still in her slippers and housecoat. Nothing on underneath. It was warm in the kitchen, and he took off his jacket and hung it on the back of the chair. Brooks Brothers.

"You look like you could use some sleep," he said.

"I look like I fell out of a car." Her face was still swollen and bruised; she'd spent half an hour that morning at her makeup table, not knowing where to start. She'd spent the last four days not knowing where to start. He looked up at the ceiling, where a light swayed gently as the workmen moved around.

"Howard Hughes's plane crashed into the roof right after the war," she said, "and they still haven't gotten the lattice right. I never much cared, but Alec couldn't let it go. That was the way he was. I should probably just send them home and forget it."

"Here?" he said, "That happened here?" The crash had been a big story in the newspapers, pictures everywhere of Hughes in the hospital, his head bandaged, his arms in casts, a nurse holding his cigarette.

"They still occasionally find little pieces of the plane in the neighborhood," she said. "People take them home after parties." She gestured toward the backyard, as if she were offering him whatever he might want.

"I'm not much on souvenirs."

She understood he was intelligent, and when he said that, it seemed to hold some second, hidden meaning, but she was fogged in and couldn't see what it was. A moment had passed and he was looking at her more closely. "Are you faint?" he said.

She thought about that and said, "No, but the day's young."

"Your color drained. You looked scared."

"I probably am."

"Of me?"

"Of everything."

He shrugged. "I'm harmless."

"I was there," she said, and then wished that she hadn't. She hadn't decided about him yet. He reached into his pocket for a cigarette, then changed his mind.

"It's all right," she said. "Alec smoked. . . ."

He said, "I was thinking maybe I'd stop, see if I miss it."

He was staring at her in a way that kept her wondering about how she looked. If she at least looked clean. Above them, the workers hammered the lattice. Then the sound of an electric saw. "I hope this isn't anything that has to be done today," she said. "I'm not up to much right now."

He shook his head. "I just wanted to come by for a minute, see how you were doing." She looked at him, waiting for him to say what he wanted. "I would have been around sooner, but I had some business out of town."

She had another drink of the beer and began to feel better. "Is this where we get our stories straight?" she said.

He sat still, studying her, and then he smiled and said, "Let's talk about it another time." She noticed again the way he smiled. His face moved, but nothing happened; it wasn't unlike watching someone stutter.

"Does it matter? Is something going to change?"

"Let's wait. You've been through an ordeal."

The word caught her by surprise and she looked away, biting her cheek, but it was already too late. It began with a few bubbles, floating up to the surface, and then more, and then it just poured over the sides, and then she was howling, making more noise than the carpenters. She tried to stop, and couldn't, and then she didn't care. She brayed. Her eyes teared and her body cinched up in all the places she was bruised, and still she couldn't stop. She fought for air like a squalling baby. There was spit on her lips, and she wiped at her mouth with her sleeve, afraid the cuts had cracked open and were beginning to bleed. Tears blurred her vision, and he sat still, watching. She hugged herself and rocked and finally managed to speak: "Excuse me. . . . Sometimes, I don't know why, I just completely lose touch." She took a deep breath and then heard herself say, "The whole shooting match was such an *ordeal*. Although it wasn't *much* of a shooting match, of course."

It happened again, and he waited until she ran down.

The thought occurred to her that he might be dangerous. She didn't think she cared. She got up, wiping her eyes, and went to the refrigerator for more beer. "Can I offer you a tranquilizer? Perhaps a Dexedrine—you know, a Christmas tree? They're very good together."

"Just the beer is fine," he said.

She sat back down and blew her nose into a napkin. "Now, where were we? Oh, killing the Negroes . . ." He sat very still. She leaned closer and whispered. "You don't have to worry; I'm from Georgia. We're very discreet about these things."

He finished the first beer and then started on the second.

"Actually," she said, "it's all sort of romantic, when you think about it, the boat ride and all. You're the perfect first date. . . ." She looked at him coolly across the table, and then she leaned back in the chair, suddenly spent, dead tired. The hammering resumed—when had it stopped?—and the sedative was pulling her back. "I need some sleep," she said.

"One thing," he said, and she squinted, trying to focus on his face. "There was apparently a book; this Clarence Holmes kept an address book."

She felt herself go cold. "Who?"

"Clarence Holmes," he said. "The one who went over the side. He kept a book with some names in it."

"Mine?"

"Yeah," he said. "One of about sixty. I only mention it in case somebody comes by from the Orange County prosecutor's office, you'll know what they're talking about. It would probably be less complicated all the way around if you didn't know why he had your name."

A moment passed and then, very slowly and distinctly, she said, "That should be easy enough. I've always found it's easiest just to tell the truth."

Let him take that home and sleep on it.

The funerals were both on Saturday, one in the morning, one in the afternoon. She wanted it all over in one day. There had been no telephone number in Mexico, of course, no address—as far as she knew, the Mexicans had no phones or mail delivery—so she did what she could. She bought a double plot in St. Augustine's Cemetery, just over the Third Street Bridge, where other Mexicans were buried, and held a small Catholic service for him at the little church on the same property. During the service, she thought of the wife, with her narrow hips, waiting in Mexico for him to come home. She took sedatives, but she still thought of the wife and the unborn babies. She wept, thinking of the babies.

The parish priest was called Father Duncan, whom she knew from her volunteer work for the Democratic party. He was a stunted, narrow-faced man with a deep scar that ran from his left cheek to the right side of his jaw. Everything below the scar—including half his mouth—was as bloodless as flour and did not move with the rest of his face. He told her once that as a twenty-two-year-old graduate student he had decided to kill himself, hopeless and drunk one night at the kitchen table, but was unable even to fit the two pieces of the shotgun together so that it could be loaded. And then, he said, it had come to him in a revelation, staring at the scene carved in the stock of the gun itself, that even an ugly man could bring beauty to the world.

He was lying to her, of course—if there was one thing she knew, it was when men were lying—and so she lied back. She told him he wasn't ugly.

He'd phoned her early on the morning after the murders to offer his help, and even floating in Dr. Speers' sedatives, she sensed the prurient note in his voice. She was getting rid of him when she

184

thought suddenly of the other problem, Pedro, who was Mexican after all, and Catholic.

The service had been empty. Father Duncan spoke of the dead man with a familiar affection, of his love of the sea and his loyalty to Alec Rose and his wife, Norah—all of the romance he could manufacture.

After she'd cried, thinking of the babies, she was pulled back to something the priest had said, something cheap and meaningless about a simple man and the sea, words that defined the priest's limits better than she ever could.

Later, though, she stood at the grave site and allowed her hand to linger in his a moment longer than it needed to, and in the car on the way to the other funeral, he suddenly reached for it again and held it in both of his.

"If you need a friend," he said, "that's what we do. I'm always here."

She had taken another sedative when she got in the car, and washed it down with half a glass of warm scotch. She'd found the scotch in the door compartment, along with the glass. She leaned over and patted his cheek, thinking that with a few words here and there, a certain look back across her shoulder, a borderline touch, maybe a broken lunch date—she had the distinct thought that with a little work, she could have him and the shotgun back at the old kitchen table before he knew what hit him.

Another thought along these lines came to her

two hours later. The service for Alec was running long; she was exhausted and drifting, as unable to connect Alec to the things being said about him as she had been earlier with Pedro, unable even to remember, except in general terms, what he looked like, and she wondered what it meant that earlier that same day she had entertained— and *entertained* was the correct word—thoughts of driving a deformed priest to suicide. She stared at a crucifix with one eye and then the other, moving it back and forth, and then it hit her all at once.

I'm the Antichrist.

And looking around, she decided she wasn't unhappy with that at all.

She was sitting in a folding chair, accepting condolences, nodding politely at people whose names she did not remember, who came past in a line to offer sympathy, or to recall some kindness that she and Alec had done for the underprivileged or the arts. A few of them wanted to hold her hand, or knelt to speak with their hands on her back. She was nauseated—the sedatives, the scotch, the smell of food on their breath, the heat of the room, and the crush of people. She did not want to be touched. There was a hand on her shoulder, and she stood up suddenly to move it off.

And then heard the sergeant's voice beside her. "Your husband had a lot of friends," he said. She turned and looked at him, Miller something. Miller Packard. Beyond Miller Packard, she could see the reception hall, two bars, several tables of food, a hundred conversations going all at once. Most of them, she knew, were about what had happened on the boat. She didn't care about that; she only wanted this to end. This touching and talking and waiting. The milling around and talking. She saw no way that she could stop it, though. It seemed like nothing could stop it, except, she supposed, they would all eventually die themselves.

"I wish things were more specific," she said. "I mean, I wish things had a specific ending. That someone told you when it was over."

He looked out over the crowd, not impressed much with what he saw. "You could quit the pills."

"Not yet," she said. "I don't think that's a good idea yet." For a moment, she thought she heard the workmen again, hammering upstairs, and then she looked up at the ceiling and realized that she was not in her own house.

"How many did you have?"

"I don't know," she said, "a couple before the first service, more on the way over here."

Her hand went absently to her breast, and she pressed into it a little, feeling the shock of pain, wanting it. The breast itself had been stitched, and the underside was bruised and dark. The discoloration extended from there to the other bruises across her stomach and pelvis. He was staring at her hand. She did not know how long it had been there, holding herself, but she let it drop now to her side.

187

"What do the doctors say?" he asked. He had seen the wound, and in that way he was closer to her than she wanted him to be. Yet, in another way, he was not entirely unwelcome.

"Not to worry," she said, "they say not to worry." She thought he might smile at that—Christ, he was always smiling at something that wasn't funny—but he didn't. She felt him judging her and was suddenly furious. "Is something wrong, Sergeant?" she said. "Am I slurring my words? Or is it that I'm drunk? That's it, isn't it? You disapprove of my drinking. Well, at least I've stopped laughing; you have to give me that."

She stared right into his eyes and could not read them at all, and then Father Duncan was there too, the scar cutting deep from one side of his face to the other, sectioning him off.

"Is everything all right?" he said.

"Why, everything is wonderful, Father," she said. "We were just discussing my recovery." The priest put his hand on her elbow, and she could not stand to be touched. She'd been touched enough.

"Why don't we sit down?" he said.

She looked down at him and said, "Why, Father, I thought you were."

The priest backed away a step, and started to speak once or twice before the words finally came out. "This is a terribly difficult time, Norah," he said sadly.

She turned to Miller Packard and said, "I believe I have committed a faux pas." And then, keeping

188

her back strong and straight, she walked into the bathroom. She had a good back and was always aware of her posture. As a child, she was graded on it at school. Peabody Laboratory School, Milledgeville, Georgia. Always the highest marks in posture.

The priest turned to Miller Packard when the door closed behind her and said, "She isn't herself." There was a lull then, and Father Duncan, who became anxious in the absence of conversation, who needed some kind of talk going on somewhere, said, "Are you a relative?"

"No, only a friend."

"I didn't meant to interrupt," the priest said. "I just came over because it seemed the conversation was becoming . . . *animated*, and I thought perhaps I could help. She's definitely not herself."

Father Duncan looked quickly at the bathroom door. "Sometimes pain makes us say things we regret." He smiled at Miller Packard and allowed that to sink in. "I don't know how close you are to the situation," he said, "but it was a particularly brutal assault. I mention this to help you understand any . . . unusual behavior." Packard nodded, and Father Duncan moved a little closer and dropped his voice. "I'm afraid Norah was *disfigured*."

Packard waited a few seconds and then dropped his head close and studied the priest's face. "You didn't do that to yourself, did you?" he said.

★　　★　　★

She was standing in front of the mirror, naked to the waist. The bandage and gauze lay in the sink. The nipple of her left breast was small and pink, the areola pale, all but invisible. The right breast was cross-stitched and crusted black.

A woman came into the bathroom and stopped. Norah smiled sweetly and then checked herself in the mirror. "Well, what do you think?" she said.

The woman moved a step closer. She said, "My God, Norah, I didn't know it was actually *severed.*"

"They cut it off all right," she said, and then, taking the point of the injured breast between her thumb and index finger, she squeezed until a drop of watery blood appeared and then ran in a line down her stomach. She trembled at the pain, and then found the woman in the mirror again, looking stricken. *Stricken*—she found that she loved the word *stricken*. "I didn't catch your name," she said.

"Marla Hodges, honey," the woman said. "I'm Marla Hodges. We volunteered for the Stevenson campaign together."

"Oh, Adlai," she said fondly, "'Madly for Adlai.'" She dabbed at the stitches with a linen towel and then held the breast and moved it closer to the mirror. "I just can't make up my mind."

The woman began edging back toward the door.

"If symmetry were the issue, I suppose I could

190

lop the other one off too, but you can imagine what the Republicans would say about that."

And then the woman was gone.

The door opened again, and it was Miller Packard. A strange name. Time had passed; she didn't know how much. She was still undressed to the waist, and without a word, he ran some warm water into the sink, took the towel out of her hand and cleaned her breast and patted it dry, and then the skin below it.

She shivered.

He looked closely at the wound, touching it once with the back of his finger, checking for heat. She did not misunderstand what he was doing. "We don't have to be worried about infection," she said. "At least not according to Dr. Speers. He's administered penicillin."

He retrieved her blouse and bra from the bar crossing the entrance to the stall where she'd hung them, then put the bra in his coat pocket and held the blouse for her while she put it on. Then he buttoned it up. She said, "He was concerned, however—and I would say not a little disgusted— that venereal disease is apparently able to exist in the female apparatus without any symptoms at all. I believe those were his words, the *female apparatus*." She liked that even more than *stricken*.

He finished buttoning the blouse, and she closed her eyes and felt the room begin to move. He plugged the sink and ran water into it for her, she supposed to wash her face. "It's the wonder drug, you know," she said, watching the sink fill. "It fixes everything." Her finger went to her lower lip, which had been bruised on the boat. Three distinct lumps had formed there, and she felt them whenever she spoke or swallowed. The water kept coming out of the faucet.

"Let's go home," he said, and turned it off.

"I can't leave," she said. "I'm the widow." She bent to splash her face.

"By now," he said, indicating the room, "they've all heard that you're naked and crazy and talking about lopping off your other tit." She waited, looking up at him from the sink. "It's a party," he said.

She felt an unexpected wave of affection. For the way he looked at her, even now, for his clothes and his shoes, for the way he got to the point, right from the moment she saw him on the old fisherman's boat. For his intelligence and his haircut. She forgave him the Negroes, and forgot that he seemed to smile at odd times, that he laughed at things without making any noise. It didn't matter. He was kind, but he didn't make any noise when he laughed. She saw it clearly now; she saw everything clearly.

She stood up, a few inches from his face. She touched his face. "I think you are the most considerate man I ever met," she said. And then the room spun and she stumbled, and sat down in the sink.

★　　★　　★

He brought her out of the bathroom, heading for the door. The priest was suggesting to a woman in a yellow suit that Norah should be hospitalized for a few days of observation. He stopped when he saw them coming out and stepped forward, as if to greet them, and Packard moved him out of the way effortlessly, holding on to her hand, and pulled her through a sea of faces toward the door. She smiled politely and followed along, making soggy noises, the water trickling down the backs of her legs.

He called the limo and then held the back door with one hand and helped her in with the other. The priest came out of the reception hall, looking worried. Miller Packard climbed in on the other side and shut the door. She saw other people behind the priest, the mourners, Alec's friends, trying to catch a glimpse through the windows.

"The lady is going home," he said to the driver, and then gave him the address, to make sure he had it right. She was surprised that he would remember her address—he'd only been there once. She wondered if he had a photographic memory. She had that one thought, and then she leaned across the seat and dropped her head into his lap and closed up for the day. A moment before she went to sleep, she felt his penis crowding up through the material of his trousers, pressing into her cheek.

She felt safe and liked him very much.

CHAPTER 7

BEVERLY HILLS

She wanted to see where he lived. She wanted to look at his bed and in his closet; she wanted to open the refrigerator and see what he ate. She wanted to know what music he listened to, what books he read.

"Well," he said, "I knew somebody once who played the English horn."

He was sitting on the edge of her pool; she was beneath him, resting an elbow on each of his legs. A wild scar ran the length of his upper leg, from his knee to the hip. His suit was lying near the drain at the bottom of the pool. They were still flushed, just catching their breath.

It was two months now, and he would not talk to her about what had happened on the boat. When she brought it up, he would tell her to think of it as a story with other people in it. He didn't tell her what those people did afterwards.

Maybe he only wanted her to smile; he wanted someone to smile with him at strange times.

He came to the door the day after the funerals

with an Orange County sheriff's report, which he'd typed up himself, and she initialled all six pages and signed at the end without looking at it, and then he'd stepped in and closed the door and sealed the deal, right there on the stairway, and she was looking up at a chandelier all the time, seeing herself and Miller Packard in a thousand tiny reflections, and no one from Orange County ever called or came to the house, and no one ever asked how her name might have ended up in Clarence Holmes' address book.

She looked at him now and wondered what he'd done to head them off. She guessed the address book was gone, misplaced in some evidence room or thrown over the side of some other boat into the ocean, or ashes now, but the book had been a fact, and her name had been written inside it. And he had seen it there. Matter cannot be created or destroyed—that was right out of Mr. Sanders' science class at Peabody Laboratory School. And she had seen an execution—another matter. They had each seen what they'd seen, and he wanted her to think of it as a story about other people.

They were already like a little family, the kind that kept busy all day and never discussed unpleasantries at dinner.

And he wanted her. In the car, on the lawn, in the pool. Morning, noon, and night. He stopped the Mercedes once on Wilshire Boulevard, suddenly pulled it to the side, without a word, two wheels on the curb, and dragged her into the lobby of the

Beverly Wilshire Hotel, paid for a room in cash, and took her to the ninth floor. And even then he couldn't wait; he lifted her skirt in the elevator and had it inside her on the way up. Her back pushed into the buttons, and the door began opening on the fifth floor.

Another night, as she collected herself in a small kitchen adjoining an art gallery in Hollywood, a hundred people milling around on the other side of a thin door and the damp print of her buttocks still visible on the surface of a wooden table, she looked over and saw her panties hanging from the edge of the refrigerator. In those moments when he was crazy in that particular way, she felt safe. Afterwards, she looked at him sometimes and could not get the feeling back. Afterwards was when she tried to think of what happened as a story with different people.

She pointed behind him now to the suntan lotion, and as he reached for it she touched his penis in a medical way, as if she were checking for a pulse, and then set it back against his leg. He looked at her—it had only been a few minutes; they had only just caught their breath—and gave her the lotion. She turned his hand over and squeezed the lotion into his palm until it spilled over his wrist and onto his legs. A few drops floated in the water and began to dissolve.

"I want to see how you do it," she said.

He paused, and she glanced over his shoulder to the second floor of the house next door. The house was a brick and wood Tudor on two fenced acres of manicured gardens. The Moffits kept a koi fish pond on the grounds, and a small waterfall, and flamingos. Mrs. Moffit was long and angular and kept her face stretched tight. About twice a year, she took it in and had them ratchet it back another notch, which was how it happened that she was the one person in Beverly Hills who looked more beat-up than Norah in the days after the attack on the boat.

You could not tell much about what went on over there, except to say that Mr. Moffit appeared to be the one in the house who rode sidesaddle.

Norah had been noticing Mrs. Moffit's face in various windows over there ever since Packard began showing up.

The Moffits were Democrats, and the morning Howard Hughes bounced his plane off the roof, they'd volunteered to host the fundraiser for the Waycross boys themselves, in their own backyard. Had insisted, in fact, and helped the caterer move the tables and the food and the liquor over there.

The next morning, all the koi fish were dead. Someone had spiked the pond with the gin— there were three empty fifths of Beefeaters lying in the grass—and Mrs. Moffit mailed Alec several pictures of the dead fish floating on their sides, along with the bill to replace them—no note, just the bill and the pictures—and neighborwise, it was never quite the same.

Norah saw movement now in the upstairs window.

"Instead of looking in the refrigerator?" Packard said.

She looked back at him and saw he was already hard. "No," she said, "but one thing at a time."

She stood still in the pool, her face a foot away from his hand, watching. Upstairs, the glass door opened and the maid came out to the balcony to shake the mop. She saw what was going on in the pool and stopped moving for a little while, dead still, and then disappeared back into the house. Before the door shut behind her, they heard her say "Mercy."

He moved into her house a carload at a time, all that week. Twenty suits, handmade shirts. More shoes than she had herself. An elaborate brace for his leg—it must have weighed fifty pounds. He lived somewhere in Newport Beach, and between the drive and the loading, he was gone three and four hours at a time. She offered to help, but he made excuses, the kind that meant he didn't want her in his place.

When he was gone back to Newport Beach for more, she looked over each load that he'd brought. It was mostly clothes. There were some old newspapers from Philadelphia—she couldn't tell, scanning the headlines, what he'd kept them for—but no books or records or paintings or furniture. No family pictures or yearbooks, no diplomas, no papers or medals from the army.

From what he didn't bring, she knew he hadn't given the other place up, but she didn't ask about that.

He left the house at odd times in the morning, and seemed to come and go as he wanted, and she wondered sometimes what sort of job he had with the Orange County Sheriff's Department. And why he worked for the police at all. He had money, although she didn't know how much, and seemed to have always had it. It was one of those things she could sense. But his work was a mystery, like the house or apartment in Newport Beach, none of her business. One more thing that lay between them unexplained.

He moved more of himself in all the time. At night, they went to movies and art galleries and once to a Harry Belafonte concert out in Griffith Park. He fucked her everywhere.

They went to the show at the planetarium. She sat long minutes in the dark, looking up at the starry ceiling, with her hand in his lap and his fingers moving inside her. He walked out of the planetarium into the afternoon sun with his zipper still open, two hundred children in uniform coming past them from the parking lot, Catholic kids on a field trip. And in front of all the children and nuns and the volunteer parents, she stopped walking when she saw it and turned around and fastened him up herself.

There was a brown envelope in the mail. The mail came every morning at ten. She had no idea what Alec had tipped the postman at Christmas, something else to figure out. There were several magazines today—*Time, Esquire, The Saturday Evening Post*—a bill from the funeral home, which had already been paid, a postcard from the Belgian Congo. An old friend was on safari—the world seemed full of Alec's old friends—and reported he'd made some excellent kills. "Alec—by God, this country is full of game!"

And then the brown envelope, her name handwritten in tiny letters with a pen that had been dipped in ink. No return address.

She opened the envelope, two pages inside. A petition on one page, written in the same hand that had addressed the envelope, signed and dated on the second page by eleven homeowners along the block. She went over the names and addresses and some of them she recognized, and some of them she didn't. She imagined Alec had introduced her to all the neighbors at one time or another. She imagined they had all been at the funeral.

The petition did not mention her specifically. It said only that certain recently observed acts of flagrant turpitude and immorality had threatened the character of the neighborhood, as well as the potential values of the properties therein, and would not be heretofore tolerated.

Later in the day, she went through the cards of condolence that had come in after the funeral, and found the one with the same tiny lettering. "With Deepest Sympathy, the Moffits."

She made a drink and walked through the house, feeling suddenly free. She felt like dancing.

CHAPTER 8

PARADISE DEVELOPMENTS

The day rates at Paradise Developments were posted on the wall behind the cash register. Four dollars for eighteen holes, two-fifty for nine. Weekends, it was a dollar more. Prospective home buyers—brought in occasionally by Cooper's only salesman, a part-timer named Jim Yard, who worked strictly on commission—were allowed to play free.

Near the door there were two bins of used golf balls, some marked ten cents each, and the others, mostly scuffed or cut, was a nickel. A handful of tees also cost a nickel, and you could rent a set of clubs for a dollar, but that required a ten-dollar deposit, refundable at the end of the round. The sign said NO EXCEPTIONS, although if Jim Yard brought somebody by, they let them use the clubs free too.

Customers sometimes complained that before Mr. Cooper bought the place, the tees were free.

Train had Sundays off, but he always came

around anyway, sometimes before Whitey got there to open the gate. He liked to take off his shoes and walk around in the cold, wet grass, seemed like he could feel the place waking up.

The ball-droppers began showing up a couple of hours after Train did, somewhere around eight. They were people that liked to gamble, couldn't afford a membership in a club, or, in the case of the Chinese and the coloreds, couldn't get into one anyway. The Chinese wore silk shirts and drove everybody crazy, talking that Chinese. Sound like five people learning to play the clarinet at once.

The ball-droppers had to paid Whitey their five dollars before they went out to the driving range, and they usually bought a beer or a cheese sandwich too—everybody but the Chinese, a people that would bet on anything, who Train saw one day out behind the doublewide, squatted down, shoulder bones and knees and skulls, betting on crickets, but that wouldn't spend a quarter for food. They just went out to the putting green and waited to see what other Chinese would show up.

The players dropped balls to decide the foursomes, and there was one player called Melrose English that nobody like to had in their group.

Everything come easy to Melrose English, and he wanted you to know it. There was a picture about him in the *Standard* a year ago, said if he was white, he could be out on the tour with Ben Hogan. The picture was from high school, though, when he was the state champion at a hundred yards. He looked hard even then. The paper said his nickname back then was "Modern."

As far as Train could tell, Melrose never went out his house looking like a ordinary human being. He came to the golf course dressed all in white or powder blue or pink, drove a black Lincoln that went with everything he wore. He kept his hair wavy and was always touching it to make sure it wasn't misplaced. People said he thought he was white, but it wasn't that. Train seen it wasn't that. What he wanted was everybody to know that the world had saw him coming and made room in the good seats.

Melrose was a pimp and liked saying that there was a new busload of girls coming into town every day. He talked sometimes about how he sent one home to Iowa, a hard-headed girl, would not suck the customers, so he made her an example, cut her across the face, got her sewed up and put her on the bus out of town.

Sometimes while Melrose was laughing over something on the course, Train pictured the girl from Iowa, had her hair in pigtails, the way Mr. Cooper's wife did when he met her, and she was laughing away too, maybe sitting at a bar in a new dress from Iowa, looked something like Bo Peep, touching Melrose's hand, thinking she was special to him, not paying attention that he gone moody. That was the thing

204

about Melrose, moodiness. Train could picture a cigarette on the table with an ash as long as her finger, and then in one movement, the one that would be froze in her history, his hand would move and her expression would change, a little at a time, while she realized there was something wrong with her pretty face, and she didn't know what it was yet, but it felt wrong and it was wet. And sometimes when Train pictured that, he imagined coming in himself and saving her. Sometimes it felt like he loved her.

Melrose mentioned the Iowa girl around the schoolteachers whenever it could be brought up into conversation. The teachers was the easiest ones to scare, and in his business, he scared who he could. When the balls fell wrong and one or two of them ended up in Melrose's group, you could hear them laughing all over the course, trying to guess what was supposed to be funny.

It wasn't just that he cut a girl. The man was moody, go stone-cold over a ten-dollar bet, so cold people were afraid to even look at him. Train had seen the schoolteachers and even the Chinese miss little putts so they wouldn't be in Melrose's pocket for the day. And nobody ever had Melrose himself putt out, nothing under five feet. There was even an expression about that—"Pick it up, Melrose"—when they was playing among themselves. But they were careful not to say it around Melrose himself. Nobody knew minute to minute what mood he was in, or what he liked, and everybody walked around him scart to say the wrong thing.

As far as Train could tell, an old man called Pincus Lewis was the only one immune. Pincus didn't care who Melrose English was or who he said he cut. When the boy got like that, he just turned off his hearing aid and just kept on pushing the ball around the golf course.

Melrose was in a group on this day with Pincus, a Chinese, and a boy called Silverman, whose father owned Ruby's Liquor Emporium in Inglewood. Train tagged along behind, not bothering nobody, just watching the game.

The foursome come to number five, a blind shot from the tee, and Melrose hit it down the right side. Everybody else went left, the safe play, and when they walked over the hill, Melrose's ball ain't there. He stood still, looking around himself like he dropped his keys. Below them, down by the green, there was a shallow pond, and two colored boys in their underpants were out waist-deep, diving for balls. One of them had goggles. There was snappers in that pond, and Train noticed snakes down there sunning on the rocks.

Train seen that Melrose's ball bounced once on the fairway before it disappeared over the hill, but the fairway was sloped right, and there were rocks in the rough. Mr. Cooper was always after

Whitey to get those rocks out of the rough, but nothing been done and people lost their ball over there all the time, and when they did find it, they couldn't hit it without breaking a shaft. That's why you aim it left.

"That ball have got to be in the fairway," Melrose said.

Pincus said, "Why is that?" even though he and Melrose was partners that day. The low handicap and the high.

"I ain't no fucking Chinaman, is why," Melrose said. The Chinese had lost a ball on the last hole, kept them waiting fifteen minutes while he looked for it. The Chinese all hated to lose a ball, and Melrose hated to wait. Train was already thinking he might just walk back in. It made him nervous to be around Melrose in a bad temper.

Pincus didn't care nothing about that, golf was golf. He nodded toward the empty fairway and said, "If it's there, then go hit it." Silverman look around for the exit. Nobody but Pincus would talk like that to Melrose.

Melrose spotted the two boys in the pond then, diving for balls. A bicycle with a large basket was parked at the edge of the water, and there were at least a couple hundred balls lying in a blanket on the ground. "I see where it went," he said.

Pincus looked at the boys, and then back at Melrose. "Not unlest you hit that drive four hundret yards," he said.

"One of them must of got up here and took it," he said. He turned and looked at the old man. "Whose side you on anyway?"

"Shit, those boys ain't bothered your ball. They in the water."

But Melrose wasn't talking to Pincus anymore. He estimated the distance to the pond and took out one of his irons and dropped half a dozen balls on the ground, new Wilsons, and then began hitting them in where the boys were wading.

The first one hit the bank; the second one hit the water so close that it splashed up into one of them's face. The boy looked up, like he didn't understand, and Melrose took another swing, put this one behind him in the bank.

"What the hell you doing?" Pincus said.

"They ain't got no business out here," Melrose said, and swung again. The boy saw this one coming and stumbled back and fell under the water. He came back up looking like the tar baby from the muck on the bottom. The older boy pulled the younger one away from there, both of them scrambling up the bank to the bicycle. The older one got on first, to pedal, and waited until the little one got on in front, and then they rode away, leaving all the balls they'd pulled out of the pond there on the ground. Half a day's work.

Train thought they must be brothers or cousins, for the older one to wait like that for the little one to get on the handlebars. Pincus watched them go. "They was only boys," he said. "Just trying to make a dollar."

"The balls belong to the people that hit them," Melrose said, but Pincus seen all he cared to see and heard all he cared to hear. He stared at Melrose, and for a second he seem to shamed him, and then turned around and walked back toward the clubhouse, pulling his golf cart.

Melrose called after him. "Where you going, man? We got a game here." Pincus reached up and turned off his hearing contraption. Quitting like that, it might be the last time the old man would ever play out here. Might have to stay home with his wife on Sunday now, maybe take her to church. Train remembered once when Melrose and Pincus was friendly, Melrose asked him what that old stuff was like. "Cactus," he said. Made Melrose laugh so hard he cried. But that was all bygones now.

"What now?" the Chinese said.

"We play skins, Chinaman. The other game is moot," Melrose said.

The Chinese nodded, as if he understood *moot*, and maybe he did; it sounded like something they eat. And then they were looking back at Train. They were all looking at Train. Then Melrose said, "You got any money on you, man?"

The news that Train had took $260 off Melrose English and a Chinese and the Silverman boy in a Sunday-morning skins game, without strokes, borrowing clubs out of Melrose's own bag, passed through the regular players at Paradise Developments and then spilt out into the street.

The boy didn't just won all the money, he made Melrose English putt out from two feet on the last hole. Melrose put the ball in the hole to save himself another fifty dollars, but the audacity was the boy made him putt it at all.

Melrose handed over the money like he didn't care. The Chinese and Silverman was afraid to breathe.

"You make it next Sunday, man?" Melrose said, cold as the icebox. And then, before Train could answer, he said, "Bring your money."

CHAPTER 9

THE COAST HIGHWAY

They got drunk and went to Mexico. They went to a live sex show, a woman and a bear, woke up in the morning in a room with a cat in the corner and cockroaches all over the ceiling, and went out and got drunk again and got married. She thought of herself, the grieving widow, watching a bear given a hand job.

Another day passed, and they were in the Jaguar, on the way home. The car had been Alec's favorite, even though it was in the shop nine or ten months a year. In a way, he'd liked it because it was so hard to keep clean. He'd liked putting effort into little things that didn't matter to anyone else. The car was painted black, and inside, anything that touched the wood or glass left smudges. Whenever she got in it now, she thought of the print of her behind on the little table at the art gallery. She'd watched it evaporate as she got into her clothes.

Miller was driving, lost in his thoughts. It was nothing new to her—he seemed lost most of the time, but she didn't know yet what it meant. It hadn't occurred to her that she never would. They were on the Coastal Highway just north of San Diego and the sun was lying on the water.

She looked down at her legs, and then laid a hand between them, on the inside of her thigh. Her thumb rested a moment on the slight rise at the border of her stocking, and she moved it back and forth, feeling the texture of her skin, then the nylon. She slid a finger underneath, feeling a small, clear pain as it passed over the little bump of scar tissue that had formed where she had been torn in the rape. It was the boy who had done that; it turned out he was only eighteen years old. She let go of the thought and slid her finger inside.

A convertible came past from the opposite direction, three boys who might have been eighteen too, all of them in Navy uniforms, headed back to San Diego. She felt a small sadness watching them, at the parts of her life that were gone. Later, they came across a pickup full of Mexicans, stopped along side the road with the hood up, children spilling out the windows, too many adults to count drinking in the truck bed. Having the kind of good time that only Mexicans could have. He remarked then that you almost never saw their children crying.

He kept the car at seventy a little while and then eighty; it seemed to her that he was happiest when he was taking chances. She reached across his arm, throwing a shadow across his lap, and slowly wiped her wet finger over his lips. He tasted what it was and closed his eyes, and because of that

212

she saw the animal come up over the railing before he did.

He stood up on the brakes and the back end of the Jaguar began to skate sideways, the wheel useless in his hands, the deer straight ahead, not moving, and then the car left the pavement and the deer left it too, but not in time, and there was a noise, unmistakably something alive, the end of life, and then the thing reappeared and the windshield shattered and the car slid along the railing and then crossed back over the highway, spinning now, bounced over a small ditch and came to rest on the frontage road on the other side. She sat still a moment, her skirt hiked to her lap, staring through the shattered glass right into the animal's face, the steam blowing from the radiator behind it. She felt empty, and then, strangely, she began to cry. Not over the deer, or even the accident. She hadn't been afraid—it seemed to her that she had lost her capacity for ordinary kinds of fear that morning on the boat—and she wasn't hurt. She was only empty, and she cried.

He pulled her out of the car as if he were trying to save her, and set her back against the trunk, her feet still in her shoes, and began to kiss her cheeks. Looking into her eyes, kissing her cheeks.

"You're all right. I've got you."

"I know, I know."

"You're not hurt."

"I know . . ."

"I love you," he said.

And she said, "I know."

He lifted her skirt up over her waist. A moving van blew past and the wave of air rocked the car beneath her, and she felt him pushing inside, and she closed her eyes, feeling the tears on her lashes, and heard the truck's horn blowing and dying as it moved away, and then he was up inside her, cars going by, trucks, flashes of the sun off the windshields, horns, brakes, tears, and then it was only them again, Norah and Miller Packard, banging away like jackhammers, so loud you couldn't even think. And for a while again she felt safe.

They walked slowly along the side of the highway, turning when they saw oncoming lights, trying to catch a ride. She was wearing uncomfortable shoes and the roadside was uneven and hard to see. There were only a few feet between the road bed and the steep rocks that defined the east side of the highway. The sun had set, and the air turned cool, and she was not sure the oncoming cars could see them in the dusk. She'd left her sweater in the Jaguar, half a mile back.

They walked for another ten minutes, until it got too dark to see the ground at all, and then they stopped beside some rocks large enough to sit on and waited. He said the Highway Patrol would be by soon, that they came up and down the road all day and night, looking for accidents. She was shaking with the cold. He put his coat around her shoulders.

Later, she looked at him and saw that he was away again, thinking about something else. There was blood on the sleeve of the coat. Without saying why, he had lifted the animal off the hood before they left and laid it in the gully near the rocks, and something in the gesture moved her. She could have asked, but there might have been a practical reason, and she didn't want to know that. She didn't want to be disappointed.

"Are you sure the police are coming?"

"Even if nobody reported the accident," he said, "they patrol up and down here all the time."

"What were you thinking?" she said a little later, wanting to feel closer to him, stalled out here on the highway, while everyone else was on the way somewhere else. "When we hit the deer, I mean. When we were out of control."

"Nothing," he said, and then turned and kissed her and smiled. "Just keeping it on the road." A truck full of watermelons passed them, headed north.

"What about when it was over?" she said.

He smiled again but didn't answer.

A few minutes passed and a set of headlights threw light beams over the crest of the hill to the north, the angles changing as the car got closer to the top, and then it came into view. She saw the car was slowing, and then that it was a black Ford. It had spotlights on both sides, an oversize antenna on the trunk, meant to look like the Highway Patrol. One like it had come past and slowed while they were on the trunk of the Jaguar. A dark two-door Ford with spotlights and the antenna, a V-8 engine. She knew cars, had always liked to drive.

The Ford pulled to the side of the road and stopped. The passenger door opened and a face appeared in the door opening, a massive bald head with tiny features. Pale as the moon. "You all need some help?" the man called. He had an accent she estimated was North Florida, and sounded a little drunk.

Packard walked toward the car. She was behind him, holding on to his hand, shivering with the cold. The man in the car was smiling. "I thought I saw a wreck back there," he said. "I'm afraid to tell you what else."

Packard got to the open door and bent a little to look inside. The man was enormous, half-lying across the lap of a heavy girl who had lipstick on her teeth and a black brassiere beneath a white blouse. The blouse was bunched open, the buttons in the wrong holes. She might have been nineteen or twenty years old. She was smiling and holding on to a six-ounce bottle of Coca-Cola with a straw in it. Even from behind Packard, the car reeked of tequila.

"We hit a deer," Packard said.

The man sat up, and the girl tried to smooth her blouse and then saw the problem with the buttons and gave up without trying to straighten it out. She sipped at the straw instead, watching Norah. "You're lucky nobody was hurt," the man said. "This stretch of road . . ."

She saw there was barely room for him behind the steering wheel. He was wearing a Hawaiian shirt, and there were crosses tattooed on both his forearms. He had fingers like a baby's, though. Short, plump fingers. Dimples.

"At least y'all still walking and talking," the man said. "Praise the Lord for that." Then he pushed the back of the girl's seat forward—she didn't seem to mind being bent over—and gestured toward the backseat. "Hop on," he said.

Packard held her hand while she got into the backseat, and then got in himself. The man's neck was two rolls of fat between his head and his shoulders. The backseat smelled of dogs and humans. The girl in front slammed the door and had another sip from her straw, and the man pulled the car back onto the highway and lifted himself to look them over in the rearview mirror. A cross swung beneath it from a chain.

"Where you all from?" he said. "Hollywood?"

"I think there's a telephone up here somewhere," Packard said, indicating the road. "A station where we can call a garage."

"Well," the man said, "there is a gas station, in fact, and a diner out behind just four, five miles up the highway." He looked into the mirror again. "But, you know, me and Cindy are going back to the big city ourselves, could give you a lift."

"No," Packard said, "we want to take care of the car."

"Well, I don't blame you for that," the man said. "That looks like an expensive automobile." He smiled in the mirror with tiny, even teeth. "Besides, I know my appearance scares the ladies." The girl in the front seat giggled and had another sip from her straw. Packard sat still, and she saw a certain look come over his face, and the car drove up the highway. "Lord knows," the man said, "sometime I look in the mirror, I even scare myself."

She touched Packard's leg, not wanting him to forget she was there.

"The fact is," the man in the front seat said, "I'm rather gentle." And the girl up there snorted and then coughed, because she was drinking when he said that, and some of the drink came out of her nose. She wiped it with her sleeve. He moved a little and found Norah in the mirror. "Where did y'all say you were from?" he asked.

A few minutes passed, and they came around a long curve in the road and saw the gas station. "A lot of people presume that a man's oversized, that makes him slow," the man said. "In both senses of the word." He was looking at her in the mirror again.

"That's the station there," Packard said.

"Why don't we just go up the highway here a little bit," the man said, "see what we can see.

You all ain't in a hurry, are you?" It was quiet a few seconds, and then the man said, "You know, this highway is like my hobby. You never know what you gone run across here at night. You might see a wreck; you might see the bodies lying in the trees."

The car went around another long turn, and in the darkness of the backseat she felt him move slightly, slightly shift his position.

The man said, "There's a little dirt road up ahead here where the teenagers go to park. We go up there sometimes with the spotlight, scare them to death." He laughed, as if he were remembering frightened teenagers, and then tapped the brakes and slowed for the turn. A new smell came back to them from the front; the odor was damp with excitement. "Yessir. Let's all just drive up this here a little ways, see what we can see. That all right with everybody?"

The car turned off the highway and onto the dirt road. It dropped into a swale and the back axle scraped against the ground. The man slowed down and turned off his headlights. They drove a little farther, until they were hidden from the highway, and then he stopped. He put one of his stubby, massive arms across the seat back and smiled at them, showing them his teeth, and then, as she watched, he cupped his hand beneath his mouth and spit them out. The whole upper plate.

"A lot of people, they have an accident in their panties now," he said, looking directly at her. "That's what Cindy likes, when they lose control."

She slugged him playfully on the arm, embarrassed. "Carl," she said.

The man was breathing harder, through his mouth. His gums shined in the dark. "Here's a surprise for everybody," he said to Norah. "Cindy here's developed a certain preference for the female figure. . . ."

For a moment there was no sound except the man's breathing, and then she heard Packard, sounding like he was interested in that too. He said, "You wonder how something like that could happen." The man went very still, as if that remark had hurt his feelings. It made the girl angry.

"Shake him a little bit, Carl," the girl said. "See how funny it is then."

Packard turned to the girl. "Isn't there a little voice in your head yet, sweetheart, telling you something here isn't right?"

"You wait and see," she said. "You just wait till Carl comes over the seat, see what voice you're hearing."

And in that same moment, the man did start over the seat back. His arms were short and thick and pushed in opposing strokes as he wedged his body into the back. It was like watching a turtle. When he'd got about halfway over, he reached for Packard with his dimpled fingers.

"Cover your ears," Packard said, very matter of fact, and she did, without asking why, as if this kind of thing happened all the time. The gun came out just as the man got his hands on Packard's collar. He let himself be pulled forward but turned his head away before the man could butt him, and laid his cheek against the side of Carl's bald head for a moment, as if they were dancing, and then he put the gun beside the man's far ear and pulled the trigger.

For a moment she thought he'd killed him too. The flash lit up the car; she felt the concussion of the air against her face and it felt wet, like blood. The man grabbed himself violently and jerked sideways and back. The girl began to scream and then to cry. Packard sat farther up in the seat, looking at her, then at him, and then up at the roof, where there was a hole about the size of a dime, and the cotton lining around it was singed and smoking. He patted at the spot with the back of his hand, putting out the fire. The girl was holding her ears and looking at Carl and crying. Norah guessed it wouldn't be the same between them now.

"Carl?" Packard said, and when the man didn't move, Packard tapped him in the head with the barrel. Not a soft tap. "Carl?" He came up slowly, steadying himself against the dashboard, looking at his hands to see where he was shot. Packard saw the man couldn't hear well and so he raised his voice and spoke slowly. "We'll just go to the gas station now."

The girl lay against the door, crying bitterly all the way there.

★   ★   ★

221

They ate dinner in a small, dimly lit diner behind the Sinclair station while they waited for the tow truck. Barbecued chicken sandwiches and potato salad and beer. The waitress had a cigarette in the corner of her mouth, and there were stains on her blouse; it looked like she was leaking milk. They were the only customers in the place.

"It's not safe around you, is it?" she said.

He said, "I was about to ask you the same thing."

He leaned forward and kissed her, and then reached into his pocket. She had a stab of apprehension that it was another ring, a real one. The one he'd given her in Mexico was silver and already turning her finger green, but that was the one she wanted. He'd bought it from an Indian on the street, and it was perfect.

What he had wasn't a ring, though; it was Carl's teeth.

Somewhere in the back, a baby began to squawl, and the waitress hurried through a curtain in that direction. He set the teeth on the table between them. "You don't hear much about it," he said, a different tone completely, "but a friend of mine, a dentist, told me that puppies chew up more dentures than shoes and slippers put together. Dentures are the hidden cost of buying a dog."

She stared at him, and a minute passed. "You enjoyed it, didn't you?" she said. "That whole thing in the car."

He just smiled, moonstruck. It was like she was speaking French and he had fallen in love with her anyway, without knowing what anything meant.

"You saw what he looked like," she said. "Why else would you get in?"

"We both got in," he said.

"You sound like my psychologist." She'd been seeing one of those the last couple of months, a man who thought it was interesting that she'd urinated on herself to get away from the Negroes. He'd asked her if she sensed there was a connection to her father. Twenty-five dollars an hour for that.

Packard shrugged and said, "Well, Carl's the psychologist. How did he put it? 'Let's drive up this here a little ways, see what we can see'? Isn't that what psychologists try to make you do?"

She waited a moment, feeling herself react to the mention of his name, and then she looked again at the teeth. "Jesus, that head."

"Yeah, that was some head Carl had." And that fast, it happened again. Somebody let out all the bats, and she laughed out loud until she was hoarse and tearing and the waitress came out of the back thinking he'd hit her, and that was funny too. She had the idea then that if she could keep laughing, everything would be all right. Laughing, dancing, drinking, smiling, just like Packard. If she could just keep moving she was safe. When things caught up, then you had a problem. Once you stopped moving, then you couldn't move. She looked at her new husband and thought, for the first time, that she understood what he'd meant when he told her to try to think of it as a story about other people.

When the tow truck came, Miller Packard tossed Carl's teeth to a mongrel lying in the dust near the pumps. He was already making crunching noises when they climbed in for the ride home.

CHAPTER 10

PARADISE DEVELOPMENTS

Friday afternoon, Mr. Cooper was not his usual self. There was problems with the building permits again, problems with the bank. He didn't have no speech today for them about being ambassadors for Paradise Developments, or how America was opportunity for the taking. He didn't say much of nothing, in fact, just went through the alphabet, paying the men, and paid Train last, like always, and then told Train to hang around awhile, there was a man coming over later to see him.

A man that had heard about him beating Melrose in a game of golf.

"What man was that?" he said.

Train didn't want anybody coming around to see him. He thought of Mayflower, of the policeman who stuck the paper spike through his hand. A man coming around to see him—that couldn't go nowhere good. He looked at the door, afraid for a minute that Mr. Cooper's wife said something to him about the barn. That the man had called the authorities, and they were waiting now for them to come pick him up.

"Have you heard of the Indiana Klan?" Mr. Cooper said. "This is the man who stood up to them. You'll see for yourself." Then he went back to balancing his balance sheet, and time crawled along, and then Train heard somebody coming, sounded like a man sweeping the cement as he come up the steps, and then the door opened and it was the Vengeance of the Lord in person, wearing a hat.

The man walk like it hurt him to move, dragging one leg behind him. His arms were scarred and thin, and his face was about half pink, looked like somebody sewed a quilt, and his ears were little crisp-looking nubs. His skin was creased and tucked, and some places there was too much and some places it look like they wasn't enough. The man took his time studying Train, looking at him like he was the one that looked like a campfire marshmallow.

"This is Mr. Hollingsworth," Mr. Cooper said, "publisher of the *Darktown Standard*. He's been a good friend to our cause ever since we started in business."

Mr. Hollingsworth's eyes were small and alive in the middle of all that disrupted skin, and they was focused on Train from the minute he walked in the door.

"I hear you play golf," the man said finally, and when he talked, he talked like a professor. It looked

226

like a strain with his lips, which was situated like somebody sewed them on backward.

Train nodded.

"And you caddied at Brookline?" he said. Train blinked, not knowing if he could lie out of this or not. It seemed like Mr. Cooper must of told him where he come from, or how else would he know?

"Did you know those two boys well, son?" he said. "The ones got into that trouble on the boat?"

Train recoiled to be called *son*. That was another signal things was about to get worse; plus, it recalled people putting their hands on your back or shoulder.

"Everybody know them," he said.

Next thing, Hollingsworth would be asking about the police, what happened at the station, and the conversation already gone further into the area of law enforcement than Train wished to go.

"From what I've been told, those boys didn't have anything to do with it," Mr. Hollingsworth said. "Innocent victims. The police just took them out in the ocean and shot them, pure and simple, to cover up what really happened."

Hollingsworth seemed to think of something and went to write it down, and Train looked at the man's wrist, narrow and strange-colored, and the watchband hung loose and jiggled. On top of everything else about him that was fucked up, it looked like something was eating him away. It looked like grave robbing.

"The woman was white and rich," he said, almost a question, but not quite, "and she shot her own husband. Pure and simple. Somebody had to be blamed." Then he sat there waiting, and Train seen what he was waiting for was him to say it happened just like he said. Waiting for *verification*.

Train looked at the door. He wanted out of the room and away from this man Hollingsworth and his fucked-up ears. Wanted to stay away from the subject of Brookline and everything that happened over it. But all he did was nod along.

"Yessir," he said.

Hollingsworth sighed. "The ones with enough money can always find one or two of us to blame for a shot husband, right?" he said. Mr. Cooper seem to agree with that version of it, like he had a vote in what happened out there too.

"Was there much talk about it afterwards?" Hollingsworth said. "Perhaps speculation from a superior, or another caddy who works there? Someone I might contact . . ."

Train didn't say so, but they wasn't no question that whoever shot Sweet had their reasons.

All he told him was there wasn't no work out there after that. "They took away all the jobs. They said they were making a clean breast."

Mr. Hollingsworth nodded like that was exactly what he expected. "That's the pattern," he said, "as old as time. Divide the people. Divide and conquer." He looked across the table and dropped

228

his voice to a place you couldn't argue with what he said, no matter what it was. "I promise you this," he said. "Your friends Clarence Holmes and Arthur Tobin, those lives will not be lost in vain."

Train saw that the time was past to mention Sweet had done two years at Vacaville and stole $350 from old Florida's widow. He only stood still, tried not to look at the man's ears, and waited. The man leaned closer and touched him. "You're a good boy," he said. And Train thought he could smell something burnt.

Sunday morning Train was at the club at dawn. Whitey came in about 6:30 and opened the gate, looked like she slept in the woods.

Hollingsworth showed up two hours later, right after Melrose, still wearing the hat, raised the question in Train's mind of what things looked like underneath. He walked that painful way down to the first tee, where the golfers were waiting. Dragging his bad leg.

"Might you have another moment?" he said to Train.

Melrose and the two players he brought with him were sitting on the bench; they seem to enjoy the way the man spoke. One of the players called Alexander Pokey was a jockey, little bowlegs, look like a child from a distance. The other one was older and took up as much space as a Steinway piano. The jockey called him Girth, but that hardly did the spectacle of him justice.

Train waited politely and Hollingsworth said, "I was wondering if you might remember anything about the younger boy. The one who was killed." Train thought of Arthur, didn't know a thing, even if he did want to say it. Just the slow eyes and smell of baby powder, the way the boy's flesh moved under his shirt.

"What do you weigh, Girth?" the jockey said behind him, "four hundred?"

"Didn't talk to nobody," Train said.

Hollingsworth waited, wanting him to try harder. "Did he have any family you knew of? Mother, father, siblings? Any idea where I could find them?"

"The reason I'm askin'," the jockey said to the big man, "there's a mare in the barn, bit me on the back." He lifted his shirt, exposing muscles Train never would have guessed was there, and turned on the bench to show them the bandage. It was about the size of a washcloth, and the bruising spilled out of the bottom halfway to his waist.

"I'll pay you to come around once and sit on that bastard for me," the jockey said. "Just put the thought in her head."

"I can't get on no goddamn horse, Poke," the big man said.

"This bastard bit me so bad, I had to sleep sitting up," the jockey said. "I just want a little satisfaction."

"Shoot it," Melrose said.

"No sir," Train said to Hollingsworth. "I never heard him talk about nothing like that."

Train stood on the tee box, swinging the rental clubs, getting used to the weight. Some of the irons were Wilsons, some were Spalding, and while Train got used to the way they felt, Girth and the jockey sat on the bench and talked about ways other than being sat on by a four-hundred-pound rider to surprise a horse. Melrose chuckled along, and bent over and spit between his shoes. He had a way of laughing like he knew more than anybody else. The newspaperman stood by, ignoring them, still hoping Train had something to tell him.

Suddenly Melrose said, "You come out here to watch the boy lose all his money, pop?" The newspaperman turned his stare on him, and then on them all. A little while passed and it got less comfortable, and then Girth decided to retie his golf shoes, and then Melrose stood up and swung his club, said it was making him queasy to be looked at by somebody all burnt up.

He looked down the fairway awhile, waiting for the foursome ahead to hit and clear. "Gone be slow today," he said. Then he turned to Train. "I hope that don't bother you, man, to play slow."

Train shrugged. "Slow or fast," he said.

"What kind of game you want?" Melrose said after Hollingsworth left. Train looked at the jockey and the big man, remembering the sandbaggers

231

he'd seen back at Brookline. Melrose said, "How 'bout me and Alexander against you and Girth, twenty-dollar Nassau? . . ."

Train shook his head.

"Twenty dollars too rich?"

"Man," the jockey said, "I'm out here wasting my precious time."

"Skins," Train said. "Everybody for themself."

Melrose shrugged, and the two other players shrugged too. The big man looked bored. Melrose said, "Fifty for eighteen, that all right with everybody?" Testing him somehow. Train tried not to think about fifty dollars, how long it took him to earn that toting bags.

Melrose won the first four skins, chipping it in from the back side of the green, playing his game. Train felt everybody watching him, seeing if he was scared and bothered. "You got this covered, man?" Melrose said as they went to the fifth tee. Then he stepped up and hit it down the middle, deep for him, feeling good. "I mean, if we get done and the money ain't right, you know, that's bad for everybody."

But the way Train was looking at things, he was playing out of Melrose's pocket. He could lose every hole all day, still be up $210. He was beginning to get the feel of the rental clubs, waiting on the head just a little longer with the ones with the whippier shafts, and Melrose wasn't gone chip the ball in forever. He waited on the driver now and hit the ball past Melrose fifty yards.

Melrose chipped in again on five, but this time it was to tie the hole. And that was the last sniff he got.

At the end of it, everybody but Girth sat down at the picnic table outside the double-wide to settle up. Girth couldn't fit in. It wasn't until the money came out that Train saw they been playing fifty dollars a hole, not fifty for the eighteen. He picked up the cash in front of him and counted it—nineteen hundred dollars—and felt his fingers shaking.

Melrose couldn't stand the sight of him now, but the other two didn't seem bothered by the game, and they was out nine hundred each, and they sat there cool and happy, drinking gin and 7UP. One of them, the jockey, was the best putter Train ever seen. Another day, the little man might have took all the money himself.

Train kept the money in his back pocket, and in a week was already tired of carrying it around, tired of hiding it when he went to sleep or took a shower, hiding it even from Plural. When he was on the tractor, it made his leg numb. Folded in half, it was three inches thick—over two thousand dollars, more money than he ever expected to be sitting on in his life—and he worried over it like he used to worry that old Lucky was dying under the kitchen table, running from the bus home to make sure he hadn't passed on while Train was at work.

In some ways, two thousand dollars was more trouble than no money at all.

The grounds crew at Paradise Developments took an hour for lunch. The hour was unpaid. There were five regulars, and they ate their sandwiches and fruit and boiled eggs and Hostess cupcakes and then sprawled out on the grass under a big live oak behind the barn until Whitey come down and yelled at them that it was time to go back to work. They always groaned getting up, and one of them always told her that they didn't have no watches, that she ought to give them a watch, and that got under her skin, to have them asking Mr. Cooper for something more, and she would say she noticed she never had to come down and tell them it was time to lay down.

The grounds crew liked to see her worked up like that, especially when they got her mad enough to grab poor Lester by the belt and scold him, flop him around like a doll. Lester was scared to death of Whitey.

Train didn't care to be around for the bemusement of Lester, and after he ate, he usually took the old brakeless Ford pickup out to the pond on number five, where the boys had been diving for golf balls, and sat out on the hood, feeding a one-footed duck pieces of sandwiches that people left in the trash. He called the duck Marliss. Sometimes, if he found a dead snake or rabbit on the course that day, he brought it along for the snappers. There were eight or ten of them at least, some that had to weigh a hundred pounds.

All Train could figure out about what was going on at the pond was Marliss lost her foot to one of the turtles and refuse to leave the scene of the crime. Twice, Train had got off a tractor and ran her down himself and took her to the other pond over on sixteen, but both times she was back at number five in the morning. She settle herself in right next to the snappers while they laid out in the water, moving closer and then a little closer, and then closer again, until finally one of them went for her, and the second it moved, she was gone, honking and flapping out the way, leaving a trail of feathers in the wake.

The duck had been there ever since Train started. The first time he saw her, she limped out in front of the tractor, beating her wings to stay upright, look like she was trying to commit suicide. That wasn't it, though; she'd just fell into the daredevil life, and couldn't go back.

He was sitting on the hood of the truck, tossing bread to Marliss, when a person in a suit and a straw hat came toward him from the direction of the road. Vagrants had broke down the fence again, so anybody could walk onto the course, and Mr. Cooper hadn't brought in the fence company yet to put it back up. Everywhere you looked, there was things Mr. Cooper hadn't did; all he cared about was to keep those bulldozers pushing dirt.

235

The person was built on the slight side, and appeared to had a crick in his neck, maybe looking up all the time at adults. He rolled when he walked, recalling Sweet.

The person came up a dirt hill on the other side of the pond, trying not to get his shoes dirty, and then stood still a minute, popping his knuckles, staring at one of the big snappers. His shoes shined in the sun. Train waited; never first, never sorry. The little man looked up from the turtle, the straw hat throwing a shadow across his face. All Train could see was his teeth. Train threw more bread to the duck, just like this person wasn't there.

"How come you ain't killed them snappers?" the little man said. He had a deep voice for somebody that size. Delicate hands, polished nails. A mustache as thin as a pencil line across his lip.

"Ain't done nothing to kill them for," Train said.

The duck stood up straight and shook. The person moved in for a closer look, careful where he put his feet. Must of bought his clothes in the boy's department. "They'd do it to you—that's a reason." He made a gun of his thumb and finger and aimed at the turtles, pretended to shoot. His hand jumped and he made shooting noises three times. "They thinking they all safe in their shell. Probably ain't afraid of nothing."

"I don't know," Train said.

That remark seem to aggravated him, turned him ugly. "I didn't ast you what you know," he said. Train noticed that before with little people, they fly off the handle without the regular reasons. When he spoked again, though, he already forgotten he was mad. "You ain't never killed nothing for sport?" He waited a little, but Train didn't answer. "You missed the great outdoors."

Train had a sudden cold moment when he thought he felt Mayflower's hand on his neck. One of the snappers slipped under the water, drawing the little man's attention. "Lookit there. They got a head on them like an old man's dick," he said. "You could kill them for ugliness. That's a reason too." He took a cigarette from his shirt pocket, letting Train see what he had under his coat, then lit it and flicked the match into the pond. Maybe smoking stunt your growth after all.

Train threw the last of the bread to the duck and pushed himself off the hood. "Where you going?" the person said. "I thought we was talking."

"Work," Train said. "I got to get back to work."

"You cutting the grass around here, picking weeds and all? That's what you do?" Train opened the truck door to climb in, then stood where he was, still holding the door handle, and waited while the little man came toward him now, still careful where he put down his feet.

"You ain't believe what people downtown been talking about," he said. "They saying that this boy out at Paradise Development got into Melrose's pocket. Made a fool of Melrose English, saying this boy just lull him to sleep and took his roll."

"How am I gone lull somebody to sleep?" Train said.

"That ain't the point," the little man said. "The point is, it's going around this boy did it without nothing in his pocket." He was watching Train's face to see if that was true, and then he was shaking his head and smiling, like he caught him red-handed.

The little man dusted his hands and then his clothes. He looked back at the pond, but the snappers were gone now, underwater. "You know," he said, "I believe you found the right place, out here with the ducks and shit. You see what I mean? I was you, I'd stick to it." And then he reached up, the cigarette still between his fingers, and patted Train on the cheek. Train felt the heat from the cigarette and pulled away.

The little man started back toward the pond, the way he'd come. Walking that rolling walk, like the world was his.

"He want it back, then?" Train said. "He sent out his little midget to get it back?"

The little man turned around, then came back halfway to the truck, showing him again what was under his coat. There was a wrench lying on the front seat, and Train reached in and picked it up. The little man smiled at that, but then, so did Mayflower when he saw the chair leg.

"He want you to know he's thinking about you," the little man said; "that's all he said, people saying you played him with money you didn't have. He see

238

you around, something might happen. That's why if you got any sense, nigger, you stay out here with the frogs, where it's safe."

"He knows where his money's at," Train said. "All he got to do is come out and take it back."

The little man looked again down into the water, trying to spot one of the snappers. "Sometime I like to see that," he said. "See that look on their face when the bullet come through the shell."

CHAPTER 11

BEVERLY HILLS

She missed a period, which was nothing new. Since the rape, it was a crapshoot anyway. Spotting all the way through the cycle. Something seemed different now, though. She sensed it was different.

She was lying on her back in the pool when she heard the phone. She had been thinking about Packard, worrying how she would tell him about this, if she would be able to see what he was thinking when she told him.

She could not picture him holding a baby, but you never knew.

The phone rang a dozen times, then stopped. A minute later she stood up in the water to go inside, and it began again. She wrapped a towel around her waist and noticed Mr. Moffit was in one of the downstairs windows next door, watching her. She stared directly at him, and he moved slowly away into the shadows. She walked into the house, and thought she might have seen him wave. Maybe telling her the petition wasn't his idea.

She counted the rings as she went through the kitchen, picked up at fifteen. She thought it might be Packard, although he did not ordinarily call. The phone made him uncomfortable; he liked to be able to see how he was doing.

"Hello?"

"Mrs. Rose?"

She stood very still.

"Mrs. Rose? Have I reached Norah Rose?"

"Who is calling please?"

"Is this Mrs. Rose?"

"Who is calling?" she said. She thought it might be the old man from the funeral home again. The son was running the business now, but his father came in a couple of days a week, and dunned people for payment. The son had apologized for him but said there was nothing he could do. Technically, he still owned the business.

"My name is Luther Hollingsworth," the man said, "with the *Standard*."

"The what?" She laughed out loud.

"The *Darktown Standard*. A newspaper for the Negro community. I was calling for Mrs. Rose." She waited and he said, "In regard to Mr. Rose."

"Mr. Rose has passed away," she said.

"Oh, I'm aware of that," he said; "that's what I'm calling about. In fact, I was wondering when it might be convenient to have an interview."

"What are you referring to?"

"An interview," he said, "about Mr. Rose. About the circumstances surrounding his death."

It was silent again and then, slowly, distinctly, he said, "We just need to verify what happened." And she hung up.

CHAPTER 12

PARADISE DEVELOPMENTS

He drove the truck back to the barn from the pond, tired out from whatever had got into him when he picked up that wrench, thinking now about what might have happened, how far he been ready to go. He stayed in the barn all afternoon, replacing the truck's brakes, wondering what the hell happened to his sense, trying to calm himself down. His fingers was shaking again and unmanageable. He kept going over how the little man incited him at the pond, at how close he come. What else was he gone do with a wrench in his hand? And then what? He thought of the way Mayflower's head blossomed open, and pictured it happening again.

He got tired of thinking after a while, and forgave himself for what he almost did, because there wasn't nothing to be done about it one way or the other now, and went on from there. A little later, though, he caught himself wondering how much of the little man the snappers could eat.

He was thinking about the snappers, in fact,

when he forgot where he was with the brake job and smashed all eight of his fingertips at once, slamming the drum back on the wheel. It was a hundret times worst than running his toe into the root after Florida died, the only time in Train's life something hurt too bad to make any noise. He started to, but nothing come out.

Train staggered out of the barn, breathless, his eyes blind with tears, and walked bent over to the street and waited for the bus. He sucked on his fingers; he made his hands into fists. Everything he did hurt him worse. It was a confusion of pain. He felt his pulse in his fingertips, and his pulse in his head too, only faster, pounding like it was trying to keep up. The bus came and he could barely get the change out of his pocket for the ride.

Back at the gym, he turned off the lights and rolled up into a ball, his hands between his legs. Plural came up the stairs later, drunk and in the company of a woman a yard wide, and the first thing he done was turn the lights back on.

"Lookit here, Lionel," he said, "I brung enough for us both." She laughed and lift him up off the floor, and Train rolled over and moved his fingertips under his armpits and held them there, tried to hold himself like that, see if it did any good. Nothing helped, though, and when Plural asked him what was wrong and he never answered, Plural had the girl put him down. He come over and unrolled Train like a shirt he was going to iron and saw his fingertips was swollen and red, except the nails, which was now turned purple.

Plural laughed and pulled him up off the mat and walked him to the sink. He laid Train's hands on the edge, the girl watching over his shoulder, and then opened his wallet and found a sewing needle—a sewing needle—and begun turning the point into the nail of the pinkie on Train's left hand. Train jumped at the pressure, but things already hurt as bad as they could, and a minute or two later he heard a little popping noise as the needle broke through, and then a line of blood squirted three inches in the air, and then relief.

The girl squealed and ast if she could do one herself.

Plural went through each nail like that, and one after another they squirted blood two or three inches in the air, and he felt better after each one.

The day had worn Train out, start to finish, and he went back to where they slept and crawled into the bottom shelf and fell asleep. He woke later in the night, Plural and the girl up there above him, both of them snoring, and saw the boards bending under their weight. He pulled his mat off the shelf and all the way into the ring and went to sleep in the shadows of the ropes, not wanting to be an accident victim twice in the same day.

He woke up again and the girl was gone. He sat up and checked his pants pocket; the money was still there. Plural slept with the windows open, and the place was never completely quiet, not even at four in the morning. Always something going on in the street, people yelling or drinking or fighting, horns—you could always hear horns somewhere.

An hour passed. Cars went by outside; then a siren wailed its way into the city. When it was gone too, he looked over at the window screen, and it was covered with a thousand moths.

CHAPTER 13

BEVERLY HILLS

She watched Packard park and walk through the back door into the kitchen. He took off his coat and his shoes and got a Pabst Blue Ribbon out of the icebox. He dropped into a chair and closed his eyes and rested his head against the back. She came into the room and sat next to him, not knowing what to tell him first. He put his arm across her lap without looking up. They had been arguing earlier; she couldn't remember what it was about. His arm was uncomfortable and heavy.

"Somebody called today," she said. He opened his eyes, but nothing else moved. He didn't like her to answer the phone when he wasn't home. His feet were crossed at the ankle and there was a tiny hole in one of the socks. She knew they would be in the wastebasket tomorrow. "He wanted to talk about Alec. I didn't get his name."

She saw his feet tense. They mentioned Alec only when there wasn't some way to avoid it. Packard was impatient with the past, her past and his. On the whole subject of things that were over, he was like a dog wanting to move on to the next scent, a dog who only knew there was something up ahead to put his nose into next. He took a long drink of his beer, then offered her the bottle. He thought for a minute and watched her drink.

"What did he say?"

She tried to remember the exact words. "That he wanted to verify what happened. He was with a newspaper. And he kept calling me Mrs. Rose." She finished what was left in the bottle.

"What newspaper?" he said.

"That was the funny part," she said. "Something called the *Darktown Standard*? It's supposed to be in Watts." He moved his arm off her lap and put it underneath her, and then stood up. He carried her upstairs, and up there, on the bed, she thought about the tiny thing inside her, bouncing off the walls as he drove it in and backed it out, again and again, and wondered, when it was over and things in there were quiet again, if it would imagine it had been in a storm.

"Nobody can verify what happened," he said later, indicating somehow that he included himself in that, and her.

CHAPTER 14

DARKTOWN

Plural was giving some rounds these days to a young white boy that was getting ready for a ten-rounder at the Olympic. The white boy's trainer had turned Plural around left-handed, paid him a dollar a round to move with him but not do nothing to take away his confidence. The boy was always late—come in sometimes at seven-thirty or eight o'clock, after all the regulars had left. The trainer looked like he gone bleed out the ears if he don't get into another business.

Train watched them night after night. Plural with his mouth all misshaped by whatever mouthpiece he found that night lying around the sink, letting the boy touch him now and then, but always turning with the punch, turning away just as it got there, like a door somebody opened from the other side just as you were going in. The boy had half a foot and twenty, twenty-five pounds on Plural and it frustrated him not to be able to hurt him.

Plural had the stumbles, of course—Train

watched him bend down to tie a shoelace one day and just stop cold, trying to remember how, and then it was like a child going through the steps one by one—but in the ring, with this young bull coming after him, trying to break him up, Plural was as natural as the breeze. He just moved where the dance took him, this way and that, and nothing ever hit him solid.

Ten o'clock at night, Train was just drifting away when Plural's head drop over the ledge like it was disconnected off his shoulders. He had a cigarette in his lips and a smile on his face. One of his eyes didn't move; the other one did.

Plural said, "That white boy's trainer, you know what he said? Said he give me three dollars a round tomorrow, I let the boy hit me."

"Three dollars a round?"

"He can't get no other work for that boy. Not turned around. Now he's worried about the boy's certitude, wants me to let him hit me." He finished what he said but stayed where he was, grinning, his head hanging over the ledge.

"You don't need that," Train said.

Plural chuckled and said, "Sometime that man forgot to pay me, and then I told him I might had to see about his chickens. . . ."

He could tell Plural couldn't quite remember now who the man was, and he was tired of all this talk about chickens. Sometime, it seem like Plural was turning back to his childhood.

"That's hard work for him to be forgetting to pay."

Plural chuckled at that too. "Ain't too hard," he said. "That boy come back in two years, then it's hard money indeed."

Indeed. He remembered old Florida working his totes.

Plural had a pull off the cigarette again and tapped the ashes into his hand, and then he ate them. He never used ashtrays in his life. "The first time I got a thousand dollars, Train, you know what I done? I took off my clothes and throwed the money on the bed and just rolt around in the bills."

It didn't surprise Train to hear that; Plural went wherever his thoughts took him. He remembered his own money.

"I put my feet in my socks sometimes—that's where I kept mine," Train said.

"Damn, how that felt?"

"Not too good."

"No," Plural said, "it don't, do it?"

Plural lay back on his mat, disappeared from view. A little later he said, "This white boy's trainer, he come up after the boy left today, said he pay me three dollars a round, I let him hit me some." A horn honked out of the street; someone yelled and glass broke, and then tires squealed off into the other sounds of the night.

"You don't need that," Train said. "You come with me Sunday, I'll give you more than that."

"Three dollars a round," he said. "That's good money."

Plural was a long time getting to sleep that night. Train always knew when he fell off, even if he wasn't snoring. He knew he was up there now with his eyes open, smiling, thinking of three dollars a round, all he got to do is let this white boy hit him.

Train woke up Plural Sunday morning with a crutch that been sitting in the corner with cobwebs as long as Train had been here. Plural been drinking Mogan David and eating White Castle hamburgers the past evening, and you didn't want to be the first thing standing in front of him on the morning after that. Train poked him ten, eleven times, and Plural's eyes suddenly opened, looked like you just took the lid off two cans of tomatoes. His head didn't move an inch; he just lie there staring with one live eye. Didn't recognize Train at all.

"Plural?"

No answer.

"You gone come along today?"

Plural got out of bed naked and picked up his box of Tide and walked without a word across the floor to the shower. He turned it on and got in before the water had time to turn warm—it was only a trickle anyway—and stayed in there a long time.

He came out wrapped in a towel, but he still had that wild red color in his eyeballs, and Train could see that he wasn't all there in the room yet. He sat down on the ring apron and began to put on his shoes and socks, which was the normal way he dressed himself, bottom to top.

Train left him to get into his pants and went to the diner on the corner for coffee and sweet rolls. Came back and Plural was still sitting where he was in his shoes and socks, nothing else on. Thinking. He drank the coffee straight down, scalding hot, and then ate four sweet rolls. All that time, he seemed to be looking hisself over, taking some kind of inventory. Trying to remember. Train stayed quiet, giving him room. And then, suddenly, he looked up and spoke.

"Who is this cat again?" he said.

"Name is Melrose English."

Plural thought for a minute and then nodded his head. "Yeah," he said, "I heard of him." And for all Train knew, maybe he had.

They took the bus to the golf course, and had to wait half an hour downtown to transfer. The bus companies been fussing at each other, and now they wouldn't honor each other's transfers no more. Thousands of people were paying fifty cent a day to get to work instead of twenty-five. Some of them had a riot one weekend and put a bus on fire. The governor asked Ike to send in the National Guard, and the president of one of the companies, a man named Appleby, had his picture in the paper with the soldiers, saying if these people had enough money to get drunk and set buses on fire, they had enough money to pay for their own transfers.

Plural had gone quiet again, and Train kept looking for some sign he had a finger in the pudding, but it never come. They got on the next bus and Plural went to sleep, the smell of alcohol sweating through his skin. Train looked at the way the man perspired, and reasoned that even if he wasn't right yet, he'd sweat all that confusion out of him by the time they were walking down the fairway.

Which might of happened, and might not. They got off the bus stop nearest Paradise Developments and Train collected some clubs from Whitey and loosened up, and then he walked to the practice green and putted. Plural sat down on a stone and threw crackers to the crows, laughing out loud at the ways they ganged up and stole from each other.

Melrose rolled into the parking lot ten minutes to eleven and let his white boy Peter take the clubs out of the trunk. He hit two or three putts to check the speed of the greens and pronounced himself ready. That was as much as he ever done before he played. Wanted everybody to know he beat you without half-trying.

Melrose and his boy Peter came over to the spot where Train was throwing up some soft lob shots like the ones he used to drop through the hoop back at Brookline, watched him a minute, dropping shot

254

after shot in the same place, and then shook his head. "You gone have to be better than that, man," he said.

Melrose's white boy stood behind him holding his bag, the strap tight against his chest, all the veins and the muscles popping out of his neck and his head, smiling like the muscle man at the circus when he held up two show girls and a pony. He said something of his own then, to Train.

"Ain't gone be like last time, boy."

And that was true enough. Hearing those words, Plural—who up to that moment had gave no indication that he even seen Melrose and his white boy arrive—Plural stood up, tossed the rest of the crackers to the crows, causing a riot, and then ambled across the putting green, walking about like you would to the refrigerator, and put Melrose's white boy to sleep before he could even raise his hands.

The white boy had his mouth half around the last half of the word *cocksucker* when it occurred. He was saying, "Well, look at this bandy-legged cocksucker—" and Plural caught him flush on the chin, and the white boy never saw it at all. He was still holding the bag, and it hit the ground first, making a noise that scattered the crows, and then the white boy crashed down on top of it, and while Train was trying to lucidate what he just saw—while there was still a part of his brain arguing that he didn't seen what he just did—Plural hit Melrose with the same hand, and the same tight little arc that just seem to uncoiled.

Melrose might of been trying to say something too, and Train distinctly saw his jaw slide out from under his face. It all happened in one second, maybe less, and Train saw it and had the thought that even if he only had six rounds in him, Plural could do this for another eighteen minutes before he got tired.

Plural stood over them a moment, studying his work, and then turned to Train with that peaceful expression he got when he thought things was all out of his hands. He said, "Sometime it happen."

A small crowd gatherered, and Whitey came running out of the double-wide, her stomach jiggling under her shirt, and a minute later Mr. Cooper came out, too, looked horrified to have Melrose and his white boy lying on the ground bleeding. Train stood there not knowing what to do with his hands, Mr. Cooper's ambassador of goodwill and integrated housing.

"Dear Christ," Mr. Cooper said.

Plural moved a step closer to Train and asked quietly if Mr. Cooper was the reverend.

Then Mr. Cooper got behind Melrose and tried to help him up, but it was too soon for that, and Melrose issued a short, horrible noise and grabbed his face with both hands, like he was trying to hold it together. Melrose's white boy got to his knees, try to put a good face on it, but he considered Plural again and sat back down where he was. Train seen an indentation in the grass where he fell on top of the bag.

"How did this happen?" Mr. Cooper said, and Train was relieved to see that he was talking to Whitey and not to him. Like it was up to her to sort this out. Train himself had no idea what set Plural off.

"It's just a misunderstanding," Whitey said, like she was begging somebody not to hurt her, "the kind of thing that happens on a golf course." She looked around then for help, and Train felt himself begin to nod like she was right.

"We all clear on it now," Plural said, sounding reasonable and calm. "We just come to a meeting of the minds."

Mr. Cooper turned on Train, careful not to look at Plural. He had white shit in the corners of his mouth. "You're suspended," he said.

Melrose sat up slowly, hung his arms over his knees. A line of blood drooled out one side of his mouth and dropped between his feet. Mr. Cooper said, "Sir, should we call an ambulance?" And then, when Melrose don't move to answer, he looked over the scene, like he was taking in the whole Grand Canyon at once, and said, "Thank Christ susan wasn't here."

"A-men to that," Plural said.

CHAPTER 15

DARKTOWN

Hollingsworth was late for his meeting with the Reverend Willie Green, who was a political man too. They carried the same angry message to the people, but somehow the people preferred to hear it from the reverend, would walk across the street to talk to him, to touch him, sometimes to give him money, but nobody ever went out of his way to touch Hollingsworth. In that way he was shunned.

He worried at times that someone had somehow found out how he'd been burned, about the grease fire on his ship. Or that they'd known all along it wasn't the Klan. He was a cook and they gave him a Purple Heart. He'd never been in Indiana in his life.

He was on the bed in his underwear, with his arms crossed, while his wife ironed his white shirt and trousers—it made her nervous to be watched when she worked, and this was the best he could do right now to punish her—and the clothes were still warm when he put them on. "You want something to eat?" she said.

He walked past her out the door and was pleased to notice that she trembled. He went into the bathroom to comb his hair, and that was when he heard some fool banging on the screen door. A man banging like that was probably selling insurance by the week.

He walked down the stairs in his stocking feet, the banging still banging, and then stopped when he saw a white man standing on the other side.

"What is it?" he said.

The white man was well dressed, as well dressed as the Reverend Green, and unlike the reverend, he looked like he was hard under his coat. There was a Cadillac parked behind him on the curb. "This is the *Standard*?" he said, looking around.

"You've got the wrong place," Hollingsworth said.

The white man looked at him, up and down. Something disrespectful about his manner, like this was all part of some joke. Hollingsworth trembled in anger at the man's disrespect.

"No, this is it," the man said.

"What do you want?" Hollingsworth said. He walked closer to the screen door, and then opened it. He didn't know why. He and the white man stood a yard apart.

"I want to talk to the man who called my wife," the man said.

Hollingsworth felt a sudden fear; the words came

out of the man with an ordinary, experienced quality. He knew this was the kind of man who would hurt you.

"You think you can come around here and scare me?" he said, raising his voice, thinking somebody would be listening. That this might be a chapter in the story later. "After what white people have done to me"—and now he indicated his face, his arms, his hands—"you think I'm afraid of you?"

The man looked in all the places Hollingsworth indicated with that same insolent expression. "My name is Miller Packard," he said. "My wife was formerly married to Alec Rose, and I don't believe either one of us have had the pleasure of your acquaintance." He looked at the man's skin more closely and said, "She doesn't even smoke." And then he moved a step closer again, so close that Hollingsworth could smell the soap on his skin.

"If you have any questions about that," he said, "you come see me." And then he looked behind Hollingsworth and smiled. Hollingsworth's wife was standing at the bottom of the stairs. "I hope I didn't disturb you, ma'am," he said, and then he turned and walked back to the Cadillac.

When the man was almost at the car, Hollingsworth called out. "You think I'm afraid of you?" he said. He felt his wife's hand on his arm, and that pushed him further on. "After all you people have already done? You think I'm afraid of you *now*?"

CHAPTER 16

DARKTOWN

Monday night, the trainer brought his boy to Sugars Gym, and Plural went five rounds with him for three dollars a round, letting the boy hit him on the button a few times to build his confidence. After they took off their cups and gloves, the kid come over to Plural and said, "You don't want no more, pop?"

Plural smiled at the white boy and spoke to the trainer, "That's fifteen dollars, Collie."

The kid looked at the trainer; fifteen dollars. Then he followed him into a corner of the room and asked in a loud voice why they were paying this old coon three dollars a round, money that came out of his purse. The trainer told him to shut up and do his bag work and be there on time tomorrow.

Train watched the white boy slide his hands into the bag gloves, noticed the size of his wrists, saw how the bag jumped when he set himself and hit it, and even though he didn't understand yet much of what went on in a boxing ring, he knew this boy

261

wasn't somebody you wanted to hit you in the head for any three dollars a round.

The kid did five rounds on the bag and then got into his jacket to leave. "You sure, pops?" he said to Plural. "I got a couple more rounds in me if you got something coming up and need the work." But Plural didn't care what the boy said. He had fifteen dollars in his pocket for fifteen minutes' work, and he always liked getting paid.

The next morning, Train went out for coffee and sweet rolls and found a *Mirror News* lying outside the store. Plural was lumped up a bit, and he picked up the paper and then set it right back down.

Train looked over at the paper to see what it was. The Rosenbergs had been executed in Sing Sing, went to the electric chair for giving away the bomb plans. Him first and then her. They sung to each other the night before from their cells and then it was two thousand volts, and she took it five times before it killed her. The body was too hot to touch, the paper said, and they had to let her cool down before they could got her out of the chair. A witness said it smelled like bacon frying.

Plural got up and sat in the window that looked out over the street, eating a roll. Train wondered if he had a relation on death row himself.

Plural gave the white boy another four rounds that afternoon, and afterwards, coming out of the shower, he walked into a water pipe. The white boy was still in the gym, hitting the heavy bag, and saw it happen. He stopped—but then he was always stopping, looking for some reason not to do the work—and smiled down at his hands. "Collie," he said, loud because the trainer was over by the shower, "you got to get me some new meat. I fucked this one up."

There was younger fighters around, and they all laughed at that. Collie didn't laugh, though. He turned red, and for a little while Train thought he might come over and take a swing at the boy himself.

"Do the work, all right?" he said finally. "After you done something, then you can talk about who you fucked up." Then he turned around and walked out of the gym, talking to himself like he was both sides of an argument. "You see what I mean, you stupid fuck?" he said. "You see what I mean? And this ain't nothing. You wait awhile and then you see some real problems."

Plural sat down on the toilet, which was in the corner next to the shower, and stared at the floor between his feet, and after the blond boy finally left, he stood up, turned around, and vomited, then made his way back to the corner of the room and lay down. Didn't seemed to notice that he never got paid. "Well," he said, "sometime it happen."

Suddenly, everybody was talking to themself.

Then Plural went still, not looking at nothing, a dead man's stare, and that scared Train, until it was all he could do to stand up. Recalled to him how it felt when he was in the kitchen, Mayflower told him it was jail or the road.

"Plural?"

Plural chuckled, which was his reaction when things went bad or good; it was his reaction to the spin of the earth. *Sometime it happen.*

"What's wrong?" he said. Plural moved his head in Train's direction and paused there a long time, trying to find him. Train wondered what he was gone do with him now. How it got to be him that had to do it.

"It happened before," he said. "Everybody just look like an angel, all slow motion and soft, with a black hole in the middle. Like when you get caught in the side of your head with somethin' you don't see, only your head don't clear." And he chuckled at that too. "And then later on, the hole just grow bigger."

Hearing him talk about angels, Train saw how it fit together if Plural died. The loss and the relief at the same time. That was one of the troubles with the connections he got: He was always thinking of things he never wanted to think about in the first place. "What kind of angel?" he said.

Plural shook his head. "I don't know, man. Like a cloud or something, and a empty hole in the middle. Nothing in it but the color black."

A few minutes passed. It was hot outside and the smell of sewage from the street floated up into the room. Train said, "This was the same thing that happened to the other eye too?"

Plural pulled the skin below his eyeball down so Train could look for himself. He chuckled again.

The next morning, Train had to put the coffee cup in Plural's hand. Plural played like nothing was wrong, but Train could tell from the way he held his head when he looked up that he was having trouble finding him.

"Maybe if you went to the hospital, they can fix you up," Train said. He was never in the hospital himself. He watched Plural set the coffee down next to his foot, where he could find it again, and then he picked up the sack of rolls in his lap and ate one like nothing was wrong.

"What hospital is that?" he said.

"Wadsworth, down on Wilshire."

Plural seemed to thought that was comical. Everything struck him humorous. "The vet hospital?" he said. "Man, you look acrost the street, you know what you see? The vet cemetery. They wheel you in the front, and out the side, and stamped you *Return to sender*. And the nurses in there, they as soon to touch you as bad pork. That's how welcome you are."

"You fought in the war," Train said.

"Yes I did," he said. "Yes I did."

The blond boy and his trainer came up late that afternoon for some light work. The fight was that weekend, so the sparring was over. Plural sat in a chair over by the windows in the sun, his face held up into it. The trainer saw that he wasn't right

265

and gave him the fifteen dollars he owed from last time, and then saw his boy staring at Plural too, sitting there by the window in a block of sun and a thousand specks of floating dust, and tried to hurry him out.

It was too late for that, though. Once somebody saw what they saw, you can't just erase it off the board.

CHAPTER 17

BEVERLY HILLS

She told him she'd missed her period, and for a little while she didn't think he'd heard her. Then he looked up from the paper—he was reading a story about the Rosenbergs' execution. She'd read it herself earlier; they had two sons.

"It's stress," he said.

"It doesn't feel like stress."

"Whatever it is, we can take care of it."

"What does that mean?" she said. *"We can take care of it?"*

"It means that whatever you want to do, we can do it. You don't have to go to Mexico. I have the name of somebody here in Beverly Hills. If that's what you want to do."

"You want to kill it?" she said.

"No, just whatever you decide to do about it is fine with me," he said.

She stared at him, and he saw that was the wrong answer.

He'd only had her a little while and wanted her to himself. He looked at her, wishing he could start the conversation over. He would tell her later on to think of it as a story, with two different people.

CHAPTER 18

DARKTOWN

Train waited out his suspension, counting the days until he could go back to work. He went for coffee and rolls in the morning, usually found a newspaper somebody had left behind and read the sports section out loud to Plural while they ate. There was a story on Monday about the blond boy freezing up in the ring, said that the manager had put this kid in too deep too fast.

"You can't blame nobody for that boy," Plural said. "Sometime they is only so much you can do."

Two or three times a week, Train rode the bus out past Paradise Developments, looking out the window to see who was on the tractor, if they were cutting the grass too close for this time of year, if the course was getting enough water. It looked worse every time he went by—spots on the greens, everything turning brown and bare. Mr. Cooper had the bulldozers clearing lots along two more fairways, looked like pulled teeth. There was dandelions in the fairways, trash cans by the tee boxes that wasn't been emptied, and whoever been running the tractor had gone right over a flower bed on number one.

After he rode past the course, he sometimes caught an afternoon movie downtown, lost himself for a while in a story. He was always worried about Plural back at the gym, though, and some of the time he begun to think about Plural so much, he got up and left the show early. He was afraid of having him there by himself after everybody took off.

Once in awhile, usually when something recalled it in the movies, he found himself thinking about the big-money skins game with Melrose English, how all that money looked on the table, the excitement to have people cared who he was. He wanted that again, but he was tied to Plural now, and couldn't even think about nothing like that in the future without thinking how Plural fit in too.

Sunday night, Plural put "Twenty Questions" on the radio. He never missed "Twenty Questions," even had Train send in an entry for him on a postcard once, trying to win *The Book of Knowledge* if he stumped the panel. He was sitting with the radio over by the window, where the reception was best, hoping tonight was the night.

The panel was from New York, and sometimes Train could hardly understand what they said. He loved the ladies' voices, though; he imagined touching those soft throats while they sang. He heard somewhere that all the ladies in New York were singers; they called them "nightingales."

The show moved along, and so far they didn't used Plural's idea, and it seemed like they'd used everything else: Jack Benny's violin, the bluegrass of Kentucky, and the eggs of a duckbill platypus. Plural had sent in "Dale Evans' saddle." He sometimes reminisced how he like to come home to Dale, get one of those big lipstick kisses and sit down to dinner. Said he didn't care if she ate with her hands.

Plural had ran the pencil off the page when he printed his entry on the postcard—"Dale Evans sadil"—and Train had to fix it before he sent it in. He had to read it back to him, too, twice. Plural seem to loved the sound of the words—*Dale Evans' saddle*. He sniffed the air like there was beef in the oven.

Plural enjoyed the show best when the panel got stumped, and when they guessed Ben Franklin's pipe on their eighteenth question, he blew a little air through his nose in disgust and said it ain't that hard to guess a pipe.

The show ended and the moderator signed off and Plural looked in the general direction of New York and said, "What the fuck is a moderator, Train?" and then listened carefully to everything Train knew about that, like he might be thinking of a new career.

★   ★   ★

Train had a stab of worry time to time about what to do with Plural when he went back to work. He was getting around a little better—he could find the toilet by himself, and the shower—but anything out of the familiar on the floor could trip him, and that seem to mixed him up about where he was. When he lost his place like that, he could walk right through the window. There was something else too. He'd got the idea in his head again that people owed him money, kept saying that he might have to go outside and steal somebody's poultry. Train wisht Plural would talk about stealing something else.

Train went downstairs one afternoon to see Mr. Sugars and told him that Plural wasn't seeing good, and asked if somebody could check in on him from time to time, make sure he wasn't mixed-up. That he had to go back to work. Mr. Sugars was sitting at his table, wearing a visor like in the movies, counting dimes and quarters and putting them into paper rolls. A coin-operated man.

"He can't see?" Mr. Sugars said.

"Not good."

Mr. Sugars kept counting coins, didn't want to lose his place. He wasn't a person that had an easy time counting. "You know," he said, "when No-Tank come in here, I told him I don't mind helping out an old fighter, as long as there ain't no complications. And now he gone blind? I can't have complications like that. I could be liable."

He mulled it around his head while he counted

271

his money and kept coming back to the same spot. "There was a girl stayed up to the gym for a week a few years ago," he said, "a loose kind of girl off the street that smelled like Kool-Aid, and she made up a new language when she fucked.

"Afterwards, though, getting that chick out the door was like flushing a tomcat down the toilet. I still got the marks to remind me. And the lesson I learned from her was that in business you have to be heartless."

And then he told Train that he and Plural better find a new place to stay.

CHAPTER 19

BEVERLY HILLS

She was sick in the morning again. She hadn't brought it back up with Packard, though. Lately, even more than before, he seemed to sense when she wanted to tell him something important and held her off.

She sat down on the edge of the bathtub now—it felt ice-cold—her fingers covering her lips, waiting to see if the nausea had passed. There was a window on the far wall cracked open, and she heard a car door slam outside.

The nausea passed—she realized she was hungry, and that was the signal it was gone for the morning. A moment later, she was starving. Steak and eggs, she thought, and a dish of sherbet at the same time. She ate everything these days with sherbet. It wasn't just the sweetness mingled with the other taste of meat; it was the cold with the hot. She felt a new wetness in the corner of her mouth and, wiping at it with the back of her hand, realized she was starting to drool.

She stood up and washed her face. She was

brushing her teeth when she heard truck brakes outside. A minute later, she thought she heard people talking. The kind of low hum you hear walking into a church before a funeral. No specific words, just the sound of talk.

She rinsed her mouth and went downstairs and into the dining room. There was a floor-to-ceiling window there that looked out over the long yard to the road. And she saw a yellow bus parked against the curb in front of the house, with the words *First Baptist Church Bible School* stencilled along the side. She stood still and counted the people on the sidewalk—there were thirteen of them, all Negroes, some of them carrying signs—and she went straight to the kitchen and tried to call Packard. He didn't pick up the phone, though. A secretary asked if there was a message.

She hung up and sat at the kitchen table and listened to them outside, furious with Packard.

The police came in about half an hour—there were half a dozen calls in ten minutes—and dispersed the crowd. She'd watched from the kitchen as the Negroes got back in their bus, all except a thin older man who had skin that reminded her of peeling paint, and who sat down in the middle of the street and refused to move until he was handcuffed and arrested.

The bus went off down the street, pouring black smoke, Negroes hanging out the windows, the driver blowing the horn as it went.

Packard arrived half an hour later. He came up

the walk to the house with a happy, expectant look on his face, and it reminded her somehow of the way the husband in the movies always looked when the little woman told him she was knocked up.

The police took Hollingsworth into an interrogation room. They did not have any questions for him, though. One of them closed the door, and the other one—the one who had thrown him into the car—began slapping his face. Just that, no nightstick, no hose, just his open hand.

Unaccountably, Hollingsworth felt himself shaking, and then beginning to cry. "There were witnesses," he said, and he heard the panic in his own voice and realized he was not meant for this. Realized he was meant to stay behind his typewriter. "There were a dozen witnesses who saw me, saw there wasn't a mark on me."

That stopped the policeman for a minute. He looked Hollingsworth up and down, then glanced at his partner, who was still standing at the door. "I don't know how to tell you this, Remus," he said, "but you're already so fucked-up looking, there's nothing we could do that anybody would notice at all."

And then he slapped him again, not too hard, just making his point.

CHAPTER 20

PARADISE DEVELOPMENTS

The day Train come back to work was a Tuesday, a month after the suspension. Mr. Cooper was at his desk, worrying over some letters he was reading. There was two small windows in the room. One held the air conditioner, which had leaked a puddle of water on the floor, and the other one looked out over the course, where the trees was now the color of dirt, and there was fungus on half the greens. The spots had got so big they bled into each other, sucked the color out of the grass. Everything you saw outside was dead and dying.

Mr. Cooper took his time getting around to Train, like this business about the suspension was the sixth or seventh thing on his mind. And maybe it was. Train had some other things on his mind too, mostly how to tell him about Plural, that somehow he had to bring him along to work.

Mr. Cooper stubbed out his cigarette, closed his book suddenly, blowing the ashes out of the ashtray, and then he leaned forward and lit a fresh one. The smoke seem to crawl up his nose. He sized Train up awhile, like he couldn't make up his mind, and then finally he said, "I just want to make sure we're all on the same page. From now on, you report to Whitey everywhere you go. I want her to know where you are. You understand?"

Train just been standing there waiting, looking out the window, thinking how Mr. Cooper had got into this business without knowing nothing about the way things grew, or probably nothing about building houses either. He just naturally went from one thing to another in the assumption that a man that could kill roaches could do anything else, and this is where it ended up. All the time Train spent out on the course, and it all come to nothing. Less than nothing, because things had died that were alive and kicking when he first came.

Mr. Cooper turned in his seat and looked out the little window—which was a long time since it was washed—over the first fairway, and the bulldozers smoothing over some lots in the distance. A little noise come out of his mouth now and then that sounded like he was sucking his thumb. "First those two boys hack each other to death," he said, "and then you." Train heard that he was being scolded. It seemed out of place somehow. Mr. Cooper swung back around suddenly and turned dead serious, like Gary Cooper strapping on the guns.

"Tell me something," he said. "Is it in the blood? After this business with the other two boys, you seemed like the other side of the coin. The truth is, my friend, I thought you might be running the course for me someday, and then this. What happened? Does something just call you people back?"

"The suspension run out. That's what called me back."

Mr. Cooper looked at Train first like he was disappointed, like he thought there was some discussion Train might wanted to hold about "Is it in the blood?" Train held still, and presently Mr. Cooper seem to ran out of air.

"This kind of thing could ruin us," he said.

Train nodded like he agreed with that, just like he cared.

"Maybe it's a blessing in disguise," he said, "a kind of message. Maybe what we need out here is some sort of screening committee, to assure buyers that we're only taking the right kind of people."

The next morning, Wednesday, Train stepped off the bus at the corner and then turned around and led Plural off by his hand. He'd been leading him around enough by now that touching each other's hands seem an ordinary-enough thing. Both of them was still stinging clean from the shave and shower, dressed in fresh clothes. They walked up the street, and Mr. Cooper's car was already in the parking lot, and on the way in they went past two signs that said wagering was strictly prohibited.

By now, Train decided not to say nothing about

278

Plural to Mr. Cooper or Whitey neither. He just decided to hire him on his own.

None of the machinery in the barn was took care of during the suspension. The John Deere was almost three quarts low on oil, and the blades of the mowers was so dull, they couldn't tossed a salad. Probably shake you out of the seat pulling them around. He gave Plural a broom, started him at the back of the barn, and then spent an hour on the tractor; added oil to the crankcase and sharpened the blades, and then rode it out of the barn into the sun.

He turned off the mower reel and drove the course backward, starting at eighteen and going to number one, noticing uneven patches of grass in the fairway looked like somebody been grazing cattle. Clover everywhere.

The dust from the lots Mr. Cooper was clearing blew in the air and was on the leaves of all the plants. Someone thrown a bag of garbage over the fence on number seventeen that nobody cleaned up, and there was a deer carcass laying by the pond on the sixteenth tee. Must have been out there a week; the coyotes and birds had took everything but the spine and the feet and the skull. Half a foot of scum covered the pond itself. Train stopped the tractor to take in how bad it was, and in the sudden quiet he heard the bulldozers in the distance, clearing more lots for Mr. Cooper's development.

Gophers had took over the whole fairway on

number ten, but Train decided to fix that later, put off killing them until everything else was done. He stopped the tractor again to look at a dried-out camellia, dead to the roots.

All that work for nothing. When he finished looking around, he went up to the office without even washing off the dust to tell Mr. Cooper what he had to do to get things back in shape. Mr. Cooper's door was closed, though, and as Train got closer, he heard Whitey inside, telling Mr. Cooper there was storm clouds on the horizon and trouble waiting to happen.

It made him suddenly timid, to realize that she was trying to push him out the door. He wondered how it get to that this time.

He went back to work. Plural and him come every morning at six, and in spite of what Mr. Cooper said, he didn't wait around for Whitey to tell him what to do. She didn't arrived until seven-thirty or eight anyway, about the time the bulldozers fired up for the day.

The rest of the crew—all except Lester—didn't see the point to starting till she yelled at them to move. By then, Train was long gone and Plural was usually walking the perimeter of the the barn with his broom, talking to himself, sweeping. He worked slowly, stopped dead as a bug whenever he ran into anything unfamiliar—boxes and bags or attachments to the equipment, all the things people hadn't put away the night before—and then moved it to the side or found his way around.

Train paid him Friday out of his own pocket, half of what he made himself. Plural always liked getting paid. Never did nothing with his money though but save it, and once a week go out for Mogan David and White Castle hamburgers. As the black spot took his eyesight away, he ruminated on things more, sometime went all day without saying a word to the rest of the crew, not even to Train at lunch. When he did say something, it usually only meant that he come to a place in his thoughts where he saw something about the way things fit together. He'd chuckle and shake his head and say, "Well, nigger, sometime it happen."

More and more, though, whole days passed without a report from the dark regions. Then one afternoon, laying out in the shade of the barn after they ate, Plural suddenly picked up his head and said, "Uh-oh, now. Look out."

Train had been watching vultures circling in the sky half a mile south, wondering what had died out there now. Plural was laughing at something. He said, "A woman about to get flammable on you, man."

"What woman?"

Train sat up, the pine needles and specks of dirt dropping off the back of his head and sifting down his back, and a moment later she appeared on the path coming down from the double-wide, her shirt tucked into her cowboy belt, her stomach jiggling

281

like it always did. She walked like she was holding a wheelbarrow—little jerky steps, like it was pulling her down the hill. It came to Train that Plural must of heard her before she even come out of the double-wide, that he must of known from how she was walking that she was mad. He wondered if the blind could hear things that nobody else did. He heard of that someplace before. She stopped, standing right over him, damp, trying to catch her breath. She liked to stand over you when she talked.

"Miss Whitey," Plural said.

She shook her head. Didn't like having him around, and made that plain. "We're taking down the big oak Monday," she said to Train.

"What oak is that?"

"The big one, on the edge of fifteen."

"That tree ain't bothering nobody."

"It's obscuring the view from the lots," she said.

"The view," the blind man said. "You got to have a view."

Train did not think it was a good idea, having Plural doing the talking.

He sat still, which was the only thing he could do. When she reported it to Mr. Cooper, anything he said was going to sound like he was arguing. So, because she was waiting for him to say something back, he said, "Which lots?" even though he already knew what lots she meant; the foundations had been laid on the hill over there and the framing was already going up. They was supposed to be the first houses completed on the back nine.

"I ain't got time to stand around talking about it," she said. "This is straight from Mr. Cooper. He wants that tree down Monday; there's investors coming in later in the week to look at the property."

"Miss Whitey, I don't know how to take a tree like that down," Train said.

"I never said that, did I? To take it down. Mr. Cooper's hired somebody for that. We're just going to clean up afterwards. That's what I came down here to tell you, to plan on it for Monday."

The tree cutters showed up four days late in a prewar Chevy pickup with the words TREES STIRGEONS hand-painted on the sides. Train went out to watch; thought it couldn't hurt to learn how a person was supposed to take down a tree. It look like the first step was, you sat for a while in the shade of the tree itself and passed around some reefer.

The Mexicans laughed and coughed and talked, and lit each other up, and Train saw that like everything else he did, Mr. Cooper had hired them on the cheap, and Train knew that last month the Trees Stirgeons was probably housepainters or electricians. The Mexicans just decided they like the way some occupation look, and the next thing you knew, that's what they were. When you seen a dentist sign in their neighborhoods on the other side of the bridges, that meant a Mexican with a pair of pliers.

Half an hour passed, and Whitey showed up in the company truck and stared at them awhile, but the Mexicans was immune to that and hardly seemed to notice her standing there with her arms folded across her chest. She might as well been staring down the tree. She went over to them finally, a hundred keys jingling from her belt, to ask if they ever planned to take down the damn tree. She was one of them people that never gave up a key.

It turned out, though, that none of them understood her kind of English. They just smiled and offered her a toke. She got back in the company truck, slammed the door, and went to find Mr. Cooper.

Another half hour passed, and one of the Mexicans—the smallest one, he look like about thirteen years old—threw a thick rope from the back of the truck over his shoulder and shinnied halfway up the oak, looking down more and more often the higher he got, laughing with the ones left on the ground, and then tied it off as soon as the tree was narrowed enough to get the rope around it.

While he was descenting the tree trunk, the other two fastened the end of the rope to the truck bumper and then pulled it taut—it didn't especially look like anybody planned out how to do this before the little one monkeyed up the tree—and then the three of them took turns on a two-man saw that got stuck more and more often as they worked deeper into the wood. When that happened, whatever Mexican who was not on the saw picked up another, smaller saw and angled in from above until the two-man saw could be wedged loose. Then they all traded places and started over again. It was hard work, and they took off their shirts and sweated and took breaks to smoke another joint every few minutes.

Then they stopped for lunch, looked like they might be a third of the way through, and Train went back to the barn to check on Plural and to look for the poison. Whitey been after him to kill the gophers ever since he said he'd do that last—once she saw something he didn't like to do, that's what she wanted him to do right now—and he was in the barn, hunting for it, when the tree fell.

The noise gathered and rolled and broke like a storm, and by the time he got back out there, the tree was laying one side of the fairway to the other, bits of splintered limbs scattered all over hell, and there was huge ruts in the ground where the branches had hit and broke off. A jagged spike, six foot high, was sticking up out of the stump like somebody broke the last tooth in their mouth.

The Mexicans was in the bed of the pickup, celebrating. The trunk of the tree had fell no more than a yard from the trunk, the rope still attached, and the Mexicans was half-hidden by the limbs and leaves. The one that had went up the tree looked over at Train and smiled, the beginning of a soft mustache over his lip.

Mr. Cooper and Whitey arrived a few minutes later. The Mexican who seem to be in charge stood up in the truck bed and greeted Mr. Cooper like lost family, held out his hands as if Mr. Cooper might have missed there was a tree laying across the fairway and half across his truck. "*Veinte y cinco, señor,*" he said.

"My ass," Mr. Cooper said. "Look at this fucking mess."

"Yes, *señor,*" the smiling Mexican said, "thees fucking mess." And they all smiled, proud as a marching band. Then the Mexican said "*Veinte y cinco,*" again, politely, and offered to shake hands. Mr. Cooper turned away from him and spoke to Whitey.

"Get them off the property," he said, "and then get this cleaned up." He looked up the hill at the lots along the fairway, the house frames going up, probably trying to picture how the fallen tree would look from there. The man was nervous now, as if he suddenly come to realize that his time was almost up.

Whitey saw it too, and she turned on the Mexicans. "Get out of here," she said, looking up into the truck. "Vamoose, *hasta luego* . . ."

The Mexicans checked with each other to see

if anybody understood what this was about. "Vamoose," she said, "shoo . . ."

"*Veinte y cinco, señorita*," said the one who had smiled. Who wasn't smiling now.

"No *veinte y cinco*," she said, pointing at the tree. "You fucked it up."

The Mexicans shrugged, wondering what did she expect tree cutters to do. Like it was none of their business now. Meantime, Mr. Cooper walked across the fairway to the far end of the tree to look at it from there. He got himself in a line between the tree and the lots up on the hill and studied it from there. "Good Christ," he said. "How long is this going to take?"

"I'll get on it right away," Whitey said.

The Mexicans were now worried about getting paid. Train sat on the tractor, staring at the tree. It looked bigger laying down than it did standing up, and heavier. It had dented the roof of the Mexicans' truck and tore off the gas cap. It looked like the ceiling was about a foot shorter inside the cab.

Train noticed that Mr. Cooper had gave up on Whitey now and was looking around in his direction for help.

"That friend of yours," Mr. Cooper said, "can he saw?"

"You never know," Train said, "he might." He imagined Plural in the tangle of branches—strange new shapes all around him, closing him in—and was not necessarily sure about putting a saw in his hands.

"He's built for it," Mr. Cooper said. "He looks like he could saw forever."

It took them two days—Train, Plural, and Lester—to cut the branches off the tree and then cut the trunk into pieces that they could tow off with the tractor. Another whole day to drag off the big branches and then rake up the pieces of wood scattered all over the fairway.

The three Mexicans was there every day, sitting in their dented truck, smoking joints, watching the claim jumpers. Waiting for their money. Mr. Cooper saw them whenever he come down to check on the cleanup, and once Train heard him say to Whitey that he handled these people before, that if you waited them out, they'd forget about what they were doing out here and leave. Train knew better, though. Mexicans were the best waiters in the world, and eventually Mr. Cooper would have to pay up or call the police.

Mr. Cooper been putting off paying Plural too. The money was drying up. Plural been on the saw two days, twelve hours a day, baking in the sun, cut up most of the tree by himself. He had insect bites and cuts and blisters everywhere you look. All Mr. Cooper said about settling up was that he'd put something extra in Train's paycheck that Friday for his friend. Train seen the way things was going around Paradise Developments, though, and guessed it wouldn't be but a dollar or two. Then Friday came and went, and there wasn't nothing extra in his paycheck at all.

Plural knew when he was being cheated, but kept it to himself.

Monday morning, here come Whitey down early to tell Train the Mexicans had left too much stump, that Mr. Cooper wanted it took down level with the grass. Mr. Cooper had postponed the investors twice already, and now they were supposed to come in Friday, and he wanted everything just right.

Plural smiled at the sound of that, then made a sound of his own, like he just sat down for Sunday dinner. She turned on him and said for his information she was conducting business here with Train, and certainly not with him. Plural just kept smiling and shook his head.

"That man done confused me with his tools," he said.

"What's he saying now?" she said.

Train said, "He ain't gone take down the stump."

"Tell him to," she said. "Tell him Mr. Cooper and me been putting up with this blind business all along, and now he's got to do something useful for us."

"Tell her the man forgot to pay me," Plural said to Train. Sound like he was making fun of Whitey, but you could never be sure of exactly what his intentions was. "Been forgettin' for the whole time I been out here, lettin' you take care of it for him, got me confused with his tools."

She looked at Train, who had no idea how Plural figured that out.

"A man do me like that, I ain't taking down his stump," Plural said, talking to her now. "More politely, he better stay up to watch his chickens."

"Well, how much do you want?" Whitey said. "Just to take down the stump—how much do you want me to say that you want?"

Plural thought it over, seemed to be adding and subtracting in his head. "Six hundred dollars," he said.

The next morning, Whitey drove down to the barn in the pickup and told Train to fill one of the big cans with gasoline and put it in the back. They rode out to the fifteenth and she parked near the stump. It was eight feet wide, two feet high all the way around, except at the spike. "Mr. Cooper decided to burn it down," she said.

It seemed reckless to Train, lighting up a stump with gasoline. She saw the look on his face. "No arguments," she said. "We don't have time to explain every damn thing we tell you to do."

The Mexicans were back again, sitting in their truck, watching. Train got out and lifted the gas can over the tailgate. Whitey lit a cigarette and stayed where she was. The Mexicans sat up when they saw the gas. Whitey crossed her forearms on the open window and leaned out, her chin resting on her wrist. Looking younger and something like a woman.

Train carried the gas to the stump and set it down. He thought of how this all looked a few days ago, what it would come to after it was burnt. It seemed ignorant to be part of it, like he somehow stepped into the middle of a golfing joke. *And then the nigger pours gas all over the tree. . . .*

"How long you think it might take to get this done?" Whitey said from the truck. He unscrewed the cap and gave himself another minute, not wanting anything to do with it, and then he turned the ten gallon can upside down and walked around the stump twice, watching the gas soak into the ground. Some of it leaked onto his hands, cold and dry. He could see fumes in the air, and then heard Whitey start the truck, and when he turned, she was backing away to a safer distance. "Light it," she said from the window. "We got other things to do today."

Train took matches from his front pocket, lit one, and tossed it onto the stump. There was a noise like shaking out a rug, and then smoke and heat, but he couldn't see the flame itself; in the sunlight, he could not see the flame.

★   ★   ★

The fire burned all day and all night, and there was still smoke coming out of the stump the next morning. Mr. Cooper come down to see for himself that the job was done right. "Once that's gone out," he said to Train, "I want you to pull out the stump with the tractor."

The fire didn't go out, though. Not that day or the next. On Thursday morning, the smoke was still coming up, and on Friday, the fourth day, Mr. Cooper told Whitey to have Train run a hose in from the irrigation system and soak it down.

Train did what he was told, but the smoke was there again on Saturday. And Sunday and Monday. By then, you could smell it all over the course. Mr. Cooper put off his investors again, and meantime, the bulldozers stopped levelling out ten staked lots along number seventeen. Five on the course, five across the road. The name of the road was Bobby Jones Drive.

Train took the John Deere out to the stump, but it was like trying to pull a tooth with your fingers. When he reported back to Whitey, she threw a pencil into the wall and yelled, "Do I have to do everything around here myself? I can't stand this anymore." She'd be wetting herself next.

He thought he might wait till she was feeling steadier to tell her that early in the morning he'd seen smoke laying on the ground a hundred yards farther up the fairway, near the green. Then he thought he might just as well let her find that out for herself. He'd got off the tractor and put his hands flat on the ground and felt the heat. Somehow they'd caught the earth itself on fire.

Mr. Cooper got on one of the dozers off seventeen, drove it down Bobby Jones Drive and then over the drainage ditch to get to the stump. He put the blade down, and the stump and ten feet of thick roots rolled out underneath it.

The stump come out black and smoking, a huge ball of roots and dirt and tentacles. Left enough hole to bury a pony. Mr. Cooper got off the dozer, seemed like he just won an argument, but then he stood in the smoke at the edge of the hole a long time, just staring down into hell. He heard the Mexicans talking to each other in the cab of their truck.

Whitey got out of the truck they come down in and walked over and stood awhile with him. "Whose idea was this?" he said finally.

She looked around, scratching at her fanny. Not going to answer that one for anything.

It turned out to be the last they saw of the Mexicans, though. It turned out one way to get them to leave was to set the ground on fire under their truck.

Two weeks passed and the fire spread. There was smoke all over the back nine, and Train found one of the snappers—one of the huge old ones—dead over by the pond on number five. When Train lifted it up the shell broke in two. The old investors

293

backed out, and Mr. Cooper begun to bring in new ones, had different ones out three Fridays in a row, but they all seen developers before, and knew what they looked like going broke.

Meanwhile, Mr. Cooper quit talking to Whitey, walked past her like she wasn't there. And she quit talking to Train. Then he saw her sitting in the cab of her truck one afternoon, smoking a cigarette, crying. It never occurred to him until that moment that such a thing was possible.

CHAPTER 21

BEVERLY HILLS

She was in the pool every morning that week, and twice Mrs. Moffit had walked out into the yard next door, seen her there, and walked right back into her house. Once it seemed funny, the next time she almost cried. Both of those things made her want to eat. And that's how it was all the time. Her moods blew in from six directions a day, independent of outside events. She was happier and sadder than she'd been in a long time.

Packard noticed the change, and began taking her to lunch, showing up early in the afternoon two or three days a week, taking her each time to a new restaurant and watching her eat, transfixed at the piles of food she was putting into her mouth.

After lunch sometimes they would make love, and he was so tender, but he never asked if she had been back to the doctor. It was one more thing he didn't want to talk about, and because of that, in some way, she didn't want to talk about it either. It seemed like too much work and maneuvering even to bring it up.

They had just pulled into the driveway Wednesday afternoon—she was stuffed with Chinese food, craving sherbet—and another car, a white-and-pink four-holer Buick, pulled in right behind them. Packard stopped his car, looked in the mirror a moment, then got out.

A woman got out of the Buick, and one way or another, everything she had on matched her shoes. Her breasts were pointy and ridiculous, like somebody had thrown a sheet over a gun turret. She hurried up the driveway to Packard, holding out her hand. "Dixie Finnity," she said. "I've just been sitting over there, admiring your house," and she indicated the other side of the street.

The woman held on to Packard's hand a second too long, and then squinted across the hood of the car into the front seat and smiled at Norah, too. "You have a lovely home," she said. You couldn't tell who she was talking to.

"I'm sure you do too," Packard said, and she stumbled a moment over that.

"I wonder if I could have a little of your time this afternoon," she said. "I have something to show you that I believe you'll be very interested in seeing." Then she winked at Packard, as if she'd forgotten Norah was there.

"She winked at me," Packard said. Norah opened her door and got out, feeling heavy and tired.

The woman patted his hand. "Oh, you," she said, and then winked at Norah too.

Norah saw that Packard was smiling back at the woman now, curious where this would go. She took a step closer, looking at her more closely, and the closer you got, the more you saw, and none of it could be good news in the mirror. She was pitiful in a way, but not in a way that Norah pitied.

They walked to the house. Packard held the door for the woman, and then gave Norah a shiver before they followed her in. The woman went into the living room and turned in a small, girlish circle, taking it all in at once. She made a noise that seemed to go with the circle she'd just turned, and covered her mouth with her hand. The place was just too much for her.

"My goodness," she said, a vaguely southern accent now, "this is spectacular. Even better than from the outside. It's just spectacular. I can see why they want it so badly."

Packard went to a chair and sat down. The woman did not know what to make of that, and turned to Norah. "You have a lovely home," she said again.

"Thank you," Norah said. "Would you like some sherbet?"

The woman began to say yes—thinking she was offering coffee—then heard the question and stopped. She patted her stomach, pulling her blouse tight against her chest. "I'd love some, but I just can't," she said, and had another quick look at Packard, her hand still holding the blouse tight. He sat where he was, smiling in that not quite finished way he had of smiling. He looked at the business card she'd given him, and then read it out loud. "'Dixie Finnity, Exclusive Properties.'"

"May I sit down?" she said.

"Certainly," he said, but did not indicate a spot.

She took a seat on the davenport, in front of the coffee table. Trying to look confident, which was probably important in real estate. She tugged at her skirt, trying to get it to cover more of her legs. Norah went into the kitchen, got a quart container of sherbet out of the freezer, and picked up a spoon off the counter. She went back into the living room and sat cross-legged on the floor, and ate out of the carton.

"Well, you're wondering who I am," the woman said.

"No," he said, "this happens all the time."

She couldn't get started. "To get right to the point," she said, "but first let me assure you this is really quite unusual, almost unprecedented, but I have a client who would like to make you a cash offer on your property." Packard dropped her business card on the table in front of him, leaned back farther into his chair and closed his eyes. A moment passed. She waited for him to open his eyes. It seemed like he might be napping.

She turned to Norah then. "Now, before you say anything," she said, "let me just add that my agency is not in the habit of making blind offers for properties that are not on the market. As I said, I realize this is unusual, but the offer is extremely generous, and that was the only reason I agreed to represent the parties."

"Somebody wants to buy the house," Packard said without opening his eyes.

"Exactly."

"Who?"

She winked again at Norah and leaned forward, as if this were a secret. "I'll bet you mean how much," she said.

Packard didn't answer. She looked through her purse, which was about a yard deep, and finally found a notepad and a pen. She opened the pad and wrote "$500,000" in large numerals across the page, and then underlined it twice. Hearing the sounds of a figure being underlined, Packard opened his eyes to see what it was. Then he turned to look at Norah.

"Half a million," he said. "Are places around here going for half a million these days?"

"I don't think so," she said.

He turned back to the real estate woman. "Who wants to buy it?" There were no houses in this part of Beverly Hills selling for half a million dollars. Some of the mansions where the movie stars lived might be worth that, or more, but this was not a mansion. Five bedrooms, four baths, the pool, a guest house. A beautiful house, but not a mansion.

"This is the most unusual part of all," the woman said. "The buyers, for now at least, wish to remain anonymous."

Norah pulled the spoon slowly out of her mouth, upside down. The woman looked fondly at the figure she had written on the pad.

"This is a very generous offer," the woman said. "Unheard of, really . . ."

Packard sat looking at her, stared until her thumbnail went to her mouth, checking for food or lipstick on her front teeth.

"Of course, it's always possible they might go a little higher," the woman said. "They love the house."

Packard looked at Norah again and said, "I don't think we could consider any offer without knowing who was making it. It could be Mickey Cohen."

"Oh no," the woman said. "Nothing like that. These are excellent people. Excellent people, really."

"The neighborhood has very high standards," he said.

The woman began to nod. "The buyers are very well acquainted with the area. It wouldn't be a problem, I can assure you of that."

Packard seemed to think it over, then shook his head. "No, we couldn't do it. Not without knowing who it was. We owe it to our neighbors." He let the room go silent for a moment and then said, "Unless, you know, you told us and it could stay right here in this room, just between the three of us." And he left that hanging. He seemed good at this, and Norah wondered if it was something he did at work to make people confess.

The woman was still smiling, but she couldn't make up her mind. For a long time she didn't answer, and then, finally, she leaned forward and said, "Cross your heart?"

After the woman left, Norah and Packard sat in the living room while Norah finished the sherbet. She was puzzled at his expression. "What are you thinking?" she said.

"Our neighbors are trying to get rid of us," he said.

"And?"

"I don't know. I was sort of thinking of going outside and fucking you on the front lawn."

CHAPTER 22

PARADISE DEVELOPMENTS

Friday night, Mr. Cooper come in sweating and out of breath, announced they had a mistake at the bank with the payroll. That they have to wait for their envelopes until Monday, when they straightened it out. Mr. Cooper was wearing a green suit, looked like something his mother bought, expecting him to grow into it. His wife was waiting outside in the car for him to take her to the big art opening.

Train looked out the window and saw her sitting in the front seat with the door open, fanning herself with one hand, smoking with the other. Blowing the smoke up and away from her face. It was still hot outside, and he guessed she was trying not to sweat. She looked up once and seemed to find him in the window. She held on point a moment and then looked away, annoyed. Nervous about her show, he thought.

CHAPTER 23

HOLLYWOOD

The opening was on Sunset, where all the galleries were, a photography exhibit called "Men Working," by a young artist who did not use a last name. susan.

All the big galleries, in fact, were on the same block of buildings, and all of them, as far as Packard could tell, were operated by people who owned only black clothes. Packard drove her to the exhibit in the Jaguar, which they'd just gotten back from the body shop, quiet all the way there. He didn't like these things, didn't like the people.

The centerpiece of the show was a sequence of photographs, two Negroes hacking each other to death with farm implements. Fourteen pictures in all, hanging from the ceiling, beginning in a barn of some kind and then leading up a weedy path as the men died in stages, the camera registering their looks of shock as they realized what was happening, how far it had gone, and then the other kind of shock, as they bled out, and even then they kept after each other with their tools.

The first twelve photographs were framed in black and of slightly different sizes and led, as you walked through the gallery's main room, to the last two—of the bodies—which hung in identical frames, side by side at the end of the room. Beneath them stood the photographer herself.

She had packed herself into a small black dress and was standing inside a circle of admirers, pale makeup and a stab of red lipstick. Pretty in a doughy way, faintly Asian eyes. Remarkable, the men said. The pictures were remarkable. The place was smoky; everyone was smoking something. Patrons and art dealers and poets and beatniks. An older man seemed to be there with the photographer, but she was ignoring him and turned away whenever he moved in her direction. Ashamed of him, it looked like.

Norah watched the photographer choose and flirt, touching a man's hand, another man's sleeve, touching herself. She had known women like this one all her life, had grown up with women like this, who were careless in familiar ways, and she knew that sooner or later the carelessness, or what was beneath it, would begin to show, and the photographer would not look very young or pretty anymore.

For the moment, though, it was her world. The exhibit was already famous; the critics had fought it out in all the art publications, bitterly, personally, poisonously, until in the end it couldn't have been more entertaining if they'd hacked each other to pieces with farm tools too.

Norah looked quickly at the first two photographs—in one, there was flesh open to the bone—and could not look at the rest. She felt them hanging near her in the air, though, and then, without knowing exactly why, she was sick in the way she had been back on the boat. Packard, she noticed, was not affected. He walked into this art gallery as he walked into all art galleries, the way she imagined he would walk into a hospital room—the kind of visitor who begins inventing errands to run as soon as he arrives.

He went past the pictures without any particular reaction, and then ducked into a smaller, less crowded room, where they had set up a bar. He had been to half a dozen of these things now, and could instinctively find the liquor. She went outside and took a pill and smoked a cigarette, calming herself down, and waited. Sorry she'd come, wanting to leave. Half an hour passed, and he did not come out.

She found him still in the smaller room, standing in front of a photograph of a young Negro with a child's face and an erection, who was sitting barefoot on a tractor. The boy had been posed with his legs in an awkward, unnatural position to show his feet, and there was something patient in his expression, as if the posing were only one indignity among a hundred, another imposition.

Packard was drinking punch, very pleased with

something in the picture. Or perhaps pleased with himself.

She looked at the picture again. The boy had a beautiful face, a face that would have been beautiful on a woman too.

There were other photographs in the room, portraits of Negroes taken in the same barn where the blood was spilled first, but they were all unremarkable, one-note and careless, as if the men in them didn't mean anything at all. She began to reach for Packard's arm, to ask him what it was about the boy on the tractor, but he turned away as she moved her hand, not seeing her, and walked back into the main room of the exhibit. Happier than he'd been all night.

She looked once more at the picture and then followed him back in. There was no way to know what Packard was thinking.

The photographer was still standing where she had been before, smoke and admirers all around. She was smoking herself now, the hand with the cigarette bent at the wrist, as if she were reaching out the door to check for rain, the elbow beneath it resting against her side. Remarkable, they were saying. She had a remarkable eye. Some of the admirers were as old as the man the photographer had come with. Norah saw that he was distracted, sitting off to the side on a folding chair with a piece of cake on one part of his lap and a glass of punch between his knees. He'd seemed to have forgotten where he was and was saying something, apparently talking to himself.

The photographer checked her reflection in the window and was smoothing her dress over her rump when she suddenly found herself staring up into Miller Packard's face. She smiled as if this were more like it, as if he were just what she'd been looking for—and maybe he was; she made no secret of it that she was out looking— and gave him a certain encouragement over her shoulder. Packard stepped more in front of her and smiled his two-thirds smile until she was uneasy, and she excused herself and moved slightly away. He moved with her, though, keeping himself right there in front.

She was beginning to wonder now who he was. He did not carry himself like a patron of the arts, and some of the men moved to get out of his way. He did not belong here; the photographer saw that.

"May I help you?" she said. Letting him know she was annoyed.

"I hope so," he said. There was a long pause. "The thing is, I'd like to know where you got these pictures."

She looked at him a moment, blinked, as if she didn't understand. "Excuse me?" He did not repeat the question, though, but continued to stare in a way that was entirely inappropriate in an art gallery. She looked around for help, but no one stepped up to defend her. She hiked her dress a little in front and faced him down. She probably thought she was good at that, facing down the bullies.

"Oh, I see. You're rude," she said, and looked quickly down at his wedding ring. "Let me guess. You wife finds it exciting."

He kept grinning, and in spite of all her admirers and supporters in the gallery, she edged farther away.

"I just want to know where you got the pictures," he said.

"What you see in the pictures is everywhere; that's the point," she said. There was the beginning of panic in her voice now.

Some of the men began talking to each other, or excused themselves to get a drink. A whole pocket of the room had gone quiet. "Just these," he said. "Just where you took these."

"In the first place," she said, speaking more to the men who had stayed than to him, "I don't take photographs; I make them." She was frightened, though, and couldn't keep it out of her voice.

"That's cool," somebody said. "That's cool."

"Did you make them do that?" he said, and pointed in the direction of the dead men on the wall. The photographer glanced again in the direction of the man who had brought her, but he was lost in his thoughts, his lips moving, his hands absently brushing cake crumbs off his pants.

"Has it occurred to you," she said, sounding like

308

it occurred to everyone, "that every time you define art, you diminish it?"

Norah saw the photographer was back on familiar footing. She could talk about art. "That every time you discuss a piece, it limits the connections?" And then, when Packard only continued to look at her in that way that made her want to cover herself up, she said, "Everything you need to know is right there in the photographs."

"Miss," he said, changing everything except the tone of his own voice, "there is nothing in these fucking pictures I need to know except where they were taken." She stared at him a moment, checking his clothes again, his shoes, his wedding ring, as if there might be some mistake, and then suddenly her face turned ugly and she began to cry.

The man set his cake dish on the floor and stood up. He moved to her slowly, excusing himself as he walked by Packard, and then held her as she wept, held her in a tired, mechanical way, as if he were still thinking about something else, or perhaps it was just that he was used to her weeping.

"He's ruining everything," she said into his coat.

The man looked at Packard, patting her on the back. "At the golf course," the man said, "Paradise Developments. It's out about three miles east of Griffith Park."

"That was nice," she said to him on the way home. Everything she had on felt too tight. She hadn't been embarrassed by what Packard had done as much as surprised. She was surprised he'd spoken to the photographer at all. She reminded herself that with Packard, you were never sure what was next.

He was running the engine hard through the gears—"driving happy," he called it. "This is perfect," he said, "perfect."

And she felt perfect herself for a few minutes and didn't ask what he meant.

CHAPTER 24

PARADISE DEVELOPMENTS

Monday morning, Mr. Cooper come in at nine o'clock with a twitch he develop sometime over the weekend. He assembled the staff in front of the barn, nervous as the Rosenbergs in the chair, and when they all collected in one place, he fired everybody, Whitey to Lester. Didn't said the word *fired*—he called it "laid off"—but they all knew what it was. Everybody but Lester, who thought Mr. Cooper wanted them all to laid down, and so he did.

The bank had cut off the funds, Mr. Cooper said, and there wasn't any funds to pay nobody until the loan was restructured, so the only fair thing to do was suspend operations. Then he also gave his word of honor that they would all get every penny they had coming, that he just needed a little time to work out the details. That was when even Lester knew they was shit out of luck.

Why this would happen to him, he said, after all the years he been a successful businessman, he

311

didn't know, and he scratched his head and looked around the place for an answer.

He said, "It's still the idea of a lifetime," but the way he said it, he knew whatever else it was, it was come and gone.

A hot, dry wind blowed in hard from the desert every afternoon for a week, and from what Train could tell, the fire beneath the ground seem to be following it west now, across the whole back nine and up into the lots themselves, where the bulldozers were parked.

The course was strangely sunlit that morning, and quiet—there was no carpenters pounding on the houses they been framing, and the bulldozers all gone quiet. Train guessed the last of Mr. Cooper's money had went out their exhaust.

And then, a few minutes after Mr. Cooper left, there was a noise, something as vulgar as the bulldozers themselfs. Most of the crew was trudging up toward the street by now, carrying their lunch pails, moving heavy, like they was climbing a ladder. Train and Plural hadn't left yet, and Train followed the noise around the barn and saw Whitey out back, leaning her weight with one hand against a tree, blowing breakfast. She looked up at him, red-eyed and evil and a line of drool hanging off her bottom lip, and Train thought, Even Jesus don't lay hands on that.

Plural, who ain't seen Whitey and could eat—

312

Train guessed there was some advantage to everything, even gone blind—Plural helped himself to a sandwich in the office, and they walked out to the street to catch a bus.

As they got to the gate, though, a Cadillac pulled to the curb and stopped. It stopped and they stopped too. It took Train a little while to remember the man's name was Mr. Packard, but he knew him as soon as he saw the car. The Mile Away Man.

Mr. Packard opened the door and got out, wearing a suit that shined like leaves in the late sunlight. He seemed relieved to found him. "Mr. Walk," he said. "Good to see you."

It surprised Train, but it didn't surprised him too much. In the same world where you burn down a stump and it sets the ground on fire, what could sneak up on you then?

"You remember me?" Mr. Packard said. Then he looked behind Train at Plural, who was carrying the box of Tide that he used for his personal hygiene. He got into the habit lately of showering under a hose here at Paradise Developments, where they had better water pressure than they'd had back at the gym.

"Who's this?" Mr. Packard said. Seemed so happy, Train was afraid the man gone hug them both.

"Who's you?" Plural said.

Mr. Packard liked that; he seem to like everything. "Nobody," he said.

"Us neither," Plural said. Mr. Packard held out his hand to shake, and Plural set down his bag without another word and bust him in the nose. It happened before Train could move a muscle to stop it. Train stood there remembering the gun the man had in his golf bag, which meant he got it under his coat now, but Mr. Packard just sat on the cement where Plural had put him, holding his knees, looking surprised, dripping blood onto his shirt and tie and over that smooth, shiny suit.

Presently Mr. Packard shook his head, clearing things up, the blood running out his nose into his teeth, some of it dropping off his chin—he cupped his hand beneath it, looked like he was trying to save what he could—and then he begun to hiccup. Once, twice, and then on and on. Train tried to think of a way out of this that did not end with him and Plural shot or in jail, but nothing came. The ground was on fire, they was unemployed and out of a place to stay and generally shit out of luck.

Mr. Packard hiccuped again, and then looked up from the ground, the blood coming almost black out of both sides of his nose, and Train seen he was laughing. Plural had already heard it in the sound of the hiccups, and the sound appealed to his nature, and he laughed a little himself.

Mr. Packard pointed at Plural and said, "He's blind, right?"

"Yessir," Train said. "He don't know what he's doing."

And that just pop Mr. Packard's toast. He leaned

his head back, trying to stop the bleeding, but it only seem to made it worse. Plural gave him his handkerchief. To Train's certain knowledge, that handkerchief had never been washed except inside the pants' pocket, and now Mr. Packard was pressing it into his face.

"A blind man," he said, "we should of sold tickets." He used the handkerchief to dab at his eyes, which were tearing—you couldn't say if it was the punch or just the man enjoying himself— and then moved it back to catch the blood. "This just gets better and better," he said.

"It do, don't it?" Plural said.

Mr. Packard held out his hand and then grabbed at his leg when Train helped him up on his feet, but regardless of that and his nose, it didn't seem to be any hard feelings.

Mr. Packard loaded them into his car, put Plural up front, where he could keep an eye on him, and drove to the police station. Train lowered himself in the seat a little when he saw where they were. In the parking lot, Mr. Packard climbed out of the car, then leaned back in and spoke to Train. "You two be all right out here a few minutes? I want to go in and see if they'll let me use the shower. I better change clothes before I go home. I don't want to upset Mrs. Packard. . . ."

"I could used a change myself," Plural said.

Mr. Packard looked him over and saw that he

had a point. "Why not?" he said. Then, to Train: "You too?"

"I believe I'll wait here," Train said.

Mr. Packard opened the trunk, took out some clothes, and then got Plural out of the front seat, and then the two of them went into the station, Plural carrying his box of Tide.

Train sat in the backseat of the Cadillac, scared to death, thinking that if it wasn't for leaving Plural behind, he could be on the way to Union Station right now, headed out of town.

They were a long time inside. Train stayed low in the seat, watching the police come and go. Sometimes they had a prisoner in handcuffs— Mexicans and colored mostly, some of them been tuned up on the way in.

Mr. Packard and Plural were gone thirty, forty minutes, and the longer they stayed inside, the more Train expected Mr. Packard would find out in there that he was a wanted man. Or that somebody would walk by and see him in the Caddy, and take him inside to straighten it out. People in that building were still looking for him; that much he knew.

A police car stopped, and two cops pulled a boy out of the backseat, had to pry him out, screaming and kicking and crying, might have been eleven years old. It took them both to carry him up the steps, one of them holding his feet.

Train remembered being taken through those doors himself. He'd tried to stop just before he went in—it seemed like he needed a little more time—and then somebody pushed him from behind, and the sounds of voices was coming at him from every direction. It was a clammy, cool place and all you heard was orders, and all the orders came too fast and piled up on each other as one noise bounced into the next. You went through the doors and found out how people went crazy—which he begun to understand wasn't what people thought. Everything didn't look upside down; you didn't get no glass of water and see a fish swimming around inside. It was more like you become pressurized until you blow a leak.

He watched the boy and felt a certain pity, but then, things happened when they did, and sometimes you could do something about it, and mostly you couldn't. He wondered what crime a boy that size did to be in so much trouble with the law in the first place. Train leaned back and closed his eyes, just trying to get out of the way of things and let time move them along, the way it does.

He heard them before he saw them, right next to the door. Plural was wearing a clean white shirt, a tie, and new pants. The pants was half a foot too long and cinched just under his chest with a belt, and the shirt was buttoned all the way to the collar. Mr. Packard was carrying the clothes they been wearing before. He had on pants of a lighter color than Plural's. He also washed the blood off and combed his hair. His nose was swole by now to where you couldn't exactly say it started somewhere and his forehead stopped. The swelling had moved under his eyes too, give his whole face a flat look, and colored the skin under his eyes.

Mr. Packard didn't seemed ashamed, though, to be walking around looking like pudding. He opened the door for Plural and took his arm to help him into the car, like they on the way to the big dance.

They drove all the way into Beverly Hills before Train could breathe in and out again without reminding himself to do it. Mr. Packard seemed not to lost the amusement of the situation while he was inside. He whistled along awhile; then he turned to Plural and asked him about a fight, like he was continuing on a subject they been talking about inside.

"So what were you thinking with this guy, then?" he said. "Climbing into the ring, I mean."

Plural puckered his lips and thought it over. "The first thing is," he said, "you always think, This can't be the motherfucker *I'm* fightin'. They got to made some mistake. He look as big as two of me."

Train was leaning into the door, his cheek against the window, listening to the hum of the tires. He could feel a little push of cool air somewhere, couldn't tell exactly where it was coming from. Plural talked a little longer about fighting at the Olympic and finding out he didn't have no tank, and then for a little while it was quiet.

"You ever do any building?" Mr. Packard asked, still talking to Plural.

"What kind of building you mean?"

"I don't know. Carpentry, electricity, plumbing, roofing. There's always things to do around a house. They don't take care of themselves."

"I don't touch electricity," Plural said. "I helped a man stole a roof once, but I don't touch electricity."

Stole a roof? Train sat up at that.

"Stole a roof?" Mr. Packard said, like he wondered why he hadn't tried that himself.

Plural shrugged. "A man puts it up, a man can take it down," he said, "although as it develop, I don't enjoy the height."

Mr. Packard drove them along the road awhile, turning here and there, and then he looked in the back, where Train was, and said, "Your man and I were talking about your current situation, and I told him I have a guest house nobody's using, and there isn't any reason you couldn't stay there. At least until you get on your feet. Except you'll probably want to fix the roof." He drove on a little longer and then said, "Maybe keep an eye on Mrs. Packard for me if she needs anything while I'm not at home."

He caught Train's eye in the mirror and said,

"She had a bad time of it the last few months. Lost her first husband."

Plural said, "I wonder does she know Digger Love."

"Who?" Mr. Packard said.

"A man in the funeral business," Plural said. "Out in Ohio. Sometime he put on boxing shows too."

"No," Mr. Packard said, "it was here. It happened here."

"All I know," Plural said, "that Digger, he gets around."

CHAPTER 25

BEVERLY HILLS

A small guest cottage sat just inside the iron gate, behind the garage. Weather-yellowed stucco with fingers of ivy growing all the way to the roof. The roof itself was bleached of its intended color, warped and cracked by the ivy, and leaked when it rained.

The cottage was divided into four rooms, and the floors listed to the south, as if it were sinking. The place had termites and spiders and a hornets' nest under the sink. Alec had intended to gut the whole thing and remodel, and they'd argued when she asked him to leave it alone. She was new to money then, and liked the way the place looked, liked the idea of an eyesore in the landscape.

She woke up, still half in a dream about throwing the good china at Packard. He was dodging and laughing. She lay still, trying to remember why she was throwing china, and then she heard a sound from the backyard, something breaking.

She rolled out of bed, feeling swollen, and looked out the window. A Negro on the roof of the cottage, holding a crowbar. Shirtless and smooth, a boy. She watched him for a few minutes from the window, not even wondering at first why he was there. He took the shingles off one at a time and dropped them down into the yard. They fell on top of one another with a clapping noise like a rifle. Sometimes they broke.

She suddenly saw it, what it was about—the Moffits. One way or another, he was always playing; he always had some kind of game going somewhere. It was his nature. He'd come home last night with both eyes discolored, his nose spread across his face. Neither one of them had said a word. That was a different kind of game—one she played with him—who would say something first.

Even so, it was strange that Packard would have the roof fixed without telling her ahead of time. He ordinarily kept a respectful distance from all the things that were here before he was.

She hadn't felt queasy yet and hoped her luck would hold. Perhaps the morning sickness was over. She was late in the third month, not really showing yet.

Little Otis, she thought, conceived in an elevator.

The boy dropped another shingle into the yard, and she noticed a second worker, an older, shirtless Negro, reclining on his elbows beside a wheelbarrow, the sun shining off the bunched muscles in his shoulders blades. He made no move to help the boy, and she thought he must be the boss.

Two Negroes in the yard, and she was alone. Three months pregnant. She was suddenly conscious of the breath going in and out of her body. Furious with Packard for putting her in this position, for not seeing how she would feel after what happened on the boat, for not even asking if she'd been to the doctor. He was either too much or too little, all the time.

The Negro on the ground turned slightly and seemed to follow something across the sky, his head rolling strangely, and she stepped quickly away from the window, hiding, holding still behind the screen, hoping, without knowing why it would matter, that he was the boy's father.

It seemed to her that she had seen the boy before, but decided it was probably only a resemblance to one of the defendants from Waycross. She couldn't say which one. She still had all their pictures somewhere, and it came to her suddenly that she hadn't looked at them in months. She did not wake up anymore outraged by injustice in the Deep South. These days, she did not think much about changing the world.

She moved closer to the window again and watched the boy work, the muscles under his skin. She put her hand on her stomach, as if she were holding the baby still, and watched. The man on the ground was nodding and seemed to be talking to himself, like the drug addicts you saw on the street in Venice. She wondered why Packard insisted on this, why he couldn't just let things go. She walked into the bathroom and put on a pair of shorts and a T-shirt and tennis shoes. She brushed her teeth and ran a comb through her hair and went downstairs and out the door and got the newspaper out of the bushes where the delivery kid had thrown it.

She saw them again from the kitchen window, transfixed for a moment by the strange, easy way the boy worked. The roof seemed to come off almost by itself; the work somehow went faster than he did. There was a steady clatter of shingles falling on one another in the grass. She scrambled four eggs and ate at the kitchen table. Scrambled eggs and most of a quart of orange sherbet, watching them, listening to the sounds through the open window.

The boy on the roof stood up, and she saw he was taller than she'd thought, and younger. The man on the ground was talking, and she was beginning to pick out a word here and there, not that any of it made sense. She thought he said that a chicken never knew who stole it.

She left her spoon balanced across the top of the sherbet container when she finished eating, and it fell onto the table. The man on the ground heard the noise and turned, and she was terrified—almost screamed—when she saw that he was blind.

She held still, trembling, afraid for the baby's own eyes.

The blind man turned away. She guessed the boy on the roof was about the age of the one who'd come on the boat with the mulatto. The news-papers—when she'd finally read the newspapers, forced herself to read them—had said that he was only seventeen. She'd been trying ever since to see if that changed what had happened.

She noticed the old ladder propped against the storm drain at the far end of the roof and wished she'd thrown it out when she went through the things in the garage. She was afraid, though, then and now, of what it would mean if she began cleaning Alec's things out of the house. She had not touched the clothes in his closet, the books and papers on the desk in his den, his paintings, the pictures of his parents. She'd only gone in his den once, and left right away, feeling like a thief.

The boy walked to the ladder—he seemed unaware of the pitch of the roof—and came down easily, facing the front, the way you come downstairs, trusting the rungs were there for his feet. He went to the hose, turned on the spigot, and cooled the back of his head and neck before he drank. The water beaded in his hair.

Packard came home in the middle of the afternoon, driving a flatbed truck with *Orange County School District* stencilled across the door. The truck didn't sound like it had a muffler. There were a dozen bundles of new roofing shingles in back, and several long, heavy-looking rolls of tar paper. He backed the truck into the driveway, past the house, where it could not be seen from the street. He was wearing an off-the-rack blue suit, one he usually only wore when he had to testify in court, when he wanted to look simpler, plainer than he was.

Which, of course, was another game, a different kind of game.

He got out of the truck, said something to the boy on the roof, and came into the house. Two minutes later, the shorts she'd put on were lying in the sink and she was on the kitchen table with him inside her. She turned her head while he did it, and, through the windows in the kitchen door, glimpsed the boy on the truck, handing down new shingles to the blind man, who stacked them carefully in the grass along the edge of the cement.

"Who are they?" she said later. Packard was sitting in his underwear, peeling a line through a beer label. The frying pan she'd used to scramble the eggs was still on the stove. His shoes were on the floor with the cheap blue suit. And outside, the boy was still moving shingles.

He looked up from the beer, thinking he'd explain it to her now, explain the beauty of it, and that she would see it too. When he looked, though, there was a lynch mob waiting on the other side of the table.

The last couple of months with her, it was full moon around here every other night. He tried a smile, but it hurt to move his face.

She watched him smile and stop. He tipped the chair back on two legs and reached into the refrigerator for another beer. "The boy's had some bad luck," he said finally. "The other one, I guess he's had some bad luck too."

"He can't see," she said, and he shrugged, as if that were what he meant. "You aren't going to let a blind man on the roof. . . ."

"No, don't worry about that," he said. "The boy watches out for him. He won't let him near a ladder."

"Who are they?" she said again.

"Roofers?" he said.

"Well, that's what we need all right," she said, "more roofers."

"There's always things that need to be done," he said. "The kid's very handy. . . ."

She waited, stared at him and waited.

"You want the whole story? He's just a kid who got into something that wasn't his fault," he said. He swallowed some of the beer and told her. "He was a caddy at Brookline."

She stood up, barefoot and naked below the T-shirt, and walked to the freezer and took out a glass, and then a fresh quart of sherbet. Then she went to the cabinet where they kept liquor and filled the glass halfway with vodka and added a scoop of sherbet, and then waited a minute for things to melt and killed it in four swallows. She sat back down at the table, feeling suddenly warm. She tasted the eggs and sherbet and vodka all at once. Not too bad, really.

"What was that?" he said.

"A float." Then she sighed, and felt herself giving

in. She wasn't sure to what. "Why do you have to do things like this?" she said.

"It isn't anything more than it is," he said, and she could see he was disappointed in her. "It doesn't have any meaning." It was quiet a moment, and then he said, "Look, nothing's permanent. If we don't like having them around after a week or two, say so and they're gone."

"You're moving them into the guest house, right?"

"The kid's got a way with plants, making things grow," he said. "There's a lot of things to be done around here."

She sat still, already sweating vodka. The boy was climbing the ladder back to the roof now, carrying a roll of tar paper over his shoulder. The ladder bowed under the weight, and she waited for it to break. He was fearless, though, and young, and took it for granted that it would be there under his feet. He was like Packard.

"Let's give it a couple of weeks," he said. Then he lifted his beer bottle and touched the edge of her juice glass and smiled. "To the Moffits."

She got up to take a shower then and there was a peeling noise as her bottom broke the seal with the seat of the chair.

The boy and the blind man left late in the afternoon with Packard, went back to wherever he'd found them, and were in the backyard again in the morning when she woke up. She stood behind the window again, just watching the boy. She was feeling safer today, and for a while she imagined the Moffits next door and saw that Packard was right: It *was* funny.

The boy tore off the last section of old shingles and then walked to the very peak of the roof and squatted, shading his eyes to study the job. He gave no more thought to falling than the birds did. The blind man sat beneath him on the grass, quiet today, not saying much.

She noticed a long, narrow bruise along the inside of her thigh—she guessed you couldn't be laid out and used on a kitchen table and not show some wear and tear—and the skin felt cool when she touched it. She went over again what he'd said when she told him she'd missed a period, the thing about Mexico. She thought of Pedro and his wife, still waiting for him down there somewhere, and she was afraid Packard would talk her into that, the way he talked her into everything else. He wanted her to himself.

It came to her now that from the very start, they had been giving each other permission to do anything.

She walked into the bathroom and turned on the shower. The drain was slow, and she watched the water cover her feet. She shaved her legs, nicking one of them below the knee, and the blood washed down over her ankle and into the water, turning pale and thinning from the line of the cut down, and then disappearing completely. She turned away to protect the cut from the spraying water and watched herself bleed.

A little later, when the bleeding slowed, she moved the razor to the other leg and deliberately cut herself again.

The blind man was missing a front tooth, and there was some suggestion in the way he moved that he hadn't been blind very long. That he wasn't used to not seeing. She found herself worrying about him, where he would go after this. She watched him in the yard; he seemed fascinated with the water hose, with the water itself. Sometimes when the sprinklers were on, he trapped one in his bare feet and stood over it in the yard, grinning, the water squirting up over his pants legs.

She thought that perhaps he and the boy had worked together before it happened, and took a narrow comfort in that. Allowed herself to believe somehow that made it easier for him now.

It took the boy three days to finish the roof, and the morning after that, he and the blind man moved in. They carried their belongings in grocery bags while the Moffits watched from the windows.

On that same day, the Moffits began to visit their backyard at odd hours of the evening. One or the other of them was always watching, although you could see Mr. Moffit was not paying much attention. Sometimes they sat out in the yard together, slapping at mosquitoes, reading magazines by the spotlights in their trees, or just feeding the fish or the flamingos, Mrs. Moffit glancing up at any sound, any movement from the other side of the fence.

To Packard, it was more fun than the circus.

He left the house open now when they went out to lunch, as if to prove he trusted them. He left money and keys on the table beside the pool when he swam.

She looked across the table at the restaurant now, and, with the swelling and the bruises under his eyes, his face was only vaguely familiar. It reminded her of her own face after the boat.

"Does it hurt?" she said. The first mention either of them had made of it.

He picked up his salad fork and poked himself gently under both eyes, then straight into the holes in his nose. He thought about it, looking for the answer, and then nodded his head. "Yes," he said.

She smiled at that without meaning to. "Something at work?" she said.

He shook his head no. "The blind guy?" he said. "I was teaching him to drive."

She looked at him more closely and he motioned to the waiter and asked for a clean fork.

"Certainly, sir," the waiter said. He'd been watching their table awhile with a certain familiar interest, but you couldn't say for sure which one of them he liked. "I apologize."

"Don't give it a thought," Packard said.

The waiter looked at Packard's eyes, then at Norah. "Perhaps it would be safer for you with spoons," he said, and Packard laughed out loud. He was smiling at her, happy, pleased with himself. She remembered the blind one standing in the yard with his foot over the sprinkler, the simple pleasure of that, and felt a sudden pang of conscience.

"You can't just use people like this," she said.

"Use them? I'm giving them a place to stay."

She could see she'd bothered him with that, though, maybe touched his conscience, too. "You know what I mean," she said.

"They need a place to stay," he said. "They were sleeping in a gym and the guy threw them out." He thought for a moment and then said, "Plus, I'm going to spend some time with the kid, working on his golf game. That kid could turn out to be a player."

"There's a lot of future for him in that," she said. But the truth was, there was as much future for a Negro in that as anything else.

"You know I'm going to keep the baby," she said.

"There's plenty of time to think it over," he said. "You don't have to decide anything right now."

"If you don't want babies," she said, "you shouldn't be fucking people in elevators."

CHAPTER 26

BEVERLY HILLS

It was the middle of the morning when he saw her. The old roof creaked under his feet and begun to smell of tar as it collected the sun's heat, and he could feel the sweat drops falling from his armpits to his ribs and then running down into his pants. It was just a glimpse—she come out to collect the paper and then hurried back inside—but she was beautiful and her hair was pulled back off her face, and what he remembered clearest afterwards was her ears. He never seen such delicate, perfect ears. (The ears Train was used to seeing in fact was Plural's, which were all gnarled and swollen, and it hurt him to lie on them at night, which was why he slept on his back.) Mrs. Packard's reminded Train of the seashells they sold off card tables along the Santa Monica Pier, pink and pearly down to where they narrowed into the dark, and beyond that was the hidden place where the thing itself had lived.

He tried to think what it might be like in there, but nothing came.

★   ★   ★

Three days later they moved in. Him and Plural.

Somebody had laid out sheets and pillows and blankets on the beds, but Plural said the floor was fine for him. "Folks got a place like this, they read the sheets," he said. "You don't know what might set them off."

Train hadn't slept in a bed or a room of his own since he left home, and he looked away from the bed, trying not to remember all that, because it had a way of leading back to the situation there in the kitchen. In spite of himself, it come to him anyway. He thought of the chair leg dropping on the floor, how it startled the dog. Until then, Lucky been peacefully asleep.

"Besides that," Plural said, "you lay in a feather bed, it come up around you, feels too familiar."

It took Plural awhile to get used to a new room, and until he was used to it, he talked in his sleep. Before when he dreamed, he just made that whinny noise.

"They didn't have to do her like that," he said that first night.

Train had just slipped off the edge, but he wasn't all the way gone yet. He sat up straight in bed. "Plural?"

"Little bitty thing like that, she wasn't but four, four and a half feet tall."

"Who's that, man?"

"Didn't have to do her like that at all." Getting louder now.

Train got up and touched his shoulder, being careful not to stand where he could be hit. "Plural," he said, "you talking in your sleep." The muscles jumped under Train's fingers and then Plural's eyes opened. Except for that he lay still.

"You talking in your sleep," Train said again.

"She didn't have nobody to save her," he said.

"Who?"

"Joan of Arc," he said. "Who you think we was talking about?"

Mr. Packard came out in the morning with ham sandwiches. "I hope the beds were all right," he said.

"No sir," Plural said, "we didn't bother them beds at all."

That stopped him a minute, but then he just continue on. "Well, if you need more blankets or pillows, Norah put some in the closet." He started to leave, then remembered about the paint, ast what color they wanted inside. Plural mulled that one over and said, "Salmon is always nice."

It turned out, though, that fresh paint gave Plural headaches and made his nose run, and he took to sleeping outside, and Train took his blanket and pillow out there too, to make sure Plural didn't talk in the night and walk into the house or the swimming pool. He didn't know if Plural could swim; it wasn't something that ever come up in conversation. Their conversations—the ones where they knew what each other was talking about—

tended more and more in the direction of poultry. That or the water pressure. Plural been in Watts and Darktown most of his life, never had water pressure all the time like they did here. He loved the water hose.

So they lay outdoors together at night, Train looking at the stars, Plural at whatever it was you saw when you was blind. The neighborhood was quiet, and a long way off you could hear cars and sometimes music. The swimming pool made noises, too, sounded like a human stomach, and from time to time the flamingos stirred in the neighbor's yard.

"You know," Plural said one night, "I never ate a duck."

Mr. Packard came home at two o'clock in the afternoon and looked over the inside of the house. He went into all the rooms that Train had painted, then spoke to Plural, who was sitting at the kitchen table, eating crackers and milk. "It looks good," he said.

Plural shrugged. "We like it," he said.

"You be all right for a while?" Mr. Packard said, looking around again. The truth was, he never was truly comfortable around Plural since he got hit, even now they knew who each other was. Always kept an avenue of escape. "I want to take Lionel out to Western Avenue." It had been two weeks now, and the bruises beneath his eyes had faded to yellows and browns, colors where he looked like he been sick rather than punched in the face.

"I been all right all my life," Plural said.

Train didn't know what Mr. Packard wanted with him at Western Avenue, but he seen all along that the man didn't just wake up one day and decided he needed a couple extra Negroes for houseguests. A thousand thoughts floated past, and then one of them stuck—that Mr. Packard had found out what happened to Mayflower—but then that floated downstream like the others. It was no point worrying over spilled milk. That was one Mayflower himself used to say.

Mr. Packard drove out to Inglewood using side streets. They passed into city limits and saw a sign: INGLEWOOD, A PROUD CAUCASIAN COMMUNITY.

Mr. Packard kept headed to the west, out toward the airport. In the distance, planes took off and come in, and Train tried to think what it would be like, being inside one of them, leaving Mother Earth.

Mr. Packard turned left two times, and a little later Train saw the golf course. He remembered he been out here one day a long time ago when he was looking for a job. Right after he moved into Sugars with Plural. It took him three buses and two and a half hours to get here, and when he told the man behind the counter he was hunting for work, the man leaned over his lunch plate to cover it, like Train just asked for half his sandwich.

They pulled into the parking lot and Mr. Packard stopped the car. It coughed a few times before it died. "All right," he said, "let's go see what we've got to work with." It seemed like a strange thing to be finding out now, after the man already moved him in.

Now that Paradise Developments was closed due to the ground being on fire, there was only two places left in Los Angeles where Negroes could play golf, Western Avenue and Griffith Park, and there was stories around about things had happened at Griffith Park. Colored people going off into the tree branches after their ball and end up hanging from one, or all beat-up and in the ER.

Everybody heard of those stories, and some of the white community *abhorred* them, had wrote letters to the paper how they abhorred them, which Train had read, and which he guessed must have been what Mr. Cooper had in mind when he come up with the idea for Paradise Developments.

The man had seen the future and it was harmony of the races.

The engine finally gave up and quit and Mr. Packard set the emergency brake and got out, and when he opened the trunk, Train saw there was two bags of clubs inside, one of them brand-new Tommy Armours. He picked up that bag and handed it to Train. Never said a word. Then he shut the trunk, leaving his own bag inside.

Train stood still, looking at the clubs. Until this moment, nobody had gave him anything in his life that somebody hadn't finished with it first. Even his dog was all broke-up when he got it.

He walked a little behind Mr. Packard, carrying the new clubs and looking at them at the same time. There was a certain excitement to it that went beyond the clubs themself. The last time he played golf, he gone home with nineteen hundred dollars, and a day hardly passed when he didn't think of what it was like seeing all that money at once.

They walked out to the driving range, and Mr. Packard left him there and went inside the office for some balls. When he come out, he found a comfortable spot on the ground and sat down to watch. Train tipped over a bucket of balls, the ones on top spilling over the ground, and he took the nine iron out of the bag, noticed he could see hisself in the shaft.

It was awkward at first, with Mr. Packard there, but then Train began to feel the weight of the club head in his hands, to feel where it was, and after that, the swing happened by itself, like it always had, like something he hid and then remembered where it was.

He changed to a longer club, but it didn't matter what he had in his hand now, 'cause it would swing itself. The balls came off the iron low and long, and he hit a half dozen on a line into the same spot in the bottom of the fence, a little over two hundred yards away.

He felt Mr. Packard stir behind him and he remembered he hadn't thanked him yet, didn't know what to say, and a minute later, thinking about that, he caught one of the balls thin and felt the sting all the way to his elbows.

"One thought," Mr. Packard said. "Focus on one thought."

Train heard that advice before, of course—all the twenty-six handicappers in the world was somewhere on a golf course right now, giving each other swing thoughts—but himself, he didn't think one thing at a time, and didn't know how. To start with, everything he saw had names—the ball, the grass, the club, his shoes—and he looked at those things and knew the names, and the names were thoughts. Just like being cold was a thought, and being hungry, and being worried. And besides the thing he was worried about, the worrying itself was a thought. Things came and went away; you couldn't stop it if you tried. He wondered if it was the same way for people that did the big thinking—Eisenhower and General MacArthur—or if somehow they could turn off the names while they was envisioned in a better world.

"What's your swing thought?" Mr. Packard said behind him. "What are you telling yourself over the ball?"

"I don't know," he said. "I just get out the way and let it go."

That seem to amuse Mr. Packard, and he leaned back on his elbows and shut up to watch. The thing that made it work right wasn't a thought anyway. It was whatever moved the ideas and thoughts along, the breeze that kept things circulating in and out of your head at a speed where nothing was hurried but nothing stayed so long you had to notice. That was all you wanted in your head to swing a golf club, a light breeze to empty things out.

Didn't mean you had to be stupid to play the game, but it didn't hurt.

A brittle old man and his wife come out of the office half an hour later, carrying balls and their clubs. She had smoke blue hair and more makeup than she was lying in a casket, and her hat matched her socks and her lipstick. The man walked ahead of her a little ways, not looking back. You could see it wasn't his idea, her taking up the game.

They went to a spot not too far from where Train was still hitting balls, and she bent over and picked a ball out of the basket, looking it over like she was shopping for apples, and then knelt down and took a long time to get it to stay on the tee, and then creaked coming back up. Train couldn't tell how old old people were—after about fifty, they all looked the same—but he could see these two were older than most. She stood still a moment, out of breath and getting herself back together, and then took one of the clubs out of her bag and swung. The ball stood where it was.

It was quiet a minute and then the husband started in. He corrected her grip; he flexed her old knees; he straightened her elbow and her back and lifted her chin. He told her to stick out her fanny and not to hit so much from the top. And then he told her to relax.

She set the club down on her bag, very dignified, opened her purse, and pulled out a cigarette. She lit it, staring at him, and then gasped at the smoke like she was surprised. There was a kiss of pink lipstick on the cigarette, and a tiny bit of the cigarette paper attached to her lip.

"What now?" he said.

"Relaxing," she said. "You told me to relax."

"If I'm not mistaken," he said, "I was not the one who thought this was such a wonderful goddamn idea in the first place." Mr. Packard was watching them now, smiling like a baby with gas. He couldn't help it; Train could see that. Made him smile himself.

"Why, of course not, Phillip. Of course not. It was all my idea." There was something in the tone that Packard just loved.

"I told you you wouldn't like the game," the man said. "It takes too much practice."

"We haven't played the game," she said. "So far, all I have done is attempt to hit a single ball, which has somehow provoked ten minutes of criticism of every aspect of my posture."

"What do you expect? You can't just go out on a golf course." She stared at him and her eyes narrowed. "You'd have people backed up behind you all the way to the parking lot. You have to be able to play the game to go out on the course."

"You're saying one has to be able to play the game to play the game," she said.

Mr. Packard covered his face.

"You have to be able to hit the ball somewhere," he said.

"How, pray tell, does one learn?" she said. The woman had a way of saying things; you had to gave her that.

"One listens by example," he said, and picked up her iron and swung it himself. He was an old man and had an old man's golf swing. He hit one ball, and then another and another, like he was punishing her. Train pictured him and three old men just like him out on the course, smoking their cigars, quarreling over the rules and quarter bets. Telling jokes about penalty strokes for killing wives with golf balls.

The old man looked up suddenly and noticed Train watching. He stared a moment, stepped away from the ball he was about to hit. A Negro staring at him while he was fighting with his wife— he looked to Mr. Packard, like he want him to do something about it, but then he seen Mr. Packard been staring at him too. Staring and laughing. The old man seem to hold his breath and then turned bluish.

"Fucking public courses," he said.

"Pardon me, Phillip?"

"Let's go," he said, and picked up his bag to leave.

She stood where she was. "Phillip," she said, "you are making a perfect ass of yourself."

"Are you coming?"

"We haven't played yet," she said. "I want to play."

The man headed off without another word. She crossed her arms and watched him go. He walked into the parking lot and disappeared, and she turned back to the bucket of balls on the ground, knelt, and set another one carefully on a tee.

All the way home, Mr. Packard was amused with the world at large. The old man had come back for her about ten minutes after he left, wild-eyed and wild-haired and deranged, looked like somebody was asleep when the house caught fire. The old woman hit about six balls by then, and she seen him coming too, stood there steely-eyed waiting for him, and for a moment Train thought she might brain him with the iron. In the end, though, she only picked up her clubs and followed him to the car.

Mr. Packard reached over and polished Train's head, and for a little while everything was more comfortable between them than it ever been before.

They stopped at a store on the way home, and went up and down the aisles, throwing things in the grocery cart. Crackers and cheese and mayonnaise for Plural. Mr. Packard had seen Train drinking grape Nehi back at Brookline, and he bought a crate full of that. He got canned spinach, Spam, devilled ham, potato chips, and baked beans. He bought a bag of carrots, a can opener.

Train looked in the cart, and it was the most food in there that he had seen in one place since he left home. Toilet paper, napkins, paper plates. They went down an aisle where they had the jelly and peanut butter, and Train remembered a night upstairs in the gym when he and Plural ate a jar of strawberry jelly for supper.

The people in the store stared at Train from behind and around from the ends of the aisles, wondering what he was doing in here, wondering what him and Mr. Packard were doing in here together. He heard a man say this to the woman with him: "Why don't they just take it back to Pershing Square?"

Train and Mr. Packard walked into the guest house that evening carrying four sacks of groceries. Mr. Packard set his on the kitchen sink, keeping his safe distance from Plural, and then went on over to visit the missus. That's what he said, "visit the missus." Seemed like he wanted to stay around there, but something was calling him home. Plural helped Train put the groceries away, touching the food all over, interested in the shapes of things, like a possum.

"What do he want?" he said later on, after they had ate.

"All he want so far is to go hit golf balls," Train said. "He just sit there and watch me hit golf balls."

"But what do he want?"

And it was quiet there in the little house, and then they heard the flamingos. One of them went off, and then they all did, and then they settled down, a little at a time, like every one of them had to get the last word. It was getting dark in the guest house, but Train saw him smile at the noise.

CHAPTER 27

BEVERLY HILLS

For as long as she had known Packard, he had come and gone at irregular hours, showing up at the house in the afternoon or morning, sometimes in the middle of the night. Sometimes not going to work for a week at a time. Now, he took the boy to the golf course at the same time every afternoon, and it was always just after dark when he brought him back. It unsettled her in some way, thinking of him on a schedule.

The blind man was alone in the guest house all afternoon, and rarely came out. He kept the doors and the windows open, and at five-thirty every night he turned on a radio and listened to "Sky King" and then "Sergeant Preston of the Yukon."

Afterwards, sometimes, after the radio went off, she heard him talking to himself about one of them or the other, about what they should have done.

Mr. Packard took Train to the store for golf shoes before they went out to hit balls. The shoe man

347

had him look through the fluoroscope to see how they fit. Showed the bones in his feet. Train put the shoes on when they got to Western Avenue, and then walked across the parking lot in them, feeling like he was on high heels. The shoes embarrassed him at first, but nobody else paid no attention. And when he thought about it later, it was no more out of place to see a colored boy in golf shoes than to see him playing golf at all.

Mr. Packard got balls from the office again, like he always did, and sat down to watch Train swing. The new shoes felt strange at first—his feet didn't slide in the grass the way they did in his tennis shoes—but once he got used to them, the swing begun to happen in a tighter space, and it felt more easy and natural to do than it did before.

Then on the way home, Mr. Packard said, "You seem to lay the club off at the top a little. That's the only thing I noticed." Train thought about that, couldn't see it at all. "At the top," Mr. Packard said. "Try not to lay it off at the top. . . ."

"What did the man want today?" Plural said.

They were outside, lying under the moon.

"Bought me spike shoes," he said. "Told me I was laying it off at the top."

Plural chuckled at that, but Train didn't know which part of it struck him funny.

The next time at the driving range, Mr. Packard pulled his own clubs out of the trunk and showed

Train what he meant. The boy tried it Mr. Packard's way, aiming the club shaft behind his shoulders at the flag, but thinking where the shaft was supposed to be, he couldn't get out of the way of the swing. He did it over and over, a hundred times at least, but it was always the same: Thinking one thing led to thinking about another, and once you got started in that direction, once you begin taking questions, then you couldn't do it anymore. You took a living thing apart to see how it worked, you killed it.

Mr. Packard watched from the grass for an hour and then stopped him, said to forget everything he said.

"What do you do all afternoon?" she said.

"Mostly, he hits balls and I watch."

"That's all?" She wanted to talk about the baby, but she didn't know how. Whenever she tried, he told her there was still time to think it over.

"It's something to see," Packard said. "I'm not sure I've ever seen anything like it."

CHAPTER 28

WESTERN AVENUE

It was the end of the week before Mr. Packard finally told him what he had in mind. They'd began going out on the course late in the afternoon, when they had the front nine all to themselves and Mr. Packard could drop a ball under a tree or in a divot for Train to hit and wasn't nobody behind them acting like they was passing kidney stones because they had to wait.

They came down a hill, where Mr. Packard spotted a snake hole in the fairway, a little over a hundred yards to the green, and he took a ball out of his pocket and set it on top. Set there about like ice cream on the cone. Train did not like snakes, never had. He looked at the flag and then at the ball and the pile of fresh dirt it was laying against and took the eight iron out of his bag instead of a wedge, and shortened his swing. The ball came out low and spinning, and stopped where it hit the green. Stopped dead.

Mr. Packard looked at that shot and said that he been playing the game most of his life, and there was nothing he knew about hitting a golf ball that the boy didn't already understand. Seemed to got sentimental over it too. "Ben Hogan couldn't hit that any better than you just did," he said.

The truth was, it never occurred to Train that anyone could. He never seen nobody personally that was close. He remembered he did see Ben Hogan once in a newsreel, laid out in the hospital after a car accident. The doctors pronounced he would never walk again, but this year he just gone out and won the Masters. It wasn't the first time Train heard of that—the doctors said somebody never walk again, and then they win a dance contest or walk across Death Valley. It seemed to Train that it might be the first thing that went through a doc's mind when they brought you in.

Train put his club back in the bag and they started toward the green, and on the way there, Mr. Packard mentioned he heard of a game in Milwaukee, a man there named Frankie Cassidy would play a two-thousand-dollar Nassau. Mr. Packard seem to know the man, but didn't say exactly how. He checked on Train to see if the money scart him off.

"Milwaukee?" Train said.

"Wisconsin, where they make all the dairy products. The man's famous in the Midwest, but he won't leave his own golf course. That tells you something right there."

Train shrugged. "Two-thousand-dollar Nassau," he said.

"It's his brother Happy's money, Happy Cassidy from Cicero? Just outside Chicago city limits?"

Train shook his head.

"He runs the Cassidy crime family. Little people with enormous heads, every one of them. And they've all been shot in the head, and they never die. They believe it's the luck of the Irish—they walk around thinking they were all born lucky— and it never occurred to any of them yet that if they were that fucking lucky, they wouldn't keep getting shot."

"I heard Chicago's a hard place to get paid," Train said. He heard that from Plural, in fact, who fought there once and said they put him up in a hotel on the South Side, had to open the windows and build a fire in the trash can because there wasn't no heat, and didn't feed him nothing but white bread the whole time he was in town.

"That isn't a problem," Mr. Packard said. "The brother with the money, Happy, the last time he was shot, it was in the spine, and now betting on his brother is all he does for fun. To keep on the sunny side of life. He didn't pay his bets, it wouldn't mean anything."

Mr. Packard was still watching Train, see if any of this bothered him. "So what about it?" he said.

"How we gone get there?"

"Airplane. You see the curvature of the earth and the stewardesses bring you anything you want."

Train felt the excitement and the let-down at the same time. He'd wanted to fly in an airplane for as long as he could remember, and he wanted to see the curvature of the earth as much as anybody else, but now it was right in his hand, he couldn't leave Plural that long to do it. How it happened, he didn't know. Somewhere along the way, he just picked him up—the longer you went, the more weight you carried, like a racehorse. That was a saying from Brookline too, said by the old men, and it seemed to Train that he was too young to fit into their sayings, but here Plural was, and there wasn't nobody else to watch him.

"I got to look after Plural," he said.

Mr. Packard shrugged. "It's only a couple of days. Leave next Thursday, be back Sunday or Monday. I'll have Mrs. Packard check in on him, if you want. He seems to know his way around the yard pretty well."

Train thought about Plural and Mrs. Packard in the backyard, maybe setting out by the pool, eating lunch off a silver tray. The only time he seen Plural in a social situation before was the night he brought that heavy girl up to the gym. What did he said? "Lookit here, Lionel, I bring enough for us both"? Train thought about that, about Plural and Mrs. Packard and the tea set—whatever that was—and he thought again about the airplane.

"And then what happen if I beat the man in Milwaukee?"

That seemed to make Mr. Packard more interested in going than he already was. "Then people like Happy Cassidy are going to be coming to us."

Train took a minute. "And everybody playing with somebody else's money. . . ."

"Yeah, that's usually the way it's done."

"And whose money I'm playing with?"

"Don't worry about that." Mr. Packard reached over and patted him on the back. In spite of the day he rubbed Train's head in the car, it was not usual for him to touch Train, and it fuddled them both.

"The thing to remember about money," Mr. Packard said a little later, "is when you get enough of it together in one place, it smells bad."

Train thought of the bags he'd toted, putting together the money that Mayflower had stole from his socks. All those pictures of George Washington with blue eyes. He remembered it smelled good to him.

There were two bedrooms in the guest house, but the night was warm again and they slept outside.

"What he said today?"

Train didn't want to talk to him. He wanted to think about money and the curvature of the earth.

"He wants to know about my thoughts," Train said.

"Oh shit."

"Yeah."

It was quiet again, and then: "What kinds of ideas you been having?"

"Nothing much," he said.

It was quiet awhile and then Plural said, "You

ever think about how you can't leave a bone outside your door, something come and eat it?"

"No, I never did," Train said. He had other things on his mind.

"The world is a hungry place, man." Plural thought about it awhile longer and then he said, "And whatever kind of thing you is, there's something out there that likes to eat it. It's natural. That's how the world keeps tidy."

Train couldn't say why, but that left him uneasy.

CHAPTER 29

BEVERLY HILLS

It was a good day again—it had been nothing but good days since she'd made up her mind about the baby—and then she'd cried twice just before dark without knowing why. Cried in the bathroom and then washed her face and felt better and went downstairs and cried again.

Packard pulled into the driveway after she'd finished, and she watched him and the boy get out and then separate, and he came toward the house, slowing down as he got to the back door, as if he were afraid to come inside. She caught her reflection in the kitchen window, and her face looked wide and white, like a peasant's. She wondered why he hadn't remarked on the change. If he would just ignore everything until the day the baby came out.

"I'm going away a few days next week," he said.

She felt herself panic, tried to hold it in. She didn't want him to see her panic. "You're leaving me alone with them?" she said.

He laughed at that the way he laughed. "You're not afraid of those two?"

"I just don't want to be left here alone."

"You ought to get to know them better," he said. "You'd like them."

"I like them enough already. I just don't want to be alone."

He was playing with the salt shaker now, spinning it on the table. "Well," he said, "as a matter of fact, I'm taking the kid with me, so you won't be here with them both."

"Why? Where are you going?"

"Milwaukee," he said. "To play golf. I think he's a player." He waited a minute, something there between them, and then he said, "And I told him maybe you'd check in on his friend."

CHAPTER 30

WISCONSIN

Wisconsin looked green from the air and green from the car and green when they got out of the car at the golf course. Train saw they had different grasses from L.A., and they left the rough deeper here.

He and Mr. Packard walked around the clubhouse, Train carrying his clubs, excited to see this man Frankie, looking everywhere at once. They turned the corner and stopped. There was people all over the putting green, holding their cocktails, eating food that seem to drip when they bit in, old men with their hands in their pockets rocking back and forth on their golf shoes, pants like a box of green crayons. Mr. Packard stood still, looking them over, and then found what he was looking for and pointed out a man sitting in a wheelchair.

The man had a tall drink in a holder attached to the arm of the chair, with two long pink straws and an umbrella in the glass. He was wearing a cowboy hat that was too big for his head and cowboy boots at the end of those dead legs. You could just see his red hair under the hat. A woman in a yellow dress had her hand on the back of his chair, leaning down to him, talking, and suddenly everybody broke out laughing at something he said.

He laughed like the world was a balloon and he was trying to fill it up.

"Albert Cassidy," Mr. Packard said, "the happy cowboy. He's the money." Mr. Packard looked around again and then nodded at another man, also with red hair, this one standing up. "And there's brother Frankie, the player. And there's his brother Tommy, and Arthur. There's about half a dozen of them in all. All redheads, I think. The whole family comes up for this; everybody brings along their girlfriends, it's sort of a reunion."

Train followed Mr. Packard in closer to the crowd, looking everywhere at once. The air hum to him with the excitement. The man in the wheelchair saw them first and smiled at Mr. Packard in a certain way that recalled what Plural said about how the world was a hungry place.

Mr. Packard walked straight toward him, smiling too, like it was a contest, and Train was a step behind, still carrying the bag. The people standing around the wheelchair with drinks began looking up, and then moving away like they was afraid. Train had a sudden uncomfortable feeling he turned visible at the wrong time. Then brother Frankie the player looked over and saw Train too. They stared at each other a minute, and Frankie turned back to his brother in the chair.

"That's the caddy, right?" Frankie said.

Albert just kept smiling at Mr. Packard, had a look like he didn't have nothing to lose, and Mr. Packard kept smiling back.

"He's the player," Mr. Packard said.

The brother acted like Mr. Packard and Train wasn't there. "You didn't say it was a nigger," he said to his brother. "I can't play a nigger here."

The man in the wheelchair said, "Do me a favor, Frankie. Work it out. We're having a nice time here, got the whole family together. Buy some drinks and slap some backs. Me and Miller ain't seen each other in a long time."

His brother looked around. "Albert," he said, "it's a nigger." Then he glanced back at Train again, like to make sure. "They ain't going to let him play out here. What are you thinking?" Then he looked from Train to Mr. Packard and seem to get prickly all of a sudden and said, "Who is this fucking guy anyway? What kind of people you know, shows up here with a nigger?"

The man in the wheelchair didn't answer, and Frankie the player turned around, knowing everybody was watching, and stalked off in the direction of the clubhouse. To show the ones that couldn't hear that he didn't have nothing to do with it. By now there was fifty, sixty people out on the green, and more all the time. Every time the clubhouse door opened, there was another three or four coming out. The new arrivals asked the ones who was already there what happened, everybody talking in quiet voices about the nigger on the putting green. The Cassidy family—which, it turned out, included some black-haired cousins—stood together off to the side.

Train heard someone from the clubhouse say Frankie had done the right thing, standing up to his brother, that here in Wisconsin the rules were the same for everybody.

Frankie already disappeared into the clubhouse, though, and the boy carrying his sticks went around the side, and the man in the wheelchair looked over to Mr. Packard and shrugged. "Well, that's an anticlimax for you," he said. "After you spent all that money to get out here."

Mr. Packard walked over to the wheelchair, and Train saw the beginnings of the decline of civilized behavior. Train thought he might like to hit a few putts himself, or swing an iron, to do something familiar. Looked around for somewhere else to be.

"What can I tell you, Miller?" said the man in the wheelchair, "Frankie won't play the shine."

"That's all right," Mr. Packard said, and patted him on the shoulder.

"He won't do it. I tried to talk to him—you heard me—but he's hardheaded. Besides, I guess you could say that the rules are the rules. That's why people join a country club."

"You knew," Mr. Packard said. Train heard that and began to walk away. Did not want to hear Mr. Packard discuss at what point he told the man he was colored. He took a step or two, but then saw there wasn't no place to go, and stopped. They was surrounded. Train looked off into the distance, feeling all that excitement turning into scart, wishing he'd stayed home with Plural.

"You can appreciate Frankie's situation," the man in the wheelchair said. "They could bring him up to the board. It was supposed to look like your boy was his guest, supposed to be strictly on the sly."

Mr. Packard nodded like he agreed with all that. "Thirty-six holes, a two-thousand Nassau, that's twelve thousand," he said.

The man in the wheelchair looked around at his relatives, and then he was chuckling and laughing and shaking his head. "Miller Packard," he said, "the one and only."

Mr. Packard poked at something under the man's shirt and said, "Albert, you shit in that bag, or is that your lunch?" A murmur went through the clubhouse crowd; somebody said that was definitely uncalled for, but if it bothered the man in the wheelchair, he didn't let it show.

"Let me ask you a question," he said to Mr. Packard. "You think you're still in California? You see any fucking coconut trees around here?"

Mr. Packard looked up into the trees for coconuts, then shrugged and reached out suddenly and grabbed the cowboy hat off the man's head and set it on his own. "You're right," he said, "we'll call it even."

For a moment nobody moved, and then one of

the Cassidys come up behind Mr. Packard and hit him in the back of the neck with a judo chop. Mr. Packard turned around and grabbed a handful of red hair. Another one jumped him from the side, took a head lock on him, and then come off the ground like Gorgeous George, and there was three of them in a pile on the ground, and then other relatives ran over and began kicking anything that moved and then jumped into the pile themselves, yelling words that sent a portion of the female membership running for the clubhouse.

In the stampede, a woman screamed and tripped, and then other people tumbled over her. A purse spilled lipstick, dimes and nickels, and a feminine napkin. Train saw a hearing aid lying beside a pair of sunglasses.

Back at the other pile—the one with Mr. Packard in it—somebody rolled into the wheelchair and tipped it over. Albert dropped out of it sideways and splayed across the practice green, his legs bent across each other like somebody tossed their pants on the floor when they got in bed. He was red-faced and embarrassed, but dead from the nipples down, and after awhile he give up trying to get to his feet and just lay still, looking at the sky, and waited for the end of the family reunion.

Train heard a distinct snap, like a bone, and then somebody screamed, and a second or two later Mr. Packard crawled out of the pile of bodies with the cowboy hat in his teeth, grinning like the last day of school.

CHAPTER 31

BEVERLY HILLS

She did not want Packard to leave and then, once he was gone, she did not want him back. She thought of things that happened around him, that he caused to happen, and did not want him back. She remembered exactly the way he had picked the mulatto's shoe off the deck and tossed it after him into the ocean, as if to demonstrate the point that nothing that happened could be undone. She remembered the plink the shoe made in the water after the splash. She remembered the crack-up on the ocean highway, the deer in the windshield, and then the man and the girl in the car. Oh yes, Packard would go to the end of the road too. She thought of the scene with the photographer at the art opening, the places he decided to have at her, the Negroes in the guest house. He was drawn to movement and friction, to chance; he had to have something in play.

In their best moments, they seemed to be in it together.

She lay awake that night, thinking of all reasons

to leave him, all the qualities that were different now that she was going to have a baby.

In the morning she missed him so badly she wept.

Later—evening—she felt safe and quiet and happy, and knew that in some way the tiny thing taking shape inside her felt safe too. She found herself thinking of the blind man in the guest house and remembered that he liked eggs, and that Packard had asked her to look in on him while he was gone.

She went out the back door, carrying a tray of sandwiches, thinking what a beautiful yard it would be to grow up in, as happy as she had been in a long time. She knocked on his door and waited, alive and full of life.

She sat in the guest house's kitchen with the blind man, watching him eat, glad she'd decided to come over. Thinking she should have done it earlier. He was shirtless, wearing trousers and shoes without socks. The room was tiny and the windows were shut and the air was close and warm. There was something familiar between them, as if they'd known each other a long time.

"My husband said you were a fighter," she said.

He smiled and put one of the sandwiches in his mouth. Half of it, actually—she'd cut them in half. "Not consequentially," he said. "Turned out I don't have no tank." The food rolled in his mouth—it reminded her of a clothes dryer—and she wondered if he'd missed breakfast and lunch. She'd made four sandwiches and he picked up the second half, with the first one still in his mouth, and held it a few inches off the plate; he seemed to be feeling its weight.

"They's this man Art Love—they call him 'Digger'—he running the program out of his own pocket. Digger's the promoter, the referee, and the manager of one of the fighters in the main event, and he got me in there with Irish Jack McKinney, and we moving around a little bit, you know what I mean, and then along about the third or fourth round, everything suddenly gone black. Then Jack scream like he was bit, which I can't see the reason for that, except Irish Jack was a primal man. That man could hit you in the head and break your legs. Neverthemind, I'm about niney percent sure Jack ain't knocked me out, but how can you be sure of something like that, standing there in the dark? I says, 'Jack? We still here?'

"And Jack says, 'Shit, I thought a spider got on me.'

"And I says, 'I was hoping you ain't knocked me out.'

"He says, 'No, but I think I might of got Digger.'"

"Who's Digger again?" she said.

"Digger Love, the ref."

"Right, Digger Love, the referee . . ."

"Shit, this boy of his named the Duke come into the ring with a flashlight and says they blown the main fuse, and this was at a little club out in Ohio, where they had all their connections down in the cellar, and as long as me and Jack was already dirty, would one of us mind going down there and putting a penny in the box, get us through the night so they don't have to give refunds and everybody could get paid.

"Jack says, 'I don't touch electricity'—that man always knew his mind—and so I guessed it's up to me do we get paid, and I gone down there with the Duke and he holding the light while I crawl in that cellar space and put a penny behind the main fuse. And that motherfucker light me up like Christmas. We go back upstairs—I'm all covered with dirt and bugs and Jack is lost his sweat—and they got a new referee 'cause Digger is too embarrassed to continue in the public eye, and I can still feel that feeling when the electricity lit me up. 'Jack,' I says, 'I don't touch electricity neither.'"

She looked at him, waiting for him to finish the story, but to Plural that was the finish. "What happened?" she said.

He didn't understand the question.

"The fight," she said. "Who won the fight?"

Plural thought for a moment, trying to remember; then he gave up. "Jack might knowed that," he said. "He kept track of them things better than me. The last time I seen him, though, we was cracked wide open together about old Digger Love, how it wasn't no spider at all, he just knocked poor old Digger right out from underneath his hair.

367

It lit on Jack's arm, and Jack throwed that thing off like fire."

"The referee's toupee?" she said.

"Yes ma'am. Couldn't face his public without that rug on his head. It takes all kinds, I guess."

She looked at the blind man with tenderness, felt herself beginning to weep.

CHAPTER 32

WISCONSIN

At eleven in the morning, Train was setting with Mr. Packard at the gate when Mr. Albert Cassidy and all his brothers and cousins from West Chicago come past on the way to their plane, limping and stitched up and depressed. Looked like the Confederate army in retreat. Albert was back in the saddle, pushed along by a younger black-haired man with a ordinary-size head—might of been an in-law—that Train didn't remember from the tussle. The man been in it, though. He had a bandage on his forehead looked like an earmuff.

Albert hisself wasn't busted up like some of the relatives, but he looked sore and gloomy, and you could tell it was a long ways up the hill to the bright side of life this morning.

Mr. Packard watched the procession move past their seats, and then, about the volume they used to announced the flights, he said, "It must be a goddamn chain gang, Charlene." Who Charlene was, Train didn't know.

369

Hearing that remark, some of the Cassidys of West Chicago looked around and spotted Mr. Packard, and saw that he was playing with them again, and then they seen Train too, and the one pushing the wheelchair changed directions, tried to save Albert from any further rumination over yesterday's indignities, and how fucked up things had generally got. Albert saw them, though, and leaned out his seat, like a dog riding half out the back window, staring pitchforks as he went by.

Mr. Packard just smiled and opened up his travel bag and pulled out the cowboy hat and set it on top of Train's head. The hat fit his head like a lamp shade, balanced on top and hung loose around his ears.

That event seem to of blessed the whole day, seeing the Cassidys in their present condition, and Mr. Packard was blithesome on the way home. Felt luckier than Moses in an inner tube. They sat up in front together, Train at the window, the stewardess calling him "sir" when she brought him his menu. The plane was entitled the *Constellation*. The stewardess served three drinks before dinner, and Train was afraid that the alcohol would make Mr. Packard talk more than he liked to and that afterwards, when it wore off, he would realize what he'd did and there would be resentments.

But Mr. Packard didn't talk that much after he started to drink, mostly just dropped his head back into the cushion and watched the stewardess walk up and down the aisle. Train did the same. The girl had a bottom that just made you want to eat her skirt, although when he looked over, it didn't seem like Mr. Packard was on the same page with him on that. Blithesome, but out there in the distance. The Mile Away Man rides again.

Sometime after dinner the plane banked south, and for a few minutes the sun was right out Train's window, hanging on the lip of the world. And then it dropped over the other side, and a little later the plane dropped with it. The stewardess come past, picking up the glasses, and she waited while Mr. Packard finished his last drink. When Train looked outside again, the city of Los Angeles seemed to be floating up to meet them.

He heard Mr. Packard sigh. Wherever he been at, he wasn't ready yet to come back. He finished what was left in the glass and handed it to the stewardess. She smiled and said, "Going home?" A girl from the South.

Mr. Packard nodded and said, "Home from the hunt."

"You-all hunters?" she said. She was sweet on Mr. Packard; Train could see that. Mr. Packard looked up at her, seemed surprised at the prettiness of the girl. It made Train wonder what he been looking at the last several hours.

"Me, I'm just the gun bearer," Mr. Packard said. "This here is the hunter. I only carry the guns." That tickled the stewardess and she sissy-slapped him on the shoulder and walked on up the aisle.

Mr. Packard sighed again, like he just ate. Then

he closed his eyes. A little later, after Train thought he'd went to sleep, he suddenly begun talking. "You know how sometimes you read a story in the paper," he said slowly, "that a person out in the valley somewhere stepped out the front door to get the milk and was run over by the milk truck? You know the kind of thing I'm talking about?"

Train nodded, thinking he had an understanding of how that might feel, at least afterwards when you were splayed out over the rosebushes, trying to figure out how you got there.

"Well," Mr. Packard said, "from what I've seen, it happens more than you think. In fact, if you live long enough, something like that is bound to happen. And afterwards, some people get over it fast, and some people can't seem to get over it at all. The doctors can put their legs back together and tell them they're as good as new, but they never really believe it, and every time the victim stands up, they wonder if something in there might come loose, like somebody pulling a can out of the bottom of a display at the grocery store, and the whole pile is going to come down on top of itself. Inside, I mean. They walk around waiting for their bones to crumble. Or maybe they got hit by lightning while they were on the phone, and now it rings even on a clear day and they can't bring themselves to pick it up."

Train waited, and for a long time it seem like that was as much as Mr. Packard had to say. But then he opened his eyes wide—for a moment, it

372

was like he just seen the milk truck with his name on it bouncing acrost the lawn—and his expression was so fierce, it made Train pull back in his seat. "I only mention it," he said, calmer than he looked, "because Mrs. Packard's going through a bad time again. So you understand what's happening."

"No sir. I haven't seen nothing like that."

Mr. Packard continued to stare; then he seem to focus in more on Train, like he was draining the lake to see what was on the bottom.

CHAPTER 33

BEVERLY HILLS

The rest of the month, every weekend, Mr. Packard found a game for Train at Western Avenue. Sometimes he said what Train was playing for; sometimes he didn't. Mr. Packard collected the money in the parking lot, or in the bar inside the clubhouse. Always gave Train something. Fifty dollars, sometimes a hundred or two. Train counted the money and hid it away, but the thing he liked best was the importance of it. When he was on the golf course and there was money down, everybody knew who he was then.

Some of the players he beat made the regular excuses about they had tennis elbows and foot blisters, and some of them just threw their sticks in the trunk and drove away. The worst people played, the more they discussed illness and injuries. It was always like that. He remembered sometimes he caddied a foursome, it was like they was having a contest, who was gone die first. He liked winning, and he liked hearing the excuses. He liked that feeling when he took the heart out of other players

374

with shots they never thought of hitting. He liked it every time he made them re-assess him up.

He begun trying to think of some way to keep it like this, looking beyond tomorrow. Begun to think like it was his.

At the house, it didn't seem like things was going Mr. Packard's way. It was two weeks since Train even glimpsed Mrs. Packard. For all he knew, Mr. Packard kept her tied up.

The next week they went to New York, and the week after that to Texas—he thought he'd played in the wind till he got to Texas—and then for two weeks there wasn't no games, and Train and Mr. Packard just went back out to Western Avenue and played each other for a dollar or two. Mr. Packard wouldn't take no strokes, and by then Train seen all the game he had, and it wasn't no fun really playing the same course, beating the same man that couldn't never beat him, with nothing come of it in the end anyway. Not after he played for thousands of dollars in places even Plural never seen.

CHAPTER 34

BEVERLY HILLS

She took some food over to the blind man on a Saturday night. It was her habit these long days when Packard was out of town with the boy. It was hot and she'd gained eight pounds, and nothing fit, not even her Mexican wedding ring. She'd gotten it off that morning, but her finger was still indented and green all the way around. She sweated all the time now and stayed away from bathroom mirrors. She tried not to look at herself when she dressed. Her feet were swollen and a small vein appeared one morning, blue and lumpy, on the inside of her thigh.

She was fat-faced and lonely, and found that she craved the company of the blind. She brought him scrambled-egg sandwiches and some carrot sticks. She presumed finger food was the easiest for him to eat.

"I thought you might be hungry," she always said.

She was sitting with him at the little kitchen table

again, feeling comfortable with him in a way she didn't feel with Packard, or anybody else. She slipped off her shoes. The strap lines were red and ugly, and he suddenly sniffed the air, and she thought for a moment it was her feet.

"Eggs," he said, like he was in love.

"It's practically all I eat these days," she said. "Eggs and sherbet." Then realized he might notice she hadn't brought any sherbet for him. "I just ran out of the sherbet," she said. "I might have some ice cream." Did he even know what sherbet was? He seemed to be thinking it over.

"Well, any way you look at it," he said finally, "it got to hurt. Great big egg like that come out that little pucker hole."

She could not think of a word to say.

He edged a sandwich into his mouth and talked around it. "Y'all hear people complain this chicken won't lay, that chicken won't lay, but shit, I wouldn't lay neither. Of course, in regard to that, they ain't unsimiliar to womens. The skinny ones ain't used to it scream like to die, and the ones with more meat and experience, they just spit out a baby like a watermelon seed."

Then he smiled politely, showing the eggs in his mouth, and said, "Did you had children yourself, ma'am?"

"Excuse me," she said, and picked up her shoes, and once she was out of the guest house she ran barefoot into her own house and upstairs to her bedroom, locking doors as she went through.

She got into bed and lay still, listening to crickets, and then the flamingos. There was a faint hum from the hallway light, and she could hear a faucet dripping downstairs in the kitchen. The house made the occasional noises it made at night, something like popping knuckles. She lay with her face against the pillow and heard herself breathe.

She thought about what the blind man had said, and wondered at what horrible things he'd done. They—the Negroes—all had something hidden in the basement; she'd known it all along. And he'd been laughing at her. He'd made her embarrassed and afraid and ashamed of herself, and she knew he was over there now, still laughing.

They could smell fear.

CHAPTER 35

COLORADO

They was on the airplane again, this time for the Rocky Mountains. The player there was a college boy, wasn't much older than Train. He hit the ball a long way, shaped his shots to the course, left and right, but Train seen he was thinking too much. Maybe about the money, maybe about the men whose money it was, taking little looks at them after he hit, see how they liked what he was doing. Trying to please everybody at once.

The player's name was Otto Stiles, and he just been to the quarter finals of the U.S. Amateur, and Train beat him six and five in a course six thousand feet up in the mountains. Never hit a bad shot.

They finished in less than two hours, late in the afternoon, and the ball had hung in the air longer than it seem like it could, like it didn't want to come down. Train could hear it land from the tee box sometimes, the soft, solid thump hundreds of yards away. Without putting it into words—there wasn't no reason to put it into words—it was the purest day he ever had. There would be better scores—it wasn't but a sixty-six; there was already lots of better scores than that—and days he hit it farther, and straighter, but somehow on this afternoon, nothing was wasted. In the end, that's as much as there was to it: Nothing was wasted. There was owls in the trees, and the college boy and him played a nice speed and nobody talked too much. It wasn't no "Nice shot" or "Fuck me" or "Hit it, Alice" all the way around. Nobody laughing or crying the blues or saying they was hurt.

The men with the college boy had little meetings with each other as they went along and saw the match getting out of hand, but they kept what they said to themself, standing somewhere away from Train and Otto Stiles, where they couldn't hear. They quit after thirteen holes, with the college boy down six.

Afterwards, they went to the parking lot to settle up; Mr. Packard and the people that brought the college boy was taking care of the money. Train was used to that by now. They let him play the course, but it was understood he couldn't be took inside. Didn't bother him any; he was what all of them was there about. He was the stick.

Mr. Packard sat on the trunk of the gamblers' car while they counted out the bills. The wind had come up and it was getting cold, and the car shook him as the engine warmed up. Train saw the lace ends of his shoes dancing against the leather. Then the money changed hands—looked to him like fifteen thousand—but Otto Stiles didn't see it. He was over to himself, staring at the ground, thinking, How could this happen? The boy was blinking tears.

"Tomorrow?" Mr. Packard said, putting the money away. He always give them a chance to play again. Train seen Otto Stiles hunch up at that, but then it could have been just the cold wind.

The man who paid him the money checked the college boy, like he had a delicate situation on his hands. "I don't think so," he said.

"We don't have to play for anything," Mr. Packard said. "You want to, we can just play for dinner. Whatever you want." Then he looked over at Otto Stiles. "He's a nice golfer," he said. Otto Stiles had fell apart at the turn, gone nine over the last four holes after he seen how far the game had got away from him.

"I think he might need some time off," the man said.

In the diner that night, Mr. Packard counted out fifteen one-hundred-dollar bills and handed them to Train. Train put the money in his shirt pocket without checking it himself, which was how Mr. Packard had did it when the gamblers gave it to him.

CHAPTER 36

BEVERLY HILLS

It took all day to get back to L.A., and the closer they got, the faster Mr. Packard ordered his drinks, and about ten minutes after Mr. Packard went into the house, Train heard them arguing upstairs, him and Mrs. Packard. Something wrong, but she wouldn't tell him what. One minute, she shouted for him to leave her alone, the next minute, she went quiet, and Train knew somehow that was harder on him than when she yelled. A door slammed and he called her, but there wasn't no answer. He called her again and again, sounded injured and impatient at the same time, like she caught his peeder in the door.

Train and Plural was sitting outside by the pool. The night was hot and windy, and Train been telling Plural about the owls, and the snow in the mountains. Plural been to Denver himself, he said, didn't remember no owls. It wasn't much of a story, but mostly he was talking now to overcome the embarrassment of what was going on inside. The only time lately that Train wanted to hear him talk, to cover up the sounds in the other house.

"I knocked out a local boy name Milton Hopper in Denver," Plural said. "They call him 'Little Rhino,' the boy trying to butt me all night, and then the crowd threw pennies when I left the ring. Shouting, 'Don't come back here, boy.'" He smiled at that, a memory of his life in the ring.

He ruminated on it awhile and got a little sad. He said, "Then I come to find out they was only six rounds in the tank."

He turned in the direction of the house. "She come out to take the car somewheres, and I try to open the car door to help her out like Mr. Packard said, but that woman see me around and run back in the house. Once she yelled '*Stop it!*' and another time she get in the car and gone squealing down the driveway like she just rob the First National."

They sat still, listening to Mr. Packard's voice coming from inside. Lights went on in a different room, went on and then went off. Like he was hunting for her now. The wind rattled the trees, and then they heard the flamingos settling in for the night next door. Sounded like a yard full of pigs.

"The man gave you money again?" Plural said.

"Some," Train said.

Plural shook his head and spoke almost in a whisper. "What do he want?"

Train didn't answer—he didn't know—and in the quiet, they heard Mr. Packard upstairs, begging her to tell him that same thing.

CHAPTER 37

BEVERLY HILLS

The Beverly Hills police arrived late in the afternoon; the sun coming through the windows flat and rich. Packard and the boy were still out at the golf course. The police knocked at the front door and waited.

She cracked the door, still in her housecoat, and noticed some of the neighborhood had already collected across the street. Cigars and sandals, an old woman in blue hair and curlers.

One of the policemen was young, and he took as much of her in as he could through the crack. There had been a complaint that someone was menacing the neighbors' flamingos, he said. She heard in his voice that he was enjoying the novelty of police work.

Alec's double-barrel Parker twelve-gauge shotgun leaned against the wall, a foot from her hand. On bad days now, she hauled it around with her, room to room, always knew where it was. It was useless, of course—even if she'd known how to shoot it, the barrels were so heavy, she could

384

barely lift it to a shooting position. On good days, she thought of donating it to the Boy Scouts or whatever charity took shotguns. This day, like a lot of them, had started bright and turned black later in the afternoon. It was all the waiting and worrying about the baby and Packard. Too much had happened in too little time. Sometimes she felt like there was no room left inside her. And the baby continued to grow.

Both of the policemen were polite, held their hats under their arms. Sunglasses. She saw the shine of scalp under their crew cuts.

"Ma'am?" he said.

"I'll get my purse," she said. There were more people on the sidewalk across the street now, an older couple with a white poodle. She didn't like having the police around her house, and was about to offer a donation for the rodeo. Wait— that was the sheriff's department. This was the city police. They had a yearly drive for the widows and orphans, although she didn't think there had been a policeman killed in Beverly Hills since the war. It seemed like one had been injured by a limousine at a big Hollywood funeral, but she couldn't remember whose funeral it was. She thought of offering them the shotgun.

"It isn't necessary to get your purse, ma'am," the young policeman said. "We were just wondering if we might speak to your guests."

The way he said *guests*, he knew what they were. She smiled at him, trying to think of something to say, trying to get something to come out, then trying to remember whose funeral it was where the policeman was hurt, and then she couldn't see that any of it was worth the effort. Any of it. Everything was too hard.

"Ma'am," the young one said, "if you could do me a personal favor, it could make my life a lot easier. What I'd like to do, I'd like to just go back and have a word with your guests."

Oh, he was charming her.

She closed the door. The policemen stayed where they were awhile, perhaps thinking that she was getting dressed. Five minutes passed, then ten. She watched from upstairs, sitting behind a window screen.

"You know, Dick," the younger one said, "you might not of noticed, but that was some nice leg there, she put some makeup on and wash her hair." And she touched her hair to see if it felt stringy, and he started up the driveway alone, toward the backyard.

And sixty seconds later he was unconscious.

The older cop was still out in front of the house, sitting in the patrol car, when Packard and Train came in from the golf course. It was getting dark.

Packard set the parking brake and got out, ignoring the neighbors standing across the street, and headed straight for the cruiser. The policeman watched him come, and then took his time before he rolled down the window to talk, not caring for the way the man came at him across the lawn.

"Problem?" Packard said. Nothing friendly about it, but nothing puffed up, either. The policeman understood instantly that this was not an ordinary citizen of Beverly Hills at his window, that this one probably never threatened anybody in his life. He would skip that step. A certain fright stabbed him, something like falling, something like little monkey hands all over his balls.

"We're just checking out a neighborhood complaint," he said, hearing the change in his own voice. Packard waited, and the policeman turned away to light a cigarette. To regroup. "Something about flamingos. My partner's in the back."

Packard gazed down through the window, and the policeman said, "He didn't think you'd mind if he went back there and talked to them. Just a talk, a conversation about flamingos. The missus came to the door, but she didn't appear responsive."

"He went back there alone?"

"Just for a conversation, chief. A little talk."

Train was still waiting by the car, and Mr. Packard came past him hurried and worried, and Train fell in behind, as he always did.

The other policeman was laying on his side next to the pool, moths flying orbits in the light around his head. Looked like the tweety birds after somebody been knocked out in the comics. Plural was on a lawn chair not far away, rocking up and back.

Could of been somebody's grandmother, baby-sitting a sleeping child.

Plural looked up at the sound of the footsteps, recognized who it was. "The golfers," he said, and broke into a smile. Like he'd forgot he spilled a policeman on the patio.

The policeman lay still, looked to be pretending to be dead. Thinking, as it develop, that he could be shot. Mr. Packard checked him over and then picked him up, like he was no weight at all, and sat him into a chair not far from Plural's. A swelling covered the side of his head and disappeared into his hair, looked like a half a potato.

The policeman put his face in his hands, trying to get his bearings. His pistol was still in his holster and his hat floated in the pool. The frames of his sunglasses was still on his nose, but the glass part themself was back where he'd been laying, spaced about like they were when they was connected. Train seen Plural hit people before, but it was hard to understand how he knocked the glass out of his glasses.

Mr. Packard got the pool strainer and fished out the hat. The policeman took it without looking up, without seeming to notice it was wet. He held it on his lap and kept his head down, sick and sweating and waiting for all this badness to pass.

"What are you doing back here?" Mr. Packard said.

Train froze at that question, and for a second it felt like Mayflower was laying on the patio where the police was. That everything was out in the open. Wished in that second that he never met Plural in the first place. Wished all this trouble was with somebody else.

Without looking up, the policeman made a gesture of some sort into empty space and said, "Am I shot?"

"No," Mr. Packard said, "you're all right."

"You fine," Plural said. The policeman reached down to make sure his weapon was still in his holster. "I think I'm going to be sick," he said.

"Here we go," Plural said, and lifted his feet.

The feeling passed though, and the policeman dropped his face back into his hands and looked through his fingers at his feet. Shiny black shoes, white socks. He put his fingers through the empty glass frames. It stopped him a moment, trying to figure out what was wrong. "Shit," he said, "I can't remember where I am."

His hat dropped on the ground and rolled a foot or two, and he pulled at the skin on his face, like he would liked to take his head in his hands and hold it out where he could see it for himself.

Train recognized that the situation was still broke into pieces for him, though, and he couldn't fit it together. The policeman looked again at Plural, seemed to know him now. "That man shot me," he said.

"You aren't shot," Mr. Packard said, "but around the blind, you should be clear about your intentions."

Plural nodded at that, as if it was what he was thinking too, and then something stirred the birds on the other side of the fence, the low grunting turned into shrieking, and they beat their wings and yelled, then gradually settled back down to graze the south end of the pool. No reason, the birds just did what they did. The young cop jumped at the flapping and the noise, and then looked up, and either what he saw or just the motion itself seemed to make him sick all over again.

"Jesus Christ," he said, "how do you people live in all this confusion?"

Train heard them arguing that night again, come from downstairs in the kitchen.

"He didn't know who it was," Mr. Packard said. Inside, Train saw their shadows moving on the wall. "He was just protecting the house."

No answer, though. Nothing at all.

CHAPTER 38

SEATTLE

Another match that weekend at Western Avenue, and then up to Seattle. Mr. Packard had the first drink before the plane ever took off.

Train was supposed to be playing a man for fifty in Seattle—that was what they called fifty thousand these days, fifty. It wasn't the money, though, that they was going for. As far as money went, Mr. Packard seemed just as happy to took Albert Cassidy's cowboy hat.

Still, Train had won him something everywhere he played, and when the games got bigger, Mr. Packard start to gave him five hundred or a thousand afterwards. He told Train to put it in the bank, but Plural told him to keep it hisself.

"They always somebody in this world that want to hold your money," Plural said.

Train saw his line of thinking was connected to why he kept wondering what did Mr. Packard want.

★ ★ ★

The stewardess came past, and Mr. Packard caught her eye and pointed to his glass. She smiled at him, but he'd already turned back out the window. She let the smile spill into the next seat, and asked Train would he like another orange juice or some peanuts. He didn't look old enough to drink— he could see that himself—and wondered if he ever would.

The pilot came on the loudspeaker to announce they should be arriving in Seattle in forty-five minutes. Train stood up to stretch his legs and walked up toward the place the stewardesses had made dinner, and looked out the windows. It was dark, and there was a line of scattered lights below, trucks and cars. Everybody going their own way, and Train up there above them, going to Seattle to bet other people's money and then go back home. As important as Native Dancer himself, on the way to the Kentucky Derby.

Two other stewardesses was in their seats, talking away, and when they saw Train standing at the window, one of them stared at him and the other one glanced away. Both of them up here thinking the same thing, that he didn't need to be in any airplane. They had to see him play to know he belong on the plane.

He went back to his seat and Mr. Packard sipped at his drink. "I'm afraid we got a little bit of a situation, Mr. Walk," he said. It sounded like life had wore him out. Train waited to hear what it was. He knew somehow that it was over for him now, that he had to go find something for himself. He tried to remembered what it was like before, when he didn't matter.

Train felt the engines change pitch, and then the plane itself pitched down with it into the night. Sometimes it seemed like everything that happened, he felt it first. Seemed like he had too many connections, knew too many things ahead of time.

"Your friend, Plural . . ."

Train waited, felt it coming.

"It's getting to be a problem."

Train started to say he'd get rid of him, but he stopped himself short. He thought of what that meant, how he would tell Plural he had to go.

"About them birds?" Train said, but he knew it wasn't.

"Not the birds," Mr. Packard said.

The man in Seattle was named Skagstead, bald as a baby and born to have a good time. The first player since they started in this business that fooled with him while they was going around, try to maintain cordiality in the game.

Skagstead and the man with the money rode in a golf cart, kept a cooler of beer in there, and he would had one and then Skagstead would had one too, like a duel of tap dancers, all the way around. They gave one to Mr. Packard and offered one to Train too, and when Train said no thank you, they ast if he want a soda pop instead. They was cheerful like that all the way around, and somehow in all the beer drinking and pleasantness, they got to number eighteen just one hole down. The bald man didn't looked that good hitting it, but he could play.

Number eighteen was a par five, and the bald man got hold of a driver off the fairway and rolled it on in two. Train hit next, left his ball forty feet.

The bald man was away by a little bit and hit his putt, the best putt he hit all day, from the bottom edge of the green. It looked too strong, but then it took the break of the green hard left and slowed down, and then stopped right to the edge of the hole.

The ball quit on the spot, sniffing the hole, teetered half in and half out. Train and Mr. Packard look at each other, and in that same second a butterfly—not even a monarch, just a little white butterfly—floated into the picture and landed on that ball where it settled, and the ball dropped in the hole.

And none of them ever seen that before, and they all know they never were gone see it again. Just like they know the bald man never gone get this close to Train again in a golf match.

Mr. Skagstead was nicely comported, said to check the rules to make sure there wasn't no penalty for being helped by a butterfly—which, in Train's experience, was the kind of thing the rule book would in fact have a rule for—but that started Mr. Packard to laughing until he choked, and when he could talk again, he said, shit, he don't care about that, what happened happened, and Train missed his putt to the high side and they left it like that, all even.

And golf felt good in a new way it never felt before. Something besides being the center of things and winning money. Train thought about how long he played this game before he found out that he liked it for itself.

Mr. Skagstead and his man knew a place with a peanut bowl on the table and sawdust on the floor, and nobody looked twice at Train when they all come in together, and they all ate dinner and drank tequila—even Train tried it, but it tasted like sweat to him—and while they was eating, Mr. Skagstead suddenly looked up, like he just remembered something, and smiled across the table, his eyes all cannonballed from the liquor, and his head was streaked with sweat, and he said this just to Train, like only the two of them would understand. "That was some fun," he said.

CHAPTER 39

BEVERLY HILLS

She had a nap that afternoon and woke up feeling clearheaded and thinking of how to decorate the nursery. An hour later, she thought about the blind man, the way he was always trying to get the car door for her, trying to help with the groceries. Trying. In the safety of the afternoon, she was surprised at herself for the way she'd treated him.

And she knew better than to say the things she'd said to Packard; she knew they weren't all the same. She touched her stomach and wondered if he'd felt it in there, if she'd been scaring the baby too.

She fixed a plate of cookies later and went over to see him again. Practicing her apology. It was dusk; the air was hot and still. She knocked and waited, and was suddenly aware of a certain odor, something damp and vaguely metallic. A noise rose and died inside, and then the door opened, and he stood in the threshold, shirtless in his undershorts, his face aimed at the moon, his arms and chest spotted with blood and pink feathers, and there were more feathers in the air and all over the floor and furniture, and one of his hands was closed into a fist just beneath the animal's head, and beneath that, hanging limp, twelve inches of neck that had been torn from the body.

He seemed to know what she was thinking. He grinned at her and there were bits of feathers and blood in his teeth. He'd bitten off its head. "The lady of the household," he said. "What you got for me tonight?"

She stood still, thinking that he meant to rip out the baby too. That it would happen now.

What began on the boat had come full circle.

He smacked his lips as she backed away. "You know it's a hungry world," he said.

CHAPTER 40

COMING HOME

On the runway Mr. Packard was quiet and restless, and Train knew the time had come for Mr. Packard to tell him what he been trying to tell him all along—to find another place. Mr. Packard waited, though, until the plane was in the air.

"So it turns out you're a player," he said. "At least you got that much out of all this." Like everything between them was settled.

"I had that already," Train said. Not arguing, just trying to hold on a little longer.

Mr. Packard ordered two double bourbons from the stewardess and closed his eyes. "Look," he said, "something's gone wrong at home. She's scared to death all the time, and it's getting worse instead of better."

"Of what?"

"Plural, I think. It's hard to say for sure." And now they were talking like people talked to each other, like there was nothing in between them to consider.

Train nodded, thinking again of putting Plural someplace else. A home for the blind, or back in a gym somewheres. The stewardess brought the drinks and Mr. Packard killed one and gave her the glass back empty before she left the spot. "Oh my," she said. "Somebody's having a good time tonight." He smiled in a weak way, like somebody just tucked him in bed with the mumps.

"I hope you can understand it," he said a little later. "That you won't hold it against us." *Us.* "It's not even actually about your friend, I don't think. She's afraid of him because of something that happened before. It went away for a while, and now it's come back."

There was a certain sound to his voice that reminded Train of how Mr. Packard been sounding at night from inside the house. The man was looking for relief.

He turned to Train, got nothing back at all, and then put his face in the window. "I don't know how all this is going to come out," he said. "But at least you found out that you can play, you can play with anybody. That's worth something."

But he already said that.

The plane stopped in San Francisco, where they picked up passengers off another flight. One of them, an old red-faced priest, had Train's seat number on his ticket. The stewardess checked both tickets while the priest looked down the barrels at Train.

The rest of first class was full.

"We could reseat you in the back," the stewardess said to the priest. He turned to her, to eyewitness this person going to put the body of Christ or whatever they call it into coach.

She gave it up fast and turned and smiled at Train, not wanting to be in the middle of this at all. Train noticed the rings on the priest's fingers, four of them on one hand; he could hear him breathing. Sounded like an iron lung. The priest swayed slightly, and Train smelled alcohol, something he couldn't quite place, maybe vodka. He noticed the blood vessels in the old man's nose and cheeks. Train stayed where he was, waiting for Mr. Packard to straighten it out. He held on to the thought that Mr. Packard could straighten things out.

But Miller Packard was six drinks into the flight and gone staring out the window again, watching the suitcases come up the ramp to the plane.

"Let me get the pilot," the stewardess said, and stepped through the door into the cockpit. By now, everybody in the cabin but Mr. Packard was watching. The priest rested one of his hands against the back of the seat; Train smelled cigarette smoke on it, felt the man's weight. Felt himself running out of time.

The pilot came out, putting on his cap. He looked at the tickets, shaking his head, and puckered his lips. Then he leaned forward, smiling politely, and said to Train, "Sir, I'm sure you wouldn't mind if we reassigned your seat?" Train waited one last minute, but Mr. Packard was off somewhere else. Already left him behind. And that seemed like the last chance he had. The pilot leaned a little closer and whispered to him, like he wanted to keep this away from the rest of the passengers. "It's a man of the cloth," he said.

Train got up and followed the stewardess toward the back of the plane. As he passed through the curtain separating the compartments, he turned back and saw the priest brushing off the seat with a handkerchief before he sat down.

Mr. Packard was waiting for him at the gate when he got off the plane. "What happened?" he said. "I look around, I'm sitting next to a priest."

He didn't wait for an answer, but went mile-away and sad, staring at an old woman sitting on a crate, talking to a dog named Barney that was inside it.

And then the same thing all the way home. A mile away.

He come out of it long enough to give Train an envelope three inches thick. It was full of money, but by now it smelled bad, just like Mr. Packard said. It was probably all the money they won since they started.

Mr. Packard started to say something, and then just let it go. Probably to tell him again that at least he found out he could play.

CHAPTER 41

BEVERLY HILLS

She lay in bed in the dark, her arms crossed over her stomach, staring at nothing. She'd taken three sleeping pills and a Christmas tree, but it only seemed to make her more awake, more aware of things moving, patterns on the ceiling, dark shapes coming and going; everything was familiar but indistinct. She wanted something distinct. And then she looked into the corner of the room, and for an instant she saw the dead bird's head spilled over the blind man's fist.

She lay still, unable to see it again, knowing it was there. She was aware of the baby, of frightening the baby, and Christ, she wanted them gone. She wanted them all gone.

All the Negroes in her life, past and present. She did not want them in the guest house, or sitting out by the pool before Packard got home from the office. She did not want to know they were being executed in Waycross, Georgia; she didn't want the boy in the yard with the lawn mower or cleaning the pool; she didn't want to see the blind man smiling like an idiot in the sun, with his foot cupped over the sprinkler head while the water bubbled up between his toes. She didn't want him listening for her in the driveway, trying to open doors. She didn't want him knowing where she was.

What did she want? She tried to think. *What did she want?*

Nothing. That would be enough.

She wanted to lie in the bathtub, just that, lie in the tub doing nothing and have nothing done to her or for her, lie there until the odor of wet feathers and bird blood was off her skin. Just lock the door and lie in the tub, but she couldn't do that. With the noise of the water, she might not hear him coming in. Or he might slip in after she was already in the tub and she wouldn't see him in the bathroom steam. How would she know? She imagined rising up out of the water and somehow clearing a path of sight—clearing it the way you would clean the fog off the bathroom mirror—and finding him sitting on the floor, his back against the closed door, holding her baby in his fist.

What had he said? "You know it's a hungry world"?

She gagged, and then waited until the feeling passed and then tiptoed to the window. He was sitting by the pool now, talking to himself. As she watched, he stretched, and even in the half-light of the patio, she saw the deep-etched muscles in his back and his arms. His tiny mis-shapen feet. Her arches began to cramp, and she came down off her toes. She sat back on the bed and did nothing, and a long time later she heard the door open downstairs. A minute passed and there were no more sounds, and then she felt him there, standing at the bottom of the stairs, gazing toward the second floor, finding her. Fixing on the heat of her body.

She caught a reflection of herself in the window, a dark glimpse of her face. It seemed unfamiliar, vulgar and thick, the way it had felt when she'd touched it after the beating. She wasn't pretty anymore, and it occurred to her that she never had been, that people had only assumed she was because she'd tried so hard to be that.

She moved into the corner and waited for him to come up the stairs. Waited a long time, and then a light went on suddenly overhead, and she saw him in the doorway, swaying, smiling, as if he were about to laugh but couldn't, like a man waiting to sneeze, and realized in the second before she pulled at the trigger who she had been afraid of all along.

CHAPTER 42

BEVERLY HILLS

Train and Packard had drove home together; neither one of them could find nothing to say. Like it was already tomorrow or next week, and they both just gone their own way.

It begun to feel eerie between them now, and when they got home, Mr. Packard turned off the engine and let the car coast to the curb, not to wake up his wife. He steered in close and stopped. The street outside Train's window glowing red in the brake lights.

Mr. Packard got out, sad and patient, seem so tired he could barely shut the door, and walked up the driveway to the side of the house. The man was inside that house before he was inside, and never even said good night.

Mr. Packard stopped at the door to find his keys, and Train went past him to the back, everything happening slow motion and a hundred miles an hour at the same time. He heard Mr. Packard slide the key into the lock, and Train made a deal that the lock itself was one more last chance to straighten this out, that Mr. Packard could still turn around and fix things up, but once the bolt slid open, it was like he open the car window, everything would fly out into the wild.

And the bolt slid open.

The door opened too, and Mr. Packard walked inside. Train went on back through the gate to the guest house. He heard the whinny noises Plural made when he dreamed, could hardly stand to hear it now.

Train opened the door and let himself in. Plural was naked, asleep in the rocking chair, his cheek resting on his shoulder. Feathers all over the room; the place smelled like blood and poultry. Plural had high arches, and the toes of his feet barely touched the floor.

Train moved quietly into the kitchen and stared at the bird lying across the table. The neck and the head anyway. The rest was in the sink, half-plucked. He went back outside to get away from it and Plural both.

He sat down on one of the deck chairs and took off his shoes and his socks and lay down on the cool plastic. He felt like he ought to go up to the house and tell Mr. Packard that he didn't want this to end like everything else did, just everybody gone their own ways.

And then the connection come in like lightning on the telephone. It echoed through the dark, and then things broke and splintered inside the house, sounded like a collapse of the keepsakes, and in that second, he seen that he missed the whole point. That all this time he been thinking how he could keep what he had for the future, keep what him and Mr. Packard was together—all that money and importance—but the point all along was Plural.

He had to take Plural along or there wasn't no point.

He looked up at the house, imagining how Plural would look to the police when they come, covered with feathers and blood, and somebody shot upstairs.

He went into the guest house and Plural was still asleep and innocent in the rocking chair. Train shook his bare foot to wake him up. Sticky with blood. "C'mon, Plural," he said, feeling his fingers peel off the blind man's skin. "C'mon, man, we got to go."

CHAPTER 43

THE BEDROOM WINDOW

Nothing could be taken back, or taken over. Things were what they were.

He'd seen the empty bed; he'd seen something move. He'd turned on the light, and she was sitting on the floor, up against the bed, her knees pressed together, with the shotgun resting in the space where they forked open. The gun from the boat. He saw her, and she saw him. Recognized him over the barrel, and whatever her intentions had been, there was no misunderstanding. A second passed and he began to tell her the boy and the blind man were leaving. He began to ask what she was doing out of bed.

The shot blew his leg out from under him, and at the same time blew him backward, out of the room. He rolled himself into a ball in the hallway and felt for his knee, but there was an empty, warm place where it had been. He moved his hand to the side, feeling the tear in his pants, looking for his kneecap, and then in fact came across part of it, lower than it should have been, beneath the material, and it

408

moved when he touched it, and then moved again when he put his hand back into the wound itself.

There wasn't much pain—the blood was all over, but not much pain—and he moved the hand above the wound, trying instinctively to hold the parts of his leg together, pressed into the wound with his other hand, and rocked his forehead back and forth into the cool wall, barely moving. He wasn't dying—it wasn't that, not yet—but he was hurt in a way that couldn't be fixed.

It hadn't been a mistake. She had seen who it was. "I just wanted your attention," she said, so quietly that he was not even sure she said it.

Now he heard her dialing the phone. "My husband's been shot," she said, and then he felt her watching him. It felt like whatever was wrong between them, they'd talked it over now. He was paying attention.

And then he was pulling away—an old, familiar detatchment sliding into the picture from as long ago as he could remember—and he moved away until he could see it all clearly, from a distance, from behind her, looking over her shoulder from the window. As if he were outside looking in.

He looked and saw himself on the floor, holding off the bleeding, holding his ruined leg together, feeling a rush of fear, and not knowing whether to laugh or cry.

She was speaking into the phone slowly, clearly, repeating herself. "My husband's been shot. Could you please pay attention?"

If they know what's good for them, they will, he thought.

She gave the police the address twice, and then said thank you and hung up the phone.

The room was quiet and ringing at the same time, and in the silence, the familiar, ringing silence, he heard something else. Packard was weeping. Weeping and bleeding in his own hallway. Knowing he couldn't stop one any more than the other.

He watched from the window and understood that it was all out of his hands.

May 20, 2003
Whidbey Island, Washington